TO
SPEAK
FOR THE
DEAD

TO SPEAK FOR THE DEAD

Paul Levine

BANTAM BOOKS
NEW YORK · TORONTO · LONDON · SYDNEY · AUCKLAND

TO SPEAK FOR THE DEAD
A Bantam Book / August 1990

Grateful acknowledgment is made for permission to use an excerpt from "The Lawyers Know Too Much" from Smoke and Steel by Carl Sandburg, copyright 1920 by Harcourt Brace Jovanovich, Inc., and renewed 1948 by Carl Sandburg, reprinted by permission of the publisher. "It's Still Rock and Roll To Me" by Billy Joel, copyright © 1980 by Impulsive Music. All rights controlled and administered by EMI April Music Inc. All rights reserved. International copyright secured. Used by permission.

Library of Congress Cataloging-in-Publication Data

Levine, Paul (Paul J.)
    To speak for the dead / Paul Levine.
      p.   cm.
    ISBN 0-553-05747-2
    I. Title.
  PS3562.E8995T6   1990
  813'.54—dc20   89-18460
                                CIP

Published simultaneously in the United States and Canada

Bantam Books are published by Bantam Books, a division of Bantam Doubleday Dell Publishing Group, Inc. Its trademark, consisting of the words "Bantam Books" and the portrayal of a rooster, is Registered in U.S. Patent and Trademark Office and in other countries. Marca Registrada. Bantam Books, 666 Fifth Avenue, New York, New York 10103.

PRINTED IN THE UNITED STATES OF AMERICA

BVG   0 9 8 7 6 5 4

For my wife Alice,
Who moved me then,
And moves me still,
And taught me all I know of love.

ACKNOWLEDGMENTS

I gratefully acknowledge the assistance of South Florida medical examiners Dr. Joseph Davis and Dr. Ronald Wright, orthopedic surgeon Dr. Joel Kallan, the great trial lawyers and friends Stuart Grossman, Edward Shohat and Philip Freidin, my indefatigable secretary Gayle Bouffard, my agent Bob Colgan and my editor Kate Miciak. The rest of you know who you are.

I also acknowledge the hellish paradise of Miami, a tropical Casablanca of sultry days and pastel sunsets, where buzzards endlessly circle the courthouse, some on wings and some in Porsches.

"The Coroner shall view the body and the woundes and the strokes, and the bodye shalbe buryed. And yf the Coroner fynde the bodye buried before his cominge, he shall not omitte to digge up the bodye.

"And when the inquest is sworne ye Coroner must inquire if ye person were slayne by felony or by misadventure. And after it shalbe enquired who were presente at the dede, and who be coulpable of the ayde, force, commandement, consent, or receite of suche felonies wittingly."

ANTHONY FITZHERBERT,
The New Book of Justice, 1545 A.D.

TO
SPEAK
FOR THE
DEAD

Prologue

TABLE DANCER

He would remember the sounds—the wailing sirens, the moans of the injured—and the smells, a smoky ashen stench that clung to hair and clothing. Late the first night, he slipped into the parking lot for some air, and he tasted the sky as the smoke rose above Miami's inner core. He heard the city scream, the popping of wood and plastic aflame, short bursts of gunfire followed by silence, then the crackle of police radios. Later he would remember slipping in a puddle of blood on the tile floor of the Emergency Room.

He would not leave the hospital for seventy-two hours, and by then, he had treated more gunshot wounds than most doctors see in a lifetime. Blacks against police, whites against blacks, savage violence in a ghetto hopelessly misnamed Liberty City. By the time the shooting stopped and the fires were out, an eerie silence hung over the area, an inner-city battle zone where neither side surrendered, but each put away its weapons and withdrew.

"That's a real poster ass, huh?"

Roger Salisbury shot a sideways glance at the man next to him. A working guy, heavy boots and a plaid shirt open at the neck. Thick hands, one on a pack of cigarettes, the other on his drink, elbows resting on the scarred bar. "Like to frame that ass, hang it in the den next to Bob Griese."

"Uh-huh," Salisbury mumbled. He didn't come here to talk, didn't know why he came. Maybe to lose himself in a place crammed with people and noise, to be alone amid clinking glasses, laughter, and the creaminess of women's bodies. He strained his neck to see her above him on the stage.

"Not that one," the man said, tapping the bar with a solid index finger. "Over there at the stairs, the on-deck circle. A real poster ass. Never saw a skinny girl with an ass like that. Eat my lunch offa that."

She wore a black G-string, a red bikini top, and red high-heeled shoes. If not for the outfit and the setting, she could have been a cheerleader with a mom, dad, and grandmom in Kansas. Good bone structure, fair complexion with freckles across a button nose, short wavy reddish-brown hair, wholesome as a wheat field. The face belonged in a high school yearbook; the body launched a thousand fantasies. Her thin waist accentuated a round bottom that arched skyward out of both sides of the tiny G-string. Her breasts were round and full. She was warming up, fastening a prefab smile into place,

2

taking a few practice swings, tapping a sequined shoe in time to Billy Joel, who was turned up way too high:

What's the mat-ter with the clothes I'm wear-ing?
Can't you tell that your tie's too wide?
May-be I should buy some old tab col-lars.
Wel-come back to the age of jive.

The working guy was looking at Salisbury now, sizing him up. Looking at a blow-dry haircut that was a little too precise for a place like this. Clean shaven, skin still glistening like he'd just spanked his face with Aqua Velva at two A.M., as if the girls in a beat-your-meat joint really care. The hair was starting to show some early gray, the features pleasant, if not matinee idol stuff. A professor at Miami–Dade maybe, the working guy figured.

Salisbury knew the guy was looking at him, now at his hands, just as he had done. Funny how hands can tell you so much. Proud of his hands. Broad and strong. They could have swung a pick, except there were no calluses. He had washed off the blood, scrubbing as hard after surgery as he had before the endless night began. Seventy-two hours with only catnaps and stale sandwiches until the hospital cafeteria ran out. But he stood there the whole time, one of the leaders, the chief orthopedics resident, setting broken bones, picking glass and bullet fragments out of wounds, calming hysterical relatives.

After showering at the hospital, he had tossed the soiled lab coat into the trash and grabbed a blue blazer from his locker. Now he was nursing a beer and trying to forget the carnage. He could have gone home. Twenty-seventh Avenue was finally open after the three-day blockade. But too tired to sleep, he wound through unfamiliar streets and was finally lured out of the night by the neon sign of the Tangiers on West Dixie. He would think about it later, many times, why he stopped that night, what drew him to such a strange and threatening place. Pickup trucks and old Chevys jammed the parking lot. Music blared from outdoor loudspeakers, a rhythmic, pulsating beat intended to tempt men inside just as the singing of the Sirens drew Greek sailors onto the rocks. It might have been the flashing sign. The throbbing colors got right to the point——NUDE GIRLS 24 HOURS . . . NUDE GIRLS 24 HOURS——blinking on, blinking off, proof of bare flesh moment after moment after moment.

The working guy was talking to him: "I say let'em burn colored town down to the ground if they want to, no skin offa my nose. I mean, the cops was wrong, killing one of the coloreds, had his hands cuffed behind his back, no need for that. But some of 'em just looking for excuses to behave like animals. They burned a poor Cuban alive in his car, heard it on the radio."

"We tried to save him," Salisbury said quietly.

The guy gave him a look. "Sure! You're a doctor. Should have known. Jesus, you musta seen it all. Wait a minute, Sweet Jesus, here comes Miss Poster Ass. She's worth a twenty-dollar dance, or I'm the Prince of Wales."

Roger Salisbury watched her walk toward them, an inviting smile aimed his way. The other men around the small stage hooted and slapped their thighs. Roger Salisbury lowered his eyes and studied his drink.

"Your first time?" the man asked. Silence. "Yeah, your first time. Loosen up. Here's the poop. First the girls dance out here on the bar stage. No big deal, they take it all off, you stick a dollar bill in their garter and maybe one'll kiss you. In the back, where it's darker, you got your table dances, twenty bucks. That's one-on-one and I may buy me an up-close-and-personal visit with Miss Poster Ass. Haven't been able to get here all week what with the jungle bunnies staging their block parties."

On stage now, grinding to the music, no longer the Kansas cheerleader. *Ev-ry-bod-y's talk-in' 'bout the new sound. Funny, but it's still rock and roll to me.* In a few moments, the bikini top was off, firm breasts bounding free. The G-string came next, and then she arched her back, bent over, and propped her hands on her knees looking away from the men. The poster ass wiggled clockwise as if on coasters, then stopped and wiggled counterclockwise. Salisbury stared as if hypnotized. The ass quivered once, fluttered twice with contractions that Roger Salisbury felt deep in his own loins, then stopped six inches from his face. His fatigue gone, the swirl of blood and bodies a dreamy fog, Roger Salisbury fantasized that the perfect ass wiggled only for him. He didn't see the other men, some laughing, some bantering, others conjuring up their own steamy visions. None of the others, though, seemed spellbound by an act as old as the species.

The dance done, the girl smiled at Roger Salisbury, an open interested smile, he thought. And though she smiled at each man, again he thought it was only for him. She sashayed from one end of the small stage to the other, collecting dollar bills in a black garter while propping a red, high-heeled shoe on the rim between the stage and the bar. Other than the garter and the shoes, she was naked, but her face showed neither shame nor seduction. She could have been passing the collection plate at the First Lutheran Church of Topeka. Roger Salisbury slipped a five-dollar bill into her garter, removing it from his wallet with two fingers, never taking his eyes off the girl. A neat trick, but he could also tie knots in thread with a thumb and one finger inside a matchbox. Great hands. The strong, steady hands of a surgeon.

Her smile widened as she leaned close to him, her voice a moist whisper on his ear. "I'd like to dance for you. Just you." And he believed it.

Roger Salisbury believed everything she said that night. That she was a model down on her luck, that her name was Autumn Rain, that all she wanted was a good man and a family. They talked in the smoky shadows of a corner table and she danced for him alone. Twenty dollars and another twenty as a tip. He didn't lay a hand on her. At nearby tables men grasped tumbling breasts, and the girls stepped gingerly from their perches in four-inch spikes to sit on customers' laps, writhing on top of them, grinding down with bare asses onto the fully clothed groins of middle-aged men. "Didja come?" the heavy girl at the next table whispered to her customer, already reaching for a tip.

"I've never seen anything like this," Roger Salisbury said, shaking his head. "It's half prostitution and half masturbation." He gestured toward the overweight girl who was gathering her meager outfit and sneaking a peek at the president's face on the bill she had glommed from a guy in faded jeans. "You don't do that, do you?" Salisbury asked.

She smiled. *Of course not,* the look said.

He asked her out.

Against the rules, she said. Some guys, they think if you're an exotic dancer, it means for fifty bucks you give head or whatever.

But I'm different, Roger Salisbury said.

She cocked her head to one side and studied him. They all thought they were different, but she knew there were only two kinds of men, jerks and jerk-offs. Oh, some made more money and didn't get their fingernails dirty. She'd seen them, white shirts and yellow ties, slumming it, yukking it up. But either way, grease monkeys or stock-brokers, once those gates opened and the blood rushed in, turning their worms into stick shifts, they were either jerks or jerk-offs. The jerk-offs were mostly young, wise guys without a pot to piss in, spending all their bread on wheels and women, figuring everything in a skirt—or G-string—was a pushover. Jerks were saps, always falling in love and wanting to change you, make an honest woman out of you. Okay, put me in chains, if the price is right. This guy, jerk all the way.

I'm a doctor, he said.

Oh, she said, sounding impressed.

He told her how he had patched and mended those caught in the city's crossfire, how he wanted to help people and be a great doctor. She listened with wide eyes and nodded as if she knew what he felt deep inside and she smiled with practiced sincerity. A doctor, she figured, made lots of money, not realizing that a resident took home far less than an exotic dancer and got his hands just as dirty.

She looked directly into Roger Salisbury's eyes and softened her own. He looked into her eyes and thought he saw warmth and beauty of spirit.

Roger Salisbury, it turned out, was better at reading X rays than the looks in women's eyes.

1

THE RONGEUR

When the witness hesitated, I drummed my pen impatiently against my legal pad. Made a show of it. Not that I was in a hurry. I had all day, all week. The Doctors' Medical Insurance Trust pays by the hour and not minimum wage. Take your sweet time. The drum roll was only for effect, to remind the jury that the witness didn't seem too sure of himself. And to make him squirm a bit, to rattle him.

First the pen *clop-clop-clopping* against the legal pad. Then the slow, purposeful walk toward the witness stand, let him feel me there as he fans through his papers looking for a lost report. Then the stare, the high-voltage Jake Lassiter laser beam stare. Melt him down.

I unbuttoned my dark suitcoat and hooked a thumb into my belt. Then I stood there, 220 pounds of ex–football player, ex–public defender, ex–a-lot-of-things, leaning against the faded walnut rail of the witness stand, home to a million sweaty palms.

Only forty seconds since the question was asked, but I wanted it to seem like hours. Make the jury soak up the silence. The only sounds were the whine of the air conditioning and the paper shuffling of the witness. Young lawyers sometimes make the mistake of filling that black hole, of clarifying the question or rephrasing it, inadvertently breathing life into the dead air that hangs like a shroud over a hostile witness. What folly. The witness is zipped up because he's worried. He's thinking, not about his answer, but of the reason for the question, trying to outthink you, trying to anticipate the next question. Let him stew in his own juice.

Another twenty seconds of silence. One juror yawned. Another sighed.

Judge Raymond Leonard looked up from the *Daily Racing Form,* a startled expression as if he just discovered he was lost. I nodded silently, assuring him there was no objection awaiting the wisdom that got him through night classes at Stetson Law School. The judge was a large man in his fifties, bald and moon-faced and partial to maroon robes instead of traditional black. History would never link him with Justices Marshall or Cardozo, but he was honest and let lawyers try their cases with little interference from the bench.

Earlier, at a sidebar conference, the judge suggested we recess at two-thirty each day. He could study the written motions in the afternoon, he said with a straight face, practically dusting off his binoculars for the last three races at Hialeah. A note on the bench said, "Hot Enough, Rivera up, 5–1, ninth race." In truth, the judge was better at handicapping the horses than recognizing hearsay.

Another thirty seconds. Then a cleared throat, the sound of a train rumbling through a tunnel, and the white-haired witness spoke. "That depends," Dr. Harvey Watkins said with a gravity usually reserved for State of the Union messages.

The jurors turned toward me, expectant looks. I widened my eyes, all but shouting, "Bullshit." Then I worked up a small spider-to-the-fly smile and tried to figure out what the hell to ask next. What I wanted to say was, *Three hundred bucks an hour, and the best you can do is "that depends." One man is dead, my client is charged with malpractice, and you're giving us the old softshoe, "that depends."*

What I said was, "Let's try it this way." An exasperated tone, like a teacher trying to explain algebra to a chimpanzee. "When a surgeon is performing a laminectomy on the L3–L4 vertebrae, can he see what he's doing with the rongeur, or does he go by feel?"

"As I said before, that depends," Dr. Watkins said with excessive dignity. Like most hired guns, he could make a belch sound like a sonnet. White hair swept back, late sixties, retired chief of orthopedics at Orlando Presbyterian, he had been a good bone carpenter in his own right until he lost his nerves to an ice-filled river of Stolichnaya. Lately he talked for pay on the traveling malpractice circuit. Consultants, they call themselves. Whores, other doctors peg them. When I defended criminal cases, I thought my clients could win any lying contest at the county fair. Now I figure doctors run a dead heat with forgers and confidence men.

No use fighting it. Just suck it up and ask, "Depends on what?" Waiting for the worst now, asking an open-ended question on cross-examination.

"Depends on what point you're talking about. Before you enter the disc space, you can see quite clearly. Then, once you lower the rongeur into it to remove the nucleus pulposus, the view changes. The disc space is very small, so of course, the rongeur is blocking your view."

"Of course," I said impatiently, as if I'd been waiting for that answer since Ponce de León landed on the coast. "So at that point you're working blind?"

I wanted a *yes*. He knew that I wanted a *yes*. He'd rather face a hip replacement with a case of the shakes than give me a *yes*.

"I don't know if I'd characterize it exactly that way . . ."

"But the surgeon can't see what he's doing at that point, can he?" Booming now, trying to force a good old-fashioned one-word answer. Come on, Dr. Harvey Wallbanger, the sooner you get off the stand, the sooner you'll be in the air-conditioned shadows of Sally Russell's Lounge across the street, cool clear liquid sliding down the throat to cleanse your godforsaken soul.

"You're talking about a space maybe half a centimeter," the doctor responded, letting his basso profundo fill the courtroom, not backing down a bit. "Of course you don't have a clear view, but you keep your eye on the rongeur, to be aware of how far you insert it into the space. You feel for resistance at the back of the space and, of course, go no farther."

"My point exactly, doctor. You're watching the rongeur, you're feeling inside the disc space for resistance. You're operating blind, aren't you? You and Dr. Salisbury and every orthopedic surgeon who's ever removed a disc . . ."

"Objection! Argumentative and repetitious." Dan Cefalo, the plaintiff's lawyer, was on his feet now, hitching up his pants even as his shirttail flopped out. He fastened his third suitcoat button into the second hole. "Judge, Mr. Lassiter is making speeches again."

Judge Leonard looked up again, unhappy to have his handicapping interrupted. Three to one he didn't hear the objection, but a virtual lock that it would be sustained. The last objection was overruled, and Judge Leonard believed in the basic fairness of splitting the baby down the middle. It was easier to keep track if you just alternated your rulings, like a kid guessing on a true–false exam.

"Sustained," the judge said, nodding toward me and cocking his head with curiosity when he looked at Cefalo, now thoroughly misbuttoned and hunched over the plaintiff's table, a Quasimodo in plaid polyester. Then the judge handed a note to the court clerk, a young woman who sat poker-faced through tales of multiple homicides, scandalous divorces, and train wrecks. The clerk slipped the note to the bailiff, who left through the rear door that led to the judge's chambers. There, enveloped in the musty smell of old law books never read much less understood, he would give the note to the judge's secretary, who would call Blinky Blitstein and lay fifty across the board on Hot Enough.

"Your Honor, I'll rephrase the question," I said, as if I had a choice. "Doctor, I think you would agree that the rongeur blocks your view of the disc space, correct?"

"Substantially."

A twenty-five-cent word. What does it take to get a *yes* out of this guy? Dr. Watkins let his tongue dart over his lips. Getting a little dry, are we? Eyes just a bit cloudy and bloodshot. Cefalo put you up at the Sonesta Beach, I bet. Room service probably brought up a bottle of Russia's best. Maybe one of Finland's too. A Winter War in a tenth-floor suite overlooking the Atlantic.

I walked to the rear of the courtroom so that the jury was between the witness stand and me. I wanted all eyes on Dr. Watkins as I broke him like a rotten mast in a gale.

"Doctor, isn't it true that, because of the narrow disc space, any time a surgeon performs this kind of surgery, a known risk is that the rongeur will go too far, will pierce the aorta?"

"A risk? Of course, it's a risk, but . . ."

"And that's what happened here, the occurrence of that risk, that statistically will occur—"

"Objection! Your Honor, Mr. Lassiter refuses to permit the doctor to finish his answer. He's interrupting." This time Cefalo banged his knee on the plaintiff's table as he stood up and his tie flopped out of his misbuttoned coat like the tongue of a thirsty dog. Most days Cefalo dressed as well as the next guy, but in trial he figured he gained sympathy by looking like a vagrant. He'd drop his drawers if it would win one juror's vote. This day his suit was old and wrinkled and smelled like an overheated horse. But Dan Cefalo knew his stuff. Best to remember that or get blindsided when he transformed from Buddy Hackett to Gregory Peck in closing argument.

"Overruled," the judge said without looking up.

Thank you, Nathan Detroit.

I took a few giant steps toward the witness stand, feeling my oats. I wanted to finish with a flourish. Dr. Watkins had nailed us hard on direct examination. Now just trying to get even, or close to it. I walked to the clerk's table and picked up the stainless steel instrument that resembled a small, delicate pair of pliers. The clerk never looked up, leaving me staring into the top of her Afro. She was reading a paperback with a castle and a dark-eyed woman on the cover.

"Now, this rongeur, Plaintiff's Exhibit Five, is the perfect instrument for removing the herniated disc material, isn't it?"

"I don't know if it's perfect, but that's what's used."

They'll be examining his liver under a microscope before he'll give a defense lawyer a *yes*. I walked to the rear of the courtroom, the doctor's eyes tracking me, suspicion wrinkling his brow. He wouldn't trust me with the petty cash.

"But perfect as it is for one job, it poses a real and known danger to the aorta, doesn't it?"

Dr. Watkins smiled. The eyes seemed to clear. His chin thrust out and he shot a look at the jury, just to make sure they were paying attention.

"The rongeur poses no danger," he said in deep, senatorial tones. "The surgeon who is too hasty or too rough or loses track of where he is, that's the danger. A rongeur does not do the damage except in a most elementary way, the same way a gun kills, but it is the man pulling the trigger who is brought to justice. A surgeon who is negligent, that is the danger. It is professional negligence, or as you lawyers like to call it, malpractice, to damage the aorta while doing a laminectomy—"

"Your Honor!" I am much too loud, a wounded boar. "The witness is not being responsive. He is the one who is speech making for the benefit of the party that pays him royally." Anything to distract the jury from my blood spilling across the floor. One question too many, the classic bozo move on cross.

Judge Leonard swiveled in his cushioned chair. "Is that an objection?"

I toted up the judge's prior rulings like a blackjack player counting face cards. "Yes, Your Honor, I ask that the jury be instructed to disregard the witness's self-serving soliloquy."

"Sustained. The jury will disregard the last statement of the witness."

Fat chance, the jurors figuring that anything they're supposed to forget must be worth remembering. How to rescue the moment? I caught sight of Cefalo. If his smile were any wider, his uppers would fall out.

"No further questions are necessary, Your Honor," I said with more than a touch of bravado. Then I swaggered to my seat, as if I had just vanquished the witness. I doubted the jury bought even a slice of it. *Lassiter, why didn't you shut up when you had the chance?*

Ramrod straight, white hair in place, Dr. Watkins strode from the witness stand, pausing to nod graciously at the jury, a general admiring his troops. Then he walked by the plaintiff's table, bowed toward Dan Cefalo and tenderly patted Mrs. Melanie Corrigan, the young widow, on the arm. As he passed me, he shook his head, ever so slightly, a compassionate look, as if this poor wretch of a mouthpiece couldn't help it if he was on the wrong side and an incompetent boob to boot. What a pro. The jurors never took their eyes off him.

My eyes closed and behind them were visions of green hills and cool streams, where the courthouses were only for marriage licenses and real estate deeds. Then I wondered if it was too late to coach powder-puff football at a prep school in Vermont.

2

THE
GOOD GUYS

Roger Salisbury was pouring black bean soup over the rice, then carefully layering a row of chopped onions on top, building a little mound. Not a drop of the dark soup spilled. The Cuban crackers, which in my hands crumble into dust, he split down the middle with a thumb and index finger, a clean break like marble under a sculptor's chisel. Steady hands, the hands of a surgeon. Not hands that would have slipped, letting the rongeur puncture the aorta, leaving Philip

Corrigan to die of internal bleeding and Melanie Corrigan to live as a young, beautiful, and very rich widow. Which is why Roger Salisbury was questioning my strategy in cross-examining the white-haired baron of bombast who nearly blew me out of the courtroom this very day.

"If our defense is that I didn't nick the aorta, why were you trying to get Watkins to admit that a surgeon can't see what he's doing in a laminectomy? It sounded like you were trying to excuse me for something I didn't do."

When a client thinks that you are letting him sink into the treacherous waters of the justice system, it is best to appear calm and knowledgeable, even when you are floundering about, looking for the nearest lifeboat yourself. This is easier to do when not distracted by two young women who are appraising you with large, luminous, and inviting eyes.

"It's called alternative pleading," I said with authority and a polite smile toward our observers, perched on barstools at the counter. When confronted with large, luminous, and inviting eyes, I am polite without fail. "We say to the jury, first, the good doctor didn't come within a country mile of the damn blood vessel. Second, even if he might have sideswiped it, that's not negligence. It's an accepted risk of this kind of surgery because of the small disc space and the proximity of the aorta."

"I get the feeling you don't believe me," Roger Salisbury said. He ladled more soup onto the rice with those sturdy hands, and I watched the steam rise, a pungent aroma enveloping us. One of the women was smiling now. At me, I thought. Or was it at Roger? He was handsome in a nondescript way. Medium height, medium build, medium features. The kind of guy who gives police artists fits. Nothing to work with, no missing teeth, bent nose, or jagged scars, nothing protruding, nothing receding.

I dug into my palomilla, a tough piece of flank steak marinated in oils and spices and likely left on the hood of a '59 Chevy in the Miami sun. I was talking with my hands, or rather my fork, which had speared a sweet fried plantain.

"It's a historic legal strategy. In olden times, a plaintiff might sue his neighbor and say, 'I lent him my kettle, and when he returned it, it was cracked.' The neighbor answers the lawsuit and says, 'I never borrowed the kettle, but if I did, it was cracked when he gave it to me.' "

Roger Salisbury shook his head. "Your profession is so uncertain, so full of contradictions. I'll never understand the law."

"Nor I, women." Their eyes were lighting up with magical, come-hither glints. I stayed put and Roger kept talking.

"Jake, I have a lot of faith in you, you know that."

Oh boy, I got fired once by a client who started off just like that. "Sure, and you should have," I said, showing the old confidence.

"But I can't say I'm happy with the way the trial's going."

"Listen, Roger. There's a psychological phenomenon every defendant goes through during the plaintiff's case. Try to remember it's still the top of the first inning. We haven't even been to bat yet. Wait'll old Charlie Riggs testifies for us. He's honest and savvy, and he'll make Wallbanger Watkins look like the whoring sawbones he is."

"Sure."

"You don't sound convinced."

"Riggs is on the verge of senile dementia, if not over it. He speaks Latin half the time. He's the friggin' coroner—or was until they retired him—not an orthopedic surgeon."

"Roger, trust me. We need a canoemaker, not a carpenter. Charlie Riggs is going to tell the jury why Philip Corrigan died. It's a hole in their case, and I'm going to ride the U.S. Cavalry through it."

Finally the two women set sail for our table. One looked straight at me from under a pile of auburn hair that reached her shoulders and kept going toward Mexico. She had caramel skin and lustrous ebony eyes. The other had thick, jet black hair that only made her porcelain complexion seem even more delicate. She wore one earring shaped like a golden spermatozoan and another of ivory that could have been a miniature elephant tusk. Both women wore tourniquet-tight slacks, high-heeled open-toed shoes, and oversized cotton sweatshirts, with spangles and shoulders from here to the Orange Bowl.

"May we join you for a moment?" Miss Caramel Skin asked. The *you* was a *chew*.

Roger Salisbury looked up and grinned. Even the punitive damage claim hadn't sent his hormones into hibernation. I could have used the distraction. My social life was as empty as a Miami Beach hotel in July. But I took inventory quickly, knowing I had several hours of work ahead. There is a time for dallying, but the middle of a trial is not such a time. I wanted to finish the postmortem on the day's events and prepare for tomorrow and the widow's testimony. Still, an old reflex, maybe eons old, had the mental computer figuring a sort of cost–benefit analysis—how long it would take—the flirting time, make-nice time, bone-jumping time, and call-you-again time. Too long.

They already were sitting down and Caramel Skin was chattering about her ex-boyfriend, a Colombian, and what a scumbag he was. *Skoombag*. She was Costa Rican, Miss Earrings Honduran.

I shouldn't have brought Roger to Bayside, a yuppie hangout with shops, restaurants, and bars strung along Biscayne Bay downtown. It was a pickup place, and these two probably assumed we were in the hunt—two decent-looking guys under forty in suits—when all we wanted was solitude and an early dinner. Outside the windows, the young male lawyers, accountants, and bankers headed for the nearby singles bars, suitcoats slung over shoulders, red suspenders holding up Brooks Brothers suit pants. They slouched against open-air bars waiting for their frozen margaritas to ooze out of chrome-plated machines that belong in Dairy Queens, not taverns. Nearby the young women—mirror images in business suits or no-nonsense below-the-knee dresses—their mouths fixed in go-to-hell looks, struggled with the degree of toughness and cool necessary to beat the men at their own game. Altogether, a smug clique of well-dressed boys and girls.

"Carlos had a Cigarette," Caramel Skin was saying. "Used to go like a son-of-a-bitch." *Sunavabeach*. "Liked the Cigarette more than he liked me. Now he's at FCI."

Salisbury wore a blank look. I said, "Federal Correctional Institution. Probably used the boat to bring in bags of the white stuff."

"*Si. Hizo el tonto*. He played the fool for others. And, *como si esto fuera poco*, he used to beat me. Tie me up and spank me with a hairbrush. It was fun at first, but then . . ."

Roger Salisbury was into it now, asking Caramel Skin whether Carlos the Con used leather or plain old rope. Scientific study or kinky curiosity, I wondered. Miss Earrings was telling me that they were fashion models—aren't they all?—who really didn't have work permits. Came here on tourist visas. Which meant they also were following the scent for the Holy Grail, green cards. Bagging American husbands would do the trick.

The earrings dangled near my face. Our knees touched and her voice dropped to a whisper, a ploy to get me to lean closer. Do they teach this stuff or is it in their genes? A long fingernail traced the outline of my right ear. In the right time and place, it could have been erotic. In a brightly lit restaurant with my mind on business, it itched.

"Thick hair, Mister Broad Shoulders," she said. *Theek and Meester*. "Some of the Yankees, their hair is like, how they say, *telaranas?*"

"Cobwebs," Caramel Skin said.

"*Sí*, cobwebs. But yours, *chico*, is thick like *cáñamo*. And *rubianco*."

"Like hemp and almost blond," Caramel Skin said, helpfully. Her friend gave a tug on my theek *rubianco cáñamo*, which did not help me get a fried plantain into my mouth. "And *ojos azules*," she said, giggling, looking into my eyes.

The women excused themselves to go to the restroom, probably to divide up the spoils. Caramel Skin would get the smaller guy with neat, salt-and-pepper hair who was practically smacking his lips over images of sweet bondage. Earrings was stuck with *Meester* Broad Shoulders, who at least had neither cobwebs nor spiders in his mop but who seemed distracted.

Salisbury lit a cigarette, dragged deeply, and sent a swirl of smoke into the overhead fan. Doctors who smoke puzzle me. You know they know better. Maybe lack of discipline and self-control. I couldn't imagine a personal injury lawyer riding a motorcycle, not after seeing those eight-by-ten glossies taken by the Highway Patrol. Need a shovel to scrape up body parts.

I wanted to draw Roger away from his Latin American fantasy and talk about tomorrow's testimony. But he was saying something about a doubleheader that had nothing to do with Yankee Stadium. I shook my head no, and he gave me that puzzled look. I'd seen the same expression the first time he walked into my office about eighteen months earlier.

"You must like representing doctors," he said that day, after we exchanged hellos.

"Yeah, it's a great honor."

He gave me that look and dropped the malpractice complaint on my desk as if it carried the plague. While I read it, he walked around my office, ostensibly admiring the view of the bay, but surreptitiously looking for merit badges on the walls. He couldn't find any. No diplomas, no awards from the Kiwanis. I hung my Supreme Court admission ticket above the toilet at home. Covers a crack in the plaster. He stopped in front of a photo of my college football team, one of those posed shots with a hundred twenty guys filling the bleachers.

"You played football," he said. Impressed. He couldn't be sure I ever graduated from law school, but he was happy I could hit a blocking sled.

"A lead-footed linebacker," I said. "Better at lawyering than covering the tight end over the middle."

"Been defending doctors long?"

"Not as long as I played games in the PD's office, keeping some very bad actors on the street."

"Why'd you leave?"

"It made me puke."

"Huh?"

"Realizing every client I ever had was guilty. Not always with what they're charged, but guilty of some crime, sometimes worse than the charge."

I told him how it felt to see some slimeball go free after a warrantless search, then pimp-roll back into the courtroom for pistol-whipping a sixty-year-old liquor store clerk. *Ja-cob, my man, they got no probable cause.*

19

Told him I quit and did plaintiff's PI. Half my clients were phonies. Phony injuries and phony doctors or real injuries and no insurance.

"So representing doctors is a step up," Roger Salisbury had said brightly.

"From the gutter to the curb."

That look again.

"I sold out, joined the high-rise set at rich, old Harman & Fox," I told him. "Ordinarily, the dark-wood-and-deep-carpet types wouldn't give a guy like me a second look. Afraid I'd spill the soup on my vest, if I owned one. But they woke up one day and figured they didn't have anybody who could try a case. They could shuffle papers and write memos, but they didn't know how to tap dance in front of a jury. So I won some cases, a few for very dangerous doctors."

Now his puzzled look changed to one of concern.

"Bottom line," I said, using a favorite expression of the corporate gazoonies who ruled the firm. "I've spent my entire career looking for the good guys and have yet to find them."

He was quiet a moment, probably wondering if I was incompetent. Good, we were even. I always assume the worst. Fewer surprises later.

Things improved after that. I checked up on him. His rep was okay. Board certified and no prior lawsuits. He probably checked me out, too. Found out I've never been disbarred, committed, or convicted of moral turpitude. And the only time I was arrested it was a case of mistaken identity—I didn't know the guy I hit was a cop.

So here we were, waiting for *dos chicas* to powder their noses or inhale something into them, and my mind was stuck on the mundane subject of the pending trial.

"Roger, let's talk about tomorrow. Cefalo will put the widow on first thing. Today I was watching you out of the corner of my eye and you were staring at her. I know she looks like a million bucks, but if I saw it while I was getting blindsided by Wallbanger Watkins, I'm sure the jurors did, too. It could be mistaken for a look of guilt, like you feel sorry you croaked her old man. That's worse than having the hots for her."

"Okay, didn't know I was doing it. Probably just staring into space."

"Yeah sure. The point is, she's likely to be a very good witness. The men in the jury all want in her pants, the women want to mother her."

"Okay already, I get the point."

"Good. I don't want to concern you, but the lovely widow is a real problem for us. She can make the jury forget all our medical mumbo jumbo. That gray silk dress today with the strand of white pearls. Classy but not too flashy."

Salisbury laughed. "You ought to see her in a strapless cocktail dress."

"Uh-huh." *Uh-huh* is what I say when I don't know what to say. I would have liked Salisbury to fill me in here, but he didn't give me any help. After a moment I asked, "Since when are you Mrs. Corrigan's fashion consultant?"

"Oh that. I probably never told you. When Philip started seeing me for the back and leg pain, we became friendly. I wasn't dating anybody. They were just married. He started asking me over to their house in Gables Estates. Cocktail parties, dinners, sometimes just the three of us."

"So you know Mrs. Corrigan?"

"Melanie. Sure."

"Melanie, is it?"

He looked at me with a what's-the-big-deal look and I didn't have an answer so I polished off the palomilla and thought it over. No big deal. I just would have liked to have known about it sometime before trial.

In a moment our new friends cruised back, eyes a thousand watts brighter, ready to roll. I mumbled my apologies to Miss Earrings, who, with no apparent regret, shifted her electrified look to the blandly handsome doctor. I left them there, two women with a buzz on, and the man who had entrusted his career to me, the man who hadn't told me everything. What else, I wondered, had he left out?

I paused at the door to look back. The restaurant was filled now.

21

Some of the yuppies were crowding the bar, making too much noise, pushing limes into their Mexican beer, a trendy brand aged about as long as their attention spans. If you have to put lime in your beer, you might as well drink Kool-Aid.

Back at the table, one woman sat on each side of Roger Salisbury. They all laughed. I left the three of them there, the mathematical possibilities of their union crowding Melanie Corrigan's testimony into a dusty recess of my mind.

3

THE WIDOW

"Mrs. Corrigan, do you love your husband?"

"I do." A pause, a catch in the throat, a quiver, the beginning of a tear, then like a lake swollen by a summer storm, an overflow cascading down sculpted cheekbones. "That is, I did. I loved him very much."

Blessed timing. They don't teach that in finishing school. Dan Cefalo continued his questioning. "Do you miss him?"

Another leading question, but only a dunce would incur the jury's wrath by interrupting the soap opera with a news bulletin.

"Very much. Every day. We shared so much. Sometimes, when a car pulls into the driveway, I forget, and I think, well, maybe it's Phil."

And maybe it's the paperboy. God, could she lay it on thick. She looked toward the jury and then away as if the memory was too much to bear. A lace handkerchief appeared out of a navy leather clutch and the big, brown, wet eyes were dabbed dry. The pain radiated from her, but I was the one who was dying. Every question launched an arrow, and every answer pierced my heart. The widow was majestic, thick russet hair swept straight back to lay bare those chiseled lines, to expose her suffering. All for the glory of justice and a seven-figure award for mental anguish, loss of society, comfort, and consortium.

"Tell us about your husband, your late husband, Mrs. Corrigan. And I know it's a painful subject, so if you need a recess to gather yourself, please just say so." Cefalo extended his arms toward the widow and bowed from the waist, as if she were royalty. And she did look regal, white gloves setting off a navy and white double-breasted cardigan that covered a matching skirt. Maybe the gloves hid Racy Red nail polish, already slathered on for a night of romping through Coconut Grove clubs. Maybe on cross-examination I should order her to take off the gloves and bare her claws. Sure, or maybe I should just grab a sword and mutter a hara-kiri chant.

"I don't know where to begin, there's so much to say," she said, obviously knowing exactly where she would begin. I wanted her to say: *He was boffing half the stewardesses in town while his first wife lay dying; he made millions bribing county commissioners to grant zoning variances; and if it weren't for high-placed friends in Washington, he would have been indicted for tax evasion.*

What she said was: "Phil was the most giving man I've ever known. The way he cared for his first wife when she was terminally ill, if you could have seen that, if you all could have seen it." Then she turned to the jury, an actress facing her adoring audience. "He never thought he could love again, but I brought something to his life. And to me, he was everything—a lover, a friend, even the father I never had. Then for him to die like this, in his prime."

Clever. Very clever. So well rehearsed it didn't look rehearsed. Explaining how a twenty-six-year-old woman marries a fifty-five-year-old man. A father, for crying out loud. No mention that the champagne corks were popping only six weeks after he buried his beloved first wife. And if I bring it out on cross, I'm a cad. It was a virtuoso performance. Even Judge Leonard was listening, practically a first. He had been in a fine mood at motion calendar in the morning, as well he should after Hot Touch paid $10.40, $5.40, and $4.80.

When Dan Cefalo turned to me and said, "Your witness," he was smiling so broadly I almost didn't notice that his fly was half undone and he had buttoned his shirt into his suitcoat.

The occasion called for brilliance. Roger Salisbury looked at me as if I were his last friend in the world. I approached the witness stand with a solicitous smile. I still hadn't made up my mind. Behind those tears I saw a flinty toughness that I would love to bring out. But make a mistake, reduce her to tears or hysterics, and the jury would lynch me and nail enough zeroes on the verdict to buy an aircraft carrier. She looked straight back at me. The full lips lost a bit of their poutiness and set in a firm line. It's there somewhere, I knew. But my investigators couldn't find it in six months and my pretrial deposition came up empty. I couldn't risk it now.

I turned to the judge. "Your Honor," I said, as if seeking his approval, "I believe it would be unfair for us to keep Mrs. Corrigan on the stand to discuss this painful subject. We have no questions." Roger Salisbury sank into his chair looking hopeless and abandoned. Men on Death Row have brighter futures.

"Very well," Judge Leonard said, aiming a small smile in my direction. "Mr. Cefalo, call your next witness."

"The plaintiff rests," Dan Cefalo said, his goofy grin still lighting up the room.

"Any motions?" the judge asked. We approached the bench and the judge sent the jurors out to lunch.

"At this time, the defense moves for a directed verdict," I said without a great deal of conviction.

"On what ground, Mr. Lassiter?" the judge asked.

"On the ground that there's insufficient evidence of proximate cause, first that the surgery caused the aneurysm, and second that the aneurysm caused the death."

"Denied," the judge said before Cefalo even opened his mouth. "The plaintiff's expert testified to that. Whatsa matter, Jake, it's a jury question at least."

I knew that. Somewhere between his Bloody Marys and his White Russians, Dr. Watkins had stuck us on proximate cause, at least sufficiently to beat a directed verdict, but I was giving the judge a little preview of our defense. Oh Dr. Charles W. Riggs, I need you now.

The judge looked over the courtroom, which was emptying, and waved us closer to the bench. With a hand, he signaled the court stenographer to take a hike. "You boys talk settlement?"

A practical enough question. If he could clear us out of the courtroom, he could spend the rest of the week at the track.

"Judge, we offered the policy," I said apologetically. "A million dollars even, all we've got, no excess coverage. They oughta take it and spare the court all this time and effort."

Cefalo shook his head. "Our liquidated damages alone, lost net accumulations for the estate, are over three million. To say nothing of the widow's mental anguish and consortium claims."

The judge laughed. "Danny, your widow lady don't look like she'll be without consortium for long."

Good. I liked hearing that. Maybe the jurors will feel the same. Then we only get hit with three million, enough to wipe out the good doctor several times over.

The judge straightened. "All right, boys. Let's cut through the bullshit. Danny, how much will you take, bottom line?"

"Two-point-five. Today. No structured settlement. All cash."

The judge raised his eyebrows and ran a hand over his bald head. "Attaboy. I always figured you to bet the favorites to show, but you're no ribbon clerk, hey? Jake, whadaya got?"

I turned my pockets inside out and shook my head. "A million, judge, just the policy. Client's only been in private practice five, six years. Just finished paying off his debts. He's pulling down big income, but no assets yet. We can't pay it if we don't have it. Besides, he's simply not liable."

"Okay, Jake, but it's halftime, and you're getting your ass kicked from here to Sopchoppy. You see what's coming, don't you?"

"Sure judge, but you haven't heard my halftime speech."

"Fine, we start with your first witness at one o'clock. Court's in recess." With that, he banged the gavel, and the hollow explosion echoed off the high, beamed ceiling. Roger Salisbury slumped onto the defense table as if felled by a rifle shot.

I headed into the corridor, nearly smashing into the lovely widow. She didn't notice. She was toe-to-toe with another young woman. Each was jawing at the other, faces inflamed, just a few inches apart like Billy Martin and an umpire. I didn't recognize the other woman. No makeup, short-cropped jet black hair, a turned-up nose and a deep tan, blue jeans and running shoes, maybe the last pretty woman in Miami with thick glasses. Tortoiseshell round frames, giving her a professorial look. Her language, though, was not destined to win tenure. "You're a conniving slut and a little whore, and when I get to the bottom of this, we'll see who's out in the cold!"

The widow's eyes had narrowed into slits. No tears now. Just sparks and flames. "Get away from me you ingrate, and clear your junk out of the house by six tonight or your ratty clothes will be floating in the bay."

Dan Cefalo stepped in and separated the two. "Miss Corrigan, I think you best leave."

Oh, Miss Corrigan. The one with the colorful vocabulary must be Philip Corrigan's daughter by his first marriage. I followed her down the corridor.

"May I be of assistance?" I asked politely. Trying not to be your typical lawyer scavenging on the perimeter of misfortune.

She lowered the thick glasses and studied me with steaming eyes the color of a strong cup of coffee. The eyes had decided not to make any friends today. She looked me up and down, ending at my black wingtips. I could check for wounds later. Her nostrils flared as if I emitted noxious fumes.

"You're that doctor's lawyer, aren't you?" She made it sound like a capital crime.

"Guilty as charged. I saw you discussing a matter with Mrs. Corrigan and I just wondered if I might help . . ."

"Why? Are you fucking her or do you just want to?" She slid her glasses back up the slope of the ski-jump nose and headed toward the elevators.

"No and yes," I called after her.

4

THE SPORTSWRITER

My desk was covered with little white telephone messages. Office confetti. You think the universe comes to a halt when you are locked into your own little world, but it doesn't. It goes on whether you're in trial or at war or under the surgeon's knife. Or dead. Dead rich like Philip Corrigan laid out on smooth satin in a mahogany box, or dead poor, a wino facedown in the bay.

Greeting me in my bayfront office was the clutter of messages that would not be answered—lawyers who wouldn't be called, clients who wouldn't be seen, motions that wouldn't be heard while my world was circumscribed by the four walls of Courtroom 6-1 in the Dade County Courthouse. Next to the phone messages were stacks of pleadings, letters and memos, carefully arranged in order of importance with numbers written on those little yellow squares of paper that have their own stickum on back. What did we do before those sticky doodads were invented? Or before the photocopier? Or the computer, the telecopier, and the car phone? It must have been a slower world. Before lawyers had offices fifty-two stories above Biscayne Bay with white-coated waiters serving afternoon tea, and before surgeons cleared four hundred thousand a year, easy, scraping out gristle from knees and squeezing bad discs out of spines.

Lawyers had become businessmen, leveraging their hourly rates by stacking offices with high-billing associates, forming "teams" for well-heeled clients, and raking in profits on the difference between associates' salaries and their billing rates. Doctors had become little industries themselves, creating huge pension plans, buying buildings and leasing them back, investing in labs and million-dollar scanning machines, getting depreciation and investment income that far out-paced patient fees.

Maybe doctors were too busy following the stock market to be much good at surgery anymore. Maybe the greed of lawyers and doctors equally contributed to the malpractice crisis. But maybe an occasional slip of the scalpel or a missed melanoma just couldn't be helped. What was it old Charlie Riggs said the first day he reviewed the charts in Salisbury's case? *Errare humanum est.* To err is human. Sure, but a jury seldom forgives.

I grabbed the first message on stack one. Granny Lassiter called. I hoped she hadn't been arrested again. Granny lived in Islamorada in the Florida Keys and taught me everything I know about fishing and most of what I know about decency and principle. She was one of the first to speak against unrestrained construction in the environmentally fragile Keys. When speaking didn't work, she got a Key West conch named Virgil Thigpen drunk as an Everglades skunk and comman-deered his tank truck. The truck, not coincidentally, had just sucked up

30

the contents of Granny's septic tank and that of half a dozen neighbors. Granny drove it smack into the champagne and caviar crowd at the grand opening of Pelican Point, a plug-ugly pink condo on salt-eaten concrete stilts that would soon sink into the dredged muck off Key Largo. While the bankers, lawyers, developers, and lobbyists stood gaping, and TV cameras whirred, Granny shouted, "Shit on all of you," then sloshed twelve hundred gallons of crud onto the canape table.

The judge gave her probation plus a hundred hours of community service, which she fulfilled by donating a good-sized portion of her homemade brew to the Naval Retirement Home in Marathon.

I returned the call. Granny just wanted to pass the time of day and give me a high-tide report. Next message, the unmistakably misshapen handwriting of Cindy, my secretary:

Across the River,
A Voice to Shine,
Tempus Fugit, *Doc Speaks at Nine.*

What the hell? A headful of tight, burnt orange-brown curls popped through my door. To my eye, Cindy's hair seemed to clash with the fuchsia eye shadow but clearly matched her lipstick. If the lipstick were any brighter, you could use it for fluorescent highway markers.

"Cindy, what's this?"

"Haiku, *el jefe*."

"Who?"

"I do."

"What you do?"

"I do haiku," she said, laughing. "Haiku is three-line Japanese poetry, no breaking hearts, just recording the author's observations of nature and the human experience."

"What's it mean?"

"C'mon boss. Get with it. Crazy old Charlie Riggs is set to testify at nine tomorrow morning. He'll tell one and all what killed filthy rich Philip Corrigan."

"Good, he's our best witness."

"I don't know," Cindy said, twirling a finger through a stiff curl. If a mosquito flew into her hair, it would be knocked cold. "I've got a bad feeling about this case. Your Dr. Salisbury has a weird look in his eye."

"All men look at you that way, Cindy. Try wearing a bra."

"I never thought *you* noticed."

"Hard to miss when the air conditioning turns this place into a meat locker. Now c'mon Cindy, help me out. We have anything on Corrigan's daughter by his first marriage?"

"Sure, a little." Cindy was not as ditsy as she looked. She could turn heads with her hyped-up looks, bouncy walk, and easy smile, but underneath were brains and street smarts, an unusual combination.

"Susan Corrigan," Cindy said, without consulting the file. "About thirty, undergrad work at UF, then a master's in journalism at Northwestern. Sportswriter at the *Herald*."

"You're amazing," I said, meaning it.

"In many splendored ways unbeknownst to you."

I chose not to wade in those crowded waters.

"Wait a second," I said. "Of course. *Susan Corrigan*. I know the by-line, the first woman inside the Dolphins' locker room." I picked up yesterday's paper, which had been gathering dust in a wicker basket next to my desk. I found the story stripped across the top of the sports section under the headline, "Dolphin Hex? Injuries Vex Offensive Line."

BY SUSAN CORRIGAN
Herald Sports Writer

On a team where the quarterback is king, something wicked keeps happening to the palace guard.

And the palace tackles. And the palace center.

"It's scary the things that happened to our offensive line in the last three weeks," Dolphin Coach Don Shula said yesterday. "When injuries hit us, they come in bunches."

Sure, Susan Corrigan. Made a name for herself playing tennis against Martina, sprinting against Flo-Jo, then writing first-person pieces. I'd read her stuff. Tough and funny. Today I'd seen half of that.

"What's she have to do with Salisbury's case?" Cindy asked.

"Don't know. But there's more to the second Mrs. Corrigan than tears and white gloves, and Susan knows something."

"What's she look like, an Amazon warrior?"

"Hardly. Cute, not beautiful. Long legs, short dark hair like Dorothy Hamill, wears glasses, wholesome as the Great Outdoors. No hint of scandal."

Cindy laughed. "Doesn't sound like your type."

"Did I mention foulmouthed?"

"We're getting warmer."

"Cindy, this is all business."

"Isn't it always?"

Practice was almost over and only a few players were still on the field. Natural grass warmed by the sun, a clean earthy smell in the late afternoon Florida air. It had been one of those days when it's a crime to be shackled to an office or courtroom. Winter in the tropics. Clear sky, mid-seventies, a light breeze from the northeast. On the small college campus where the Dolphins practice, the clean air and open spaces were a world away from Miami's guttersnipes and bottom feeders.

I spotted Susan Corrigan along the sideline. She wore gray cotton sweats and running shoes and seemed to be counting heads, seeing what linemen were still able to walk as they straggled back to the locker room. A reporter's notepad was jammed into the back of her sweatpants and a ballpoint pen jutted like a torpedo out of her black hair. All business. On the field in front of her only the quarterbacks and wide receivers were still going through their paces, a few more passes before the sun set. On an adjacent practice field, a ballboy shagged kick after kick from a solitary punter.

"Susan," I called from a few yards away.

She turned with an expectant smile. The sight of me washed it away. I asked if we could talk. She turned back to the field. I asked if she was waiting for somebody. She studied the yard markers. I asked who she liked in the AFC East. She didn't give me any tips. I just stood there, looking at her profile. It wasn't hard to take.

She turned toward me again, a studious yet annoyed look through thick glasses, as if an interesting insect had landed in her soup. "Why should I help you?"

"Because you're not real interested in helping Melanie Corrigan. Because you know things about her that could help an innocent doctor save his career. Because you like the way I comb my hair."

"You're dumber than you look," she hissed.

"Is there a compliment buried in that one?"

"You're hopeless."

I can take being put down. Judges do it all the time. So do important people like a maître d' in a Bal Harbour restaurant who insists that diners wear socks. But this was different. I looked at her, a fresh-faced young woman in cotton sweats that could not hide her athletic yet very womanly body. I gave her a hangdog look that sought mercy. She turned back to the field. Dan Marino was firing short outs to Mark Duper and Mark Clayton. Though each pass arrived with ferocious speed, there was no slap of leather onto skin at the receiving end.

"Soft hands," Susan Corrigan said, mostly to herself.

"These guys are good but Paul Warfield will always be my favorite," I said. "Had moves like Baryshnikov. Stopping him was like tackling the wind."

"Sounds like you know more about football than about your own client."

I gave her my blank look and she kept going. "You still don't get it. You still don't know the truth."

"Get what? Look, I'm defending a man accused of professional malpractice. I don't know what the truth is. I never know. I just take the facts—or as much of them as I can get from people biased on all sides—and throw them at the jurors. You never know what jurors hear or remember or care about. You never know why they rule the way they do. They can right terrible wrongs or do terrible wrongs. They can shatter lives and destroy careers, and that's what I'm worried about with Roger Salisbury."

"Bring out the violins."

Suddenly a shout from behind us: "Heads up!" I looked up in time to see a brown blur dropping from the sky. Susan Corrigan's hands shot out and she caught the ball with her fingertips. A cheer went up from the wide receivers, anonymous behind their face masks.

"Soft hands," I said, "and a lot of quick." I gave her my best smile. It had been good enough for several generations of University of Miami coeds, their brains fried from working on their tans. It had lowered the minimal resistance of stewardesses from half a dozen failing airlines. It did not dent the armor of Susan Corrigan.

"Sit on this," she said, lateraling the ball toward my gut.

I felt like popping her one. Instead I took my frustrations out on the funny-shaped ball. Fingertips across the laces, I heaved a hard, tight spiral to the punter half the field away. He took it chest high and nodded with approval. The toss surprised even me.

Susan Corrigan whistled. "You've played some ball."

Her tone had subtly changed. Good, maybe if I went a few rounds with Mike Tyson, she'd give me the time of day.

"A little," I said. I decided not to tell her my right arm just lost all its feeling except for a prickly sensation where the wires had been frayed.

"Quarterback?"

"No, I decided early I'd rather be the hitter than the hittee. Linebacker with lousy lateral movement. Occasionally I'd hit people returning kickoffs if they came my way. Sometimes filled in when games were already won or lost and I'd smack fullbacks who trudged up the middle. Mostly I polished the pine, which is actually aluminum and can freeze your butt in places like South Bend and Ann Arbor in November. Gave me time to philosophize about cheerleaders' thighs."

"You look like you stay in shape."

"Used to windsurf a lot. Now I just hit the heavy bag a couple times a week and never miss a Wednesday night poker game."

"I can beat almost any man at almost any sport," she said. She didn't sound boastful. If you kin do it, it ain't braggin'.

"We should play ball sometime," I suggested.

She showed me the first hint of a smile. Her face didn't break. "Are you being a smartass now?" she asked, almost pleasantly.

"No. I just want to talk to you."

"I'll talk if you can beat me in a race."

"What?"

"The goal line," she said, pointing across the empty practice field. "Let's see who can score."

Only the punter was still on the field. He took his two-step approach and kicked the ball with a solid *thwack*. The same motion, time after time, a machine following the path designed for it on the drawing board. Like a surgeon clearing out the disc, the same motion, time after time. But the punter had shanked one off the side of his foot, and even Roger Salisbury could have booted one. There I go again, mind slipping out of gear.

"Yes or no?" she demanded. "I've got to interview Shula, and that's no day at the beach the way the Bills dropped buffalo shit all over them last Sunday."

"Okay," I said, taking off my Scotch brogue wing tips. "I suppose you want a head start." She laughed a wily laugh.

The sun was just dropping over the Everglades to the west and a pink glow spread across the sky, casting Susan Corrigan into soft focus. I stretched my hamstrings and concocted a plan. I'd run stride for stride with her without breathing hard, maybe make a crack or two, then shoot by her, and run backwards the last ten yards. I'd let her jump into my arms at the goal line if she were so inclined. Then, I'd be a gracious winner and take her out for some fresh pompano and a good white wine.

She dropped into sprinter's stance, shouted "Go," and flew across the field. I bolted after her, my tie flapping over my shoulder like a pennant at the big game. She was five yards ahead after the first two seconds. Her stride was effortless, her movements smooth. My eyes fixed on her firm, round bottom, now rolling rhythmically with each stride. Halfway there I was still in second place, the greyhound chasing the mechanical rabbit. So I picked it up, still three yards back with only thirty to go. So much for the plan. Chasing pride now. Longer strides, lifting the knees too high, some wasted motion, but letting the energy of each step power the next one. Two steps behind and she shot a quick glance over her shoulder. A mistake, but only ten yards to go, no way to catch her, so I lunged, grabbing at her waist, hand slipping down over a hip, tumbling her into the grass with me rolling on top and her glasses, notepad, and pen whirling this way and that.

We ended up near the goal line, her on the bottom looking up, moist warm breath tickling my nose. A lot of my body was touching a lot of her body, and she wasn't complaining.

"First and goal from the one," I whispered.

I looked straight into her eyes from a distance any quarterback could sneak. Was it my imagination or was the glacial ice melting? I was ready for her to get all dewy and there would be some serious sighing going on. But I had come up a yard short. She flipped me off her like a professional wrestler who doesn't want to be pinned, one of her knees slamming into my groin as she bounced up. She stood there squinting in the dusk, looking for her glasses while I sucked in some oxygen.

"You really don't know, do you?" she said, standing over me.

"Not only that, but I don't know what I don't know." My voice was pinched.

"Then listen, because you're only going to hear it once. Your client isn't guilty of medical malpractice."

"He's not?"

"No. He's guilty of murder. He killed my father. He planned it along with that slut who ought to get an Academy Award from what I saw in court today. I can't prove it, but I know it's true."

"I don't believe this."

"Believe it. Your client's a murderer. He should be fried or whatever they do these days. So pardon me if I don't get all choked up over his career problems or insurance rates. He was planking the slut—

something that doesn't exactly put him in an exclusive club—and they planned it together. The malpractice suit is just a cover."

"I still don't get it." I was starting to feel like a sap, something Susan Corrigan seemed to know the moment she met me.

"The lawsuit makes it look like the doctor and the widow are enemies. That's their cover. And the way I figure it, Lassiter, you're supposed to lose. Or at least it doesn't matter. If you lose, the insurance company will pay her, and she'll probably split the money with him. Or maybe he gets it all. She'll get more than she needs from the estate. And if she wins more than his insurance coverage, he doesn't have to worry because she won't try to collect."

I sat there with a look as intelligent as a vacant lot. "Murder and insurance fraud. You have no proof of that. And I just can't believe it."

"I can see that, now," she said. "You're not a bad guy, Lassiter. You're just not fast enough to be a linebacker, and you don't know shit from second base."

5

THE CORONER

Charlie Riggs took the stand with a smile on his face and a plastic model of the spine in his back pocket. I felt better just looking at him. Bushy gray moustache and beard, a brown tweedy jacket more at home in Ivy League libraries than art deco Miami, twinkling eyes full of experience. A trustworthy man. Like having Walter Cronkite on my side.

He'd testified hundreds of times for the state and was comfortable on the witness stand. He crossed his legs, revealing drooping socks and pale calves. He breathed on his eyeglasses and wiped them on his tie. He slipped the glasses onto his small nose that was almost buried by his beard. Then Charlie Riggs nodded. He was ready.

"Please state your name and profession for the jury," I instructed him.

"Charles W. Riggs, M.D., pathologist by training, medical examiner of Dade County for twenty-eight years, now happily retired."

"Tell us, Dr. Riggs, what are the duties of a medical examiner."

"Objection!" Dan Cefalo was on his feet. "Dr. Riggs is retired. He is incompetent to testify as to the current medical examiner's duties."

In the realm of petty objections, that one ranked pretty high, but it was the first one of the day, and you could flip a coin on it.

"Sustained," Judge Leonard said, unfolding the sports section, looking for the racetrack charts.

I had another idea. "Let's start this way, Dr. Riggs. What is a medical examiner?"

"Well, in merry old England, they were called coroners. You can trace coroners back to at least the year 1194. They were part of the justice system, part judge, part tax collector. The coroner was the *custos placitorum coronae*, the guardian of the pleas of the Crown. If a man was convicted of a crime, the coroner saw to it that his goods were forfeited to the Crown."

Cefalo looked bored, the judge was not listening as usual, but the jurors seemed fascinated by the bearded old doctor. It works that way. What's mundane to lawyers and judges enchants jurors.

"Later the coroner's duties included determining the cause of death with the help of an inquest. The sheriff would empanel a jury, much as you have here." He smiled toward the jury box, and in unison, six faces smiled back. They liked him. That was half the battle.

"The jury had to determine whether death was *ex visitatione divina*, by the visitation of God, or whether man had a hand in it. Even if death was accidental, there was still a sort of criminal penalty. For example, if a cart ran over someone and killed him, the owner had to pay the Crown the equivalent value of the cart. That got to be quite a problem when steamships and trains began doing the killing."

The jurors nodded, flattered that this wise old man would take the time to give them a history lesson. "Still later, coroners began recording how many deaths were caused by particular diseases. Sometimes I spend my evenings with a glass of brandy and a collection of the Coroner's Rolls from the 1200s. You'd be surprised how much we can learn. At any rate, Counselor, the job of the coroner, or medical examiner, is to determine cause of death. Our credo is 'to speak for the dead, to protect the living.' "

"And how does a coroner determine cause of death?" I asked.

Charlie Riggs pushed his glasses back up his nose with a chubby thumb. "By physical and medical examination, various testing devices, gas chromatography, electron microscopes, the study of toxicology, pharmacology, radiology, pathology. Much is learned in the autopsy, of course."

"May we assume you have determined the cause of death in a number of cases?"

"Thousands. For over twenty years, I performed five hundred or more autopsies a year and supervised many more."

"Can you tell us about some of your methods, some of your memorable cases?"

A hand smacked the plaintiff's table and Dan Cefalo was on his feet, one pantleg sticking into the top of his right sock, the other pantleg dragging below the heel of the left shoe where the threads had unraveled from the cuff. "Objection," he said wearily. "This retired gentleman's life story is irrelevant here."

Taking a shot at Riggs's age. I hoped the two older jurors were listening. "Your Honor, I'm entitled to qualify Dr. Riggs as an expert."

Cefalo was ready for that. He didn't want to hear any more than he had to from Charlie Riggs. "We'll stipulate that Dr. Riggs was the medical examiner for a long time, that he's done plenty of autopsies, and that he's qualified to express an opinion on cause of death."

That should have been enough, but I still wanted Riggs to tell his stories. When you have a great witness, keep him up there. Let the jury absorb his presence.

"Objection overruled," Judge Leonard said. Good, my turn to win one.

"Dr. Riggs, you were about to tell us of your cases and methods of medical examination of the cause of death."

So Charlie Riggs unfolded his memories. There was the aging playboy who lived at Turnberry Isle, found dead of a single bullet wound to the forehead. Or so it seemed. The autopsy showed no bullet in the skull, no exit wound, just a round hole right between the eyes, as if from a small caliber shell.

"The police were stumped for a murder weapon," Charlie Riggs said. "Sometimes it's best to consider everyday items. I searched the grounds and, in a dumpster near the marina, I found a woman's red shoe with blood on the metal spiked heel. The blood type matched the playboy's, the heel matched the wound, and the owner of a French shoe shop at Mayfair identified the woman who bought the six-hundred-dollar shoes two weeks earlier. The woman confessed to doing him in. A lover's spat, she didn't want to kill him, just brain him."

Then there was the mystery of the burned woman. She was sitting there, fully clothed, on her sofa, burned to death. Her clothes were not even singed. There was no smoke or evidence of fire in the apartment. The woman's boyfriend had found the body. He said she came home drunk, took a shower, and next thing he knew, she was sitting on the sofa dead.

"I took a pair of tweezers and probed the bathtub drain," Charlie Riggs told the jury. He paused. Several jurors exhaled in unison.

"It was just a hunch. Up came pieces of skin, and I knew the answer."

Charlie Riggs smiled a knowing smile and stroked his beard, everybody's favorite professor.

"Both had come home drunk, and she passed out. The boyfriend tried to revive her in the bathtub, but sailing three sheets to the wind, he turned on the hot water and left her there. The scalding water burned her to death. When the boyfriend sobered up, he panicked, so he dried her off, dressed her, put her on the sofa, and called the police."

The jury sat entranced. There's nothing like tales of death, well told. Riggs testified about matching tire treads to the marks on a hit-and-run victim's back, of fitting a defendant's teeth to bite marks on a rape–murder victim, of finding teeth in a drain under a house, the only proof of the *corpus delicti,* the body of a man dissolved in sulfuric acid by his roommate.

The litany of crime had its purpose, to shock the jury with deeds of true miscreants, to deliver a subtle message that the justice system should prosecute murderers, not decent surgeons, even if they might make mistakes. *Errare humanum est.* If that's what it was, an honest error.

. I hadn't told Charlie Riggs about the conversation with Susan Corrigan. What would I tell him, that a dead man's daughter, poisoned with grief and hate, thinks my client is a murderer? She had no physical evidence, no proof, no nothing, except the allegation that Roger Salisbury and Melanie Corrigan were getting it on. I would talk to Salisbury about it, but not now.

While Charlie Riggs testified, I watched Roger. He kept shooting sideways glances at Melanie Corrigan's perfect profile. She watched the witness, oblivious to the attention. She was wearing a simple cotton dress that, to me, looked about two sizes too large, but I supposed was in style. A wide belt gathered it at the waist and it ended demurely below the knee. It was one of those deceiving things women wear, so simple it disguises the name of an Italian designer and a megabucks price tag.

I tried to read the look in Roger Salisbury's eyes but could not. Was there a chance that it was true? Not just that he might have been diddling his patient's wife. I didn't care about that. But that he might have killed Corrigan. That it was all a plot, that the malpractice trial was just a cover, or better yet, a way to pick up another million. If that's what it was, there'd be plenty of chances for Salisbury to tank it. He was scheduled to testify after Riggs.

I continued my direct examination: "Now Dr. Riggs, have you had an opportunity to examine the medical records compiled by the physicians and the hospital?"

"Yes."

"And based on the records, and your years of experience, do you have an opinion to a reasonable degree of medical probability what caused the death of Philip Corrigan?"

"I do."

The courtroom was silent except for the omnipresent hum of the air conditioning. Everyone knew the next question.

"And what was the cause of death?"

"A ruptured aorta. Internal bleeding, which in turn caused a lowering of blood pressure. In layman's terms, the heart, which is the pump in a closed circulatory system, didn't have enough fluid to pump, so it stopped."

"And what, sir, caused the aorta to rupture?"

"There is no way to answer that with absolute certainty. We can only exclude certain things."

"Such as?" Keep the questions short, let the doctor carry the ball.

"Well, Dr. Salisbury here certainly didn't do it with the rongeur. If he had, the rupture would be on the posterior side of the aorta. But as reported by the surgeon who tried the emergency repair of the aorta, the rupture is on the anterior side, the front. Naturally a surgeon making an incision in a man's back, working around the spine, is not going to puncture the front of the aorta, the part that faces the abdomen."

Dan Cefalo turned ashen. There aren't many surprises in trials anymore. Pretrial discovery eliminates most of that. But Charlie Riggs gave his deposition before studying the report of the second surgery, the chaotic attempt to close the bursting aorta a dozen hours after the laminectomy. When he read the report, bells went off. Nobody else had paid any attention to where the rupture was, only that it existed.

For the next fifteen minutes, it went on like that, Charles W. Riggs, M.D., witness emeritus, showing the jury his plastic model of the spine with the blood vessels attached like strings of licorice. The report of the thoracic surgeon who tried unsuccessfully to save Corrigan's life came into evidence, and the jurors kept looking at Dr. Riggs and nodding.

It was time to slam the door. "If Dr. Salisbury did not puncture the aorta with the rongeur, could not have, as you have testified, what might have caused it to rupture?"

"We call it spontaneous aortic aneurysm. Of course, that's the effect, not the cause. The causes are many. Various illnesses or severe trauma to the abdomen can cause the aorta to burst. Arteriosclerosis can weaken the aorta and make it susceptible to aneurysm. So can high blood pressure. It could be a breakdown that medicine simply can't explain, as they said in the Middle Ages, *ex visitatione divina.*"

I smiled at Dr. Riggs. He smiled back at me. The jury smiled at both of us. One big happy family.

I was nearly through but had one more little surprise for Dan Cefalo. A nail in the coffin. I handed Riggs Plaintiff's Exhibit Three, a composite of Philip Corrigan's medical history. "Dr. Riggs, did Philip Corrigan have any prior medical abnormalities?"

Charlie Riggs scanned the document but already knew the answer from our preparation sessions. "Yes, he was previously diagnosed by a cardiologist as having some degree of arteriosclerosis."

"And the effect of such a disease?"

"Weakening of the arteries, susceptibility to aneurysm. Men in their fifties or beyond commonly show signs of arterial disease. Blame the typical American diet of saturated fats, too much beef and butter. In that condition, Mr. Corrigan could have had an artery blow out at any time."

"At any time," I repeated, just in case they missed it.

"Yes, without a trauma, just watching TV, eating dinner, any time."

"Thank you, Doctor." I nodded toward the witness stand in deference to the wisdom that had filled the courtroom. Then I turned toward Dan Cefalo, and with the placid assurance of a man who has seen the future and owns a fine chunk of it, I gently advised him, "Your witness, Counselor."

Cefalo stood up and his suitcoat fell open, revealing a dark stain of red ink under his shirt pocket, the trail of an uncapped marking pen. Or a self-inflicted wound.

His cross-examination fell flat. He scored a meaningless point getting Riggs to admit that he was not an orthopedic surgeon and had never performed a laminectomy. "But I've done thousands of autopsies, and that's how you determine cause of death," Riggs quickly added.

"You testified that trauma could cause the rupture, did you not?" Cefalo asked.

"Yes, I can't tell you how many drivers I saw in the morgue in the days before seat belts. In a collision, the steering wheel can hit the chest and abdomen with such force as to rupture the aorta. That, of course, is trauma from the front."

"But a misguided rongeur could produce the kind of trauma to rupture the aorta?"

Hit me again, Cefalo seemed to plead.

"It could, but not in the front of the blood vessel when the surgeon is coming in from the back," Riggs said.

Cefalo wouldn't call it quits. "The thoracic surgeon was working under conditions of extreme emergency trying to do the repair, was he not?"

"I assume so," Riggs said.

"And in such conditions, he could have made a mistake as to the location of the rupture, could he not?"

Riggs smiled a gentle, fatherly smile. "Every piece of evidence ever adduced in a courtroom could be the product of a mistake. Your witnesses could all be wrong. Mr. Lassiter's witnesses could all be wrong. But it's all we've got, and there's nothing to indicate the rupture was anywhere but where the chest buster—excuse me, the thoracic surgeon—said, the anterior of the aorta."

Fine. Outstanding. I couldn't have said it better myself. Cefalo sat down without laying a glove on him. It was after one o'clock and we had not yet recessed for lunch. Judge Leonard was fidgeting.

"Noting the lateness of the hour, perhaps this is an opportune time to adjourn for the day," the judge said. Translation: *There's a stakes race at Hialeah and I've got a tip from a jockey who hasn't paid alimony since his divorce fell into my division last year.* "Hearing no objection, court stands adjourned until nine-thirty tomorrow morning."

Roger Salisbury was beaming. He didn't look like a man who wanted to lose. It had been a fine morning of lawyering, and I was feeling pretty full of myself. In the back of the courtroom I caught a glimpse of Susan Corrigan wearing a Super Bowl XVI nylon jacket over a T-shirt. She eyed me as if I'd just spit in church.

I told Roger Salisbury I'd treat him to stone crabs, home fries, and cold beer for lunch. Time for a mini-celebration.

Time, too, for some questions I needed to ask.

6

THE VOYEUR

We walked from the dim light and dank air of the old courtroom into the sunshine of December in Miami. A glorious day. Not even the buzzards endlessly circling the wedding cake tiers of the courthouse could darken my mood. Souls of lawyers doing penance, a Cuban spiritualist told me. The huge black birds were as much a part of wintertime Miami as sunburned tourists, drug deals, and crooked cops. The buzzards congregated around the courthouse and on the upper ledges of the Southeast Financial Center, where for fifty dollars a square foot, the lawyers, accountants, and bankers expected a better view than birdshit two feet deep. Building management installed sonar devices that supposedly made unfriendly bird sounds. Instead of being frightened, the buzzards were turned on; they tried mating with the sonar boxes.

The doctor gave me a second look when he got into my canary yellow Olds 442 convertible, vintage 1968. At home was my old Jeep, but it was rusted out from windsurfing gear, and my clients deserve the best. Having already passed through my respectable sedan phase when I temporarily decided to grow up, I had regressed to a simpler time of big engines and Beach Boys' songs.

We drove to a seafood restaurant in a new shopping arcade that the developer spent a bundle making look like an Italian villa, circa the Renaissance. It's full of boutiques instead of stores, places with two names that always start with *Le,* and women who'll spend a fortune for clothes so they'll look good shopping for more clothes. Notwithstanding the glitz of the surroundings, there's a decent fish house tucked away in back.

"The tide turned today, didn't it?" Salisbury asked.

"Right. We pulled even, which means we're actually ahead. The plaintiff has the burden of proof. Riggs negated Watkins's testimony about the rongeur. Back to square one. They'll have to call Watkins again on rebuttal and attack Riggs. They're stuck. They can't bring in a new expert now. Our strategy is to lay low. We don't want to get fancy, just hold our position."

"What about my testimony?"

"You'll do fine. What you say isn't as important as how you look, how the jury perceives you. If you're a nice guy and it's a close battle of the experts, they'll cut you a break. If you're arrogant and a prick, they'll cut off your nuts and hand them to the widow."

He thought that over and I looked around for some service. We'd been there ten minutes before the waiter shuffled over to take our order. The kid needed a shave and was missing one earring, or is that the way they wear them?

"Whatcha want?" he asked, displaying the personality of a mollusk and half the energy. Service in restaurants now rivals that at gas stations for indifference and sloth.

I ordered for both of us. "Two portions of jumbo stoners, two Caesar salads, and two beers." Best to keep it simple.

"Kinda beers?" the waiter said. I figured him for a speech communications major at the UM.

"Grolsch. Sixteen-ouncers if you have them."

"Dunno. Got Bud, Miller, Coors Light, maybe."

"Any beer's okay with me," Salisbury said. Not hard to please. A lot of doctors are that way. They get used to hospital cafeteria food and pretty soon everything tastes alike. Not me. I'll start drinking American beer when it gets as good as its TV commercials.

The waiter shrugged and disappeared, probably to replenish his chemical stimulants. I was about to extol the glories of the Dutch brewmasters when Roger Salisbury asked, "Do you think I killed him, committed malpractice I mean?"

He wanted me to respect him. With most clients, winning is enough.

"Hey Roger, I checked around town. The med school has nice things to say about you. You've never been sued before, which in this town is an upset. Don't let my general cynicism get you down."

"Just so you believe me."

He had thrown me off stride. I wanted to ask questions, not answer them. "Roger, you know how important it is to tell your lawyer everything?"

"Sure thing. Soul mates."

"Right. Before you testify tomorrow, is there anything you want to tell me? Anything you left out?"

He cradled his chin in his hand. Something flickered behind his eyes but he blinked it away. "No, don't think so. I told you all about the surgery. No signs of an aneurysm, no drop in blood pressure. I didn't slip with the rongeur. I didn't do it."

"I know. Besides that. Anything personal with you and the Corrigans?"

"Like what?"

50

Oh shit. He wasn't going to help me out. Sometimes the best way to get through the chop is to trim the sail tight and just go. "Like were you screwing Melanie Corrigan?" At the next table, a couple of spiffed-up fiftyish women with fancy shopping bags exchanged disapproving whispers.

"At what point in time?" Roger asked.

My client, and he talks like Richard Nixon.

"Hey Roger, this is your lawyer here, not a grand jury." The waiter skulked by, his thumbs buried deep in the Caesar salad bowls. He wiped one hand on his apron, sucked some salad dressing off a thumb and brought us the beer, an anonymous American brand, devoid of calories, color, and taste. At least it was cold.

Roger took a small sip, a thinking-time sip, and said, "We were involved, sure."

"So why didn't you tell me?"

"Because it has nothing to do with the case."

My voice cranked up a few decibels. "How about letting me decide that? If it comes out, Cefalo would claim you had a motive for being a little careless, or worse, having criminal intent."

"I thought of that," he said casually, "but Melanie could never use that. It would hurt her case, wouldn't it, the unfaithful wife trying to profit from her husband's death."

"That's not the way it would play. You'd be the smooth seducer, or a madman obsessed with her, chopping up the husband so she'd be all yours."

Salisbury's fork stopped in mid-air. A look of concern crossed his face, but when he caught me studying him, he chased it away with a laugh. "A madman maybe," he said, smiling, "but when it comes to seduction, she's in a league by herself. Besides, I knew her before Corrigan did, and well . . . there's stuff you lawyers would call extenuating circumstances."

"I'm waiting."

"I'm not sure it's any of your business."

I drained my homogenized beer and tried to signal the brain-dead waiter to bring another. He looked right through me.

"Right now, my business is you, everything about you and the Corrigans," I said, waiting for him to fill me in.

Nothing.

The stone crabs arrived. Fresh, no black mottled spots, the meat tearing cleanly out of the shell, the mustard sauce tangy. I yelled for the second beer, and the waiter brought iced tea. It tasted like the beer.

I dug into the crabs two at a time, but Salisbury must have lost his appetite. He fidgeted in his chair and his eyes darted from side to side. Finally, he looked me straight on, took a breath and let it go. "Okay, here it is. I met Melanie eight or nine years ago. I was just finishing my residency, hadn't spent much time with women. You know how it is, premed in college, you bust your balls, then med school, internship, residency. Never any money or time. She was just a kid, mixed up, kind of an exotic dancer, but just for a while."

"Yeah, after that she probably was Deb of the Year."

"She wasn't bad or anything. Called herself Autumn Rain. Just used her body to make a buck. So I sort of fell for her. I started my practice, bought her a car, gave her things. It didn't last long. I found out other guys were doing the same. One guy paid for her apartment, another guy her clothes, another her trips."

"Sold shares in herself like IBM."

"Some guys can handle that. I couldn't. So I took off." He looked away. This wasn't a story he broadcast around town.

"Roger, it's nothing to be embarrassed about. It's an old story. You meet a pretty young thing who can suck a golf ball through a garden hose. You overlook the fact that she's collected enough hoses to water Joe Robbie Stadium. You'd be shocked how many guys fall for young hookers. Want to change them. Old male fantasy. Some guys lose their marriages over it. Not many doctors, though. Most are too scientific to get involved."

"She wasn't a hooker," he said indignantly and louder than necessary.

Now the two women were doing their best not to show that our conversation was more interesting than their own. I smiled in their direction. One recoiled as if I had exposed myself.

Roger Salisbury poked the ice in his tea. "Anyway, I hadn't seen her for probably five years when Philip Corrigan asked me over for dinner. He was seeing me for a cartilage problem in the knee. I scoped it. Then the disc started flaring up. We became friends. I had no idea he was married to Autumn . . . Melanie."

"So you started slipping out of the hospital a little early. Sneaking in nooners while old man Corrigan was littering the Keys with ugly condos on stilts."

He laughed a short, bitter laugh. "Hardly."

Then he clammed up again. I gave him a c'mon Roger look.

Finally he spoke in a whisper. "This is where it gets a little sticky."

"I'll bet."

They didn't have to sneak around, he told me over the watery tea. Why not? I asked.

Philip wanted to watch, Roger said. Sometimes to take part, sometimes to videotape. On their boat, a custom Hatteras furnished like a Bal Harbour penthouse, in their mansion on a giant waterbed, in their swimming pool.

So Philip Corrigan was a peeper and an old letch. Probably got to an age where the money bored him, and his engine wouldn't start without some kinky provocation.

"Then, after doing a few lines of coke, we'd mix it up, *ménage à trois*," Roger said. He paused and gave me a sheepish look.

If the two women at the next table craned their necks any farther our way, they'd need a chiropractor.

Are you disappointed in me? he asked.

I don't make moral judgments about clients, I told him, because it interferes with my ability to give good advice.

Just the same I tallied a moral scorecard on the yellow pad of my mind. We all do that. We try to live and let live, but underneath it, we're left with a smug sense of superiority about ourselves and vague disgust for others who don't measure up. Roger Salisbury didn't measure up. He was doing drugs and a group grope like some kind of sleaze. But he was my sleaze, my client, and his bedroom—or swimming pool—activities didn't make him an incompetent doctor, much less a murderer.

After his *mea culpa,* I thought his morale could use a boost.

"Here's how I see it," I told him. "You got stuck in a little game with a tramp who slithered her way to Gables Estates and a guy who couldn't get his rocks off in the missionary position. That doesn't put you in a class with Charles Manson, but if it ever came out in court or the newspapers, that's all anybody would know about you. You might be donating half your time to charity cases and feeding homeless cats, but the world would know you only as a sex-crazed doctor who aced his girlfriend's husband. Makes good reading. Now do you see why I have to know about this? If I make an uninformed decision at some point, it could hurt you. Badly. Understand?"

"Understood."

"Is that all there is to it?"

"I guess so. Except that I'm still sort of under her spell."

Oh brother.

"In all these years," he said, "nobody's been able to turn me on like her. She knows things, does things. She's totally uninhibited and free with herself. She's a pleasure giver. Do you know how hard it is for me to give that up?"

Dr. Ruth, I'm not, but I took a stab at it anyway. "Roger, it sounds to me like Melanie Corrigan is a taker, not a giver, and you better stay the hell out of her hot tub."

"There is a certain side to her, a kind of danger," he said. "Maybe that's part of the appeal, I don't know." He just let it hang there, his mind working something over, not letting me in on it.

"Okay then, I've got it all, right? You played hide the weenie with the missus while the old man watched, videotaped, and once in a while jumped on the pile."

"That's it." He paused, looked side to side and added, "There is one more thing."

"There always is."

"She asked me to kill her husband," he said.

7

SQUOOSHY

Waiting. Like making a movie or going to war, there is more waiting than working in a trial. First the judge hears motions starting at eight-thirty. Twenty different cases, forty lawyers, crowding chambers, spilling into the corridor, milling around like chickens waiting to be fed.

Waiting, an army of minutes slogging through the mud. The judge makes several phone calls from his chambers. His bookie, his mistress, his campaign contributors, who knows? Then a clerk is late bringing up the evidence, or a juror's child is sick, or an expert witness, usually a doctor, has an emergency.

That's how it was the morning Roger Salisbury was to testify. The seconds ticked off slowly, dulling my edge. I studied the filthy acoustical tile that covered the walls. At shoulder level, countless pencils and fingernails left signatures there. The heavy, straight-backed pews in the gallery tested the mettle and the cushioning of the spectators, a few vagrants lured by the air-conditioning. The court-room ceiling was thirty feet high. Together with the dark pews and the raised bench, it gave the courtroom the air of a cathedral. But where was His Holiness?

Just then the gleaming head of Judge Leonard poked through the door behind the bench that led directly to his chambers. He scowled and ducked back in. I unpacked my briefcase and found a note signed by Cindy:

Sportswriting Lady Buzzing Like Bee
Can't Get Number out of Me,
Maybe Has Pollen for You to See.

Apparently Susan Corrigan had been calling, maybe wanted to tell me what a schmuck I am, just in case I forgot. A few more minutes passed, and finally all the courtroom players were there, the judge, the clerk, the jurors, the lawyers, and the witnesses, all ready at the same time. Sometimes at this point, the electricity goes off or there's a bomb threat, but today, we started working.

Roger Salisbury came off well, just as I thought he would. I had told him not to overdress, and he was just right in gray slacks, a blue sportcoat, and tie. I had him wear a beeper on his belt to remind the jury that here was a man who responded to emergencies, who could be called at any moment to mend the injured. His salt-and-pepper hair was neatly trimmed and his face reflected confidence without being cocky. He looked like a skilled, compassionate surgeon who took the greatest care when working inside a man's spine. He spoke quietly, evenly, with no trace of the condescension that marks so many doctors in court.

I took him through the story. Philip Corrigan's office visits, fixing the bad knee, then complaints of back and leg pain. Even hurt when he coughed. All the usual tests, ankle jerk, knee jerk, straight leg raising. Salisbury found sensory deficits, a myelogram confirmed it. Finally the diagnosis, acute herniated disc at the L3–L4 vertebrae.

"Was there anything unusual about the surgery?" I asked.

"No, it was routine," Salisbury said.

I liked that. Here's a man who cuts into living flesh, fixes the problems inside, then puts it all back together again. And it's routine. No wonder we're in awe of doctors.

"I cut from approximately L1 to just above the sacrum," he said. "Nothing out of the ordinary. Down through subcutaneous tissue and adipose tissue. Bleeders were clamped and cauterized. I identified the L3–L4 interspace. I removed the ligamentum flavum and superior portion of L4 and inferior portion of L3 without incident."

I walked him through every step of it, sending the jurors messages that this doctor knew what he was doing. He was *there,* dammit. Dan Cefalo wasn't. Wallbanger Watkins wasn't. Now Salisbury was a teacher and the jurors, his students, listened to every word. Some might not have followed every move of the scalpel, but it didn't matter. Roger Salisbury knew his stuff, knew more than the jurors—a travel agent, two housewives, a student, two retired businessmen—ever would. The impression I wanted to create was simple: *Who are we to judge this man?*

"I removed the disc material, the nucleus pulposus." Roger Salisbury pointed to a chart we blew up to poster size. "In a herniated disc, it's like toothpaste that's been squeezed out of the tube. It's pushed out of the disc space and there's no putting it back."

Good imagery. It should have been. We practiced it for months.

"Then what did you do?" I asked.

"I removed the degenerative disc material with the rongeur."

"Was there anything unusual up to this point?"

"Nothing up to then or later," he said evenly. "The procedure was without incident."

"What were the patient's vital signs?"

"All normal. Blood pressure, pulse rate, breathing."

The anesthesiologist would confirm this when we read his deposition to the jury.

"You heard Dr. Watkins's testimony about the rongeur?"

"I did."

"Did anything unusual happen with the rongeur?"

"No, it never went through the disc space, certainly not around to the front of the aorta. In all respects the patient tolerated the surgery normally."

"When was the last time you saw Philip Corrigan?"

"I checked him in the recovery room and once later in his private room."

"And his condition?"

"Normal. No evidence of a mass in his abdomen, normal blood pressure, hemoglobin, and hematocrit. No sign of hemorrhage or aortic aneurysm."

I kept him up there a few minutes longer to say how surprised he was the next morning when he learned that Corrigan's aorta ruptured during the night. And, sounding sincere, he expressed regret at the death of his patient. I nodded gravely with my own look of sincerity, a look that took three years of law school, a dozen years of practice, and a couple Jimmy Stewart movies to perfect. Then I sat down, and Dan Cefalo stood up.

Cefalo was in a box. He had deposed everyone in the OR, and they all corroborated Salisbury's testimony concerning Corrigan's vital signs. The aneurysm had not happened simultaneously with the surgery. Cefalo needed to convince the jury that Salisbury nicked the front of the aorta, causing it to rupture ten hours later. No use asking Salisbury whether that happened. He'd get a big fat *no*. He needed Watkins back for rebuttal testimony. But that would come later. Now, the jurors watched Cefalo, waiting to see if he could counter-punch.

Cefalo looked even worse than usual today. All the courthouse regulars knew that his trial wardrobe was a hoax, the result of a case he tried upstate years ago. In the wilds of Okeechobee County he had worn a sharkskin suit when defending a man accused of stealing fruit from an orange grove, a felony akin to cattle rustling in the Old West. The prosecutor was a good old boy and in closing argument told the jury that they could listen to him or they could listen to that *Mia-muh* lawyer in the shiny suit. They listened to the good old boy.

Dan Cefalo learned his lesson. He stripped off the Rolex and the pinky ring and left the silk ties at home. He wore a selection of suits that the Salvation Army couldn't give away. As he won bigger verdicts, his clothes became more decrepit.

Today, though, it wasn't the clothing. Cefalo was pale and nervous. He came to court with a jagged square of toilet paper sticking to his chin. A spot of blood shone through. *Hands shaky this morning, my man?* He kept huddling with a young lawyer and two paralegals from his office. I picked up only three words of their conversation. "He here yet?" Cefalo asked. The young lawyer shook his head.

Cefalo started his cross-examination by asking whether it might be possible to pierce the aorta and not be aware of it.

"Not likely," Salisbury replied. "You watch how far you insert the rongeur and when you meet resistance, you stop."

I sneaked a look at Melanie Corrigan, who sat with legs demurely crossed at the ankles. She wore a simple black linen dress, probably to signify her continuing grief. I wanted to see, close up, what kind of woman plots to kill her husband. An actress, I thought. A fooler of men ripe to be fooled.

I turned her down, Roger had assured me last night. Philip was my friend. I would never kill him.

Did she take no for an answer?

Roger shrugged. Said she knew some guys who'd kill Philip and never blink.

I'll bet she did. A woman can't tiptoe through the gutter and keep her feet clean. If she'd been grinding in one of those jerk-off joints, she'd have run into pimps, dopers, dirty cops, confidence men, porno kings, and the other flotsam of the city. Plus, more than a few triggermen. Roger Salisbury was in over his head with that crowd. Of course, Philip Corrigan didn't die from a bullet or knife or garrote. He died from an aneurysm twelve hours after my client operated on him.

Dan Cefalo kept after Salisbury for another twenty minutes but couldn't shake him. Then, tripping on his untied shoelaces, Cefalo called it quits and dropped into his chair. We tidied up some of the trial's loose ends, reading depositions into the record, admitting certain medical reports into evidence. I had no other ammo so I announced that the defense rested. We renewed our motions for a directed verdict, and Judge Leonard denied them, saying we had issues for the jury. Actually what he said was, "You boys got yourself a real horse race here."

Dan Cefalo said he had one rebuttal witness, and the judge figured we could breeze through that after lunch and he'd still have time to make it to Hialeah. The Widener Cup was Saturday, and, like football fans who go to practice, he visited the stalls and watched the horses eat their oats and crap in the paddock.

Another down time, waiting for the judge after lunch recess. While Cefalo paced, I made notes for tomorrow's closing argument, Roger Salisbury flipped the pages of a medical journal, and my secretary Cindy waltzed into the courtroom as inconspicuous as a shark in the wading pool. She wore a white miniskirt, black fishnet stockings, leather earrings with chrome studs, all topped by a new hairdo that was spiked, punked, and Day-Glo pinked. Her hair shot in various directions like hundreds of porcupine quills. It looked like she stuck her finger in an electrical outlet.

"*Qué pasa, el jefe?*"

"Do I know you?" I said.

"Not as well as some men I could name."

"Not enough time for that."

"You don't look so busy to me."

"We're waiting for the judge. At least *I'm* waiting for the judge. The grieving widow is waiting for Probate Court to release the estate funds. And Cefalo's waiting for Wallbanger Watkins, his rebuttal witness."

"He's got a long wait," Cindy said.

"Huh?" That's my probing question technique.

Cindy sat down and propped her feet on the counsel table. "Got a long wait for the good doctor," she said matter-of-factly.

"What do you know that I don't, but should?"

"So many things. But I'm willing to teach."

"Cindy, this is serious. We're in trial."

She frowned. "Lighten up. I just have a sneaking suspicion that Watkins is AWOL, and Dan Cefalo is so shit out of luck he oughta buy a new suit."

"You didn't kidnap him, did you?" With Cindy you never could tell. Once in a sex discrimination case, a department store executive denied that he ever hit on my client, his young female assistant. Said he'd never been unfaithful to his wife, never even made a pass at another woman. Cindy tracked the guy to his favorite watering hole, ran an inviting toe inside his pantleg, and took him home. Luis (Long Lens) Morales, a convicted counterfeiter and part-time divorce photographer, leapt from her closet in time to shoot some grainy black-and-whites of the executive slipping out of his boxers.

"Kidnap him?" she asked, feigning indignation and arching her eyebrows, striped brown and orange like a Bengal tiger. "Do you think that's the only way I could get a man to buy me a drink?"

"You bagged Watkins in some bar?"

"How crude," she protested. "Last night, by utter coincidence, me and Margarita—the girl, not the drink—cruise into the lounge at the Sonesta Beach. And who do we run into but this nice older man with white hair and a silly seersucker suit. He's drinking vodka gimlets but leaving out the lime juice and telling us what a great doctor he is, and Margarita says she's got this back problem, and he says, come up to the room and he'll do a quick exam, so off we go, and meanwhile Harv orders three bottles of Finlandia from room service."

"Harv?"

"That's what he asked us to call him."

"Not very professional," I said.

"Neither was his treatment of Margarita. Unless all orthopods do pelvic exams. Not that Margarita cared. I'm not saying she's dumb, but she thinks the Silicon Valley is the space between her tits."

I closed my eyes and massaged my forehead. "Cindy, I can't wait to get a summons from the Florida Bar. It's just like stashing a witness."

"What? To have a drink with a nice man?"

We were interrupted by the banging of the courtroom door. In lurched Dr. Harvey Watkins, collar turned up on a seersucker suitcoat that looked like it had just cleaned all the windshields in the Baja road race. His tie was at half mast, his shirt unbuttoned nearly to the waist. He leaned back against the door as if the courthouse were plowing through rough seas. His hair was plastered against his scalp. Bluish veins popped through his pink skin. Dan Cefalo was a step behind, trying to steady his witness. Watkins angrily shook the hand off his elbow. As bad as the doctor looked, he was doing better than Cefalo, who had turned an unhealthy gray.

At that moment the bailiff burst through the rear door, shouting, "All rise! Court of the Eleventh Judicial Circuit in and for Dade County Florida is now in session!" Everyone in the courtroom obeyed, except Dr. Harvey Watkins, who sagged heavily into one of the church pews, his legs jammed at odd angles into the aisle, his ankles bare of socks.

"Bailiff, bring in the jury, and Mr. Cefalo, call your witness." Judge Leonard wasn't going to waste any time. He might miss someone brushing the mane of Crème Fraiche or taking Personal Flag's rectal temperature.

Cefalo was about to hyperventilate. "Your Honor, may we have one moment?"

"A moment! You've just had ninety minutes for lunch. Now, do you have rebuttal testimony or not? If not, we'll recess and you can both close in the morning."

In a trial you must make immediate decisions. Object or not, ask a question when you don't know the answer or not, move for mistrial or let it go. Dan Cefalo had to decide whether to put on Wallbanger

Watkins without even a chance to shave the white stubble from his chin or determine if the good—and drunk—doctor remembered his name. If he didn't call him, Cefalo would close the book on the case without rebutting Charlie Riggs's testimony that Salisbury couldn't have nicked the front of the aorta. Either way, a roll of the dice.

Cefalo took a deep breath and said, "At this time, the plaintiff re-calls Dr. Harvey Watkins."

Watkins tugged his necktie toward his Adam's apple, jutted his patrician chin forward, and, with the excessive dignity that the intoxicated muster in time of great need, walked almost steadily to the witness stand. He would have made it, too, had he noticed the six-inch step. He toppled forward into the walnut railing, which bounced him sideways until he fell, facedown, into the lap of the court reporter, a young black woman who didn't know if she should record the event on her stenograph.

"Beggar pardon," Watkins mumbled, and Cefalo leapt forward to help him.

A moment later the doctor was safely seated, gripping the rail of the witness stand and staring blankly out to sea. His shirttail hung over his belt and his tie was askew. He made Dan Cefalo look like the cover of *GQ*.

"Dr. Watkins, you are still under oath," Cefalo began.

"Oath?" Watkins ran a tongue over dry lips. Finally a light came on. "Of course. Years ago, I took the *hick*-ocratic oath. That is, of course, the *hick* . . ." A case of the hiccups was now distracting him and the clerk brought a glass of water. Watkins nodded a formal thank you.

Cefalo plunged ahead. "Dr. Watkins, you testified that, based on the medical records in this case, you could determine to a reasonable degree of medical certainty that Dr. Salisbury punctured the aorta with the rongeur, is that correct?"

"Objection! Leading and an inaccurate summary of the testimony." I didn't need to win that one, just to figure out what the next ruling would be.

"Overruled," Judge Leonard said. He started packing, dropping a cap and sunglasses into a briefcase.

"Is that correct?" Cefalo repeated.

Watkins nodded. Either he was saying yes, or he was falling asleep.

"Doctor, you must speak audibly for the court reporter to record your answer."

Watkins again nodded silently.

Cefalo pushed forward. "Now, to speed this up, let me tell you that another witness has testified that the rupture in the aorta was on its anterior side, in the front, and that a surgeon entering from the back could not have made the rupture there."

"Zat so?" Watkins asked, eyebrows arched in surprise.

"My question, Doctor, is whether it is possible for a surgeon performing a laminectomy to perforate the front of the aorta?"

Watkins stared into space.

Sweat broke out on Cefalo's forehead. "You may remember our discussing this yesterday morning . . ."

I was on my feet. "Objection! Leading. Your Honor, really, there is certain latitude, but this is too much."

"Sustained. Move it along, Mr. Cefalo."

Cefalo tried again. "The fact that the perforation was in front. What, if anything, does that tell you?"

Watkins mumbled something, his eyes half closed. The jurors were shooting each other sideways glances. *Get a load of this.* Somewhere a trillion miles away, some intergalactic god of luck was shining on Roger Salisbury.

"Doctor?"

"Squooshy," Dr. Watkins said.

"Squooshy?" Cefalo asked, his eyes widening.

A momentary brightness came to Dr. Watkins's face. "It's all squooshy in there. You might think it's like all these pretty pictures in the books, the vascular system here, the muscles there, the bones over there. Hah! Phooey!" The *phooey* shot a wad of expectorant toward the court reporter.

"It's all squooshed up. And it moves. The son-of-a-bitch keeps breathing while you're cutting him up. It's all squooshing around and moving. Front, back, in between. Who the fuck can tell the difference?"

Even Judge Leonard heard that. He aimed a murderous look at Dan Cefalo, who hastily advised that Dr. Watkins was now my witness. I didn't want him. The judge banged his gavel louder than usual and crisply ordered us adjourned. Then he shot off the bench, his maroon robes flying behind him.

Roger Salisbury was pumping my hand as if we'd already won. I told him to wait until tomorrow. You can never tell with juries. He said he felt like celebrating, maybe carousing, how about our finding a couple *chicas*. I didn't ask if they were both for him, just declined, saying I had to gather my thoughts for tomorrow. Then I asked him a question.

"What about it? If you go in from the back, could you tear the aorta in front?"

He smiled. "Our witness said no."

"Right. And Watkins said everything's squooshy. What do you say?"

He smiled again. "I say they're both right. Riggs is right in what he does. When a body is dead, it's inert. If you did a laminectomy on a corpse, you probably couldn't hit the front of the aorta with the rongeur. But Watkins was right that with a living, breathing body, there's movement. It's a mess in there, things can happen. If you pushed the rongeur too far, it's possible that on the way back, it could nick the front of the aorta. It's possible."

"But unlikely," I suggested.

"Unless you were trying," Roger Salisbury said.

8

THE
LATE SHOW

This is how I prepare my closing argument. I toss the files into the trunk of the 442 convertible and head home. Home is in the old part of Coconut Grove between Kumquat Avenue and Poinciana. You can't see the house from the street thanks to the jacaranda, live oak, and chinaberry trees that crowd the small lot. So little sun reaches the front yard that the lawn wouldn't support a hungry billy goat. The trees also shade the house, a 1920s coral rock pillbox that would be the last building standing after a direct hit by Alice, Bruce, Celia, or David. Granny Lassiter lived in the house when the Grove was full of artists and barnacled types, when there were saloons instead of boutiques. After the area became chic, Granny grabbed her fishing gear and headed for the Keys.

I leave the files in the trunk and head into the kitchen. There is a refrigerator, a microwave, some cabinets, and enough room for two very good friends to stand. The house is two stories but barely more than a cottage. It will never grace the pages of *Architectural Digest* but is perfect for someone who does not want to entertain or rub shoulders with society.

I turn on all the ceiling fans. I don't like air-conditioning. It dries out the air and shuts you off from the natural sounds of birds, crickets, and neighborhood burglars.

My porch looks into a jungle of overgrown shrubs and weeds that, like the battlement of a castle, shelters my tiny backyard. Because the neighborhood is secluded, drug dealers have been moving in. They are good neighbors for the most part, never noisy, never nosy. The ones who process the cocaine, however, are a problem. On Loquat Street last year, a house blew up when a barrel of ether ignited. Nothing left of the house or three Colombians. Charred pieces of greenbacks wafted over Coconut Grove, tiny embers blinking like fireflies in the nighttime sky. A portrait of U. S. Grant, his beard scorched, landed in my hammock.

I put on the eight-ounce gloves and hit the heavy bag that hangs on the porch. It doesn't hit back. It doesn't say ouch. I go four rounds and win them all. I think about the case, the high points, what to emphasize, what to shrug off. It all comes back, witness by witness. I don't need the files or my notes. Each jab is a scrap of testimony to push, each hook a point to drive home.

I lie on my back and do stomach crunches. When a man gets to a certain age, he has to work the stomach hard. If not, it starts to merge with the chest. The whole torso becomes one amorphous mass. I work my stomach hard.

I finish with push-ups. First regular push-ups, then elevated, with feet propped up on the porch, hands on the ground, lowering myself into the overgrowth of the yard until the weeds tickle my nose.

Then I check the refrigerator. Everything I need, starting with smoked amberjack. I find some mayo that hasn't quite turned green, some Muenster that has, a jar of Pommery mustard, half a lemon. There are fresh tomatoes on the counter, part of the Florida winter crop, pale and tough, the hide of tennis balls. I've brought home a fresh loaf of French bread. I stack some of the amberjack on the bread, slather on the mayo, layer three leathery tomato slices on top, and cover it with the cheese and mustard. Dinner is served. Life in the fast lane.

Back at the refrigerator, I buy myself a beer. The choice, a sixteen-ounce Grolsch with the porcelain stopper or Anchor Steam, my one exception to the American beer boycott. I study them both. My biggest decision of the day, other than deciding whether to get sucked into a discussion of damages, or throw all my weight into shouting, "no liability." Cefalo will have to argue both, first that Salisbury is liable for professional negligence, second that the damages should be roughly equal to Brazil's foreign debt. I have to argue there is no liability. Sometimes, if you think you're going to lose that one, you slip into the alternative argument, *but if you find the defendant liable, damages should not exceed the cost of a Dolphins' season ticket.* Problem is, that weakens your liability case.

Now about that beer, the mind still cranking away. Anchor Steam has a deep amber color. Knew a girl with eyes like that once. Every time I looked at her, I got thirsty. I go for the Grolsch.

The files were still in the trunk, an emptied four-pack of Grolsch was in the trash, and I was in the hammock, letting the mind run through it all, visualizing tomorrow. I didn't hear the phone until the third ring. Realized I wasn't visualizing at all. Dozing.

"I need to see you," a woman's voice said. "Are you busy?"

It took a moment, then I placed it. Susan Corrigan. "I'm hard at work trying to find justice in an imperfect world."

"Do you know where Lagoon Road is?" she asked.

"Sure, Gables Estates."

"That's where I live, nine-ten Lagoon Road."

"The newspaper must be paying handsomely these days."

"It's Dad's house. Please come over. Now. It's important."

Of course, Dad's house. Which means, it's now stepmommy's house.

"I don't know if that's such a good idea. Ethically, I'm not permitted to speak to Mrs. Corrigan without her lawyer present."

Not that I toe the line somebody else draws. Guys from big law firms in three-piece suits sit around hotel ballrooms at ABA conventions thinking up lots of rules. Their idea of ethics is to give the side with the most money the upper hand. My ethical standards are simple. I never lie to the court or knowingly let a client do it. Other than that I like to shoot the opposition in the kneecaps.

"She's not here," Susan Corrigan said. "Just come around back to the cabana by the pool. This involves your client."

Oh. A little bit of me knew that's what it was about. Another little bit of me hoped it was something else again. I stored a few megabytes of closing argument somewhere between my ears. Then I showered. I put on faded blue jeans that worked hard to get that way, a blue and orange rugby shirt, and a pair of well-worn running shoes in case I had to chase her again. I never got the 442 out of third gear going down Old Cutler, a two-lane, winding road heading south out of Coconut Grove. Huge banyan trees stood on each side of the road, their tangled trunks like giant snakes erupting from the ground. The thick branches met overhead, forming a dark umbrella that blocked out the moonlight. Briny smells of saltwater hammocks oozed from the bay side of the road. I turned left onto Arvida and headed down Millionaire's Row, lushly landscaped homes backed up onto canals with clear access to Biscayne Bay and the Atlantic beyond.

The Corrigan house sat on a cul-de-sac lined with royal palms a hundred feet high. You could get a crick in your neck looking up at the trees. The house, too. The first thing you notice is its height. You look up to see the ground floor. Though Lagoon Road is only five feet above sea level, if you add forty feet of fill and top it with a heap of landscaping, you have a Florida mountain. Then the sound, a waterfall tumbling through huge coral boulders.

You could look at the Corrigan house and be overwhelmed with its size or its styling, rough-hewn cedar flanking stone walls, sun decks overlooking the water. But I thought of only one word, electricity. How much juice did it take to run four separate central air-conditioning systems, to power the pump that ran the waterfall that cascaded down the man-made mountain, to illuminate with colored spotlights the palm trees and blooming poinsettias and impatiens? How much more electricity for the hot tub and the front gate and TV cameras? The Corrigan house was a one-family oil shortage.

The front gate was open and I pulled into the brick driveway and sat there a moment. No other cars, no signs of life, the four-car garage buttoned up tight. A flagstone walk ran around the house. It was bordered with three-foot-high pine posts, each topped by a tiny lamp. Heavy hemp lines were strung post to post to form a path, like queues in a theater.

Behind the house, a wooden deck led to a swimming pool. Fifty yards long but only twelve feet wide, a serious pool for laps. It smelled of salt water, not chlorine, probably a pipe right to the bay. Beyond the pool was a concrete dock, a boathouse, and a private lagoon that opened onto Biscayne Bay. Tied to the dock was a yacht that in time of war would be impounded for transporting troops.

The cabana was an architect's idea of Tahiti. Whatever the building was made of was disguised by a bamboo front and topped, chikee style, with a palm frond roof. Half a dozen coconuts sat in primitive bowls on the front porch. A machete was wedged into one of the husks. I could hear the swish of a paddle fan through the open front door. I knocked on the bamboo.

"Lassiter, come in and make yourself a drink. There's some Gatorade in the fridge."

My potassium level seemed okay so I demurred on the Gatorade. I nosed around. Her voice was coming from what had to be the bedroom. The rest of the place was one room, a galley kitchen that opened into a small living room with TV, stereo, and VCR. A bookshelf with some sports reference books, some poetry anthologies—maybe a woman's heart lurked beneath the sweats—and a survival manual for Miami, a Spanish/English dictionary.

Rustling noises women make when dressing were coming from the bedroom. She could have been changing into something sheer and flimsy and dabbing sweet essence behind her ears. But she emerged with a freshly scrubbed face, *sans* makeup, the faint aroma of Ivory soap in the air. Cut-off jeans revealed strong legs, calves that flexed with each step. Her short black hair was even shorter in a ponytail tied with a rubber band. She wore a Miami Dolphins' jersey that still had room for me inside.

"You like my place?" she asked.

"Sure. When you called, I didn't realize you *lived* in the cabana. Thought you were inviting me to a pool party. Have you been banished from the castle by the wicked stepmother?"

She shook her head. "I lived in the house until Dad married that . . . woman. Then I decided to give them some privacy. I do my mile in the pool every night. This is all I need."

"I like it. It's one of the few houses in Miami smaller than mine."

"Until yesterday I kept some things in the main house. My skis, scuba equipment, some clothes. She tossed everything out on the patio after we exchanged words in the courthouse."

"I heard some of those words. You can exchange them with the best. Mind telling me what you were arguing about?"

She was silent. I was sitting on a rattan loveseat and she sat facing me, legs crossed, enveloped in a peacock chair. She smiled. That made two smiles if you counted one on the football field.

She was doing something with her hands, buying a little time to get into whatever it was that prompted her to call me. She started slowly. "You finish the case tomorrow, don't you?"

"That's right."

"You think you're going to win."

That might have been a question. "I have my hopes."

"Would you feel badly if you get off a guilty man?"

"*Guilty* is a criminal law word. In civil practice, there's no such thing. I'm hoping for a no-liability verdict. But civil liability is a gray area. So I can't respond to the question as phrased."

"A real lawyer's answer," she said contemptuously.

"You don't care much for my profession, or is it just me?"

She laughed and put some rhythm in her voice:

Why is there always a secret singing
When a lawyer cashes in?
Why does a hearse horse snicker
Hauling a lawyer away?

"I don't know," I said. "It wasn't on the bar exam."

She grimaced and gave me another stanza.

Singers of songs and dreamers of plays
Build a house no wind blows over.
The lawyers—tell me why a hearse horse snickers
hauling a lawyer's bones.

"Do I win a new refrigerator with a correct answer, go on to the next round? Robert Frost, maybe."

She grimaced. "Carl Sandburg."

"Funny, he admired a pretty fair trial lawyer named Lincoln. And I was hoping your taste in poetry ran more to Grecian urns than lawyers' bones."

She steered the conversation back where she wanted it. "Murder is part of criminal law, isn't it?"

That didn't stir me so she kept going. "You said the other day I had no proof. Maybe you should look at something."

She hopped up and pushed a button on the VCR and another on the small Sony TV. She sat down again and turned away. The set blinked on, a typical home movie, jerky camera, panning too quickly through a lushly appointed room. It looked like a Beverly Hills hotel suite, piano bar, Lucite furniture, starlight ceiling. No people visible, just modern, expensive furniture, some lighted artwork, and a nighttime sky indoors.

"That's the main salon of the *Cory*," Susan Corrigan said.

"The *Cory?*"

"Didn't you see the boat outside?"

"Oh that. I thought it was the *Nimitz,* four thousand sailors on shore leave."

"Wouldn't that make her happy?" she asked, icily, gesturing toward the house. "The *Cory* is a custom-made Hatteras, about eighty-two feet. One of Dad's toys."

The picture broke up, some snow, then Melanie Corrigan in a bikini on the screen, cocking a hip at the camera, pouting a come-hither look to stage left. The screen went to black for a second as a shoulder blocked the camera, a man walking into view. He was medium size, wearing swim trunks and a T-shirt, and he turned self-consciously to the camera. Roger Salisbury. If it was supposed to surprise me, it didn't.

"That's the main stateroom," Susan said.

A king-size waterbed sat on a floor of black and white tile and was illuminated from below with neon tubes. The headboard was the skyline of Miami, etched into black glass. Rock music played in the background. Roger Salisbury stood awkwardly at the foot of the bed and Melanie Corrigan began doing a striptease, if that's what you call it when you're starting out with only a black bikini that must have been made during a spandex shortage. The top was a strap slightly wider than dental floss, the bottom no bigger than your average Band-Aid. She was grinding to the music, rather expertly, some very fluid hip movements. She motioned for Roger to sit on the bed and he did, obedient little puppy.

She unhooked the halter top and squeezed her high firm breasts together, taking a deep breath as if the tiny scrap of fabric had been crushing her poor lungs to death. Acting right out of a high school play or a porno flick made on the cheap in Lauderdale. She tossed the halter at Roger. It landed on his head and slid over his nose and mouth. He could have robbed a bank in a B Western.

Next the bottom came off, and she wiggled her can in Roger's face in time with the music. She wiggled left and wiggled right, wiggled fast and wiggled slow. I had a feeling this was not her maiden cruise.

It took a minute more and then they were at it. A moment later the photographer discovered the electric zoom. First the long shot of two bodies writhing beneath the etched glass Miami skyline. Then the bodies got larger until only one body part, or two parts joined, filled the screen. Finally the camera zoomed back to show us the writhing bodies.

Susan Corrigan looked at me, her back to the screen. I was half embarrassed for her, half bored for me. Like an ex-jock in the bleachers, I'd rather play than watch. It went on for a while, then a cut and roll 'em again. The scene might have been shot another day or later the same day. If there was any dialogue, it was lost in the music laid over the action. Now Roger Salisbury was wearing a stethoscope and nothing else. Compared to Melanie Corrigan, however, he was overdressed.

Roger looked down her throat.

She said something. Ahhh.

Playing doctor. A little pantomime.

Open wide.

She did.

He took her pulse. Then she inhaled and jutted her breasts out, and he tapped her chest and listened to her lungs through the stethoscope. They seemed to pass the test.

She turned over and gave Salisbury a view of a perfectly rounded bottom. He laid his right hand on her ass and tapped it slowly with his thumb. A medical procedure I'd never seen, more like checking a melon's ripeness. Whatever its purpose, Melanie thought it hilarious. Laughing, she turned over and the camera jiggled, some jollies from the photographer, too. Then Roger felt her forehead as if the poor child was fevered, and just to be sure, he took her temperature. With something too big to have been a thermometer.

The picture broke up, came back on and went to black as someone walked by the lens. I figured it was Philip Corrigan, dealing himself in, having put the camera on a tripod. But it wasn't Corrigan. It was Hercules, albeit a short one. He reminded me of the bulldog on the hood of a Mack truck, only not as cute. One of those sides of beef you see in the gym, a body builder, slabs on top of slabs of muscle, a thick neck and sloping shoulders, a tattoo of a lightning bolt on one arm. Dark complexion, a flat, broad, mean face, drooping black moustache. His arms hung out from his sides, pushed there by his overdeveloped lats. And he was naked, revealing one part of his body not pumped up to Schwarzeneggerian proportions. So now I was watching two naked men and one naked woman. There were arms and legs entwined, a couple of glances toward the camera, and much thrusting of loins.

A quick cut and the camera angle was different. I was trying to figure out how the photographer got over the bed, looking down at the goings-on like a dance number in an old Busby Berkeley musical. Then I saw the photographer on the screen, a neat trick. He was at the foot of the bed, aiming the camera up, a man in his fifties, thinning hair and pot belly, lying on his side, stark naked, shooting a trick shot at a mirror on the ceiling over the bed. Philip Corrigan. I consulted my scorecard: three men and a woman. Again, the zoom, and Philip Corrigan disappeared from view. The screen filled with the body builder's shoulders. Covered with pimples, the telltale sign of an anabolic steroid user.

It went on for a few more minutes, then the screen faded to black and then to snow. It stayed that way.

"Well, what do you think now?" Susan Corrigan asked softly.

"I think the hand-held camera technique is more suitable to documentaries. The lighting is too harsh, the plot a mite thin. The bit with the mirror is cute, but frankly, I prefer *The Lady from Shanghai*."

"Is everything a joke to you?"

"Not everything, not even this. Susan, let it go. Every family has its dirty little secrets that are best left in the closet."

"My father wasn't like that. Not before her and Roger Salisbury."

"Okay. So she corrupted him. Maybe Roger's no angel, either. But what can be gained now?"

Her eyes blazed at me. "What about catching his killers?"

That again. "I still haven't seen any proof he was killed, much less that Roger Salisbury did it. What about Mr. Universe there? What about a dozen other guys you don't even know about?"

"More lawyer's games. Your beloved client is the only one who cut Dad open the day before he died. And as far as I know, he's the only one who carried poison around in his little leather case."

"What are you talking about?"

"This." She reached into a drawer, came up with something and tossed it at me. A small leather valise, a man's pocketbook if you're the kind of guy who carries that sort of thing. A gold monogram, "R.A.S." Roger Allen Salisbury. I unzipped it. Two hypodermic needles, a clear small vial of colorless liquid, half empty. No labels, no instructions.

A nasty little package. I felt a chill. "What is it?"

"Succinylcholine, a drug used in anesthesia. It paralyzes the limbs, the lungs, too. In anesthesia, a respirator breathes for you. Without a respirator, you would just lie there and watch yourself die."

"How do you know all this? Where did this come from?"

"One question at a time, Counselor. First, I found it in Melanie's room. Hidden in a drawer with thirty pairs of black panties, which is an awful lot for someone who seldom wears any. I think she knows it's missing. Probably suspects me. That's why she changed the locks and tossed my things out. Second, I've done some research on it, had a lab test it. I'm a reporter, and I know a lot more than just box scores and yards-per-carry."

"Has this been in your possession continuously since discovering it?" Ever the lawyer, Lassiter, already thinking about chain of custody.

"The lab at Jackson Memorial took about five cc's out of the bottle. Otherwise, it's intact."

"What's this have to do with Salisbury, assuming the stuff is his?"

"Of course it's his! Melanie was screwing him, must have gotten the drug from him. She hated my father, just used him. She couldn't divorce him. She'd get nothing because of an antenuptial agreement. But if he died while married to her, she got the house, the boat, plus thirty percent of the estate."

I nodded. "Items in joint name plus the marital share."

"Right."

"So she had the motive. But that's all you can prove. For a criminal case built on circumstantial evidence, you need a lot more. Your case against Melanie is weak and you don't have anything on Salisbury. For one thing, your father didn't die of poisoning. He died of an aneurysm."

She turned her head away and blinked back a tear. "That's why I need your help."

"For what?"

"To figure out how they did it."

"Did what?"

"Oh Jake, think about it."

It was the first time she called me by my given name. I liked the sound of it.

"How they killed Dad with succinylcholine and made it look like an aneurysm," she said softly, her armor turning to tin.

I didn't buy it. "A hospital's a pretty risky place to kill somebody, doctors and nurses all around."

"That's what made it work. Who would object if Dr. Salisbury came into Dad's room after the surgery? He could have given the injection then. And who would be looking for poison when the patient dies of an aneurysm? It's a classic misdirection play. Like the old Oklahoma fumblerooski, where the center and quarterback drop the ball. Everybody goes one way and the guard grabs the ball and walks in for the touchdown."

It was crazy. No evidence. Just an angry young woman searching for villains. Blaming others for her father's descent. The old fumblerooski, for crying out loud! I looked at her. A tear came to those dark eyes and then another. I looked at the hypodermics and the tiny bottle. And back at those wet, dark eyes.

"Where do we start?" I asked.

9

PROXIMATE
CAUSE

I was cruising on autopilot. On a very rough flight. I hadn't slept or thought about closing argument since Susan Corrigan handed me the vial and told me it was a murder weapon. I still felt it in the palm of my hand, the glass cool and smooth to the touch. Succinylcholine, a laboratory name. Like the clear liquid itself, impersonal as death.

The vial added a new dimension to Susan's bald allegation that Roger Salisbury killed her father. She had an exhibit. How juries love exhibits. The murder weapon, something to take back into the jury room and fondle.

My mind bounced it back and forth. I looked at Roger Salisbury sitting next to me. Salt-and-pepper hair well groomed, an oval face that was nearly delicate, intelligent eyes. Almost a scholarly appearance, an overall impression of competence. He looked like what he was, a physician. A healer, not a killer. But I had seen him stripped bare—literally—and wondered if his taste in after-dark activities could lead him to murder.

That's what Susan Corrigan wanted me to think. Maybe I was playing the fool for an elaborate scheme, Susan Corrigan throwing me a curve. She could have had the monogrammed leather valise made up in any shopping center. The liquid could have been water. She could be in cahoots with Melanie Corrigan to get me to tank the case. Or at least to distract me enough that I boot it. Hauling me over the night before closing argument. And me leaping for the bait, a wholesome dark-haired young woman, maybe underneath the Ivory soap just as mendacious as Melanie Corrigan. But I didn't have time to think about it. Dan Cefalo was clearing his throat and approaching the lectern. He looked remarkably normal in a dark blue suit and a white shirt that stayed inside his pants. He turned to Melanie Corrigan, gave her a fatherly smile, then bowed in the direction of the judge.

"May it please the court," he began, "and ladies and gentlemen of the jury. First I want to thank you all for coming down here and spending a week listening to a bunch of lawyers and doctors. I know it hasn't been easy, but without the aid of responsible citizens such as yourselves, we wouldn't have a justice system."

This is the *thank you folks* part of closing argument. It's a way to butter up the jurors, then get down to the nitty gritty: asking them to spend several million dollars of someone else's money.

"So on behalf of Mrs. Corrigan here," Cefalo continued, nodding and drawing their eyes to the plaintiff's table, "and on behalf of all of us whose privilege it is to serve, we thank you. You had to leave your jobs and families but that's what makes our system great. I love it, the

American system of justice. It's what separates us from the barbarians and Communists."

I was starting to feel very patriotic and wondering when he would get into it.

"Now the first thing to remember when I'm up here and when Mr. Lassiter gets up here, is that what we say is not evidence. This is just lawyer's talk, and you know the old expression, talk's cheap. They call this closing argument, but I'm not going to argue with Mr. Lassiter. Think of me as a guide. I'm going to guide you through the evidence so that when you go back into that jury room, you can decide the case on the evidence you heard from that witness stand and the law as Judge Leonard instructs you."

Two of the jurors nodded. Cefalo was starting with the low-key approach. *I'm your pal; let's think this through together*. It's the right tone. Don't lecture. Schmooze with them, gain their confidence, then rev up the heavy equipment and steamroller them. I knew what was coming even if they didn't.

"You folks might remember back in opening statement I told you that we had the burden of proof, to prove that Philip Corrigan died because of the negligence, the malpractice, of the defendant. Now, when the lawyers get through talkin' at you, the judge will tell you that all we need do is prove our case by a preponderance of the evidence. What does that mean? Well, if you put two boys on a teeter-totter and one weighs fifty-one pounds and the other forty-nine, the boy who weighs more tilts the scales. We just need to tilt the scale."

With that, Cefalo moved from behind the lectern and held his arms out, pretending to be a scale. He lowered his right arm one way, just a bit, to illustrate his point. "A wee little tilt and you must find for the plaintiff on liability," he reminded them. He would make the case as easy as first-grade recess.

"I also told you back in opening statement that a trial is like a book, and every witness is a chapter. Every book has a story and this one is a tragedy. It's about a vigorous, healthy man in the prime of his life, a family man, a businessman, a husband, a philanthropist . . ."

Again Cefalo turned to Melanie Corrigan. Six heads swiveled the same way. She gnawed her lower lip and fought back a tear. Her long hair was lassoed into a knot on top of her head and again she wore black. It emphasized her fair complexion, made her seem wan and helpless.

Cefalo got back into it, building momentum. "Philip Corrigan went into the hospital to have routine disc surgery. He put his trust in Roger Salisbury, who held himself out to be an expert orthopedic surgeon. Now his widow wakes up each morning, and there's always that moment, that split second, when she hopes he's still beside her."

It went on this way for a while, Cefalo painting with a broad brush. His strategy was to dance around the evidence and avoid the expert testimony until he had heated up their emotions.

"Now you folks heard from a lot of witnesses. But the two you probably remember best are Dr. Harvey Watkins, the former chief of orthopedics at a great hospital, and the defense witness, Charles Riggs, the elderly fellow who used to be the coroner. I think you should ask yourselves one question about these two. Who's done more laminectomies? Why, Dr. Watkins has done more disc jobs than a dog's got fleas. Old Charlie Riggs, he's never had a patient that lived."

A big smile; the jurors tittered. Roger Salisbury shifted uncomfortably in his chair.

"Matter of fact, Charlie Riggs never had a live patient in his entire career. His testimony was all hypothetical."

Cefalo dragged *hypo-thetical* across his tongue, the same way a Florida politician once accused an opposing candidate's wife of being a *prac-ticing thes-pian*.

"They might as well have brought Gino, my butcher, in here to describe back surgery. You know what they call coroners in the medical profession? Canoemakers. They just chop, chop, chop it up like hollowing out a log."

"Objection, Your Honor! That's not a legitimate comment on the evidence." I don't like to object during closing argument. It sometimes angers the jurors who like hearing lawyers beat their breasts, but I wanted Cefalo to know I hadn't fallen asleep.

"Overruled," Judge Leonard said.

"Canoemakers," Cefalo repeated, needling me. "Riggs has never done one laminectomy. Not one! Mr. Lassiter should be ashamed."

With that Cefalo turned and looked toward me. So did the jurors, looking peeved, wondering if I tried to bamboozle them. Good strategy, avoiding what Riggs had said, just attacking his credentials. Sooner or later, though, he'd have to address the testimony or risk giving that ball to me on an open field. Roger Salisbury was squirming so much his chair squeaked on the old tile floor. I patted his arm, a coach telling a player to calm down.

"You heard the real expert, Dr. Harvey Watkins, on the first day of trial. It was only a few days ago, but it seems like a lifetime, so let me go over it. He said that it's malpractice to pierce the aorta with the rongeur. And it was Philip Corrigan's aorta that burst later that night. No one disagrees about that. All Mr. Riggs—excuse me, Dr. Riggs— all he said was he didn't know how the aorta got torn in front. But did he tell you what caused the aneurysm? No! He had no answer. The way I figure it, Dr. Salisbury here was poking around so much, it's lucky the rongeur didn't come out the belly button."

Roger Salisbury groaned. I had nearly forgotten how Dan Cefalo could make hokum sound like the gospel. I also had forgotten to tell Roger Salisbury not to have a stroke during the plaintiff's closing. I still had a few things to say if the jury didn't draw and quarter my client first.

"I do regret one thing," Cefalo said, lowering his voice. "Unfortunately, Dr. Watkins was taken ill shortly before his rebuttal testimony. He was not as articulate as he might have been. But I'm sure you got the drift. It was Dr. Salisbury's negligence and that alone which caused the death of Philip Corrigan and left this young woman a grief-stricken widow."

On cue Melanie Corrigan dabbed her eyes. Cefalo was gearing for the transition into the damages phase of his argument. He moved closer to the jury box and looked each juror directly in the eyes, moving slowly from one to the other.

"So, in summary, there is no question about liability. No, ladies and gentlemen, this is not a case of 'who wins.' This is a case of 'how much.' And this is a very substantial case because Philip Corrigan was a very substantial man. He was a builder, a developer, a man who employed hundreds and brought commerce to thousands with the first chain of shopping centers ever built in the Florida Keys. Before Philip Corrigan, there was no Zippy Mart south of Homestead. Before Philip Corrigan, there were no condos built in the flood plain. They said it couldn't be done, but Philip Corrigan did it."

Two jurors nodded, impressed.

"In a few minutes, the judge will instruct you as to the elements of damages, and they are all very substantial. You heard the accountants testify as to the loss of net accumulations of the estate of Philip Corrigan because of his untimely and tragic death. You will take their written report into the jury room. You heard the widow, Mrs. Corrigan, testify as to her grief. God willing, you will carry that grief with you into your deliberations and relieve some of it with your verdict."

God on the plaintiff's side. I didn't like that one bit. The widow's tears were coming now. Melanie Corrigan turned away, leaving the jury with her sculpted profile.

"The judge will instruct you that Mrs. Corrigan is entitled to be compensated for her mental anguish and the lost companionship and protection of her husband. Mental anguish is something she will carry with her every day for the rest of her life. Every wedding anniversary and holiday, every time she sees something in the house that reminds her of him, every morning when she awakens and every night when she goes to sleep, she will think of him, struck down. Negligently, mercilessly, senselessly. And for that reason we ask you for a total verdict of five million dollars for Mrs. Corrigan and five million dollars for the estate, a total, ladies and gentlemen, of ten million dollars."

He let it sink in a moment, then continued, "And I don't apologize for asking for one dollar of it. You know, folks, they auctioned off a racehorse the other day for fifteen million dollars."

Judge Leonard's bald head popped up. He wouldn't mind five points of that investment.

"No apologies," Cefalo repeated. "I'm told some Japanese fellows paid forty million dollars for a picture by . . . what's the name of that painter fellow, Van Gogh? And our very own United States Air Force pays millions and millions of dollars for each jet fighter. But you know, they build an ejection seat into each plane, 'cause if there's any trouble, they want to save the pilot's life, let the plane go down in flames. A life is worth more than a twenty-million-dollar airplane. So, no sir, I'm not going to apologize for asking you folks for ten million dollars."

Dan Cefalo was just about done not apologizing. He seemed to be gathering his thoughts for a final assault. He walked toward the defense table, where Roger Salisbury had broken a sweat. Cefalo took a deep breath and said, "Philip Corrigan went into that hospital and said, 'Take good care of me, Doctor. Use all your training and expertise. Don't cut me open and let me bleed to death.' They put him to sleep and there he was, innocent as a baby, at this man's mercy, and this man chopped him up."

With that Cefalo turned and stabbed a finger at Roger Salisbury. *J'accuse*. Then he walked to the rail of the jury box and leaned on it, a close friend of all six honest folks.

"You know, some fancy writer, I don't know his name, once wrote, 'For of all sad words of tongue or pen, the saddest are these, it might have been.' The saddest are these, it might have been. What might have been for Philip and Melanie Corrigan, we will never know. Perhaps children, other lives to share with their own total love. But Philip Corrigan, who trusted this man with his life, left this world all too soon. And now Melanie Corrigan trusts you with her life. She has only one chance. If she is unhappy with the result, she can't come back and try again. Next week this courtroom might have some fender-bender case or a dispute over a parking space at a condo. This case is here and now and it is a tragic one and a substantial one. Don't let Melanie Corrigan walk out of here and say, 'It might have been.' Thank you and God bless you."

God again. We now knew that Cefalo was for God and against communism. He sat down and Melanie Corrigan opened the faucets. She buried her head into Cefalo's shoulder. He patted her between the shoulder blades. None of the jurors even saw me stand up and approach the lectern. I felt my throat tighten. Roger Salisbury's face was frozen with panic. It was important to show him that Cefalo's stellar performance did not bother me. I did this by not tossing my breakfast into the jury box.

It was a very lonely walk, those half dozen steps to center stage. I paused and finally the jurors turned toward me, their eyes challenging. I thanked them for their attention without waving the flag in their faces. I told them I only had one chance to speak to them, and then Mr. Cefalo would get up for his rebuttal. They seemed to like that. I told them that he had a second chance because the plaintiff had the burden of proof. As the defendant, we didn't have to prove anything. And then I said, let's see what they had proved.

"A man has died, and Mr. Cefalo is right about one thing. That is a tragedy. It always is when a person is taken before his three score and ten. But the world is full of tragedies. They happen every day. And not every one, not this one, has someone to blame. Mr. Cefalo is right about something else. This is a substantial case, but not because a lot of money is involved. It is substantial because it involves the reputation and good name of a very fine surgeon, a man who has treated the poor and underprivileged in our public hospital, a man who spent years training and preparing himself in every way for life-and-death decisions."

I caught a glimpse of Dan Cefalo rolling his eyes. Give me a break, Dan. You're way ahead in the laying-it-on-thick department. What did he expect me to say, that my client spent years planning his pension fund, that orthopods are out of their league whenever they move north of ankles and knees?

I continued, "Philip Corrigan died of a ruptured aorta. We all know that. No one disputes it. Aortic aneurysms happen every day. You heard the testimony. They can occur from high blood pressure, trauma, arteriosclerosis, a host of things. It can be, as Dr. Riggs said, '*ex visitatione divina*,' a visitation from God."

I was not going to be outdone in the God department. I studied the six faces. Nothing. Not a hint. At least they seemed to be listening.

"Let me now tell you of the crucial flaw in the plaintiff's case, the weak link, the stumbling block where this house of cards comes tumbling down." No one will ever accuse me of leaving a cliché unturned.

"The weak link is proximate cause. Let me repeat that. It's not *ap-proximate cause*. It's *proximate cause*. When we sit down, Judge Leonard will read you the law of proximate cause."

I needed to make a point based on Riggs's testimony. I could have said, *here's what Riggs said*, but that might not work after Cefalo's hatchet job. The trick now was to put Riggs's testimony in the context of what the judge would tell them.

I picked up the book of standard jury instructions. I wanted to look official, the judge's helper. Then in deep tones, trying to make the causation instruction sound like the Magna Charta, I said, "Here is what the judge will instruct you: 'Negligence is the legal cause of death if it directly and in natural continuous sequences produces or contributes substantially to producing such death, so that it can reasonably be said that, but for the negligence, the death would not have occurred.' Remember, that is not Jake Lassiter talking, that is the judge, and that is the law."

The risk in discussing jury instructions is that the jurors won't have the foggiest idea what you're talking about. The instructions are complicated, and juries are noticeably light on Rhodes scholars. I needed to explain the gobbledygook. "'*But for the negligence, the death would not have occurred.*' That is what you must determine if Roger Salisbury is to be found liable for professional negligence, for violating his oath, for that is what they have charged him with. When Roger Salisbury became a physician, he promised to adhere to the Hippocratic oath. He promised to do no harm. And they have charged him under Florida law with negligently causing the death of Philip Corrigan. First, you must ask yourselves, what is the evidence that Dr. Salisbury contributed substantially to the death and that, but for the negligence, the death would not have occurred."

I couldn't tell if it was getting across, but I plowed ahead.

"That is the ultimate question of proximate cause, and on that question, the evidence is undisputed."

I paused again, this time for effect. "Ladies and gentlemen, think back over the testimony of Dr. Harvey Watkins. You can think from now until the Orange Bowl Parade, and you won't find Dr. Watkins saying that the aneurysm resulted from anything Dr. Salisbury did. You see, I agree with everything Dr. Watkins said. He said it would be negligence to allow the rongeur to pierce the aorta. Fine, but there's no evidence that happened here. That's the missing link. The surgery occurred in the morning. The aneurysm happened late that night back in the private room. No loss of blood pressure during surgery, no indication of internal bleeding. Mr. Cefalo wants you to pile inference on inference, that the rongeur struck the aorta despite no evidence of an aneurysm for another twelve hours. And what did Dr. Riggs tell us?"

I spread my feet wide and stood two feet from the rail of the jury box. There I stood motionless, a rock. I wanted them to see nothing but me, to hear nothing but my words.

"Dr. Riggs told us two things, first, that the blowout in the aorta was in front where the rongeur couldn't touch it, and second, that Philip Corrigan had arteriosclerosis, hardening of the arteries. Now, unlike the name, hardening of the arteries actually weakens the arteries. Philip Corrigan was fifty-seven years old. A lot of blood had gone through those veins, a lot of miles on his odometer. And I submit to you, ladies and gentlemen, that his time had come, *ex visitatione divina.*"

I tried to see how it was going. If they bought this, we win. If not, we get hammered. I had a decision to make. This was the point where I should move to the damages issue, register shock at the ten-million-dollar figure. Hit them with the bit about cashing in on death. But I decided to risk it.

"Ladies and gentlemen, now is when a defense lawyer ordinarily discusses damages. But I am so convinced that the evidence does not support a plaintiff's verdict on liability that I find that unnecessary. They simply haven't proved their case."

I needed a way to wrap it up. Take a risky swipe at the sympathy factor.

"Finally, one word about Mrs. Corrigan. She is a young woman and her grief will heal. Surely she knew when she married a man twice her age that at some point she would be a widow."

This was thin ice. Go too far here and risk offending the jury into a retaliatory verdict.

"Mr. Cefalo quoted you an old saw about what might have been. Another writer once said that grief is the most intense of all emotions and therefore the shortest lived. Time heals. Grief ends. Life goes on. It is natural for you to feel sympathy for Mrs. Corrigan, as I do, but it is not to enter into your deliberations. Judge Leonard will instruct you that you are not to be swayed by sympathy. Sentiment has no place here. Only the facts and the law, and they will convince you that there is no liability in this case. Thank you."

Melanie Corrigan's eyes burned a hole in my back as I walked to the defense table. Roger Salisbury's face was a mixture of hope and fear. Dan Cefalo didn't waste any time. He had the last shot.

"Ladies and gentlemen, I rise now to speak one last time for Philip Corrigan, who cannot speak for himself."

Talk about *non sequiturs*. If Philip Corrigan could speak for himself, we wouldn't be here.

Cefalo raised his voice in lawyerly indignation. "They've put this woman through the death of her husband, a funeral, a trial, a world of loneliness, and now they say, it'll pass. Go home, Mrs. Corrigan, it'll pass. Let me tell you folks something. When we're done here today, I'll go home to my family. You folks will go home to yours. Mr. Lassiter will see his friends and there will be cheery talk and hors d'oeuvres and the tinkling of glasses."

That was news to me. I was planning to open a can of tuna.

"But the Corrigan house will be dark and empty when she turns the key in the lock tonight. It'll be that way tonight and tomorrow and the next night. So Mr. Lassiter would have you split hairs over this and that, but the fact is that a man went into the hospital for simple surgery and he didn't come out, and they have a bushelbasket full of reasons why, but you and I know the truth. So as you prepare to go into the jury room, I leave you and ask that you remember you are this woman's last and only hope. God speed."

A dangerous combination, I thought, as the jurors filed into their windowless room. The intellect of man, the speed of God.

10

WE HAVE, YOUR HONOR

Waiting again, this time for a verdict. Waiting is not my strong suit. I never did the bit outside a hospital delivery room, but I know all the clichés, the pacing, the endless cigarettes, the furrowed brows. At least there, when it's over, you've got something to take home. I leave it all behind. Win, lose, or mistrial, I bury it. Winning is less joy than relief, removing the knife from the wound. Losing is not agony, just the fulfillment of promised pain.

Defending a case is particularly frustrating. If you win, you have broken even, restored the status quo. Your client wants to take you to dinner. He shows you his new bumper sticker, *My Lawyer Can Beat Your Lawyer*. If you lose, he questions what you should have done to win. And always finds something.

Roger Salisbury paced in the corridor. I sat with Cindy in the courtroom. While I read the latest *Windrider* magazine, she propped her bare feet on the defense table and painted her toenails a metallic silver that reminded me of a '71 Corvette. The bailiff came by and gave her a dirty look. She wiggled a burnished big toe at him.

Still waiting, two hundred minutes creeping along, life ticking away. Somewhere off the Canary Islands, tanned young men and women from France are sailing windsurfers at more than thirty knots. On a hundred slopes in the Rockies, skiers are whooping it up on fresh powder. Only a hundred miles away, bass fishermen are lazing across Lake Okeechobee. So why am I waiting, just waiting, in an old relic of a courthouse for six strangers to tell me if I'm worth a hot damn in my chosen field.

"Is it a good sign they're taking so long?" Roger Salisbury asked, coming in from the corridor.

"It could be," I said. Very insightful. In truth, it's meaningless. If the jury comes back with a verdict after twenty minutes, you can be sure it's for the defense. They haven't had time to order steaks at taxpayer expense, much less determine both liability and damages. After that, anything goes. They could have determined liability in the plaintiff's favor hours ago and only now be deciding how many zeroes to tack onto the verdict form.

I picked up a newspaper and turned to the sports pages. There was Susan Corrigan's by-line above a story on the Dolphins game, a loss at Cleveland. The Dolphins never did play well in cold weather, losing 24 to 10 to the Browns and their defense known as the Dawgs:

CLEVELAND—When the game was still dicey and the field was turning icy, the Browns showed the Miami Dolphins what a Dawg Day afternoon is like on the shores of frozen Lake Erie.

Cute. I wanted to see her. Maybe after the verdict, if she calms down about this murder business. My daydreaming was interrupted by The Knock. It's the knock that sets the adrenaline pumping, the knock from inside the jury room. It could mean anything, including the fact that the jurors are hungry. The bailiff hurried over, as best he could. He was a retired motorcycle cop with snow-white hair, a bow-legged walk, and a hacking cough. When he came out, he headed straight for the judge's chambers, a poker face all the way. Must have forgotten about the bottle of Jack Daniels I *schmear* him with every Christmas.

In a moment the judge flew through the rear door of the courtroom, still hooking his robe in front, its tail aflutter like a mainsail tacking. Things would happen fast now if there was a verdict. But the jury might have a question, not an answer. Usually baffling questions. *Could the court reporter read back the nurse's testimony about the patient's postsurgery constipation?* You can never tell what goes through their minds.

But no questions this time. The foreman was holding a piece of legal-size paper neatly folded at the middle. He was a retired accountant. No trace of a sense of humor or spontaneity when I questioned him on *voir dire*. I had asked him the last book he read. *"The Price Waterhouse Guide to the New Tax Law,"* he responded. Not the kind of a guy to have a beer with, but perfect for the defense in a personal injury or medical malpractice case. I tried to catch the foreman's eye. No soap. Looked at the rest of them. Still no luck. Legal folklore has it that they avoid your eyes when they've voted against you.

One of the women, a housewife, looked toward Melanie Corrigan and teared up. Now what the hell did that mean? The widow was through with her tears. She had dusted on some blush during the long break. A nice mixture of healthy and sultry, shedding her mourning widow image a mite early. Her lips were freshly painted in a pink liquid gloss, a wet look. Her hair now cascaded over her shoulders. She ran a hand through the reddish brown waves and tossed her head back, showing me a fine line of neck. A splendid pose for a shampoo ad.

Roger Salisbury could have been in an ad, too. For Plummer Funeral Home. When news of The Knock reached the corridor, he quit pacing and hastily joined me at the defense table, the color draining from his face. Now his complexion was the gray of a California scal. I wondered if he was too young for a coronary.

"Has the jury reached a verdict?" Judge Leonard asked in a grave tone suitable for an execution.

"We have, Your Honor," said the foreman, with no wasted breaths. He stood and handed the verdict form to the bailiff, who used it to shield a cough, then handed it to the judge. Judge Leonard took a thousand years to read it, and I strained with X-ray eyes to read it from fifty feet away. Not a trace of emotion crossed Judge Leonard's face as he handed the form to the clerk. Annoyed at having been interrupted, she reluctantly put down her new paperback, this one a survey of women's sexual fantasies.

"The clerk will publish the verdict," Judge Leonard said in the same stern voice.

The clerk stood up, lodged her chewing gum in the roof of her mouth, jammed a pencil into her Afro, and in a bored monotone, started reading:

"In the Eleventh Judicial Circuit, in and for Dade County, Florida, Case Number eight-seven, one-eight-three-seven-six, Melanie Corrigan, as Personal Representative of the Estate of Philip M. Corrigan, deceased, versus Roger A. Salisbury, M.D." She paused, cleared her throat, *ah-chem*. Oh get to it, already. "We, the jury, find for the defendant."

Boom. That was it. She sat down. Roger Salisbury slapped me on the back. Dan Cefalo winced once, recovered like the pro he was, and asked the judge to poll the jury. He did. Each one affirmed the verdict. Melanie Corrigan looked over at Roger Salisbury and gave him a small, bittersweet smile. Like it didn't matter. Like that's one for you. If that wasn't the damnedest thing.

Judge Leonard was doing his thank-yous to the jurors while his bailiff handed them certificates bearing a sketch of the judge that made his round face look like Abe Lincoln on Mount Rushmore. Good for a few votes in the next election.

Then it was over. The jurors picked up their things, the few spectators ambled down the corridor looking for more action. Roger Salisbury began babbling about how brilliant I was, how great Charlie Riggs was, how beautiful Cindy was. He wanted to treat me to dinner, champagne, wenching.

I was spent. I told him I would be poor company. In truth I was tired of his company. I had given him a piece of myself. The camaraderie that comes from the shared experience evaporates when the experience ends. Like war buddies, you drift apart when the conflict is over. Quickly.

So why did I feel that the case of Corrigan versus Salisbury was only just beginning?

11

THE WASP
AND THE
CATERPILLAR

Cindy headed back to the office and I aimed the 442 convertible west on Tamiami Trail toward the Everglades. No way I was going to return phone calls and compile expense account forms after coming out of trial. I wanted some open air. Tamiami Trail is *Calle Ocho* in Little Havana. I passed city parks where old Cuban men played dominoes, drinking espresso, cigars clenched in brown teeth, vowing to return to a *Cuba Libre*. They do not consider themselves *immigrantes,* a term that implies a voluntary move to a new home. They are *exilados,* refugees in exile. When their homeland is liberated from the Communist butcher, they will return.

The young Cubans, the teenagers born in Miami, look at matters differently. With their 280Z's, late nights in Coconut Grove discos, and weekends on Key Biscayne beaches, they have no desire to take up arms or swing machetes in the sugarcane fields. If they don battle fatigues, it is only because the look is fashionable this season at the Banana Republic boutique.

When hundreds of thousands of Cuban refugees flooded Miami in the 1960s, there were few directions to go. East was the small downtown and Biscayne Bay. South was pricey Coral Gables, and it would be years before most exiles could move there. North was Liberty City, officially the Central Negro District on old police reports, a place the Great Society passed by, the scorching pavement without the palm trees of the Gables or the pines of South Dade.

The only direction was west, and those who fled Castro pushed Miami that way, blowing the city out at the seams, bringing new food and music and clothing, and in a generation, they owned the gas stations and restaurants and auto dealerships and furniture stores and even banks. From the bay westward for one hundred forty blocks, onto the fringes of the Everglades, on both sides of Tamiami Trail, they lived and worked and prospered. In the middle of what was a sleepy Southern town another country grew, strange and forbidding—*Fantasias Ropas, Vistas Funeraria, Clinicas Quiropracticas*—its premises off-limits to English speakers.

The Anglo immigrants of a generation before came from Georgia and Alabama. They lived in small concrete block stucco houses with no garages, and in their front yards pickup trucks were hitched to airboats, ready for midnight frogging in the Glades. These whites— airline mechanics, truck drivers, power company linemen—already feared the mean street blacks and resented the Miami Beach Jews. Culture shock for these Southern Baptists was a Florida town turned upside down, where native-born whites got the hell out, bumper stickers pleading sarcastically, *WILL THE LAST ANGLO TO LEAVE MIAMI PLEASE TURN OFF THE LIGHTS*.

Traffic thinned after I passed the sprawling campus of Florida International University. Now it was a straight shot across the Trail, all the way to Naples if I wanted to air it out. At first I pretended not to know where I was headed. But I knew. I knew the little dirt road that came out of the Everglades near Shark Valley just this side of the phony Miccosukee village where a bored Indian wrestles a stoned gator, tourists clicking their Nikons.

I slid into the turn, sending up a swirl of dust and startling a dozen snowy egrets in the sawgrass. A great white heron with matchstick legs eyed me from the shallow water, then stutter-stepped away like a man on crutches. The high ground—barely two feet above the swamp—was a mile off the Trail, just a patch of dirt behind a stand of scraggly trees. The house was an old fishing cabin, weatherbeaten boards topped by a corrugated aluminum roof that caught the late afternoon sun. An old fishing cabin is what you're left with when your wife's lawyer is a B-52 bomber with a mouth like a nuclear warhead. A Spanish-style house with an orange barrel-tile roof on a shady Coral Gables street is what your wife gets when the mushroom cloud has lifted.

In a dilapidated lawn chair, bare feet propped on a milk carton, sat Charles W. Riggs, M.D., retired medical examiner of Dade County, Florida. He put down a dusty book and motioned me toward another plastic chair with frayed straps for a seat. I looked at the book. *Select Coroners' Rolls, 1265–1413, A.D.* Must have missed it on the bestseller list. Riggs wore khaki bush shorts that stopped just above his knobby knees. His legs were short and pale, the legs of a man with enough sense to stay out of the Florida sun. His faded T-shirt advertised an oyster bar in Key West and bulged at the middle. His graying beard needed trimming or at least combing. His half-glasses had tossed a screw and were mended with a bent fishhook. The glasses sat cockeyed on his small nose. Behind the lenses, his eyes—the color of sawgrass during a drought—took it all in and let only some of it out.

"You make a wrong turn heading for the beach?" he asked.

"No, just thought I'd be neighborly, drop by. *Qué pasa,* Doc?"

"Mosquitoes biting, fish ain't. What're you doing this far west?"

"Lately haven't known east from west, up from down."

"Sounds like one of those country ballads. You're not in love are you, Jake?"

I fiddled with the old book. "Not in love, though there's a woman. But this isn't about her, not exactly. It's Salisbury. We finished today, defense verdict."

"Congratulations. When I saw your face, I thought the jury might have stuck it to you. Would have been a shame. That rongeur never got close to the aorta."

My white shirt, angelic for verdict day, was beginning to patch with sweat. No breeze cut through the great river of grass today. "I believed you about the rongeur," I said. "The jury believed you. There's a young woman, Corrigan's daughter, who says the malpractice case was just a cover, that Salisbury and the widow poisoned her father with a drug, succinylcholine."

Charlie Riggs didn't bat an eye. "What's the motive?"

"Money. Melanie wanted her husband's. Salisbury wanted Melanie, the money, too, I suppose."

"Radix omnium malorum est cupiditas."

"Easy for you to say."

"The love of money," Charlie Riggs explained, "is the root of all evil. Not money itself. There's nothing inherently evil about money, but the love of it, that's what does them in. Money never meant beans to me. Martha, my ex, was always yammering about money. Wanted me to go into private practice, form my own P.A., start a chain of labs, pay kickbacks to the internists, the whole lousy deal. Imagine me a businessman, or even worse, looking at slides all day, a bookkeeper in a white coat with a microscope."

I kept my mouth shut and let him think about it, a brilliant career of public service, a wrecked family life. He smiled sadly and said, "Loved the scent of money, she did, and hated the smell of formaldehyde."

I navigated the conversation back on course. "I'm having trouble believing it, murder I mean. But Susan Corrigan came up with a vial that supposedly has the drug, a couple of hypodermics, all in a leather valise belonging to Salisbury."

Charlie Riggs shook his head. "Succinylcholine, a lousy way to die. You'd be conscious, fully aware, but paralyzed until your lungs and heart gave out. Ugly. Somebody must have a lot of hunger for money to do that."

"That doesn't surprise you, does it, Charlie? Man is the cruelest animal."

He waggled a finger at me. "A common misconception. There are animals in nature capable of the cruelest torture. Take the ichneumons, a variety of wasps. The ichneumon injects its eggs right into a caterpillar's body after shooting it with a paralyzing toxin. Sort of a succinylcholine in nature. When the eggs hatch, the wasp larvae begin eating the caterpillar, slowly and painfully. They keep that poor caterpillar alive so the innards don't spoil, first eating the fat and the digestive organs, saving the heart for last. Finally nothing is left but the shell. Nature is just as cruel as man."

This was standard fare for Doc Riggs, a mix of Biology 101 and Basic Philosophy. I said, "Sure Charlie, but the icky-whachamacallit does it for food, for survival."

"Is that really an important distinction?"

Pulling the old Socratic method on me. "Sure it is," I said. "Killing for food is justifiable homicide in the animal kingdom. I've watched enough Marlin Perkins to know that. Man kills for money or out of anger or passion. I've tried enough criminal cases to know that."

He looked at me over the repaired glasses that hung lopsided on his nose. "Either way, the victim is just as innocent, the pain just as real, is it not?"

I didn't answer, just sat there and listened to the sound of the swamp, the water stirred by unseen animals. Overhead I heard the short, mellow whistle of an osprey, the Florida fish hawk, and imagined its sharp eyes on full alert for catfish, talons at the ready.

Two mosquitoes buzzed around my left ear, debating who would dine first.

Finally Charlie Riggs said, mostly to himself, "Succinylcholine. Be hard to trace. Breaks down into succinic acid and choline and both substances are normally present in the body. A physician would know that. We could check for needle tracks, though."

"Isn't it a little late for that?"

He sprang from the chair and bounded into the cabin, banging the screen door behind him. "Read the book," he called out. "Right where the mark is. I'll fix us some limeade. Key limes, sour as my ex-wife's disposition."

I blew some dust off the book and it fell open to the year 1267. A crummy time to be alive unless you were handy with a sword. The book was in Latin on the left-hand pages and English on the right. Riggs had been reading the left side, making little notes. Never having gotten past *amo, amas, amat,* I opted for the English:

It happened in the vill of Goldington after vespers the eve of the feast of St. Dunstan that strife arose on the Green between William Read and John Barford concerning sheep. William received a wound on the head from which he seemed to recover. Then he died of ague and his wife raised the hue. The coroner found that William Read had already been buried and instructed that he be dug up. When he be dug up, the coroner said that William Read died of the wound, not the illness, and ordered John Barford attached.

Charlie Riggs toddled out of the cabin carrying two mason jars of limeade with no ice. I put down the book and asked, "You want to exhume Corrigan's body?"

He handed me one of the jars, dropped into his rickety chair, and studied the swamp. "You'd be surprised how well embalming preserves tissues. Might be hard to find needle tracks, though. The skin will be moldy, and if he's buried in damp ground, it's probably turned to adipocere, sort of a waxy gunk. And he isn't going to smell like Chanel No. 5."

He let that hang in the still air, then said, "If you're getting hungry, I'm about to put supper on. Fresh possum."

I passed on the invitation, thoughts of parasitic wasps and moldy corpses failing to whet the appetite. I took a swig of the warm limeade. It puckered me up; he had left out the sugar.

"Well how about it, Jake? You ready to rob graves?"

"I've done worse, but Salisbury is my client. I can't do anything against his interests."

Riggs scowled. "The case is over, Counselor."

"Not in the eyes of the Florida Bar. I can't use something I learned in the course of representing Salisbury in a way that may harm him. I try not to break more than two or three of the canons each week."

I must not have sounded convincing. I hadn't convinced Riggs, and I hadn't convinced myself.

Charlie Riggs downed his limeade in one gulp, gave me his teacher-to-student look, and said, "It's not as if you're going to the authorities. Just a little private investigation to answer some questions, settle your conscience. Besides, it'll give me something to do. And maybe your young lady friend will appreciate you searching for the truth, kind of set you apart from most members of your profession."

He knew how to push all the right buttons. "C'mon, Jake. To hell with your canons."

"Come to think of it," I said, "they're not mine."

"Good boy. Let's get to it. The grave is silent, *magis mutus quam piscis,* but you and I, Jake, we can speak for the dead."

12

KNIGHT ERRANT

The city swallowed up the Salisbury verdict just as it did everything else. A tiny morsel for the carnivorous media machines. Two paragraphs in the "Courthouse Roundup" section of the newspaper, no television or radio coverage at all. *60 Minutes* did not call me for an interview; young lawyers did not stop me on Flagler Street and ask for words of wisdom; my partners did not toast me with champagne or vote me a bonus.

If the jury had hit Salisbury with a ten-million-dollar verdict, headlines would have screamed the news from here to Tallahassee. But a defense verdict sinks into the muck of the day's events, a fallen twig barely stirring a ripple in the malevolent swamp.

I did receive a memo from Morris McGonigal, the senior partner, a guy with a gray flannel personality in a seersucker town. Or rather my secretary Cindy received a memo from his secretary. It said, "Please advise Mr. Lassiter that Mr. McGonigal congratulates him on his recent verdict."

The personal touch.

I wasn't complaining about the lack of notoriety. It probably was better for Salisbury. A doctor gets hit with a big verdict, the public thinks he's a butcher. The doctor gets off, the public thinks the jury fouled up. Besides, it was a heavy news day, even by Miami standards. Federal agents arrested two Nicaraguans who had a dozen TOW missiles and an antitank rocket in their truck, the Miami version of a firearms violation. The Nicaraguans were planning to fight the Sandinistas, a holy mission hereabouts, and would probably get probation, if not a key to the city.

A few hours later, most Miami police were busy pumping bullets into the van of a 63-year-old Cuban plumber. They had good reason. He had fired five shots at an undercover cop. But then the plumber had good reason. The cop, dressed like a thug, was stuck in a monstrous traffic jam on *Calle Ocho*. The cop waved his gun at the plumber to get him to move his van. His *motherfucking Cuban van*, witnesses would later recall the officer screaming. There was a convenience store robbery coming down a block away, and the cop, his Firebird socked in by the van, was hollering in English, a language as foreign to the plumber as Sanskrit.

The plumber figured he was being robbed and opened fire. That drew seven police cars, a number of shotguns, and forty-seven holes in the van, three in the plumber, and one in his colostomy bag. The plumber survived, and the convenience store robbers got away with seventy-three dollars and a box of DoveBars.

I was mired in my typical psychological letdown after a trial, just puttering around the office, shuffling stacks of mail, trying to figure out where to go from here. I tried calling Susan Corrigan, but a bored voice on the copy desk said she was on the west coast, headed out early for pregame stories on the Dolphins' next opponent, their old nemesis, the Raiders. I wanted to see her, and not just to talk about digging up dear old Dad. I had a little buzz about Ms. Susan Corrigan. That happens sometimes when I get stiff-armed. Don't know why, maybe my ego needs bruising. Maybe too much easy flesh in the early years. Or maybe I had matured a notch or two until I finally appreciated a strong, savvy lady more than a lusty, dim one. Whatever the reason, the image of the suntanned and sharp-tongued sportswriter was hovering just below the surface of my consciousness.

I had just hung up with the newspaper when Cindy slipped me a note:

Widow Not Merry,
Do Not Tarry;
Commotion, Line Two.

I punched the flashing button and heard shouting in the background, a man's voice and a woman's voice. I couldn't make out the words. I said hello a bunch of times. The phone must have been put down. Some women need two hands to argue. The voices came closer. "You owe me," the man's voice said, booming over the wire. Then the sound of a woman laughing. More yelling, then a woman's loud voice telling the man to get out. I thought I heard a door slam. Then silence.

"Hello." The woman's voice, under perfect control. "Mr. Lassiter?"

I told her it was.

She told me it was Mrs. Corrigan calling. I knew that.

She said there was trouble. I knew that, too.

Could you come over?

"If you have trouble, why not call the police?" I suggested.

"You wouldn't like that," she said, evenly. "Neither would your client."

It was coming into focus. "Is Roger there?"

"He is, and he's making quite a scene."

"Put him on."

"At the moment, he's pacing on the patio by the Jacuzzi. If it's just the same to you, I'd rather not have him in the house. He hit me. And I don't think he'll leave my property unless you come talk to him. Or should I just call the police and charge him with trespassing and assault?"

"I'll be there in twenty minutes."

She didn't ask if I knew the address and I didn't tell her I did. I just headed to the parking garage, and like a knight errant, saddled my steed and galloped south on Miami Avenue toward Coconut Grove and Gables Estates beyond. At the same time I wondered what Roger Salisbury was doing, screwing everything up. Why wasn't he sawing bones and scraping kneecaps? What was it he'd said? That he was still under her spell. Didn't he know she was poison?

The water still tumbled through its man-made waterfall and the house still sat, silent as a tomb, atop its man-made hill. But no cars in the driveway, no voices to break the gentle roar of the waterfall, and no Roger Salisbury. The winter sun, low in the afternoon sky, slanted narrow shadows from the royal palms, like jailhouse bars, across the Corrigan house. A chill was in the air, a cold front from the Midwest rustling the palm fronds with a crisp northwest breeze. I parked by the waterfall, patted the 442 on the rump and told it to stay put. Then, I walked up the front steps and rang the bell.

"He threatened to kill me," Melanie Corrigan said.

She had thrown open the double doors, a good trick in itself. Fifteen feet high, six inches thick, crossed-hatched by thick beams, a circus elephant could slip in sideways.

"Where is he?"

"He threatened to kill me," she repeated. There was a red splotch just below her left eye. A right-handed guy who doesn't know how to punch might have glanced one off there. "He left. Drove away like a madman. Cursing at me."

She led me into the foyer and closed the door. An electric bolt clicked into place like a bullet shoved into the chamber. The foyer had a marble floor and a cathedral ceiling. Not as big as Madison Square Garden, but you still could play basketball there. Full court. Between the foyer and the living room was a pond stocked with fat orange fish. A fountain poured water over an island where bronze flamingoes and alligators eyed each other between rocks and ferns. We walked past the pond and around a glass-enclosed elevator, crossing no more than two county lines. We tiptoed down three marble steps without disturbing an eight-foot Zulu warrior carved from teak, and we landed in an octagonal, sunken living room.

The living room was black and white, black furniture that looked plastic to me but must have cost a bundle when selected by a trendy designer, white tile that wouldn't stay clean a minute if I lived there, white walls covered with paintings of women's heads floating away from their bodies, an ebony grand piano that was probably for show. All in all, a starter home for the nouveau riche who want to make a personal statement: *We have more money than we know what to do with.*

Melanie Corrigan fit right in—she wore black. I knew it was silk, but I didn't know if it was a slip or a dress. I did know there was nothing between the silk and her satin skin. The silk thing was held up by two thin straps, was cut low at the breasts and high on the thighs and was sheer as a shadow. If it was a dress you wouldn't wear it to church. If it was a slip, where was her dress?

"Thank you for coming, Mr. Lassiter. May I call you Jake?"

"Of course, Melanie." I nodded in the direction of her décolletage. "Are you auditioning for *Cat on a Hot Tin Roof?*"

It only took her a second. "Do you think I'd be a good Maggie?"

"From what I hear, you'd get an Oscar, a Tony, and a Super Bowl ring."

"Your client talks too much." She narrowed her eyes. "He also made the mistake of underestimating me."

"And I'll bet he wasn't the first."

She looked at me straight on, sizing me up. Then a little smile like we shared some secret. "Would you like a drink?" she asked.

I said yes but she didn't ask what I wanted. She slid behind a bar, and I took a seat on a Lucite barstool that would throw your back into spasms if you stayed for more than two drinks. The designer obviously had not been in many bars where men sit and talk and drink. Melanie Corrigan bent down to get a bottle and let me see the tops of very white, very firm breasts.

I would have liked a beer. She reached for tequila and orange juice and poured some of each in a glass you could have used to put out a three-alarm fire. She dropped in some ice cubes and shook a dash of bitters on top. I don't care for a drink that needs ice and fruit juice.

"Tijuana Sunrise," she said.

"Buenos días," I said.

She poured herself one, and we each took a sip. She didn't seem to be in a hurry. Her russet hair was tumbling free today, lightly brushing her shoulders where the tiny silk straps did their best to slide downhill.

"Roger is getting to be a problem," she said finally, touching her cheekbone where the bruise was already beginning to darken. She had long, graceful fingers, nails expensively done with lots of color. "He can't accept the fact that it's over."

She tugged at one of the slippery straps. I kept quiet.

"He apparently told you about us," she continued, fishing to find out what I knew.

"Every dirty little detail, the twosomes, the threesomes."

She didn't blink, just gave a little shrug that sent the strap slithering off one shoulder. The black silk fell open, exposing a cinnamon nipple that acted like it enjoyed being watched.

"He thinks he still owns me, thinks I'm still a kid. You've got to keep him away from me or he's going to get hurt."

"That sounds like a threat."

"I could say things that wouldn't be good for his health."

"Such as?"

She studied me a moment, deciding how much to say. "He wanted to kill Philip, wanted me to do it. That's all he talked about for months. I refused, of course."

"Of course," I said with just a dash of sarcasm like the bitters in the silly drink.

"Screw you, Lassiter," she said. What happened to *Jake?*

She gave me a look with a below-zero wind chill and said, "I might not have been the world's greatest wife by your standards, but I did a lot for Philip. Whatever he asked. We had an arrangement. He got what he wanted from me, and I got what I wanted from him."

"His bank accounts and stock portfolio."

She wouldn't let me rile her. "The freedom that came with those things. Philip didn't care if I saw other men, maybe even liked it. For me things were great. I didn't depend on men's handouts anymore. Why would I kill him? There was no reason to."

"So why did you keep your mouth shut when your darling husband planned to go under the knife of the doctor who wanted him dead?"

"I was scared to death when Philip went in the hospital, but I thought, with all the nurses and other doctors around, Roger just couldn't . . ."

She let it hang there.

"He didn't," I said. "The jury found that Roger wasn't even negligent, much less a killer. Your husband died of a spontaneous aneurysm."

"He was poisoned," she said without a trace of emotion. "In his hospital room."

I took a long hit on the drink to think that one over. This conversation sounded familiar.

She kept going. "Roger had this liquid in a bottle, an anesthetic. He wanted me to use it on Philip. Get him drunk or stoned, then inject him in the buttocks. Said it couldn't be traced."

"He gave you the bottle?"

"No. I wouldn't take it then. After Philip died, I was at Roger's house. I was still seeing him until I filed the lawsuit. I knew he kept the bottle in a small refrigerator, so I took it. I wanted to turn it over to the authorities."

"Did you?"

She looked away. "No. I know I should have, but then everything would have come out in the newspapers. I've worked hard to earn respectability, and it would all be gone."

"But you sued him for malpractice."

"I didn't want to. I didn't want the attention. But I was afraid if I didn't suc Roger, it would raise suspicions. Philip's daughter, that tomboy bitch, would have thought Roger and I killed him."

Lights were flashing like a pinball machine. Susan Corrigan may have been right about Roger Salisbury but wrong about Melanie Corrigan. Melanie had to be telling the truth, I thought. She couldn't risk telling me about the drug if she had been in on it.

"What was Roger doing here today?"

"I never really told him it was over. I didn't want to hurt him. When I filed the suit, I told him we'd get back together after the trial. Today I told him to stay away and he freaked."

"Show me the drug," I said, already knowing the response.

She gave me a helpless look that I hadn't seen on her before. "I can't," she said. "It's gone, stolen."

I decided there was nothing to be gained in telling Melanie Corrigan that her beloved stepdaughter had been poking around in her under-wear drawer. "What do you want me to do?" I asked.

She half smiled and half sighed. Her eyes seemed to widen, to change from business to bedroom, a neat trick. Outside the floor-to-ceiling windows, the sun was setting, and inside, the room was bathed in pink. Melanie Corrigan's skin took on a soft glow, and it hadn't looked bad in the light. She glided around the bar to where I was planted on the hard-as-granite barstool. She pulled up the silky strap one more time and now her perky nipples poked at the flimsy fabric. Maybe they were standing at attention because of the cool evening air or maybe it had something to do with the full moon coming up over the bay. Or maybe it was the proximity of me. Or maybe, just maybe, I should have my head examined. Ready to drink that pretty poison, as big a fool as Roger Salisbury.

At that moment what I wanted most was knowledge of self. I would have liked to figure out that urge that started halfway between my knees and chest and threatened to spread northward until it flooded whatever brain cells still worked without a jump start. I would have liked to, but I didn't have time because she looked me right in the eyes, smiled, and then slapped me.

There are slaps that ring your ears and slaps that bring tears to your eyes. This one could do neither. Less sting than my aftershave. I smiled at her and stood up. She had on a funny look, watching me with pouting lips. She had a good pout.

Then she slapped me again. Harder. Not enough to take an eight-count, but probably enough to bring some color to my cheeks, as well as to hers. Especially hers. She was enjoying this, warming up around the eyes. A hot little smile now. And *crack,* another slap. I was getting used to it.

She threw her arms around my neck, pressed herself up against me, then rocked up and down on her tiptoes as if stretching her calves. What she was doing was rubbing parts of her against parts of me like a very friendly, very slinky cat. My hands slid down her back to her round, tight bottom. She was firm where a woman ought to be firm and soft where a woman ought to be soft.

I looked at her close up. She had tiny golden freckles across the bridge of her nose, and little smile lines creased the corners of her mouth. A look of innocence and mirth. But the eyes were something else, wet and wild. And her neck was fragrant with the sweetness of the tropical night. A provocative blend of the pure and the wanton.

"When your face gets red, your eyes are even bluer," she said.

"Wait'll I start bleeding. I'll be another Paul Newman."

"You like being slapped," she said. Telling me, not asking me.

"Not as much as some other things," I said.

"You could learn." She pulled me toward her, looking into my eyes from under long lashes, still standing on her toes, straining against me. "You're a big man," she said, running her hands across my back. "More man than Roger or Philip."

Then she decided to see if I could swallow her tongue.

I could.

Just then an ugly noise from outside filled the room. A shout in Japanese split the air like a police siren. It could have awakened the dead at Guadalcanal, and it nearly cost Melanie Corrigan the tip of her slippery tongue. I let her go, and she straightened her sliding strap and brushed a hand through her hair.

"Must be Sergio," she said, as if there was nothing unusual in a banzai yell interrupting a perfectly fine kiss. We retraced the path to the foyer without pausing for food or water. Then another bellow from outside, and the front door shuddered as if hit by a wrecking ball. "He probably saw your car outside. He's insanely jealous."

Yet another Oriental war whoop and again the door groaned in pain.

"Sergio?" I asked.

"Sergio Machado-Alvarez," she said, serenely. "My chauffeur, boat captain, and . . . friend. We'd better open the door or he'll just break it down."

She punched the code into the digital alarm and unleashed the deadbolt. The huge door swung open to reveal a swarthy, mousta-chioed block of concrete. Sneakers, sweat pants, and a sleeveless muscle shirt, a tattoo of a lightning bolt on his tricep. He had plenty of beef to show, huge shoulders and chest, a fireplug of muscle and malice. Recently, I'd seen even more of him on videotape.

Sergio Machado-Alvarez stepped into the foyer and shot me a sideways smile, a mean little smile under the drooping moustache. He had big gray teeth like a double row of gravestones. He needed a shave and always would.

There was only one thing that detracted from his overall appearance as a menace to society. He was short. Like a lot of little guys he probably was working hard on the compensation factor. Building huge muscles, getting tough with karate, having something to show off. Stand at any gas station and study men and their cars in relation to their size. Check out how many short guys drive Sedan de Villes and Lincoln Town Cars. They need pillows to see over the steering wheel. Then come the big guys. They have to unfold a section at a time to get out of their Alfa Romeos and Corvettes.

"Do you know who I am?" he asked. A voice of practiced toughness, a faint Cuban accent.

"Something that escaped from the zoo."

"*Hijo de puta,*" he snarled, "I'll dig you another asshole."

"Why not spare yourself the trouble and just lend me one of yours?" Even I didn't know what that meant, the mouth being quicker than the mind.

He took a few seconds to think it over, then dropped into the half-moon stance with legs spread, left foot forward, hands on hips. I needed this like I needed to be in traction, which I might be if either of us found it necessary to show off for the lady of the house. I had been hitting the heavy bag at home. But the heavy bag doesn't know karate. And this guy looked like he intended to scatter my teeth.

"*Hombre,* you think you're tough?"

"No, I'm a pansy. You're tough."

He was trying to figure out if I was pulling his chain. He was the kind of guy who needed to take a thought and spread it on the kitchen table with the comics page. "I got *cojones grandes*, balls the size of grapefruit," he said slowly, as if he had memorized the phrase.

"You can take penicillin for that," I suggested.

His throat released a growl that a Doberman would be proud to own. Melanie shook a long fingernail and said, "Sergio, Mr. Lassiter is my guest. Please mind your manners. And don't you have a class to teach?"

The sinister little hulk looked at his watch, his lips moving slowly.

"Little hand on the six, big hand on the eleven," I said, helpfully. "You can figure it out."

His eyes flicked toward Melanie. "I got to train housewives to kick their husbands in the balls." Then he looked at me and made his face even uglier. He seemed to be all forehead and whiskers. "I'll see you another time, *cagado cabrón* asshole," he said.

"How's Wednesday for lunch? Have your girl call my girl."

This time the growl became a shriek. He bolted through the open doorway and bounded down the steps as fast as his chunky legs could move. *"Ushiro-keomi!"* His yell nearly drowned out the sound of the electric-powered waterfall tumbling over the landscaping. Then, in the driveway, he spun sideways and put out the left headlight on my 442 with a back-thrust kick. Glass scattered on the cobblestones. What kind of a man hurts an innocent old car?

"Shuto!" He brought his hand down like a sword across the hood,

the sickening sound of metal giving way, caving in. Next, I figured, he would bite the tires and give me four flats. Instead, he jumped on his motorcycle, a loud Kawasaki, did a wheelie, and screamed off into the night, shouting unheard insults over his shoulder.

I surveyed the damage to the 442, then sat down on the front steps.

"Do you want to come back in?" Melanie Corrigan said, with a promise as large as a king-size waterbed. But the moment had passed. My brains had taken over. I didn't want her tequila and orange juice and didn't want any part of her. She was too available, too free with herself, but too expensive for her men. Look at the price Philip Corrigan paid, and Roger Salisbury, tangled up with lust and maybe murder. And Sergio, the muscle-bound half-wit, martial arts fueled by jealousy.

I wanted to see Susan Corrigan, wanted to tell her about Melanie's charges against Roger. I wanted some help in figuring it all out. But first, I wanted to go home and pound out the vicious dent in my wounded chariot.

13

GRAVEYARD SHIFT

A great piece of luck, Charlie Riggs was saying. Philip Corrigan entombed in a crypt aboveground, an ornate mausoleum with the design of Palmland, his largest shopping center, molded into the concrete.

"A great piece of luck," he said again, "especially with Corrigan dead two years. In Florida the ground is so damp, the tissues break down fast. I hate to tell you what corpses look like when you dig them up, mold on the outside, parasites and larvae on the inside. Mausoleum tombs are so rare these days, so expensive. But I guess he could afford it."

"Judging from his house, the tomb will have a wine cellar, an elevator, and a butler," I said.

"Just so it's airtight, that's the ticket."

Riggs was nearly smacking his lips at the prospect of popping the top on Philip Corrigan's last resting place. I had pulled the funeral bills from the case file. In a wrongful death case the estate recovers funeral expenses, and I remembered a fifty-thousand-dollar number. Sure enough, there it was, a bill from Eternal Memories Mortuary and Mausoleum. When the first Mrs. Corrigan had died, her husband bought the choicest acre plot and ordered a mausoleum built for two, and not the compact efficiency model either. The perfect touch from the loving husband, a promise that his bones would one day rest beside hers. Just not so soon, Philip Corrigan would have hoped.

Eighty-five thousand for construction and services related to Mrs. Corrigan. Another fifty grand two years later for finishing Philip Corrigan's crypt put the whole shebang into six figures for the condo-like mausoleum. According to the specifications on the bill, it had a sitting room with a concrete bench so mourners could be shielded from the midday sun, a main room with matching concrete crypts on raised platforms of coral rock, and a foyer with the inscription, "Death Pays All Debts," a fitting eulogy for a guy who leveraged construction loans into his fortune.

Charlie Riggs and I were in my Olds 442, which sported a new headlight and pounded-out hood, and responded with a happy roar coming east on Tamiami Trail. I had told Riggs about the conversation with Melanie Corrigan, leaving out the details of the slinky body and lingering kiss. Her allegations against Salisbury fascinated him.

"Fits a little too nicely," he said, chewing on a cold pipe. His forehead was furrowed in thought, and the lights were on behind his straw-colored eyes.

"How's that?"

"First the daughter tells you the doctor used the drug to kill

Corrigan. Then the widow tells you the doctor wanted her to do it with the drug. You don't even know if the liquid the daughter showed you is succinylcholine."

"What are you saying?"

"That the two women could be framing the good doctor."

"I can't buy it. Every crime needs a motive, as you constantly remind me. Melanie Corrigan might have one, just to get rid of Salisbury. He's a pest to her. But Susan Corrigan, what could she have against Salisbury?"

Riggs tried to light his pipe, no easy task with the top down and the 442 howling at seventy-five. "Maybe nothing, except they needed a fall guy for the murder of Philip Corrigan."

"What?" I nearly lost control, swerving to avoid a dead armadillo.

"How was the estate split?"

"Melanie got the house, the yacht, and thirty percent of the gross assets. Susan got the rest after estate taxes. Neither one's going hungry."

"So they each had a motive, hypothetically at least, for wanting Philip Corrigan dead."

"Hey Doc, we're talking about a girl and her father."

"As Plautus said, *lupus est homo homini*. Man is a wolf to man. It applies to women, too. Inhumanity is often at its worst inside the family. Men beat their wives or commit incest. Wives kill their husbands, sometimes in the most bizarre manner. And daughters sometimes kill their fathers."

"That's sick, Charlie."

"So it is," he said, giving up on the pipe and blinking into the wind.

We followed the stone path around the house and found Susan Corrigan just getting out of the saltwater pool. She wore a dark blue, no-nonsense Lycra competition suit. It clung to every curve and crevice of her athletic body. She put on her tortoiseshell glasses, which immediately steamed up.

"Finished with two hundred yards of butterfly," she said, puffing a little. "Gets the blood flowing."

I introduced her to Charlie Riggs, and she gave him a respectful hello and asked why the distinguished former coroner would hang around with a second-string ex-jock turned shyster. On the off chance that was a joke, I laughed like a good sport. Then I handed her a towel, but she neglected to ask me to dry her back so I didn't. Plowing common ground, I said I had read her game story from LA. *The Dolphin receivers dropped everything but their paychecks Sunday.*

"Eight dropped passes," she said, "two in the end zone, they lose by three points. And the defense played great. Did you see Tyrone Washington? Four sacks."

Charlie Riggs cleared his throat. Small talk was not his forte. "Miss Corrigan, you know what we want to do."

"Yes," she said. "Jake told me on the phone. Did you bring the papers?"

"I prepared an affidavit," I said, "but it's not going to be much good. I asked Melanie to sign it, too, to get permission from both of you, but she refused."

Susan flung the towel onto the wet pool deck. Her eyes blazed. "You did what! She killed Dad or at least helped Salisbury do it. Why would you ask her?"

"As the surviving wife and the personal representative of the estate, she technically has the right to say yes or no," I said. "And you might be wrong about her." I recounted my meeting with the widow, again leaving out the snuggling stuff.

"So," I said, "both of you accuse Roger Salisbury of poisoning your father. But she won't give permission to exhume the body. Says to let it go, she doesn't want to be involved."

"And don't you find that suspicious?" Susan asked as if I were a simpleton.

"Maybe if she hadn't tipped me to Roger in the first place, it would be suspicious. But now, I don't know."

She fastened me with an angry look I was coming to know too well. "*I* tipped you to Roger Salisbury. And now I authorize you to do the autopsy. If you won't do it, I'll go to the state attorney. He can get a warrant or something, right?"

"Right," I said. "A court order. But then you lose control of the investigation. The coroner will do it. You and Charlie and I will be out in the cold. In fact, if you tell them that you've got the succinylcholine and traces are found in the body, you'll be suspect number one."

Her eyes were flaming behind the tortoiseshell glasses. "Then what do you propose we do?"

I looked at Charlie Riggs and he looked at me. We both were thinking the same thing. We looked at Susan Corrigan, whose short black hair was dripping little puddles onto the patio. We didn't say a word but she caught on.

Great minds think alike. But maybe slightly addled ones, too.

"There are some things we'll need," I said.

"I have everything back in the Glades," Charlie Riggs said.

"Tonight?" Susan Corrigan asked.

Charlie and I both nodded.

I went home to change. A charcoal suit with burgundy pinstripes is fine for lawyering, but it wouldn't do at all for my new avocation.

The saw made a frightful noise. Powered by a small gas motor, it was biting through the concrete seam of the crypt, tossing dust everywhere and making a racket that jack-hammered off the marble walls. Susan Corrigan stood guard outside the mausoleum, keeping an eye out for the night watchman.

I had second thoughts about bringing Susan on such a grisly assignment, but she was the only one who could bring us right where we needed to be. Charlie and I shouldn't be stumbling over gravestones after midnight looking for the right tomb. That was Susan's argument, anyway. Now that we were here, I saw it would have been hard to miss. Built on the top of a small knoll, the Corrigan mausoleum commanded an impressive view of a lake and the Palmetto Expressway in the sprawling southwest suburbs. I should have figured it. Even in death, Philip Corrigan adhered to the three rules of real estate: location, location, location.

I was muscling the power saw through the concrete. Charlie Riggs held a portable lamp that threw our shadows across the marble floor and up a decorative wall into which were inscribed the names of all the Corrigan shopping centers and condo projects, even the ones that resulted in class action consumer lawsuits.

I put the saw down for a rest. "This place raises ostentatiousness to new levels."

"De gustibus non est disputandum," Charlie said.

"Gesundheit," I said.

Charlie shook his head and grimaced. "There's no accounting for taste. Or your abysmal lack of training in Latin. Didn't you learn anything in law school?"

"Only not to draw to an inside straight," I admitted.

We went back to work. Twenty minutes later we were still watching our shadows dance up the wall when Charlie said, "Help me with this. The top's ready to move."

I got my hands into the seam and tried to lift the top. No dice. It must have weighed five hundred pounds. I put my shoulder against it and tried sliding it off. It moved two inches and sent a grinding noise up my spine.

Suddenly I heard padded footsteps on the marble floor of the foyer. A whisper from behind me, "How's it going?"

"Okay, okay," I said. "Next time, Susan, call before you drop in."

"Ignore him," Charlie said. "He's a little spooked."

I kept pushing the top of the crypt, but no traction, my sneakers slipping on the marble floor. It was like trying to move a blocking sled on a rain-slicked field with John Matuszak and Hulk Hogan sitting on top. Another inch. Nothing more. Just that damn grinding sound that maybe wouldn't bother someone used to opening tombs after midnight with the wind whistling through the gravestones.

Charlie lent me a shoulder. Another two inches. Susan pitched in and we got it going and then couldn't stop it. The concrete lid crashed to the marble floor and broke into a thousand pieces. The explosion echoed in my ears. Clouds of dust covered us and rose toward the ceiling. Someone sneezed. I hoped it was Charlie or Susan. I shined the light inside the crypt. Charlie leaned over as far as he could and patted a wooden casket.

"Good, very good indeed," he said. "Dry as toast."

I looked at Susan. "Why don't you wait for us by Charlie's truck?" Why ask her to watch as you dig out her father's body, two years in the grave. She gave me a look that said she was just as tough as me and probably a good deal more so, but she left anyway. Charlie and I went back to work. Both of us leaned on a crowbar to open the casket, a task we did in the dark because the portable light was now on the floor. The body was three feet below the top of the crypt, and since I was taller and stronger than Charlie, I was appointed as the retriever.

I leaned over, the concrete crypt folding me at the waist. I reached for what I thought would be shoulders and came up with a handful of mush.

"Yuck."

"What's the matter?" Charlie asked.

"Feels like I just stuck my hands in a barrel of apple butter."

"Mold," Charlie said. "That'd be his face. Even in a dry tomb, that'd happen."

I wiped off my hands, reached lower, found some shoulders and lifted. Lighter than I thought. Charlie put the flashlight down and held open a zippered body bag, and in a minute we were traipsing across the dew-laden grass, Charlie Riggs toting his tools in a burlap sack, and me with a body bag slung over my shoulder. Transylvania's favorite couple.

"That LA detective was wrong," I said, as we neared the truck.

"How's that?" Charlie Riggs asked.

"Marlowe, Philip Marlowe. In one of the books, he said dead men are heavier than broken hearts."

"So?"

"The former Philip Corrigan is a bantamweight."

"Bodies lose weight after death," Charlie said, as if everybody knew that.

"The ultimate diet," I concluded.

Charlie mumbled something to himself and kept walking, his scientific mind still on duty after our all-nighter. We were ten yards from the truck when Charlie stopped in his tracks. Susan Corrigan was crouched on her haunches at the rear of the pickup waiting for us, alone with her thoughts.

"Let's ID the subject," Charlie said, sounding like a homicide detective.

He unzipped the bag and popped the light into it.

"Uh-oh," I said.

"What's wrong?" Susan asked, joining us, a tremble in her voice.

"Was your father buried in a yellow chiffon dress?"

"Oh God," she said. "That's Mom and the dress is pink, or at least, it was."

"How the hell!" I shouted, nearly dropping the bag.

"I'm sorry," Susan said, her voice tight. "It's my fault. I told you the crypt on the left, but that's looking out, not in. I got turned around."

We sat down on the wet grass, as much to rest as to figure out what to do next. We used a flattened headstone for a conference table, and like a good lawyer, I called a meeting. Moonbeams were bouncing off the pale tombstones, casting a gauzy, soft focus over Susan's features. Mood lighting. I looked at her, wondering. How could she make that mistake? Did she really want us to dig up Dad? I was thinking about what Charlie had said, homicide in the family. But I looked at Susan Corrigan in that misty moonlight and thought I saw tears in her eyes.

Crazy. A night without sleep hauling ass through a graveyard and the mind starts playing tricks. Susan Corrigan could no more kill her father than, than . . .

"Not much time," Charlie Riggs said, gesturing toward the east, where pink slivers of sky were beginning to show.

"Right," I said. "Let's put Mom in the truck and get Dad."

Like most things in life, grave robbery is easier the second time around. If we kept up our two-a-day practices like the Dolphins in

August, we'd be able to purloin a body in forty-five minutes flat. This time the corpse wore a dark suit and was heavier to tote. I had it over my shoulder and was just leaving the mausoleum when I heard something, a soft singing.

Esta tarde ví llover,
Vi gente correr,
y no estabas tu.

Leather soles were scraping the marble in the foyer. Charlie and I backtracked into the mausoleum just as a flashlight poked around the corner. The night security guard.

Charlie Riggs flattened himself against a back wall. I heard his rasping breaths and hoped he wasn't going into cardiac arrest. I ducked into a shadow behind the smashed crypt, but there wasn't room for my dead buddy. Crouching like a catcher behind the plate, I gripped the seat of Philip Corrigan's pants. He stood, shakily, leaning against me like a friendly drunk. The flashlight illuminated the floor, clouds of pulverized concrete still rising from it. The dust tickled my nose, and I fought off a sneeze.

The beam bounced off the walls, and I caught sight of the guard. Private security, over sixty and overweight, probably working for minimum wage on a twelve-hour shift. The graveyard shift. In a footrace he couldn't beat Philip Corrigan.

The flashlight beam struck Corrigan's black shoes and inched up his body, finally coming to rest on a waxy, moldy face, a nose that melted into soggy cheeks.

"Madre de Dios," the guard murmured.

I was holding my breath, then had to inhale. More dust, then without warning, "AH-CHOO!"

The sound came from me, but all the guard could see was Philip Corrigan, his head flopping forward as my grip loosened.

"Don't worry," I whispered from the darkness. "Dead men don't sneeze."

The guard took a step backward. *"Jesús Cristo!"*

I raised one of Corrigan's arms, stiffly pointed a rotting hand at the waxy face and said, "No way José. *Yo soy el anti-Cristo.*"

The flashlight clattered to the floor and the guard took off. A moment later, so did we, Philip Corrigan draped over my shoulder, Charlie Riggs hustling behind me, chuckling. Whistling past the graveyard.

The black night had turned to silvery morning and the early commuters were heading north on the Palmetto, tiny shafts of headlights cutting through the mist. We loaded the truck and joined in but headed south. The expressway dumped us onto South Dixie Highway, U.S. 1, the road that starts in Maine and ends at Key West. We aimed that way, past a hundred gas stations and fast-food joints, chintzy strip shopping centers with pet stores and scuba shops, boarded-up small businesses, a thousand broken dreams. Down through Kendall and Perrine, past mango groves, strawberry fields, and packing houses, through Homestead by the Air Force base, over the Card Sound Bridge, through Key Largo and south some more.

None of us said a word, not the three of us jammed into the cab up front, and certainly not the two reunited in a zippered bag in the back. The Corrigans probably hadn't been this close since their honeymoon.

I handled the driving. Susan sat next to me, the closest she'd been since I tackled her on the practice field. Charlie Riggs was slumped against the passenger door, snoring peacefully. Near Tavernier, Susan's head dropped onto my shoulder, and I put my arm around her. This time, she didn't give me the boot. I thought she was sleeping, but a moment later she whispered, "Thank you, Jake."

I looked down at her, not knowing where she was headed.

"I was wrong to be so petulant when we first met," she said. "I was hurting so much. Losing Mom, then Dad marrying that woman, and Dad dying that way . . ."

"I understand," I said, feeling her soften under my arm.

"You've taken a big risk. I know you want to learn the truth about what happened, but I know you did it for me, too. And every time you try to get through to me, I put you off. I won't do that anymore."

I started to say something, but she put a finger to my lips. So I kissed the finger, steered with my left hand and tried not to put the truck into the Atlantic on the east side of the road or the Gulf on the west. Then I felt her face against my neck, and she nuzzled me with her upturned nose, looped her right arm around my chest and gave me a good squeeze. A fine and dandy squeeze.

The sun was well up in the eastern sky by the time we pulled into the dusty road on the Gulf of Mexico side of Islamorada. The shutters were open in the small wooden house and the aroma of strong coffee and sizzling bacon greeted us. We parked in the sand under a jacaranda tree that had lost its flowers for the winter. A royal tern sat in the tree, staring at us from under its black and white cap.

"Look what the cat drug in," Granny Lassiter said from the front porch. "Jake, you look like the loser in a mud rasslin' match." Granny sat in a pine rocking chair drinking coffee from an oversized mug. She wore khaki pants and a colorful Mexican serape. A high-crowned sombrero rested on her upper back, the drawstring tied under her chin. Her features were still strong, high cheekbones and a pugnacious chin. The hair that had been jet black when I was a boy was streaked down the middle with a bright white stripe like the center line on the highway locals call Useless 1. Granny's buddies called her "Skunky," but only after downing a good portion of her home brew.

I introduced Doc Riggs to Granny. He bowed formally, complimented her south-of-the-border outfit, and recounted one of his visits to the pyramids of the Yucatan with a graphic description of Mayan hieroglyphics and burial practices.

"It's a pleasure to have a man of learning and culture in my abode," she said, swiping at some loose strands of her hair. "Perhaps you could be a good influence on that wastrel mouthpiece kin of mine."

"Granny, please," I pleaded.

She ignored me and turned her attention to Susan Corrigan, whose dark eyes were puffy from a sleepless night but still fetching. "And you must be the gal Jacob's been telling me about. Uh-huh, I see why. You're a keeper."

"Granny!" I bellowed, warning her.

"Pay him no mind," she said. "Like most men, he don't know which end is up. After some breakfast, they'll do their work, and we'll drop a line in the Gulf and do some talking. Tell me, girl, you see anything in Jacob worth losing sleep over?"

"He's got potential," Susan allowed.

Granny laughed. "That boy's gonna grow old having potential."

I had heard enough. "Maybe we should get to work," I suggested.

"Sure 'nuff," Granny said. "The beer cellar's chilled down all the way, just like you said. Plus I got this filled with ice."

She pointed at a fish box that came from her old Bertram. It could easily hold both bodies.

Charlie Riggs eyed the box. "Forty-seven degrees would be perfect. That's what we keep the coolers in the morgue. Too cold is no good. Can't let the tissues freeze."

"So let's get started," I suggested again.

"No hurry, Jake," Charlie Riggs said, beaming at Granny. "No hurry at all."

Granny straightened up the front porch, swiping leaves off the wicker chairs with a palm frond. Then she poured everyone coffee, starting with Charlie Riggs. "Say Doc, I recognized you right off from the TV. The case of the capsized dory. Off Saddlebunch Key. You haven't changed a bit."

"Twenty years ago," Charlie said, shaking his head.

"Tempus fugit," Granny said, and Charlie's eyes lit up as if he'd found a long lost friend.

We all sat on the porch and Granny made a fuss over Charlie, who sat there reminiscing with his feet propped on the fish box that now held the Corrigans. Told us about the man whose wife drowned when their dory overturned, striking her head. The water had been calm, and the husband was a strong swimmer.

"So why didn't he save her?" Susan asked, snatching the bait like a hungry grouper.

A sly smile and Charlie continued. "Maybe his lifeguard's carry was weighted down by the million-dollar double indemnity policy he just bought on the lady's life."

Aha, we all said.

"He let her drown," Susan offered.

Charlie shook his head. "Worse than that."

"How'd you prove it?"

Another smile. "I put one of those department store mannequins in the dory facing front, just where the wife had been sitting. Sat in the back where the husband had been, stood up and smacked the mannequin with the oar. Left a mark the exact size and location of the bruise on top the dead wife's head."

The man got ninety-nine years, Charlie a TV interview.

Granny put her arm around Susan and steered her into the house. I hauled the body bag into the darkened room Granny called her beer cellar. The room was actually on the first floor, it being hard to dig a cellar when your house is built three feet above sea level. Inside were vats and bottles and the odds and ends used to make the home brew Granny gave away to neighboring fishermen. Two old air-conditioning units were turned on full blast and water dripped down the walls.

I suggested we cut first, eat breakfast later. I couldn't imagine doing the job on a full stomach. Charlie said he understood, then grabbed an old brown satchel from the cab of the truck. He unbuckled the worn leather straps and looked lovingly at half a dozen scalpels glinting in the light of the midday sun.

14

DEAD MEN DON'T BLEED

"The skin is macerated and there's mold on the face, but all things considered, not bad, not bad at all," Charlie Riggs said. He was washing off the body with a hose. The remains of Philip Corrigan were spread out on an old work table in Granny's beer cellar. "Before we do any cutting, let's examine the body."

He slipped on surgical gloves and started poking and pinching various parts of the corpse, squinting hard through his half-glasses. In formal tones he continued, "The subject is a well-developed white male, age indeterminate due to deterioration of the face. The head and neck appear to be symmetrical and exhibit no masses. The chest is symmetrical and the abdomen flat. The body is in an excellent state of preservation due to the embalming and a nearly dry tomb. There is evidence of two surgical procedures in close proximity to death, unhealed wounds from both back and abdominal surgery."

He went on that way for a while, as if the tape recorder with the microphone swinging from the ceiling was still there, as if he was still the medical examiner and as if homicide detectives still waited outside for his findings. A little sad, a man retired before his time, maybe a different kind of death.

Charlie brought a lamp closer to the body, illuminating a small area of skin at a time. "Now for a closer look." He started with the arms and worked down. I helped him flip the body onto its stomach. "Hullo! What's this, Jake? Right buttock, upper quadrant."

"Looks like a freckle."

"Come closer, my boy. *Mortui non mordent,* dead men don't bite."

"No, they smell." I moved close but it still looked like a freckle.

"A puncture wound," Charlie said triumphantly. "Pretty large gauge hypodermic, too."

"You sure?"

He didn't say yes and he didn't say no. He picked up a scalpel and swiftly dissected a piece of meat that used to be Philip Corrigan's flabby ass. In a moment Charlie held a cross section of the buttock, down through the fat, all the way into the muscle.

"There it is," he announced. I looked at a red streak, maybe three inches long. "That's the needle track, just as fresh as when it was made. Had to be done *in articulo mortis,* or there'd be evidence of healing."

I wasn't convinced. "It could have been a routine injection in connection with the laminectomy or the emergency abdominal surgery."

"Could have been," Charlie said, "but it's not on the charts. No doctor or nurse recorded it."

"Maybe the puncture was made after death. Something the under-taker did, I don't know."

"No way. See the little trail alongside the track, that's the hemor-rhage. He had to be alive when the needle was injected."

"Dead men don't bleed," I said.

"You're catching on, Jake."

"Okay, so *somebody* injected *something* into Philip Corrigan. Hard to make a case of that. What next?"

He wrinkled his forehead. "The tissues will have to be checked for succinic acid and choline. Your granny doesn't have a GCMS on the premises, I suppose."

"Not unless it's used for bonefishing or bootlegging."

Charlie held the slice of Corrigan's flesh up to the light. "Gas chromatographic spectrometer. Test for toxic substances. We'll need some brain and liver tissue, but first I'm going to do the work-up in the usual way."

The usual way. Like it was something he did every day. Which it was. Every working day for over thirty years. Thousands of bodies. So he did it without pausing, opening the neck just below the ear, making a long, smooth incision to the top of the chest and then to the other ear. He pulled up the flap of skin and exposed the inside of the neck. He deftly carved a slice straight down the chest over the sternum, avoiding the navel. He showed me where the embalming fluid had gone in, the spot being hard to miss, a thumb screw in the chest where the mortician inserted the trocar.

He peeled the skin flaps down over the chest, like pulling on an undersized sweater, exposing bright yellow fatty tissue and purple organs. He snapped the sternum in two with rib shears that looked like hedge clippers, probed into the abdomen, and made a dissection of the aorta. The punctured aneurysm was in the front, right where he had testified it was. He hummed under his breath as he worked. It sounded like "Born Free."

"Let's open the aorta and look for chalky deposits," he said brightly. "Give me some light over here, Jake."

I did what I was told and Charlie went about his business. Happy to be in control, to be taking things apart and figuring them out. Alive again. "Some evidence of sclerosis, but nothing unusual in a man of his age. Not enough to block the blood flow. Probably not enough to cause the aneurysm."

"So you hoodwinked the jury with that arteriosclerosis stuff."

"Didn't mean to. I figured the sclerosis was worse."

"So what killed him?" I asked.

"Something that caused the aneurysm, and if Roger Salisbury didn't do it and the sclerotic changes didn't do it, there's got to be something else."

I was confused. "What about the drug?"

He smiled, and his eyes crinkled, and behind them his computer was whirring, a lifetime of experience filtering the information. "It doesn't add up, not yet. Even if the tests are positive for the succinylcholine, the fact remains that he died of the aneurysm."

"I don't get it. If we find traces of the drug, that means Roger injected Corrigan—or somebody did—trying to kill him. If Corrigan was still alive when he was injected, which you say he had to be, it would have killed him. But you're saying he had the aneurysm after the injection. So what killed him and who killed him?"

Charlie caught himself before he stroked his beard with a gunked-up hand. "It's a puzzle, Jake, and we don't have enough pieces yet. But if we find the what, it'll lead us to the who. So if you'll stop talking and stand back, I'll finish the autopsy in the usual way."

The usual way again. He unpacked a portable scale, removed the heart, weighed it—four hundred fifty grams—poked around in more blood vessels, snipped here and clipped there, examining organs I didn't know existed. I was okay so far. I was okay when he cracked the ribs to get underneath. I was okay when he sliced off a piece of the liver and slipped it into a plastic lunch bag. I was okay when the band saw bit into the skull. But when he pulled the brain out, tut-tutting because it was shrunken and dehydrated, I wasn't okay. Things went a little gray, the beer cellar listed like a dinghy in rough chop, and the next thing I knew, Granny Lassiter was saying something and squeezing an ammonia-soaked rag under my nose.

I coughed and sputtered and got to my feet with Susan Corrigan's help and found I was on the front porch. Granny laughed and handed me a mason jar filled with home brew. "Drink this, Jacob. It'll put hair on your chest."

"I'm okay, I'm okay." I dusted myself off. Nothing like having two women fussing over your fallen body.

Susan Corrigan had on a funny half-smile and was holding on to my arm, propping me up. "I kind of like you this way. None of your macho bullshit."

"Great, I'll faint every chance I get. Promise you won't take advantage of me when I'm out?"

"No promises. Now just hush up. You need something to eat. Granny's making conch omelets with salsa."

In a few minutes Charlie joined us in the kitchen. He washed up and wrapped both hands around a mug of coffee, letting the steam rise through a steeple of fingers. After a while he briefed us. I watched Susan's face as Charlie talked about the puncture in the buttocks. It seemed to be what she wanted to hear, but she frowned when Charlie said there was nothing conclusive. Had to test the tissues and still figure out where the aneurysm fit in.

"The doctor and that bitch did it," Susan declared abruptly. "I just know it."

"We'll find out," Charlie promised. "I still have a couple friends on the toxicology staff at the ME's office. I can sneak in after-hours and use the equipment."

"Why not just bring Dr. MacKenzie in on it?" I suggested.

Charlie snorted. "That prick, excuse my English, wouldn't piss on me if I was on fire. I didn't recommend him for the ME's job when I retired, and now that he's got it, the Ivy League twit won't forgive me. Loves his computers and statistics and that damn new building with its creature comforts. Hell, they got air fresheners in the morgue now, you can't use your nose anymore to smell stomach contents. You know one time I opened a John Doe, smelled a familiar barbecue sauce. Full of vinegar, a touch of beer. Knew right away it was that ribs place on South Dixie. Homicide went down there, a waiter remembered the decedent and the guy he was with. Got a confession when they tracked the guy down."

Charlie went on like that for a while, unhappy with Dr. Hilton MacKenzie, the new ME who didn't like getting his hands dirty. "They built him a new building, state-of-the-art morgue, full of offices, as many administrators as the Department of Public Works, a lobby looks like a Hyatt. I remember our first morgue, just an abandoned garage. Hell, we did twenty-five hundred autopsies a year in the little building on Northwest Nineteenth Street. Then, after the boatlift, between the *Marielitos* knifing everybody and the Colombian cowboys machine-gunning each other, we ran out of cooler space. No place to put the stiffs."

"What'd you do?" Susan asked, always the inquisitive journalist.

"Rented a Burger King refrigerated truck," Charlie said. "Talk about a meat wagon. We stacked the bodies inside, put the truck in a parking lot by Jackson Memorial. Next thing you know, somebody hijacks it. Probably thought there was forty grand worth of burgers inside. Would have loved to see their faces when they busted open the trailer."

Charlie Riggs was into his storytelling. Finally, as the day wore on, the activities of last night caught up with all of us. Charlie took a nap, dozing on the front porch, mouth open, wheezing like an old Chevy. I curled up on a couch in the Florida room. A cool breeze from the Gulf whispered through open shutters. Granny tucked me in with a homemade quilt, just like the old days. Maybe later she'd drive me to Little League practice. I was halfway to dreamland when a second body joined me under the quilt.

"I'm too tired to race you to the goal line," I murmured.

"No hurry," Susan Corrigan said. "Take your time."

She kissed me very gently and then rubbed my chin with her fingertips. "You need a shave," she said. She stroked the stubble against the grain and kissed my neck. She pulled up my polo shirt and started kissing my chest. Wait a second. When I grew up, it was the guy who did the tussling with the clothes, the discovering of body parts. But I was not about to object. It would have been overruled. And I was enjoying the attention. When I tried to take the offensive, she gently pushed me down, gave me a *just relax* order with her eyes, and went about her business.

I was on my back, my clothes on the floor when she slipped out of her things, her small breasts tracing circles on my chest. From nowhere she produced a condom, as indispensable as lipstick to the modern woman. She slipped it on me without either snapping it like a slingshot or gouging me with a fingernail. Then, strong legs astride me, she eased downward, taking me in, tightening onto me. She exhaled deep surging breaths, all the time raising and lowering herself like a lifter doing squats.

I was liking it, liking her. But all the time watching her, and not just the curve of the hips. Watching her face, thinking about her and Roger Salisbury and Melanie Corrigan. And very rich, very dead Philip Corrigan. And who did what to whom.

Always thinking, damn it! Instead of just feeling. Thinking about the hacked up body a few feet away. Why not just enjoy the thrusting and the swampy heat rising from amidships? Damn it to hell, Lassiter.

I slept some more and when I awoke it was dark in the little house. Susan Corrigan purred next to me, stretched a leg until the calf muscle peaked, then curled up again. I thought about her. Smart and sassy. Part of the new breed. Toughing it out in a man's world. Elbowing past male reporters to get the best quotes in a locker room. Ignoring the wiseguys—*what happened to sportswriters who pissed standing up?*— dishing it out as well as taking it. This was the Susan Corrigan I knew. Which only made me realize I didn't know her very well at all.

I got up without disturbing her and poked around in the dark. No sign of Charlie or Granny. I found some smoked mackerel in the refrigerator and, still disoriented, tried to remember if this was dinner or a late snack. The house was quiet, the only sounds the palm fronds outside, slapping against each other in the breeze from the Gulf. I padded around to Granny's bedroom. The door was open a crack, a hurricane lamp burning by the night table. I should check on her. As she checked on me a thousand nights. She was there, under her own tufted quilt, sleeping peacefully, breathing steadily, her arms wrapped around the happy, slumbering hulk of Charles W. Riggs, M.D.

15

THE CONCH BRIGADE

No cops waited to arrest me at my little house off Kumquat Avenue; no reporters paced in the waiting room of my office. For a while, I thought The Great Graveyard Robbery might have been a dream. I was sitting at my desk Monday morning, sipping black coffee, peaceful as a monk, when I found the story on page 7 of the Local section:

Vandals destroyed a double gravesite and removed two bodies from the Eternal Memories Mortuary and Mausoleum over the weekend, Metro police reported yesterday.

The bodies of Philip R. Corrigan and Sylvia Corrigan, his wife, were taken from a private crypt at the southwest Dade cemetery, according to police spokesmen. Mr. Corrigan, who died in 1986, was a well-known builder whose projects often were opposed by environmental groups. His wife died two years earlier.

"This looks like the work of the Conch Brigade," said Metro Sgt. Joaquin Castillo, referring to the radical Keys group that advocates violence to stop construction in environmentally sensitive areas.

Because the Conch Brigade refuses to identify its members, no one with that organization could be reached for comment. Police estimate the damage to the crypt at $50,000.

Wacky. So far off that, weirdly, it was not far wrong. The Conch Brigade consisted of vicious terrorist Granny Lassiter, part-time septic tank cleaner Virgil Thigpen, and two unemployed shrimpers who could be found fishing for snook in Hell's Bay when not in jail for public drunkenness.

The newspaper made no mention of the recent malpractice trial and said nothing about the security guard seeing anything suspicious. I figured the cops made no connection with Salisbury, and the guard wasn't about to describe his close encounter with a moldy ghost. No suspects except a phantom group.

There wouldn't be much of an investigation. A penny-ante crime in Dade County, particularly on the weekend a DEA agent got hit in the head with two hundred pounds of twenty-dollar bills. Sent him to the hospital with a concussion and he couldn't even keep the money. It was evidence against a North Miami drug dealer named Guillermo Montalvo. When federal agents surrounded his house, Montalvo tossed the money—trussed up like a bale of hay—out a second story window. It glanced off the head of the agent, who wore a bulletproof vest but no hockey helmet. How much money is there in two hundred pounds of twenties? Exactly one million, eight hundred thousand, one hundred eighty dollars, according to the feds, who often weigh the take because counting it takes so much time.

The same day another federal agent got shot in the gun. Not the gut, the gun. After selling a kilo of cocaine in a sting operation, the agent drew his nine-millimeter SIG-Sauer semiautomatic handgun. The stingee, one Angel Morales, did the same thing. Morales shot his weapon first, and his bullet lodged in the agent's gun barrel. Morales had little time to enjoy his marksmanship. Four Hialeah cops who had been lurking in the bushes emptied twenty-two rounds into Morales, then kicked him in the groin for good measure.

So with everything going on, the police couldn't be expected to worry about a little old-fashioned grave robbing. I did wonder, though, if Roger had heard about it. And Melanie Corrigan. Surely the police would call her. Maybe we should put a tail on her, see if she and Roger have a tête-à-tête to talk it over. My musings were interrupted by Cindy, buzzing me.

"Some bimbo for you on two, *su majestad*."

"She have a name?"

"Sure, and a voice like melted butter."

"Please, Cindy, I'm not in the mood for Twenty Questions. Been a hard weekend and a crummy day."

"Mis-sus Philip Corrigan, and she asked for *Jacob* Lassiter."

Uh-oh.

I decided not to be expecting the call, but not to be surprised either.

"Jake," she said when I gave her a flat-toned hello, "I'm afraid there's been some trouble."

She waited a moment. I let her wait some more, then said, "I saw the story in the paper. What's going on?"

"I don't know but it's tearing me apart. You can't imagine the pain. I just keep thinking about him desecrating Philip's tomb, stealing the body, it's so terrible."

"Him?"

"Roger, of course. Who else would do it, unless that little bitch daughter was involved."

Whoops. A tiny shiver went through me, an icicle dripping down my back. Let's find out what she knows.

"Why would Susan be involved? Why Roger? Why anybody?"

"I don't know, maybe they killed him together. Now they're disposing of the evidence."

"What about Sylvia Corrigan, why her body?"

Silence. Then, "Why don't you ask the good doctor?"

So many questions, so few answers. "Why are you calling me?"

"I thought I could hire you, retain you, as my lawyer."

Suddenly I'm in demand. The doctor, the daughter, the widow. "I don't think so. I'm not sure you need a lawyer, and anyway, my representation of Roger Salisbury disqualifies me."

"I'm sorry to hear that," she said, sounding very sorry indeed. "We could have worked well together."

There was a hint there, an unmistakably seductive hint, the striking of a tiny spark that could be fanned into a flame with a few more whispers or the friction of that firm, sleek body against mine. It was her petition for rehearing. I decided to let the ruling stand.

"I'm sorry, Mrs. Corrigan," I said, as proper as a councilman declining a bribe. "It just wouldn't work."

"Then I guess I'll just do what I have to without your advice or assistance."

I let it hang there and we said our good-byes. I gave my conscience a pat on the back, the vision of Melanie Corrigan's unsheathed body a shooting star across the black sky of my mind.

The appointment was for two o'clock but Roger Salisbury was ten minutes early. Unusual for a doctor. He wore a coat and tie. Unusual, too. Doctors hereabouts usually sport the open-collar look—white smock or lab coat—and scruffy sneakers. Not Roger. Blue blazer, gray slacks, penny loafers. A frat man look. He gave Cindy a big hello, peeked out the window at one of the cruise ships chugging out Government Cut, then settled in a cushioned chair next to a thirsty rubber plant.

Charlie Riggs trundled in twenty minutes later, apologizing for being late. Just came from his semiannual haircut and beard trim, a Miccosukee barber in the Everglades. You could hardly tell he used a sawtooth fishing knife, I told Charlie, and he thanked me. Then Charlie cleared his throat, stroked his newly pruned beard, and slid his warped glasses back up the bridge of his tiny nose. Which was a signal for me to start.

"Roger, this is awkward for Charlie and me."

Expressionless, Roger Salisbury looked at Charlie, then back at me, and I continued, "I have a confession to make—"

Roger laughed. "That's what clients usually do to their lawyers, right?"

"Right, but this case is different in a lot of ways. You know somebody broke into Philip Corrigan's crypt, stole the body?"

"Saw the story in the paper. Pretty bizarre. Antidevelopment nuts in the Keys, maybe."

Doc Riggs cleared his throat again. I swallowed and said, "A couple of nuts, all right. Charlie and I did it."

He raised his eyebrows. "No. Why?"

"Susan Corrigan wanted the body tested, Melanie Corrigan didn't. We chose sides. But I wanted to tell you before we deliver tissue samples to the lab. And I wanted to ask you, is there anything you want to tell us?"

Roger shrugged. "What would I want to say?"

If he was faking it, he must have taken some acting courses along with biology and chemistry. "Okay, Roger, here it is. Melanie told me you tried to get her to inject her husband with succinylcholine, and when she wouldn't do it, you did, murdered Corrigan in his hospital room."

A cloud crossed his face. A look more of bewilderment than anger. "Do you believe her?"

I paused long enough for Charlie Riggs to light his pipe. It took three matches. "No. I don't believe her. Since that day you brought the malpractice complaint to me, I've gotten to know you, and I don't believe you could kill."

Roger Salisbury beamed. I continued, "But what's been gnawing at me is that nothing about Corrigan's death makes sense. You didn't cause the aneurysm and, apparently, the sclerosis didn't either. The hospital charts show no injections in the buttocks but Charlie found one. Then there's the succinylcholine . . ."

Salisbury turned to Charlie Riggs. "Succinylcholine wouldn't be traceable, would it? Doesn't it break down into succinic acid and choline?"

I studied Roger while Charlie tamped his pipe and answered. "Yes, but those substances are detectable in various tissues. If there's too great a quantity, a reasonable inference would be that succinylcholine was injected shortly prior to death."

No reaction. Absolute calm. "You're the expert," Salisbury said in a neutral voice. "And if you want to test the tissues, I don't have a problem."

I was feeling good about Roger Salisbury. Confident in his innocence. Then he said, "Melanie knows the truth, and if you really want to know, I mean if it matters to you, Jake, just get her to tell you."

"And how do I do that?"

"I could inject her with thiopental sodium."

"Huh?"

Charlie chimed in. "Sodium five-ethyl-five-one-methylbutyl-two-thiobarbiturate. More commonly known by its trade name, Pentothal."

"Truth serum?" I asked, louder than necessary.

"A misnomer," Charlie said, "but you get the idea. A central nervous system depressant. In the right quantities, it induces hypnosis and, yes, the patient will tell the truth about past events."

"I could stick her, and we could snatch her," Roger said blithely, as if assault and abduction were standard topics of discussion. "Bring her someplace safe, and you could cross-examine her. You're so good at that, Jake. Then you'd learn the truth. I want you to believe me."

I looked at Charlie Riggs. He looked at me. In ninety seconds, my client had gone from innocent physician to lunatic kidnapper.

"Roger, I don't think we could do that," I said, gently.

He shrugged and said okay, then offered to take me bonefishing in the Keys sometimes. I made a bad joke about an orthopod bonefishing, and he headed for Mercy Hospital to do a knee replacement.

I put my feet up on my cluttered desk, and Charlie Riggs stoked his pipe. He didn't look at me, and I didn't look at him. I wanted him to say something, but he wouldn't. So I did. "Is it my imagination, or is my client sailing without a rudder?"

Charlie stood up and walked to the window. He squinted into the brightness and looked due east over the ocean toward Bimini. "Fantasies. I think Roger Salisbury has difficulty distinguishing fantasy from reality. He wanted Melanie for himself and might have wished Philip dead. Maybe told Melanie so. But judging from his reaction today, I would say he didn't kill Philip Corrigan. And he wants you to know that. He respects you, Jake. He wants you to like him—"

"So we can be fishing buddies."

"Something like that. So he fantasizes about injecting her with Pentothal."

"All of which means he's a dreamer, not a killer."

Charlie Riggs sent me a swirl of cherry-flavored smoke. "Unless the fantasies take over. Unless they become reality. Then, *Deus misereatur,* may God have mercy . . ."

I read my mail, returned some calls, skipped a partners' meeting called to debate new artwork for the reception area—Andy Wyeth was a five-to-one favorite over Andy Warhol—and headed for *The Miami Herald*. Susan Corrigan was waiting for me on the bayfront walkway behind the building. She stood silently watching a barge unload huge rolls of newsprint onto the dock. The drawbridge on the MacArthur Causeway was up, two hundred motorists waiting for one rich guy in a gussied up Hinckley to putt-putt underneath at three knots. A stiff, warm breeze from the east crackled an American flag flying above the walkway, and the Miami sun beat hard against the concrete.

Susan wore her reporter's uniform, running shoes, faded jeans with a notepad sticking out the back pocket. Her glasses were propped on top of her short black hair. On the barge a forklift kept picking up the newsprint and rolling it down a ramp onto the dock.

"They killed a lot of trees just so you could write about some overgrown boys in plastic hats and knickers chasing a funny-shaped ball."

She jumped a half step. "Oh, you startled me. I was thinking."

"And not about me."

"About you a little," she said, honest to a fault. "More about Dad and everything that's happened. Have you heard from Charlie?"

"Not yet. Expect something tomorrow."

"What do we do then? I mean, if the report says the drug is in the brain and the liver."

"I don't know. I'm taking this one step at a time. Today, Charlie and I told Roger that we had the body and were having it tested. He didn't seem to care. So far nothing makes sense."

She thought about it a moment. "You could get in trouble for this, couldn't you?"

"What, for trespassing, destruction of property, grave robbing, and turning in my own client? Nothing worse than disbarment plus a short stay at Avon Park as a first offender."

"So why do it?"

The Hinckley chugged by, a pot-bellied middle-aged guy and three smug teenagers waving at us. The drawbridge clanked into place, the groan of metal on metal as its fittings meshed. Finally I said, "I guess I'm still looking for the good guys."

"Good guys?"

"Something I told Roger Salisbury. That I keep looking for the good guys and never find them."

She leaned close and kissed me on the lips. "Am I a good guy?"

Funny, I'd been wondering the same thing myself. "I hope so, because I've joined your side, abandoned Roger. I've stopped caring about the rules of the game, just want to do what's right."

"Sounds noble."

"Stupid, maybe. Maybe I'm swayed by those deep, dark eyes and the way you snuggle under a quilt."

She stiffened. "If you believe that, maybe you should quit the game altogether. Hit the showers."

I didn't believe it. I smiled at her and she knew I didn't believe it. She had me pretty good, and she knew that, too. She popped me a playful punch in the shoulder. Her playful punch could leave a dent.

"Take me home," she said. "Let's see how much room there is in my shower stall. Afterwards, I may even put on a skirt and let you buy me dinner."

The Olds 442 found the Corrigan home just as before. Buttoned up tight. Dark and quiet. Either the rich don't make any noise or Melanie Corrigan was entertaining under the sheets. No motorcycle out front either, so little chance of running into Hercules.

We walked around back to the cabana. Dark inside, but the front door was wide open, hanging loose on a hinge. There was the moment of disbelief, that if you blink once, the scene will change, but it didn't. I flicked on the lights. The place was torn up, and a pretty good job of it, drawers pulled out, books spilled onto the floor, clothing strewn about. Susan made a small noise, deep in her throat, then ran into the tiny bedroom and hauled a golf bag out of the closet. The clubs were scattered across the floor, a three-wood jammed angrily into a planter. She reached into the bag, fingers clawing at the leather, not finding what she wanted.

"Damn, damn," she cried, tears forming. "It's gone. They've got it. They've got the evidence."

I knew what was gone. A little leather bag with a vial of liquid and two hypodermics. I just didn't know who *they* were.

16

OH NO, SOCOLOW

When you live outside the law, you forfeit certain privileges. Like calling the police when you need them. In these parts, drug dealers are frequently robbed. Sometimes by other drug dealers, sometimes by cops. It's a fact of life that dopers won't blow the whistle. Their cars get blown up, their houses riddled with automatic weapons, their drugs and cash stolen. They write off the losses as part of overhead.

So here we were, a couple of upstanding, taxpaying citizens, a journalist and a lawyer, unable to call the cops. A smart cop would ask too many questions. *You say this drug might have killed Philip Corrigan. Say, wasn't his body stolen over the weekend?* A dumb cop wouldn't do us any good.

We cleaned up the mess. Nothing else was missing. Even the X-rated tape was still on the shelf, tucked away in a stack of exercise videos and feature films.

I tried to put two and two together. I kept getting Melanie Corrigan. The drug came from Melanie's bedroom, but Susan found it more than a year after Philip Corrigan died. Why keep a murder weapon around?

To use it again.

Maybe, I told myself. But Charlie Riggs says succinylcholine will lose its potency unless it's kept cold. Maybe Melanie doesn't know that. Or maybe she doesn't care. Maybe Roger Salisbury had already used it to kill her husband.

Roger a killer? No way. Not even concerned that we've got the body. A trifle weird, maybe. Walking a little close to the border of Fantasyland, as Charlie Riggs suggested. But not a killer.

Okay, I try something else. When Melanie finally gets around to putting on some underwear, she notices the drug's gone. It must incriminate her, or she wouldn't care about it. She suspects Susan, her nemesis. She has to get back the evidence to get rid of it, so she has Sergio bust up the front door of the cabana to make it look like a two-bit B&E. Or what was it the Nixon White House called Watergate? A third-rate burglary.

But what if I'm wrong about Roger? Maybe he and Melanie snuffed the old man. She keeps the drug as insurance against him fingering her. When it's gone, she tells him to get it back or they're both looking at a Murder One.

I didn't buy it. Maybe there was no burglary. Maybe Susan Corrigan ruffled her own sheets, got rid of the drug for her own reasons. But looking at the tears in her eyes as she cradled the empty golf bag, that made no sense to me, none at all.

* * *

I didn't want Susan staying in the little cabana, not with the door split open, so we headed to Coconut Grove and my coral rock fortress. I told her to wait outside under a jacaranda tree. Then I opened the front door slowly, stepping into the stale air, seeing shapes in the darkness. Looking for a karate freak crouched behind the sofa, waiting for the hardwood floor to creak. But the shadows held only dust and the only sounds came from a dripping faucet.

I turned on the lights and Susan stepped in boldly, and with a look of amusement, examined the spare furnishings. Her eyes sized up my little house like a broker on commission. She might wear sweats and sneakers, but underneath, she was still a rich girl who knew Chippendale from flea market.

"What's a guy like you doing in a place like this?" she asked, a lilt to her voice.

"What's a girl like you doing with a guy like me?"

She just smiled and stripped off her jeans. The adrenaline rush had ebbed, but I had enough energy left to carry her up the narrow staircase.

This time she let me take the lead, maybe content that she had already established her strength and independence. Once, she whispered, "Never stop," and at the end, she gave a yelp usually reserved for overtime victories in playoff games, and I let go with a little *whoopee-ti-ti-yo* myself. She fell asleep in my arms, her face innocent as a Norman Rockwell bride. But I was wide awake. I tucked her in and went downstairs to think.

Sometimes the best tactic is to wade right into it, pour gasoline on the flames, and see what's left after the explosion. First though, I poured myself a Grolsch. Then I dialed Roger Salisbury's number. It was nearly midnight.

"Jake, old boy, great to hear your voice. Just talking about you." *Old boy*. That was a new one, maybe into a polo-playing phase. Wonder if he'll be as chipper after I accuse him of icing Philip

Corrigan. But I never got the chance. He said, "There's somebody here who'd like to say hello."

There was a short pause, a woman's soft laugh, then a silken voice. "Jacob Lassiter, how nice of you to call. We're having some champagne and caviar and other edible things. You can join us if you like. Two's company, three's a party."

Another laugh and Roger Salisbury was back on the line. "Jake, I'm so damn happy. Just like the old days. And I'll be forever grateful to you. You're a real friend."

"Sure Roger. Sure."

A little giggling, two sweethearts pressed up to the phone, ear to ear. Roger breathed a long *whoosh* into the phone and said, "Melanie, that can wait, whoa! Hey Jake, I got a hard-on that could plant the flag on Iwo Jima."

"Semper Fi," I said, thinking these two are made for each other. She accuses him of murder; he wants to stick her with a needle. One day, he's punching her out; next day, she's running it up his flagpole.

I wished him well, hung up, and tried to sort it out. Now I believed more than ever in Roger's innocence. If Roger was in it with Melanie Corrigan, he wouldn't let me know she was there. The two of them would go through the ruse of hating each other, particularly if they sensed an investigation would start up after the body disappeared. Unless it was a double twist, the old trick from "The Purloined Letter," making the fruit of the crime so obvious that it's hard to see. Too complicated. I rejoined Susan and fell asleep thinking about it, hearing a woman's laughter—mocking me—in my dreams.

At mid-morning Susan and I drove back to her cabana to look around in the light of day. I heard a motor cranking up as we walked around the house, and we caught sight of a Boston Whaler Temptation, a twenty-two-foot outboard, pulling away from the dock. Handling the wheel was a chunk of muscle who looked familiar and stretched out on a cooler in front of the console was the bikini-clad body of Melanie

Corrigan. The widow had covered a lot of territory in the last twenty-four hours.

We ducked behind a poinciana tree and watched them slowly cross the lagoon into open water.

"Gone fishin'," I said.

"Doubt it," Susan said. "I don't think that woman's ever been on the Whaler. It's really a tender for the yacht. The man is Sergio Machado-Alvarez."

"We've met. Where do you suppose they're going?"

Susan shaded her eyes against the sun and shrugged. The Whaler headed into the bay between the channel markers, lazing at low speed. Still within sight, it dropped anchor.

"Great. We may have enough time if they stay put," I said.

The ancient Olds resisted, but I peeled rubber like a teenage punk and we slid around curves on the winding road to the marina at Matheson Hammock barely two miles away. The dockmaster there was an old client, but not exactly blue chip.

Bluegill Ovelman was shirtless and barefoot. He had a belly like a rain barrel and hands like grappling hooks. He was an old salt, an ex–commercial fisherman who earned his *ex* the third time he was arrested by the Marine Patrol. I kept him out of jail each time the patrol found a mess of undersize Florida lobsters in his cooler. The last time I persuaded the jury that Bluegill measured his catch in centimeters instead of inches, and being a mite poor at algebra, got confused on the conversion tables. Tired of using his drinking money to post bond, he retired and now tended rich men's yachts at the marina.

"Ey Counselor!" Bluegill Ovelman grinned. His cheeks were redder than a broiled lobster, and the lines under his eyes could map the trails to the Jack Daniels distillery. "Wanna take the little lady fishing?" He eyed Susan Corrigan, who gave him a smile that he wasn't likely to see on his best day.

"I hate fishing and you know it," I lied. "I like my seafood caught, cleaned, and cooked by someone else."

This was a necessary routine, a dance we'd done before. He called me a leather-shoed, high-rise, pickpocket shyster and I called him a no-count, whiskey-riddled, lobster-poaching bottom feeder. Then he gave me a hug and asked what I wanted. I wanted a boat and a sailboard and he gave me both, an old Chris Craft inboard he used as a tow boat and a banged-up Mistral windsurfing rig he tossed onto the deck. I borrowed an old pair of his swim trunks that had to be a size forty-four and kept hitching them up as we motored into the bay.

"I wouldn't do any swimming today," Bluegill Ovelman shouted as I leaned on the throttle. "Water's full of men-of-war. Big ones, too. Enough poison for a week's room and board at Jackson Memorial."

In fifteen minutes we were half a mile from the Whaler, trying to be inconspicuous. I dropped anchor and peered through binoculars. Melanie Corrigan was still soaking up rays. Sergio was bent over the starboard side, away from us. He had a gaff or a fishing rod or a net in his hand. Too far to be sure.

There was only one way to get closer without attracting attention. It was awkward, but I rigged a six-square-meter sail onto a sixteen-foot mast, nearly falling over the rub rail. I dropped the board over the side, jumped in, and jammed the mast into the universal joint while treading water. The water was warm and clear. Susan stayed in the boat and looked at me skeptically. "Do you know what you're doing?"

"Trust me. I've sailed from Key Biscayne to Bimini on one of these."

I uphauled the sail in a measly ten knots of wind, and tugging at my oversize drawers, I sailed closer to the Whaler. Out of my customary charcoal gray suit, standing in the shadow of the sail, I figured they wouldn't recognize me. Just another bozo sailing standing up.

I sailed cautiously, eyeing dozens of floating purple-blue sacs with poison-packed tails trailing underneath. Our waters are filled with biters, shockers, and stingers. Sharks, of course, are biters. You see them sometimes near Virginia Key on Key Biscayne, feeding a mile or so offshore. They seldom bother anyone. There are Atlantic rays, some weighing as much as a good-sized running back, and their tails pack over two hundred volts of electricity. They can explode out of the water and scare the bejesus out of sailors and windsurfers alike. Then, each winter, we get the Portuguese men-of-war, prehistoric animals of unearthly beauty with their iridescent bluish-purple sacs and crests of orangish red. For those lured to the luminous sac, there is only betrayal. Underneath the water, hidden from view, are dozens of tentacles, undulating with the currents, straining to inject their poison into those seduced by the beauty.

I tipped the mast forward to head downwind and sailed off the stern of the Whaler. Sergio was still bent over the side, a net now visible in his hand. I saw a fishing rod jammed into a rod holder. Okay, maybe after some grouper. I wanted to get closer, so I jibed and came back the other way. About a hundred yards away, I trimmed the sail and tried to pick up a little speed. I wanted to pass by without taking too long to do it, not give them a good look at me. It would have worked, too, if I hadn't dropped my drawers. Trying not to draw attention to yourself is hard to do when your bare ass is staring at the people you would just as soon avoid.

Not wanting to make a further spectacle of myself, I headed back to our boat where Susan Corrigan was shaking her head. "Showing off for the widow?" she asked as I climbed aboard.

"Just distracting her," I replied. "A diversion from my adorable face."

"Maybe she recognizes both ends of you," Susan said without the hint of a smile.

"If that's a question, the answer is no."

She measured that one, believed me, and we took the Chris Craft back to the marina. Mission bungled. I still had no idea why Melanie was at Roger's house last night or on the bay with Sergio today. But I was starting to get the idea that the lady had a plan for everything and everybody. Inviting me to her house had to be part of the plan. I wished I knew what part.

Susan and I headed to Coconut Grove, the Olds 442 purring in third gear. I pulled into the shade of a gumbo-limbo tree in front of my house, and she turned to me.

"Jake, we have to talk."

"Uh-huh."

"About the other night."

"The other night?"

"Don't be dense! At your Granny's. And last night, in your shoebox there behind the weeds. Have you forgotten?"

I put the stick into neutral and turned off the ignition. The engine groaned and died. "I haven't forgotten. I remember every parry and thrust."

"That's not what I mean. Don't you think we should talk about how we feel about each other?"

Uh-oh. I should have known. Somehow I assumed that Susan Corrigan was different from other women. Which she was, of course, in certain respects. She cared less about clothes than whether to pass or run on third-and-four. But she was still a woman . . . and women want to talk about relationships. I went into my big, dumb guy routine. It comes naturally.

"I'm not too good at postcoital conversation," I said.

"I know," she said compassionately. "Like most men, you have trouble expressing your emotions."

"Not all of them. Anger I'm good at."

She scowled and waited. I had one hand on the door handle, but she wasn't stirring. Trapped.

"Jake, if it helps, I'm not too good at this either. But here goes. I want you to know I wouldn't have crawled into your bed unless I felt something for you. Something more than a physical attraction. I don't know how much or where it's going. But it's real, and I wanted you to know."

She waited some more.

I was silent. Overhead, a snowy egret headed toward the Everglades. Free to roam. I fidgeted, and the old leather upholstery squeaked underneath me.

"The ball is in your court, Counselor," Susan Corrigan said.

"I appreciate what you said. Thank you."

"Thank you? You big lummox! Are there any feelings inside that block of granite that sits on your shoulders? I am so tired of commitment-phobic men who panic when things get too good. Are you afraid of love, Jake? Is that it, are you one of those guys who sabotages a relationship when it gets too close?"

I looked down and noticed I was stomping on the brake pedal. My right hand had the gearshift in a death grip. The car seemed to shrink around me, caught in one of those machines that pulverizes a two-ton sedan into a block of scrap metal the size of a sofa. "Don't you think you're overreacting to my limited ability to express myself?" I asked.

"Is that code for inaccessibility and lack of emotional depth?"

"No. You're important to me, Susan. There's so much going on right now that I haven't had a chance to figure it all out. But you've gotten to me, right through the granite. You challenge me. You make me think about the way I live, my work, everything. You turn me on, and you light me up. But it's not even halftime. Let's go into the locker room, then see what happens in the second half."

She smiled. "Not a bad speech. Not a great speech, but it'll do . . ."

Then I leaned down and kissed her, and she grabbed a handful of my hair and yanked my head back. ". . . For now," she said, pushing me toward the door.

A ringing phone greeted us in the little house. Charlie Riggs was on the line, breathing hard. "Thank God you're there. There's trouble, Jake, and his name's Abe Socolow."

Oh no, Socolow.

"They must have followed me here," Charlie said. "Two investi-gators from the State Attorney's Office plus Socolow. It's his case."

"What, a lousy grave theft?"

"No Jake, the murder of Philip Corrigan."

That took the air out of me. "Where are you, Charlie?"

"At Jane's house."

"Jane?"

"Jane! Jane Lassiter, your granny, for pete's sake."

"Oh." The last time Granny was called Jane, the Wright Brothers were still tuning pianos.

"Don't worry, Jake. I'm buying her out and I won't give you up."

"Slow down, Charlie. What happened? Who's there?"

"Socolow and two of his investigators are on the front porch. This is my one phone call, just like in the movies. Best I can figure, MacKenzie heard I was in the lab after hours. Lord knows how, he never works past five. Anyway, he busted balls on the toxicology staff. They gave him the liver and brain samples, all tested positive for succinic acid and choline. So Socolow put a tail on me. They figured I had the body. I'm giving it to them. We would have done it sooner or later anyway, and they promise no charges for the grave robbery."

"Does Socolow know you're calling me?"

"Yeah, but just as a lawyer. He doesn't know you were in the cemetery. Like I said, I won't give you up. He can't flip me."

"Relax, Charlie. You sound like Jimmy Cagney."

"I'm so sorry, Jake. This couldn't have happened ten years ago. *Fugaces labuntur anni*. You wake up one morning and you're old."

I thought Charlie was about to cry, then through the phone, I heard the unmistakable sound of Granny's screen door slamming shut. Then a voice, raspy and disagreeable, a voice from the past.

"You're one rockin' rollin' mouthpiece, Jake, but you got your dick on the chopping block this time."

"Hello, Abe," I said. "Long time."

I pictured him on the other end of the line, smirking malevolently. Abraham Socolow was lean and balding, sallow of face and unpleasant of disposition. He was born mad at the world, and nothing had happened in the next forty-four years to change his mind. He believed that his fellow man was a miscreant until proven innocent. As chief of major crimes in the State Attorney's Office, he also believed it was his mission in life to personally convict and send away the worst of the low-life slimeballs who committed felonies in the twenty-seven municipalities of Dade County, Florida.

Every prosecutor's office has one Abe Socolow but could use ten. He viewed the job as a calling, not as a stepping stone to a cushy life defending drug dealers. Abe Socolow was smart, tough, mean, and unforgiving. And messianic. He considered plea-bargaining a sacrilege, probation unthinkable, and second chances were for basketball players at the free throw line.

As much as Socolow detested robbers, rapists, and druggies, he had a special contempt for murderers. On a chart above his green metal desk in a tiny office that smelled of stale coffee and cigarettes was a poster with mug shots of fifty-eight men and three women. Sixty-one buckets of slime, Socolow liked to say. A diagonal slash cut across five of the faces and a caricature of Socolow's beakish face peeked over the top of each slash. "Slimebusters," the poster said in red ink, drawn to look like drops of blood.

The greatest anguish in Socolow's life was that he had convicted sixty-one slimeballs of first degree murder but only thirty-eight had been sentenced to death, and of those, only five had been executed. The rest were tied up in endless appeals. When I was a public defender, Socolow confided to me that he sometimes dreamed he would die before his murderers, a vision that left him frightened and alone. It was the only time I knew him to confess weakness of any kind.

"You gonna defend him, Jake?"

"Defend who?"

"Hey, don't jerk me off. Roger Salisbury. Dr. X, the great white defendant, purveyor of poison, seducer of women . . ."

"You writing headlines now, Abe?"

"No, just getting indictments and convictions."

"What's the charge?"

He laughed. "I'd say Murder One after the grand jury meets tomorrow."

"You got a *corpus delicti?*"

Another laugh, like a horse's whinny. "Right here on ice, along with some hog snapper."

"And a weapon?" I asked. Might as well do some pretrial discovery if he was in a talkative mood.

"Implements of the crime. About an hour ago, we served a warrant on Salisbury's house. Found a real interesting vial with two hypodermics. Lab will have it back tonight. Wanna bet on the contents?"

So that's what happened. A lot of things about my late-night phone call to Roger's house were coming into focus.

"Sure I'll bet. I'll bet you got the search warrant based on an affidavit from a charming widow. I'll bet she swore she saw the stuff in Salisbury's house within the last twenty-four hours."

"What of it?"

"She planted it there!" I thundered. "Last night. I know she was there. She wanted me to know she was there. It corroborates her affidavit. But I also know where she got the vial and the hypodermics and it wasn't from Roger."

"I'm listening," Socolow said.

But I wasn't talking. Melanie Corrigan must have known I wouldn't drag Susan into it. Susan would swear the drug came from Melanie's bedroom but could not prove it. That left Susan holding the drug. Roger was trapped, but I was too. Nowhere to turn. Finally I said, "Roger Salisbury isn't a murderer. He may look at life through a zipper, but last time I checked, that wasn't a capital crime."

"Fine, Lassiter, argue that to the jury. And this is what I'll argue. Roger Salisbury is banging his patient's wife. He asks her to kill her husband. She refuses. He has access to a dangerous anesthetic. The husband dies after routine surgery. The anesthetic is found in the doctor's home and traces are present in the corpse. That's our case, a simple, straightforward path to Murder One."

"Anything else?"

"Only this. It's premeditated. It's a cold-blooded, calculated murder for lust and money. It's a heinous, atrocious crime without any pretense of moral or legal justification. You know where I'm heading, doncha Jake, old buddy."

I wasn't his *old buddy* but I knew where he was heading. He was reciting Section 921.141. Like the Pledge of Allegiance, he knew the death penalty statute by heart.

"I know. You want twelve men, good and true, not just six."

"You got it. Warming up the hot seat at Raiford."

Abe Socolow wanted me to sweat. And I was sweating. But thinking, too. His case all wrapped up like that. Something was missing. The same thing Charlie Riggs and I couldn't figure out: How could Roger have killed Philip Corrigan—how could anyone?—if the cause of death was a spontaneous rupture of the aorta?

But if I was right, if nobody killed Philip Corrigan, why would Melanie frame Roger? It made no sense. She only needed Roger out of the way to cover her own tracks. If her husband had died of natural causes, there would be nothing to hide, nothing to gain.

So I was back at square one. I didn't know what caused Philip Corrigan's death, or who. And I didn't know the answer to Abe Socolow's first question. I didn't know if Roger wanted me to defend him. After all, if I hadn't dug up the body, there probably wouldn't be a murder charge. If I were Roger, I wouldn't hire me; I'd sue me.

17

TELLING LIES

IN THE NAME AND BY THE
AUTHORITY OF THE STATE OF FLORIDA:

*The Grand Jurors of the State of Florida, duly called, empaneled
and sworn to inquire and true presentment make in and for the
body of the County of Dade, upon their oaths, present that on the
14th day of October, 1986, within the County of Dade, State of
Florida, ROGER A. SALISBURY did, unlawfully and feloniously,*

from a premeditated design to effect the death of PHILIP CORRIGAN, a human being, kill PHILIP CORRIGAN, by injecting him with a dangerous drug, in violation of Florida Statute Section 782.04(1)(a), to the evil example of all others in like cases offending and against the peace and dignity of the State of Florida.

The indictment was signed by the foreman of the grand jury and delivered to my house by a messenger from Abe Socolow's office. I telephoned Roger, regretful and apologetic.

"I'll understand if you file a complaint with the Bar," I said.

"Then who'd defend me? The phony malpractice case was bad enough. But a murder charge? It's crazy, and you're the only one I trust to beat it."

He made it sound easy, as if I could pull a few strings, get him a bye. I halfheartedly tried to talk him out of it. "I'm a little rusty in Criminal Court. There are some big gun criminal lawyers you could get."

"But you believe I'm innocent. None of them will."

He had me there. I *believed* he was innocent, but I wanted to know. He was surprised when I asked him to take a polygraph test. When he agreed, I believed him a little more.

"This machine is so primitive," Roger Salisbury said. "I don't trust it, not a bit."

He was squirming in a hard wooden chair, a blood pressure cuff wrapped around his right arm, pneumograph tubes circling his chest and abdomen, electrodes attached to two fingers of his left hand. He sat on an inflatable rubber bladder and leaned back against another one, trying to balance his weight.

He was right; the equipment was primitive. The polygraph hasn't changed much since a psychologist named William Marston started fooling around with blood pressure deception tests seventy years ago. Dr. Roger Salisbury would have been more comfortable lashed to a shiny chrome device with microchips and digital readouts, not this Rube Goldberg contraption.

"Just try to relax," I said. "They used to throw people into wells to see if they were demons. The ones who drowned were found innocent. The ones who floated were obviously children of Satan deserving of death. We've progressed a bit."

The technician had spent an hour with Roger getting him prepared, gaining his confidence. And setting him up. That's what polygraph examiners do. Some small talk, convince the subject he has to tell the truth, then try to solicit a lie to an irrelevant question to measure the response against the relevant one: Did you steal the petty cash, do you smoke dope on the job, then . . . did you murder Philip Corrigan?

Roger Salisbury wouldn't know this. And he wouldn't know what every con learns while still in reform school—how to screw up the test with a nail in the shoe, a hard bite into the tongue, or other ways of jacking up blood pressure. Good. That's the way I wanted it. I wanted the truth about the death of Philip Corrigan. Not to determine whether to defend Roger. I could do that either way, guilty or innocent. Even if Roger told me he planned the murder for months and carried it out, I could still give him a defense, force the state to meet its burden of proof. That's our system. But I couldn't let him take the stand and lie. So I needed the knowledge for strategy purposes and for another reason, too. I just wanted to know. I had gotten too close to this one, nearly seduced by the widow, sleeping with the daughter, and now defending Roger Salisbury a second time.

Regardless of the test result, it would not be admissible in the murder trial. Although juries frequently hear witnesses whose powers of observation are impaired by booze, drugs, or lack of intellect, polygraph tests are barred as not meeting scientific standards of proof. The courts constantly struggle to determine who lies and who tells the truth. Some judges claim to be experts on body language. A witness who raises one heel from the floor, bites a lip, or shifts his eyes is considered untrustworthy. I tell my witnesses to ogle the lawyer asking the question and not to keep time to show tunes with their feet. And I carry ChapStick for the biters.

"Do you understand that you must answer every question truthfully?" The polygraph examiner, a retired cop named Tony Cuevas, twisted the dial on the galvanic skin monitor and waited for Roger's response. Before he went on pension, Cuevas had a more direct way of eliciting the truth. A nightstick smashed against an ankle. But that was Cuevas the cop. Cuevas the security consultant was a laid-back, soft-spoken forty-seven-year-old guy of average build and pleasant demeanor. He could have been an assistant vice president at a small town bank. Today Cuevas was relaxed and informal, wearing a short-sleeved white shirt and nondescript tie, fiddling with the balance on the cardio amplifier.

"Yes sir," Roger Salisbury answered. The five pens on the charts made their little hills.

"Do you live in Florida?" Cuevas asked. That is a neutral question. The blood pressure, respiration, and perspiration are recorded, setting the lower borders for the test.

"Yes."

"Did you ever take anything that didn't belong to you?" A control question.

Salisbury paused, then a soft "Yes."

That one didn't work. The idea of a control question is to get a false answer. Nearly everybody has stolen something, if only a candy bar. If Salisbury had falsely denied it, his physiological response to this irrelevant question would have been compared to the response to the biggie: *Did you kill Philip Corrigan?* If the reaction is greater to the irrelevant control question than to the relevant question about the killing, chances are he's telling the truth. If the reaction is greater to the relevant question, chances are he's more concerned about that answer, and it's a lie.

Tony Cuevas may have wanted to stomp on Roger Salisbury's instep to get a better answer, but he simply smiled and asked, "Did you ever cheat in school, even once?"

Another short pause, then a soft "No." I couldn't see the charts, but that was the answer Cuevas wanted. An almost sure lie to an irrelevant question.

A pause for about thirty seconds to let the reactions die.

"Did you kill Philip Corrigan?"

A hasty, firm "No, sir."

"Is your name Roger?" Back to the neutral question to start the sequence again.

"Yes."

"Did you ever wish anyone harm?" Again, a control question, eliciting the lie.

"No." It's amazing how many people refuse to admit the truth to questions they believe are irrelevant. They're afraid that if they admit to skul duggery or viciousness in the past, it's an admission of guilt on the subject of the polygraph test, and figuring the question isn't the one . that's being tested, they lie about it.

The required pause, and then: "Did you inject succinylcholine or any other substance into Philip Corrigan in an attempt to kill him?"

"No."

"Were you born in May?"

"Yes."

"Have you ever told a lie to get out of trouble?"

Silence, then "Yes." Roger Salisbury was more honest than most, but he still denied two of the control questions, enough for Cuevas to evaluate the charts.

"One more question, Dr. Salisbury. Do you know who killed Philip Corrigan?"

"No sir," Roger Salisbury said.

Cuevas went through the same questions two more times. The answers stayed the same. The pens never stopped gliding up and down the moving paper. Tony Cuevas never changed his expression. When it was over, Roger Salisbury ran a hand through his neat, salt-and-pepper hair and gave me a wary look. His shirt was soaked and he seemed worn out. I told him that honest men sweat, too, and sent him home.

I used to think I was a good judge of character. Then I got burned a few times. Now I watched Roger Salisbury heading out the door. Good looking in that bland, undefined way. A mild, passive demeanor. Troubled now. He was either an honest man worried about the

161

reliability of the strange contraption or a killer fearful that his mask was about to be peeled back.

Very perceptive, Lassiter. And you are either a brilliant lawyer riding the crest of a dazzling career or a has-been ex-jock who should be selling hurricane shutters.

Cuevas kicked open a mini-refrigerator and offered me a beer. I was thirsty and he was sociable, so we polished off a six-pack while going over the charts. Cuevas measured the little lines, some forming the Appalachians, others the Rockies. He made notes, used a calculator, scratched his head with a pencil, and said, "I got a plus eight or better on two of the three relevant questions."

"Meaning?"

"Truthful. He didn't kill Philip Corrigan. Or more properly stated, his physiological responses lead me to conclude that he doesn't believe that he did."

"So what did he lie about?"

"Nothing for sure. The machine gives us three categories. Truthful, deceptive, and inconclusive. He got a minus four when I asked him if he knew who killed the guy. Minus six would be clearly deceptive. Minus four is close but still inconclusive. Here, look at this."

He pointed at some squiggly lines. They trailed off, becoming shorter, then taller, then shorter again.

"Looks like the Dow Jones," I said.

"That's called a staircase suppression. See, it's like a series of steps. It shows suppression of respiration just after I asked if he *knows* who killed Corrigan. That's one of the indications of deception."

"So does he know who did the killing?"

"A definite maybe. Sorry, best I can do is he didn't kill Corrigan but may know who did. If he clearly lied about not knowing, I'd be even more convinced he was innocent of the murder itself."

I must have looked puzzled because Cuevas continued, "It's this way, Lassiter. If the test shows clearly truthful to the denial of having committed the crime and clearly deceptive as to the denial of knowing who did, he's absolutely innocent. Money back, guaran-fucking-teed clean as a whistle. A killer will never show a stronger response to the question of who did it than whether he did it."

I fooled around with the blood pressure cuff, then turned to Cuevas: "He told me he doesn't know who killed Corrigan. I don't like it if he's lying to me."

"He might have had an itchy foot or a chest pain when he answered. Or he might know the killer and be protecting him."

"Or her," I said.

Cuevas nodded. "Or them. But your guy looks clean on the big questions, so you got what you want, an innocent lamb being led to the slaughter."

Which means someone is telling lies about Roger Salisbury. I remembered the line from Kafka: "Someone must have been telling lies about Joseph K. for without having done anything wrong he was arrested one fine morning." Which also meant we needed to prepare for The Trial.

The next morning I was at my desk at eight o'clock when the call came on my private line. "You gonna surrender that pervert murderer or should a couple boys from major crimes cuff him and bring him in the front door with all the TV assholes outside?"

Abe Socolow had such a folksy way of saying hello. He was delivering a message, just in case I missed it the day before. There would be no breaks, no special treatment because we used to break bread together. Now I was just another problem for him. After he brushed me aside, he could sweep up the scum he saw in front of him.

"You shouldn't skip breakfast, Abe. Affects your disposition."

He snorted at me. "I chew nails for breakfast."

"And spit out tacks," I said. "Roger will be there whenever you want. We aim to cooperate. But we'd like some cooperation from the state, too."

"Like what?" he asked, suspicion rising in him like steam in a kettle.

"Bond, reasonable bond for someone never before arrested, much less convicted of a crime."

"Hey, Jake, don't pee on my leg, okay. We're talking a capital crime here. No bond. You remember your criminal procedure, don't you, or is the money too good handling divorces and corporate mergers?"

Socolow was going to make my life miserable, and if I couldn't figure that out, he was telling me about it. He wanted me to grovel a little, so I did. It wouldn't help my client to insult the guy trying to fry him. "Abe, the court will grant him bond if the state stipulates to it. He's not going anywhere. He's got his medical practice here. He'll show up for arraignment, the preliminary, the trial, the whole works. C'mon Abe . . . Who'd notice the difference?" I said, without thinking. I pictured Socolow scowling at me at the other end of the line.

"Fuck him and the horse he rode in on. Let him sit in the can with all the other shitheads."

Stay in the prosecutor's office long enough, you get warped. You start thinking like a cop and talking like a cop. Cops are everywhere— homicide, vice, narcs—telling macho stories, hanging together in the paranoid world of Us against Them. Then in the corridors of the Justice Building, you rub up against the silk-suited shoulders of criminal lawyers and their depraved clients. No way you can stay sane. Not after eighteen years.

He always thought I was too flippant. Become a judge if you want to be a wiseguy, Socolow once told me. They get away with that shit.

"So what's it gonna be?" Socolow said finally.

"I'll bring him in, but I want an immediate bond hearing. You and I both know he shouldn't have to cool his heels in that hellhole across the street."

Socolow laughed. "Good enough for spicks and spades, but not for the saintly doctor. Bring him in, and I'll get you a bond hearing this afternoon. But you know your burden under *Arthur v. State*."

I knew, I knew. Unlike a trial, where the state has the burden of proving guilt beyond a reasonable doubt, at a bond hearing in a capital case, the defendant must show that the state lacks sufficient evidence of guilt. But there was something in that for us, too. I could cross-examine Socolow's witnesses. One more time to put them under oath, a great advantage, because the best trick in the defense lawyer's trial bag is to elicit conflicting statements from prosecution witnesses. Jurors love that, even if the testimony is as innocuous as the color of the tie someone was wearing on the day of a murder. So the state's case would be unfolded in front of me, and the state's star witness, Mrs. Melanie Corrigan, would have to testify much sooner than she could have expected.

"I can't believe Melanie set me up," Roger Salisbury said as we looked for a parking space in front of the Justice Building. He squirmed in the bucket seat.

"Believe it," I said. "Hey, she sued you for malpractice, planted the drug in your house, and gave the State Attorney's Office an affidavit for the search warrant. What more does it take?"

He slammed a hand against the dashboard. "I'll believe it when I see her take the stand against me, not before."

"Fine," I said, pulling the old convertible into the meager shade of a thatch palm. "That should be right after lunch."

18

CIRCUS MAXIMUS

The Justice Building hadn't changed, except to become more crowded, dirtier, and more forbidding. When I started practicing law, six Criminal Court judges handled all felony cases in Dade County. But that was before Miami became the major port of entry for various grasses, powders, and pills from south of the border, and before Miami earned its civic bones as murder capital of the U. S. of A. Now Miami has the highest crime rate in the country. That's important. Americans have a passion for being number one. Like having the highest humidity, the murder rate is the source of a bizarre sense of pride among locals. It takes a tough *hombre* to battle Miami's mosquitoes each summer and the criminals all year round.

The city *padres* can't do much about the weather, but they keep adding personnel to the justice system. Now, eighteen state judges churn through calendars stocked with up to sixty felonies each day, hurrying through arraignments, motions, bond hearings, reports, soundings, trials, and sentencings. A constant flow of humanity crowds the corridors—Liberty City blacks, Hispanics from a dozen countries, dirt-poor whites—calling out for their public defenders in a Babel of tongues, inner-city jive, machine-gun Spanish, back-country Southern drawl.

I was pacing the fourth floor, getting the feel of the place again, waiting for the bond hearing. The tile floors were filthy, the corridors dim with dead fluorescent bulbs. Acoustic tiles were missing from the ceiling, leaving gaps like missing teeth. Every thirty feet or so, huge twists of electrical wires dropped from overhead conduits, waiting for county electricians to install some new device, maybe TV cameras, escape alarms, or other technological marvels. The wires could have been there a week or a year. In the Justice Building, time is another dimension.

An ancient bailiff in a baggy blue uniform came out of a courtroom shouting, "Judge Snyder's calendar is now being called!" All aboard.

A young assistant state attorney with too much hair and an unkempt moustache sang out, "Teddy Figuero-a! Teddy Figuero-a!" A prosecutor's missing witness, a case about to go down the tubes.

A huge black woman slammed into me. She held her even larger son by the scruff of his T-shirt and horse collared him down the corridor. The son was about twenty, with shoulders like a water buffalo but a choreographer's hips.

"What day they say your trial be?" the mom demanded.

"February four, Momma."

"No. No. The ar-rangement be February four. The trial be when, March something . . ."

They trundled toward the escalators, still debating.

Shackled defendants crossed the corridor in twos, shuffling from one holding cell to another, eyes darting left and right, looking for girlfriends, mothers, lawyers, or bondsmen.

A sunburned redhead in her forties removed one high-heeled shoe and wiggled the toes of her right foot. Four toes, the little one missing. Maybe the evidence in a criminal case. Who knows? The performers are crazed at Circus Maximus.

I threaded my way to Judge Randolph Crane's courtroom, a spacious arena with thirty-foot ceilings, paneled walls on two sides, and a stained glass ornamental wall behind the bench into which was cut a door and through which the judge miraculously appeared from chambers. Under his raised bench of simulated walnut was a red panic button that summoned corrections officers in the event a deranged defendant (or lawyer) attacked him, and on a hidden shelf sat a loaded .357 Magnum in case the officers were all squeezing up against the young women clerks in the police liaison office.

I was waiting for the officers to bring Roger into the courtroom from the county jail next door where he had been booked two hours earlier. The prisoners came through an overpass that crossed the street and led directly into holding cells attached to the courtrooms. I had stayed with Roger as long as they let me in jail processing, and when they took him back through the huge steel door that clanged shut with a sound of malice and finality, he shot me a helpless look.

It hit me then, the load I carried, Roger Salisbury's life weighing a ton on my shoulders. The first rule of criminal cases and here I was emoting, instead of thinking, feeling anguish for him instead of masterminding a brilliant strategy to set him free. If any there be.

A dozen defendants sat in the jury box waiting for their cases to be called. Lawyers milled about in front of the bar, whispering to each other, poring through files, making deals, swapping stories. The courtroom resembled a basketball court before the game, players at both ends warming up, taking shots from all over the court, slapping each other on the back, a kind of camaraderie before the battle. At the same time, the judge kept calling his calendar, sometimes banging his gavel to bring the uproar to a manageable din.

Judge Randolph Crane was serving his fourth six-year term on the bench. He was tall and spare with a long, gloomy, gray face. His pale blue eyes had seen it all and not liked any of it. He spoke quickly as if he wanted to get it over with, sometimes thumbing through his calendar, shaking his head at the number of cases still to be heard.

"Rodolfo Milan," the judge called out. A pot-bellied man in a stained guayabera dragged himself out of the jury box. A public defender whispered in his ear. In a singsong voice, the judge began his mournful chant, "You're charged with aggravated assault, grand theft, breaking and entering, possession of a weapon in the commission of a felony. Rodolfo Milan, how do you plead?"

The defendant looked for his public defender, who now was huddled with a young woman prosecutor in a black miniskirt and fishnet stockings.

"Have I got a plea for you?" She winked at the defense lawyer.

It went on like this for a while, arraignments and some guilty pleas, a few cases *nolle prossed* because the state had misplaced files or lost evidence or forgotten to subpoena witnesses or violated the speedy trial rule. With all the traps, with the rules of criminal procedure a minefield for the prosecution, it's a miracle anybody ever gets convicted. Except when they really want you. When they pay attention to you, throw their resources into it, when an Abe Socolow gets a burr under his saddle, makes it personal, then it's different. Then it's all turned around.

The judge kept calling cases, and every few minutes, corrections officers brought a new load of defendants from the holding cell to the jury box. Still no Roger Salisbury.

"Ivory Holloman," the judge sang out. "You're charged with grand theft, auto . . ."

Marvin Pollack, a skinny sixty-year-old defense lawyer with a matted toupee, pushed a young black man in a muscle shirt up against one wall of the courtroom. "Ivory, you got the money?" Pollack asked, patting the man's back pocket and not finding a wallet.

"Tomorrow, Mister Po-lock," Ivory Holloman said, terror in his eyes. If he wanted to, Ivory could pick up Marvin Pollack and use him for a walking stick. Ivory didn't want to. He wanted Marvin Pollack to keep him out of jail.

"Let's see what you got there," Pollack said, jamming his hand inside the man's tight jeans, fishing out some wrinkled currency. "Shit! A fin, nine singles, and a Lotto ticket." Pollack smoothed the bills, pocketed them, straightened his tie, and prepared to negotiate a fourteen-dollar plea.

"Lazaro Arango, first degree arson . . ."

Abe Socolow strutted into the courtroom followed by his entourage. A couple of detectives from Metro, a young woman assistant state attorney, the medical examiner, a paralegal, and two clerks from the prosecutor's office. The state can always outnumber you. The detectives flanked Melanie Corrigan, who looked a trifle uneasy, but in a virgin-white cotton dress, her arrival still cut the decibel level in half as she walked to the first row of the gallery.

Socolow stood motionless and surveyed the courtroom as if counting the heifers on his ranch and coming up one short. Finally he spotted me and nodded formally. His assistant stood a half step behind. She was a good choice for the trial, a fragile blonde, small and pale with translucent skin. Give her a good squeeze and you'd leave bruises, but just what Abe Socolow needed. Sometimes, he comes on too strong. A little righteous indignation is okay for a prosecutor up to the point the jury senses he's mean-spirited and unfair. Then, for reasons psychologists can explain, jurors begin to feel sympathy for the defendant, no matter how heinous the charge. Abe sometimes treads dangerously close to the mark, his motor cranking at the red line.

A moment later, the guards led Salisbury through the holding cell door. His eyes desperately sought me, and I moved next to him.

"We have a couple minutes," I said. "Now, no matter what Melanie or any other witness says, you're not going to testify. This is our chance to find out what they've got, not reveal our case."

Judge Crane saw Socolow in the rear of the courtroom and pulled the freshly minted file of *State v. Salisbury* off the floor. He would call us out of turn, a courtesy to the chief of major crimes, not to me. Still, Socolow had kept his promise. An immediate bond hearing, and he hadn't called the papers or TV stations. Most prosecutors would salivate over the prospect of seeing their faces in the first block of the six o'clock news. Not Honest Abe. He didn't care about publicity, and instead of sucking up to the reporters the way most prosecutors did, he avoided them. We had a one-day reprieve on publicity.

"Roger Salisbury, murder in the first degree, defendant's motion to set bond," Judge Crane called out. He seemed a little more animated. Murder One beats the dickens out of auto theft for the adrenaline rush. "Is the defendant present and represented by counsel?"

I stepped forward, nodded, and said, "Jacob Lassiter for the defense. Let the record reflect that Dr. Salisbury is present in the courtroom, just as he will be at every hearing and the trial if reasonable bond is granted and he is released pending trial."

"Hold on Mr. Lassiter," the judge said, "let's get the introductions done before you start arguing. Say, haven't seen you around here lately. Getting bored with the bankers and big shots downtown?"

The players in the criminal justice system always give it to you when you've been manipulating money instead of lives.

"I wouldn't be here at all if the state had indicted the guilty party, instead of a respected physician, a lifelong resident of this county, and a man with no prior criminal record." Might as well score a few points before the other side gets the ball.

"Still relentless," Judge Crane muttered, shaking his head. "Perhaps the state should announce its appearance before you make your closing argument."

Socolow strode to the podium, his angular body splitting the mass of young lawyers like a sword. Some color had crept into his sallow cheeks. He stood there silently a moment, his hawkish face a mask. "Abraham D. Socolow for the people of the state of Florida," he announced. He bowed to the judge and continued, "Also for the state, Jennifer Logan." He nodded toward the small blonde who was invisible next to Melanie Corrigan.

I took a good look at the widow. Not as confident as in the civil trial.

A different society over here. Less civilized. Maybe once she would have fit in with the grifters, hard guys, and con men. But maybe the comforts of Gables Estates had taken the edge off, dulled the street smarts that served her so well until now. And maybe, too, she was just smart enough to know it.

The judge began the preliminaries. "Mr. Lassiter. This is a capital case. You know, of course, the burden you face in securing bond pending trial."

"I know, Your Honor. However, by examining the state's main witness, we intend to show that the proof is not great, and the presumption of guilt is not evident. I believe we will meet the standards of *Arthur v. State*. This is a case in which the state's entire case, including the evidence on which a search warrant was based, depends on the credibility of one witness. We are prepared to demonstrate the total lack of credibility of that witness."

I was prepared for no such thing. I was ready to wing it, to go with the flow, to get her to admit the old affair with Roger and ask if she didn't want him out of her life now, and didn't this seem like a swell way to do it. Time to go fishing. You never know what you'll catch until you drop a line into the water.

Again I looked at Melanie Corrigan. Edgy, tension showing around the mouth. Good. Finally getting to her. Socolow looked at her, too. Then he whispered something to Jennifer Logan, who shook her head, *no*, thin blonde strands swaying. Socolow turned to the judge. "Your Honor. Of course we vigorously disagree with the representations made by Mr. Lassiter concerning the state's case and its chief witness. However, we agree that this defendant is not likely to flee. We will stipulate to reasonable bond, perhaps two hundred fifty thousand dollars."

Just like that. Throwing in the towel.

Of course he had good reason. He hadn't had time to adequately prepare his witnesses, and his instincts told him that Melanie Corrigan wasn't ready. While Abe Socolow might take some perverse pleasure in keeping Roger Salisbury in jail for a few months prior to trial, he wouldn't risk blowing the case by having his star witness crack at a bond hearing. We took the offer, Roger putting up his pension funds as collateral for the bond.

So we left the Justice Building together. Just like the old days during the civil trial, Roger Salisbury telling me what a great lawyer I am. Then he asked what my strategy would be during the trial.

I didn't know.

Who are our witnesses?

I didn't know that.

He gave me a funny look. I told him not to worry. The state had to show us its evidence and its witness list. And the state's case was circumstantial. Nobody *saw* Roger Salisbury inject the drug into Philip Corrigan. And nobody except Melanie Corrigan could place the black valise in Roger's possession. I liked that—Melanie's testimony against Roger's—one-on-one. I just wondered how Abe Socolow planned to change the odds.

19

THE NURSE

Like fine wine, a criminal prosecution needs to age. First, a flurry of activity during the fermentation of the case, hearings, depositions, and an exchange of papers. Then, a quiet time, waiting for a trial date, files stored away in darkened cabinets, a time for brooding, waking at dawn with brilliant strategies, tossing them on the scrap heap of half-baked ideas by midday.

Judge Crane had set the trial for June, the beginning of Miami's unremitting summer. Those who can afford it are already getting away, escaping the blazing sun, ferocious humidity, and afternoon gully washers. By June the winds have shifted to the southeast—a wet, warm breath from the Caribbean—a time when each day begins with the same notion: no relief for six months. The calendar still says Spring, but in the tropics, it is not a time of renewal. It is the season of decay, streets steaming in afternoon storms that soak but do not cool, businessmen ducking from refrigerated cars to refrigerated offices while the poor, like desert dwellers, seek shade during the day, then roam free after dark, a time of short tempers and midnight shootings. And it would be our time of trial.

Six weeks after the indictment, we knew the state's case inside out. Abe Socolow detailed it for us in a bill of particulars, a witness list, and a carton of physical evidence. We knew who would testify and what they would say. No more trial by surprise, no last minute witnesses popping from the gallery.

We knew there was no wiretap evidence, no statements made by Salisbury to be used against him, and that the confidential informant, one Melanie Corrigan, would be the star witness. We learned the test results from the Medical Examiner's Office: evidence of succinic acid and choline in Corrigan's liver and brain, but strangely, none around the needle tracks in the buttocks. I would talk to Charlie Riggs about that.

On a warm, overcast day in April, I deposed Melanie Corrigan in Abe Socolow's office, staring hard at her when she took the oath. She stared right back and promised to tell the truth, the whole truth, and nothing but the truth. Once upon a time, she held a rich man's hand and promised to love and to cherish, to honor and obey.

Today she had no surprises. After her marriage, Roger Salisbury kept pursuing her. Yes, she had dated him years ago, but that was ancient history, she was just a kid. No, she was not having an affair with him. Kept spurning his advances. He said he loved her, that Philip didn't appreciate her, didn't spend enough time with her. Roger showed her a little black valise with hypodermics and a glass vial, clear liquid inside, like a miniature vodka bottle they give you on a plane.

He told her to get rid of Philip by injecting him with the drug. She was shocked, then laughed it off, thinking it was all talk. Roger always talked crazy. But when Philip died after surgery, she suspected Roger. She wanted proof. She thought something would come out in the civil trial, but nothing did.

So after the verdict, when Roger invited her over to his place, she went, and while he was fixing drinks, she looked through a desk in the study. *Voilà*, the black valise and two hypodermics. Nearby in a small refrigerator was the vial, this time with some of the fluid missing. She slipped everything into her purse and the next day called the State Attorney's Office. At about the same time, Dr. MacKenzie tipped Socolow to the brain and liver samples that came from Charlie Riggs. When both the tissue samples and the liquid tested positive for succinylcholine, the grand jury indicted Roger Salisbury for Murder One.

She told her story well. Socolow had several weeks to prepare her for deposition after almost botching it at the bond hearing. I couldn't shake her. She denied that the valise was ever in her possession, denied planting the drug at Roger's house. Nothing there for us, but at least we knew the state's case and knew we could not win unless we discredited Melanie Corrigan.

What about the valise and the drug, I had asked Roger. I wanted him to tell me that he had never seen the succinylcholine, that Melanie must have come up with it and then stolen his valise to frame him. If we could trace the drug to her, bull's-eye!

"It didn't happen that way," he said.

"No?"

"I borrowed the sucks—that's what we call it—from an anesthesiologist. Had an old Lab retriever, must have been close to twenty, comatose, but still breathing. Put him to sleep by paralyzing his lungs with the sucks. Kept the bottle in a refrigerator. Don't remember what happened to it."

"The valise?"

He shrugged. "Noticed it missing shortly after Philip died. Didn't think anything of it."

I checked it out. The anesthesiologist confirmed the story, the pet burial place, too. An unexpected bonus, it all happened two years before Corrigan died. *Ladies and gentlemen, you don't get your murder weapon and wait two years to do the job.*

One name on the state's witness list meant nothing to us. Rebecca Ingram, R.N., Mercy Hospital. I took her deposition with Abe Socolow sitting grimly at her side. Nurse Ingram was in her thirties, no makeup, close-cropped dishwater brown hair. Next to her name on the witness list was the innocuous description: *Responded to decedent's cardiac monitor alarm.*

"Did you see Dr. Salisbury the night of Mr. Corrigan's death?" I asked.

"Yes. I saw him leaving Room five-twelve, Mr. Corrigan's room, hurrying down the hall."

Okay, the state can place Roger in the hospital that night. No problem. Seeing patients, stopped in to check on Corrigan after surgery.

"And what time did this occur?"

She did not hesitate. "Ten o'clock. Almost exactly. I remember because I was checking Mr. Corrigan every half hour on the half hour."

Still no harm done. The aneurysm occurred at eleven fifteen.

"Is that all?" That's not much of a question, sort of asking the witness what the heck you're doing on the state's witness list.

"He was carrying a little leather valise. Black. With three gold initials on it, about yea-big." She held her hands about one foot apart, and I felt a knife, the same size, lodge in my gut. Nurse Rebecca Ingram shrugged and smiled a tiny, innocent smile. "That's all," she said.

Oh. That's all. I asked Socolow if he would be kind enough to find Exhibit C in his cardboard box.

"Similar to this valise?" I asked the nurse.

"Well, it looks like it. Yes. Either that one or one just like it."

I put my hand over the gold lettering. "What initials were on the valise you saw?"

She shook her head. "I don't know."

"And of course you couldn't see what was in the valise, correct?"

"No. I mean yes. I mean, correct, I couldn't see what was in there." Questions phrased in the negative always confuse.

"Did you ask Dr. Salisbury what was in the valise?"

"No. I said nothing to him, and as far as I know, he didn't even see me."

"And in your experience, is it unusual for a doctor to carry such a valise?"

"Oh no. Many physicians carry small instruments in them or keep their patient notes there."

"Was there anything unusual about seeing Dr. Salisbury on the floor in the evening?"

"No. He frequently checks on patients after surgery."

"So in summary, you saw Dr. Salisbury on his regular nighttime rounds more than an hour before Philip Corrigan suffered an aneurysm from unknown causes, and the doctor was carrying a rather ordinary valise that may or may not be the one I am holding, and you don't know what, if anything, was in it?"

"Yes, yes, that's right," she said, clearly relieved not to have buried the doctor any deeper.

I paused a moment and tried to get smarter in a hurry. At trial you worry about asking one question too many; in discovery, one too few. I couldn't seem to pump any extra voltage into my brain. Abe Socolow cracked the knuckles of his bony hands and said, "Any more questions, Counselor?"

We were sitting in his tiny office in the Justice Building, files and cardboard boxes everywhere, a flood of paper, the daily bread of lawyers. The three of us plus a court reporter taking everything down on her silent machine. Socolow seemed a little too anxious to end this one. I pretended to study the chart of his convicted and condemned killers. Buying time, I stood up and walked to the small window that overlooked the trestles of the nearby expressway. I looked for a signpost on the foggy road that runs through my mind.

"One more question," I said.

Abe Socolow sighed and shook his head in disgust. That trick might work with kids just out of law school. Pretending exasperation: *Why the fuck you wasting everybody's time here?*

I smiled at Nurse Rebecca Ingram, who sat quietly with her hands primly folded in her lap. "Did you see anybody else on the floor that night prior to eleven-fifteen?"

"Yes, as I told Mr. Socolow, sometime between ten-thirty and eleven, I can't remember exactly when, I was at the station by the elevators, and Mrs. Corrigan came up with a gentleman."

"Oh," I breathed, trying to keep still, inviting her to continue.

"Well, they must have come up the fire stairs because I didn't see them get off the elevator. But I looked down the hall and there they were."

"Did you speak to them?"

"Yes, I told Mrs. Corrigan they really shouldn't be up there then, but she said they'd just be a minute. Then they went into Mr. Corrigan's room."

"Alone, the two of them?"

"Yes, I returned to my station."

"Did you recognize the gentleman with Mrs. Corrigan?"

"No. He was very . . . very muscular looking. I could see that even though he was wearing one of those khaki jackets with all the pockets, like he was going on a safari . . ."

"A bush jacket," I helped out.

"Yes. Heavily muscled men have a distinctive way of walking, kind of rolling side-to-side. And he was not too tall. Short, actually."

"Would you recognize him again?"

"I believe so. I believe he was Cuban, kind of swarthy, you know . . . but I don't know. He could have been Italian or something." She blushed.

What a splendid break, what a wonderful witness you have handed me, Abe Socolow. A buck would get you ten the muscular, not-too-tall guy was Sergio Machado-Alvarez, the karate instructor, boat captain, and steroid freak who made a cameo appearance on the group-grope videotape and who bruised my ancient Oldsmobile with brutal efficiency. I made a note to have Cindy subpoena Sergio for the trial.

I continued, "How long were they in the room?"

"I don't know. I didn't see them leave. They must have gone back down the stairs."

"You were on the fifth floor, correct?"

"Yes."

"Do many visitors walk up from the lobby?"

Abe Socolow was fidgeting. "Counselor, I must object to that question. It's speculative and irrelevant."

"Save it for trial," I barked. "This is discovery, and it's my deposition, and if you're sorry you listed this honest lady as a witness, tough."

Socolow banged a fist on his green metal desk, sending a Styrofoam coffee cup flying. "Damn it, Jake, you know better than that! I never try to hide anything. Let the chips fall where they may. I'm only interested in the truth, and you can create all the red herrings you want, but I don't care who was in that room, only one person poisoned Corrigan."

I ignored him and turned to Nurse Ingram.

"Just one more question," I promised.

Socolow hissed at me, "You said that fifteen minutes ago."

I proceeded as if Socolow weren't there. "Nurse Ingram, did you check on Philip Corrigan between the time you saw Mrs. Corrigan and the gentleman enter Room five-twelve and the time of the patient's distress due to the aneurysm?"

"No sir."

Whoa. I had expected a *yes*. Another pleasant surprise. She continued, "I'm sorry, but I missed the eleven o'clock check. I was filling out reports. Next thing I know, at eleven-fifteen, the cardiac monitor is going crazy. He'd had the aneurysm. I called in the Code Blue, and he was taken to surgery. But as you know . . ."

"So," I began, disregarding my one-question promise, "as far as you know, Mrs. Corrigan and the gentleman could have been in Mr. Corrigan's room from ten-thirty to eleven o'clock or even eleven-fourteen."

"I don't know. I suppose. But I don't know why they would be. Mr. Corrigan was sleeping all evening. He was sedated, of course, after surgery."

"And the last time you saw him was ten-thirty, and he was sleeping peacefully?"

"Yes."

"After Dr. Salisbury left?"

"Yes."

"Then you saw Mrs. Corrigan and the gentleman?"

"Yes."

"And the next time you saw Mr. Corrigan, he had suffered the aneurysm?"

"Yes, I said that."

"No further questions," I said, regretting only that a judge, a jury, and a gallery of spectators were not there. "Your witness, Abe."

If Abe Socolow's skin were any more sallow, he'd be quarantined for hepatitis. He started in without pleasantries.

"Nurse Ingram, as far as you know, Mrs. Corrigan and her guest could have left the room at ten-thirty-one?"

"Yes, I suppose."

"And Roger Salisbury could have come back in at ten-thirty-two?"

I let out a well-planned laugh. "Sure, and maybe Santa Claus came down the chimney at eleven-ten."

Socolow ignored me. "Answer the question," he ordered the nurse.

"Well, I would have seen Dr. Salisbury if he came up the elevator. But he could have come through the stairwell, yes."

"Nothing further," Socolow said.

Abe Socolow had gambled, had rolled the dice. He wanted to place Salisbury in Philip Corrigan's room, black valise in hand. He risked our finding out that the widow and her friend were there, too. He lost. But now, how to use that knowledge. I knew where we wanted to go with it, if not exactly how to get there.

If the state intends to prove a homicide with circumstantial evidence, it had better show that the defendant had the motive, opportunity, and means to commit the crime. With Roger Salisbury the state had all three; his motive was to get Corrigan's money and wife; the opportunity was being alone in the hospital room with Corrigan; and the means were dangerous drugs and the ability to use them.

If you are defending an accused murderer who has the motive, opportunity, and means to commit the crime, you'd better have another suspect to toss to the jury. He can't be a phantom. Shadowy figures, unknown assailants without the motive to kill, get you twenty-five years to life. Or worse. To beat the charge, you need a suspect with a name, face, and social security number.

I had my suspect: Sergio Machado-Alvarez. Now all I needed was some proof.

20

THE CONTRACT

The phone call came three days after we filed our discovery with the state. We listed our witnesses and physical evidence, including a certain "videotape portraying a prosecution witness, the decedent, the defendant, and an additional party." I wanted to see if it got a rise out of Socolow. I don't know if it did. But the widow surely noticed.

"Mr. Lassiter," she purred on the phone.

"Mrs. Corrigan," I said.

"You have something I would like very much."

"You want my 1954 Willie Mays baseball card?"

"Don't toy with me, Jake," she said, impatiently.

"So sorry, that's what I thought you wanted me to do."

"And don't flatter yourself."

"Okay, a business call, you want an appointment?"

"I want to tell you things that you will want to hear."

"Let me guess. My eyes remind you of the Mediterranean at sunset." My witty repartee will never get me a table at the Algonquin or a guest shot on Johnny Carson.

She was quiet a moment, probably deciding whether to tell me to screw off. But she was after something, so she kept going. "If you'd stop being such a smartass and listen, you'd know I'm trying to help your client."

"Like you helped him by planting the drug in his house."

"Maybe I was just returning it to the place I found it. I'll tell you everything. Just bring me the videotape."

"What if I've made copies? A year from now I could blackmail you."

She laughed softly. "You're not the type. Besides, we'll sign a contract. You draw it up, that you've turned over the only copy. If you're lying, you could be disbarred, right?"

Right. She'd thought of everything.

"Tell me," I said, giving it my best Cary Grant, "how does a girl like you get to be a girl like you?"

"Practice," she said.

And all this time I thought that's how you got to Carnegie Hall. "Okay," I said, "I'll bring the cassette. There's only one. You'll make a statement exonerating Salisbury. I'll call Socolow. We'll need him and a court reporter to take your statement."

"No! Just you. Bring a tape recorder if you want."

I thought about it. Socolow might muck it up, talk her out of it, delay until morning. She was giving me the case on a silver platter. Either that or handing me my head. "Okay, I'll be there in twenty minutes."

"Not here. I don't want you in the house. Sergio might come by. Someplace else. You know where Shark Valley is?"

"What, the Everglades? I'm not in the mood for mosquitoes. Besides, it'll be nearly dark by the time we get there."

"You're not afraid of me in the dark, are you?"

I didn't trust her at dawn, dusk, midnight, or any time in between. And she might bring friends. "It's just a strange place to execute a contract, that's all," I said.

"There'll be tourists around, just no one we'll know. Meet me there in two hours. You'll have to prepare the contract and get going. I'll be on top of the observation tower."

I said okay, but I didn't mean okay. It made no sense, a meeting at Shark Valley. And by the time we got there, the tourists would be back at their hotels sipping six-dollar piña coladas. But if she gave me a statement, admitted planting the evidence, Roger's case was over.

I was dusting off a briefcase when Cindy buzzed. "Hey boss, now the other Corrigan babe wants you."

"Say what?"

"*Mizz* Corrigan," Cindy said, dragging out the name.

"What line?"

"No line. Here. The waiting room. Just dropping by, in a sweatsuit and black Reeboks, so says our sharp-eyed receptionist."

"Bring her back," I commanded.

"Black Reeboks," Cindy repeated. "Bet they're hightops, too."

When the oak door closed behind her, Susan gave me a peck on the cheek. I grabbed her by both shoulders and brought her close. The kiss was straight on, slow and soft, and Susan half gasped and half sighed at the end of it.

"You charge by the hour for that?" she whispered.

"For you, a straight contingency fee."

She feigned anger. "You only want a third of my kisses?"

"No, I only want to spend a third of our time kissing."

"The rest talking?"

"That, too. It's good to see you, but I'm on my way out." I told her about the call from Melanie Corrigan, and she leaned against the windowsill frowning. Then she paced back and forth, her sneakers silent on the thick carpeting. Cindy was right. Hightops.

Finally she turned. "Don't go, Jake. It's a set-up."

"Maybe. And maybe I'll get a statement that will exonerate my client. I really don't have a choice."

"Then at least take the police along."

"The police work for Socolow."

"You're not going to give her the videotape." It was both a question and a plea.

"Tell me more about the tape."

"You've seen it," she said. "Nothing more to tell."

"When was it shot?"

"I don't know exactly. About two years before Dad died."

"Two years! What was it, a honeymoon cruise?"

"Actually it was right before Dad married her. Mom had just died. Dad took the *Cory* to the islands with Sergio as the captain, Roger and Melanie the guests."

"So much for a decent interval of mourning."

She turned away, an old memory dragging up the pain. "It's hard for me to be objective about Dad. He always cheated on Mom, and that last year or so, when she was sick and he took up with Melanie, it was very hard for her . . . how cruel he was at the end. I can never forgive him for that. Never."

I didn't expect that tone, the bitterness toward her father. But something else interrupted the thought, something that wasn't making sense. "Roger told me he first met your father after he married Melanie."

"No. Salisbury treated both Mom and Dad. He definitely knew Dad before he married that slut."

"Strange he would lie about that." I stored the knowledge for later use. My mind is a warehouse of information like that, bushels of scrap paper filled with notes.

I told Susan it was time to grab the mosquito spray and head for the Glades. She drifted toward the door, blocking my path like a linebacker filling the hole. "What about the tape?" she asked.

I looked around on my shelves and grabbed a small cardboard box. "Maybe Melanie would like to watch *Cross-Examining the Expert in a Product Liability Case*."

"And you think that when she discovers what you've given her she'll consider it a big joke? She's dangerous, totally amoral, and capable of anything. She could seduce you or kill you. To her, it wouldn't make the slightest difference."

"Melanie? She wouldn't hurt a fly."

"Maybe not one that's zipped up. Jake, don't be foolish. You could get hurt, or worse."

"Would a hearse horse snicker hauling this lawyer away?"

"Tell me you won't go," she pleaded.

I didn't want to go. But I couldn't not go. I put some cowboy in my voice. "A man's gotta do what a man's gotta do."

"Don't be a jerk. And that self-mockery doesn't sell with me. You really believe that tough-guy stuff."

"Just locker room bravado. Inside I'm quaking."

"There you go again. What do I have to say to you?"

"You could tell me how much you'd miss me if I end up sleeping with the alligators."

"I would miss you. I . . . I care for you."

"Care for me?"

Still blocking my path, she moved closer and gave me a wistful up-from-under look. I had to fight the urge to grab her. "I think I love you," she whispered. "Satisfied?"

"You bet."

She took a half step backwards. "Somehow I expected a more eloquent response."

"Haven't we had this conversation before? Haven't I already professed my . . . my you know."

"Jake Lassiter, how can a man be so articulate in a crowded courtroom and such a bungler one-on-one? Is it so hard to say you love me?"

"Well, I do."

"Do what?"

"Do what you said."

"Jake!"

I threw up my arms. "Do love you, okay already?"

"Not okay. I forced you into it. You still can't express your feelings, and you treat me like some bimbo whose opinions aren't worth listening to."

Now it was my turn. I moved back a yard. "Did I say something wrong? I thought we were engaging in sweet talk, and all of a sudden, I'm not listening. What is it you want me to do?"

"It's what I don't want. I don't want you to prove how tough you are. And I don't want you to walk into a trap."

"Sorry. I have a duty to Roger."

"Why don't you respect me on this?"

"Hey Susan, I appreciate your opinion, but I can take care of myself. I've been around this town a long time before I ever met you, and nobody's stolen my marbles yet."

Some color had crept into her dark complexion. "Maybe you ought to keep traveling solo, you're so good at it." She turned away, looked out the window over the Atlantic. The *S. S. Norway* was lugging its way out Government Cut, a thousand tourists headed to the Virgin Islands. "You don't take me seriously, Jake. You're a big, dumb jock like all the rest of them. I don't know what I ever saw in you."

With that, she pivoted on her black hightops and stormed out of the office, muttering "macho jerk" two or three times. Through my open door, I saw loyal Cindy shrug, as if to say, "What else is new?"

21

SHARK VALLEY

There are no sharks in Shark Valley. No valley either. Just miles of sawgrass and countless animals living in their natural habitat. Bull alligators rule the Everglades, eating turtles, white-tailed deer, and any birds that venture too close to the reptiles' muddy homes. There are wood storks and egrets and great white herons that would now be extinct if women still wore feathery hats.

But no sharks and no valley. Misnamed though it is, Shark Valley is nature unrestrained. It is a vast flat slough, a slow-moving river of shallow water that has not changed in appearance for centuries. If Philip Corrigan had ever seen the place, he would have licked his chops and dreamed of draining and filling, building on stilts, and calling it "Heron Creek." Of course, then there would be no more herons and no more creek.

Black thunderheads were forming over the Glades, mountainous clouds picking up the moisture from the fifty-mile-wide river. Nearly dusk and the world was gray. It was seven miles down a narrow asphalt road to the observation tower. No cars allowed. I rented a bicycle from the chickee hut run by the Park Service and got a second look from the ranger who warned me about the weather and the closing time. He probably doesn't get many bird watchers wearing blue suits and burgundy ties. I put my suitcoat in the car, peeled off my tie, and felt only half as stupid. I went into the restroom, tossed some cold water on my face, and stared at the mirror. I hadn't gotten any better looking. I practiced my cocky look, worked up a crooked grin, and said to the mirror, "Sure I have the tape, but first I'll take your statement." Behind me, a toilet flushed, the stall door opened, and a middle-aged tourist wearing a Mickey Mouse T-shirt gave me a sideways look, then backed away, never stopping to wash his hands. I checked my gear—the videotape, the contract, and a portable tape recorder—all safe in a thin briefcase. Then I headed into the open air, hunched over the saddle of my government-issue, dollar-fifty-an-hour bicycle that was the right size for Pee Wee Herman.

The dark clouds were growing nearer and the wind kicking hard from the west as I pedaled south into the Glades, my knees under my chin. Some serious bird watchers were hurrying back on the path, their binoculars swinging, tripods in hand. One white-haired man with knobby knees sticking out of safari shorts was carrying on about having spotted "two crested caracaras, not one, but two . . ."

Blackish-green alligators slid into the water from the side of the road. Some were babies, two feet in length, looking like rubberized gags from a hotel gift shop. The bulls, ten or twelve feet, launched themselves into the water with powerful haunches. Some dug into the mud, forming gator holes to trap the water and keep cool. Stop to look, they hiss at you, blowing air out their nostrils. Keep going, they watch until you're gone.

One of the big bulls grabbed a tourist last year. A stockbroker from Cleveland had wandered into shallow water to get video footage of a blue heron feeding. Just like an Abbott and Costello movie, the log he stepped on opened its mouth. The alligator dragged him into deeper water, then with powerful jaws, crushed the man's chest and pierced his lungs. Official cause of death: drowning. Like saying the victims of Hiroshima died of sunburn.

It took only twenty minutes to pedal to the observation tower, a sleek concrete structure with a long, elevated ramp leading to a circular deck sixty feet above the sawgrass. Deserted except for the animals. Birds fed along the banks of a pond below, keeping a watch for the gators that dozed nearby. I leaned the bike against a strangler fig, grabbed the briefcase, and slowly walked up the ramp, listening for human sounds.

Bird chirps and little splashes came from the pond below. Nothing more.

At the top, I caught the glint of the sun, hidden by the clouds, preparing to drop into the Gulf of Mexico off the coast of Naples. A hawk kite flew by, carrying an apple snail. A small unseen animal rustled the sawgrass below. Then a scraping sound from above. A dozen white terns bolted from a Caribbean pine and veered away from the tower.

Another scraping sound.

I was standing on a round concrete slab, maybe thirty feet across. Above me, the roof of the tower was another slab, the same size. I looked up into solid concrete.

A voice, just a whisper, then another.

He swung down from the slab above, landing six feet in front of me, blocking the path down the ramp. Behind me, another one dropped onto the concrete. The one behind me was short, muscular, mousta-chioed, and mean. Sergio Machado-Alvarez. The one by the ramp was bigger, not as many ripples, but maybe six-two, two-twenty, a gut beginning to give way. He wanted to play baseball. At least he was holding a baseball bat. One of the aluminum models. They make a funny *clonk* when they hit the ball. I don't know the sound when they crush a skull.

Oh shit. You were right, Susan. I didn't need this. I didn't need to prove how tough I was. Coming here already proved how smart I was.

"*Hola,* asshole," Sergio hissed. He showed me his large, gray teeth. A psychopath's smile. "You've got something for me, *damelo, gimme.*"

"Say please." I never learn.

Sergio curled a lip at me. "*Hijo de puta,* you're going to hurt real good. Orlando . . ."

Orlando was smacking his palm with the fat end of the Louisville Slugger. If they were trying to scare me, it was working. But I was thinking, too. Orlando looked slow. That was a plus. But strong. That was a minus. Sergio was unarmed. Another plus. But I knew he was no stranger to the *dojang,* and from what I saw with my dear old car, he wasn't faking it. Another minus. So far I was breaking even but still didn't have a way of getting off the tower with all my parts working.

A humorless smirk twisted Sergio's moustache. He was going to enjoy this. Orlando kept plopping the bat into a bare hand the size of an anvil. I took two steps backward until I was leaning against the railing. Floating below me were five-hundred-pound wallets with teeth.

I held my briefcase in front of me. "Where's Mrs. Corrigan? This is for her."

"Home finger-fucking herself," Sergio leered, taking a step toward me.

"Whoa there," I warned, holding the briefcase over the railing. "One more step and it's in the drink." Now that was some threat. After all, they wanted the tape to destroy it. That fact escaped Sergio, who kept inching toward me.

"Throw it over, you're gator bait, *mamalón.*" He bunched his forehead into little wrinkles and dropped into the straddle-leg stance, feet wide apart facing front, knees slightly bent, hands on hips, an attack position.

My move, but what to do? If your life is circumscribed by the four walls of the courthouse, your conduct is regulated by a myriad of rules. You become, in a word, civilized. You are not accustomed to dealing with those whose only rules are their own. In the swamp there is no court of appeal, no petition for rehearing. You depend either on the mercy of the one wielding the biggest stick, or on your own wits and strength. Of course, if I had any brains, I'd have a gun, not a product liability video, stashed in the briefcase.

The briefcase.

"Take it," I offered, extending the thin case across my body. Sergio relaxed, reached for the handle, and I brought it around, a tight backhand swing with a full follow-through. Three hundred dollars of Schlesinger Brothers leather caught him flush on the nose. He yelped, and a torrent of red spurted over both of us.

Sergio fell back against the railing, stunned, blood streaming over his sleeveless muscle shirt, looking far worse than he probably was. I watched Orlando, waiting for his move. The big guy still blocked the ramp. A concrete pillar came through the center of the deck, supporting the slab above. If he rushed me, he would have to choose one side or the other. I would go around the pillar the other way and down the ramp. But he just stood there, not moving, holding his ground like a defensive end unwilling to be faked out on a misdirection play.

And here was Sergio, swiping at his nose, his eyes teary but just as mean. "Orlando. Fuck up his knees."

My knees were already fucked up. Two cartilage scrapings through the scope, one major-league scar thanks to a ligament tear.

Sergio leaned his head back, trying to stop the flow of blood. His voice was thick. "Fuck him up good, Orlando, then throw his ass to the gators."

Sometimes it is best to turn an apparent weakness into your strength. Here was Br'er Wolf threatening to throw me into the briar patch. I leaned over the railing, stretched high and let go with a hook shot, sliding the briefcase onto the deck above me. Then I hopped over the railing, took a breath, and dropped toward the malevolent swamp.

I don't know how long it takes to plummet sixty feet. Ask Newton or Galileo or one of those guys. But it's long enough to do a lot of thinking. If an alligator wants to have you for dinner, do you smack him in the snout? Or is that a shark? I thought of Susan Corrigan, the lovely tough-talking Susan Corrigan who cared for me and worried about me and now would be left without me. And then I felt the splash.

And went under.

Deep.

Never touched bottom, and a long way up.

Warm and mucky. Brown algae clung to my legs. Leaves stuck in my hair.

I was treading water, kicking off my wing tips, swiveling my head, picking up a thousand sounds, birds fluttering away, a splash on a far bank. Something bumped my leg and I jumped. Jumping is hard to do while treading water, but I popped up like a jack-in-the-box, then fell back against the branch that had impersonated an alligator.

I heard something. A hiss like the air brakes of a bus. Behind me, not six feet away, were two nostrils exhaling spray and two eyes exuding menace above a flat, broad snout. All that was visible. The flat eyes locked on mine. The hissing grew louder. He didn't like me in his territory. That made two of us.

I started doing the backstroke. Slow, smooth strokes with my head up so I could watch him. More like Esther Williams than Mark Spitz. When I was twenty yards away, I turned over, and did a wild Australian crawl until I got to the bank. Shouts in Spanish, the sounds of leather on concrete clomping down the ramp.

The bank was muddy and I lost my balance, slipping back into the water, trying to remember to breathe again. As I reached for the stalk of a leather fern, a large, strong hand swallowed mine and dragged me out. Now what?

Wheezing, I looked up into the face of a huge black man who now had me by the arm.

"You the lawyer?" he asked.

"Why, you need one?"

"You must be. She said you make lousy jokes."

She. Another of the widow's henchmen.

Then I recognized him. Two hundred sixty-five pounds of coal jammed into blue jeans, narrow waist rising to shoulders the width of a two-car garage. Stand leeward of him, you'd stay dry in a hurricane. Unlike some football linemen, there was no trace of fat. Six thousand calories a day burned off on the practice field and the weight room. Huge, yet Tyrone Hambone Washington moved with the grace of a dancer. He could bull rush an offensive tackle onto his backside, or with that high arm motion, swim by him. Strength and speed.

The big man wiped his hands on his jeans. "The little lady sportswriter said you might need some help. So here I am. All her good pub got me AFC first team, so I owe her one."

"Susan? Susan Corrigan sent you!"

"She say, you play some defense out here, only you don't know whether they run or they pass. Hambone's good at reading defenses. You just watch."

Sergio was down the ramp first. He stood there with front leg bent, back leg straight, left arm extended with fist up, right arm curled alongside his jaw, a little slab of evil. His nose had stopped bleeding, but his muscle shirt was splattered with red.

Washington looked at him and said, "Shee-it, every little fucker in this town thinks he's Chuck-frigging-Norris. But you, shitface, you look like chuck meat to me."

"Negro hijo de puta—"

Washington's forehead seemed to drop over his eyes like a knight securing his visor before the joust. "Whadid the little Cube say?"

"Something uncomplimentary about your mother," I interpreted helpfully. "Don't think he wants you to marry his sister, either."

"Shee-it. His *seester* pull the train for every brother in Liberty City. She crazy about USDA government inspected, prime cut, Grade-A African beef."

Sergio had forgotten all about the videotape and about me. Now it was personal. Orlando watched from his perch on the ramp. He was good at watching.

"*Singao,* I keel you now," Sergio spat at Tyrone, "with my bare hands."

"Anytime, you Cuboid fag, body-building steroid-sucking cornholing midget. And stop pickin' your nose with your elbow, it won't bleed so much."

"Filthy *Negro mamalón.*"

"You gotta choice, Jose. Either git the fuck outa here now, or I'll drop kick your ass back to Havana."

I wanted to tell Sergio not to get excited, that Tyrone Hambone Washington probably says worse things to offensive linemen every week. In some quarters, his banter would be considered good-natured locker room joshing. Apparently Sergio was not well versed in this form of humor. Though his mouth was closed, a guttural noise came gurgling up from deep within him, a garbage disposal trying to digest a kitchen fork.

Seconds ticked by. Behind us, I heard a gator slip back into the water. The sun had dropped beneath the horizon, and a faint orange glow provided our only light. In minutes, we would be enveloped by the blackness of the prehistoric slough.

Sergio tensed his arms, flexed his shoulders. Hambone Washington stood with feet spread, arms loosely at his sides. Finally, the eruption. With a banzai charge, Sergio launched himself into the air, a jumping side kick. As he did so, he yelled, *"Tobi yoko-geri!"* His right foot was five feet off the ground, aimed at Washington's Adam's apple. A chunky Baryshnikov sailing through the air.

Tyrone Hambone Washington was on the balls of his feet. At the last second, he stepped deftly to one side, a small step, and moved his head to the left, like the young Muhammad Ali dodging a punch. "Tofu Yoko Ono," he said.

Sergio flew by him with perfect form and landed in the muddy sawgrass. I didn't have time to watch the rest. As Sergio drew an eight-inch stiletto from the waistband of his pants, Orlando came at me with the baseball bat. I stood there, sopping wet and barefoot, watching the pinch hitter, and not possessed of any particularly bright ideas. When Orlando was thirty feet away, I stooped at the base of a coconut palm and grabbed a yellow coconut, still in its husk, big as a volleyball and lots harder.

I heaved the coconut at Orlando. He swung and caught a piece of it. Foul ball. Strike one.

He kept advancing, triceps flexing with each warm-up swing, belly jiggling. Unlike Sergio, he was expressionless. Cold, black eyes that were all business. The mud smacked under his leather boots as he advanced. I backed up slowly, letting him close a little of the distance. Twenty feet away I flung a high, hard one with another coconut. He ducked. High and away. Count even at one and one.

This time he stayed put and I had time to scoop up a smooth round one that fit nicely in my hand. Made a motion as if to throw, held up, then came at him with a submarine pitch, an upward trajectory that caught him right in the shin. A satisfying *crack,* but he didn't drop the bat. He leaned on it like a crutch, and I came at him. Four giant steps, then, out of a crouch, shoulders square, legs driving, I made the tackle. Picture perfect. Head up, arms wrapping him, running through him, my shoulder catching the point of his chin. He went down and lost three yards.

I turned around in time to see Tyrone tossing Sergio's knife into the pond. I hadn't seen how Tyrone had disarmed him, but Sergio's right arm was hanging at an unusual angle. Then Tyrone scooped up the smaller man by the seat of his pants and dragged him across the path.

Sergio was moaning, but Tyrone was short on sympathy. "Shee-it, just a little shoulder separation. When it happens to me, they jam it back into place, tape me up, and I don't miss but one series."

Sergio did not seem to be NFL material. As he hobbled away, he turned to me and said weakly, "I owe you one, *hombre.*"

"And I know you're good for it." I started up the ramp to retrieve my briefcase.

"Now git!" Tyrone ordered, and the two men took off, wobbling, limping, and cursing until they disappeared into the darkness.

PAUL LEVINE

* * *

Charlie Riggs was tending a fire and scalding peanut oil in an iron skillet when I pulled up at his fishing cabin just off Tamiami Trail a few miles east of Shark Valley. The old upholstery in the 442 was smeared with mud, and I made squishing sounds as I eased out and walked barefoot into the campsite.

"Jacob, where you been?" Charlie Riggs didn't sound alarmed. "Either I'm seeing things or you've got a water lily in your ear."

"Been up to my ass in alligators, Charlie."

"I do believe there's a story in this. You'll find a bucket, a towel, and some shorts on the porch. Then tell me."

I cleaned up and told him. As I did, Charlie fixed dinner. He bent over a slab of pine with a nail stuck through it. He jammed a Glades bullfrog onto the nail, piercing its belly, then made a quick incision with a knife, and with a pair of pliers, he pulled off the pants of the frog.

"You like frog legs?"

"Like eating them better than watching them prepared."

Charlie shrugged. "Thirty years in the ME's office, I don't get queasy about much."

He heated some fresh tomatoes in the skillet, poured milk over the frogs' legs, dragged them through seasoned flour, then sauteed the whole mess in a sauce fragrant with butter and garlic.

"Love that country cooking," I said.

"Country nothin'. This is *cuisse de grenouilles provençale.*"

We ate and I talked, Charlie listening silently. Finally I asked him what to do.

"I suggest we visit Susan at once," he said. "This has taken on a whole new dimension. Those two thugs might have killed you. They were certainly going to hurt you."

"What's this have to do with Susan?"

"They must know she gave you the tape. For whatever reason, they seem to place great importance on getting it. Frankly, I don't know why."

"That's easy, Charlie. First, it's embarrassing to the widow, prancing around with three men. Second, it contradicts her sworn deposition. She denied having an affair with Roger."

Charlie licked his fingers, sticky with garlic butter. "You may be right, but I get the feeling there's something more to the videotape than that. Regardless, the widow apparently will do anything to get it. Maybe harm anyone who's seen it. Shall we leave?"

We shall, I said. Not really believing Susan was in danger. But making a mental note to watch the videotape again, to look for something. Something Melanie Corrigan didn't want us to see, something other than her swiveling bottom.

22

FOR WANT OF A NAIL

We tried calling Susan Corrigan from a gas station on Tamiami Trail. No answer at the cabana. We roared toward town, an evening thunderstorm slanting gray torrents across the two-lane road. For a while we listened to the machine gun rhythm of the rain on our canvas top. Cement trucks lumbered along, tossing filthy spray over our windshield. Charlie was thinking so I kept quiet. Then we argued.

"Your strategy won't work," Charlie Riggs said. "You want the jury to believe that Melanie Corrigan and this martial arts thug killed Philip Corrigan, then framed Roger to cover it up, right?"

"Sure, if you can tell me how they did it, how whatever they did ended up looking like succinylcholine poisoning."

Charlie Riggs stroked his beard. "Who says it looks like succinylcholine?"

"The ME says, choline and succinic acid found in the brain and liver."

"But none around the needle track in the buttocks?"

"Right."

"Hmmm," Charlie Riggs said, tamping tobacco into a corncob pipe. "Well?"

"Regardless whether the succinylcholine played a role in Philip Corrigan's death, your strategy is flawed. The timing is way off. What motive would they have for framing Salisbury now? It would only draw attention to themselves."

"Plenty of motive once we dug up the body. They knew something was going on, needed to plant the drug and get Roger charged."

Charlie concentrated on lighting his pipe. "Foolish. They'd be better off sitting it out."

I laughed. "You're too logical. You're smarter than they are, Charlie, but you're forgetting one thing. The malpractice suit was intended to blame Roger or at least focus attention on the aneurysm. It's what Susan called the old fumblerooski."

"The what?"

"A misdirection play. A plaintiff's verdict would establish the aneurysm as the cause of death and close the case. Even the defense verdict was no problem for them because the evidence still showed an aneurysm killed Corrigan. The jury just didn't blame Roger Salisbury for it. But then we grab Corrigan's body, and all of a sudden, they need a fall guy in case the tests are positive for poisoning. They break into Susan's cabana to get the drug, then plant it and get the murder indictment against Roger. Everything's coming up roses until they learn a nurse can place both of them in the hospital room after Roger left. Plus they know we have the videotape."

Charlie's face was shadowed in the lights of oncoming traffic. "No good. The video establishes Roger's motive for the murder, his lust for Melanie."

"But it also shows Sergio was just as bewitched, bothered, and bewildered and therefore would have the same motive to kill Corrigan. The tape furnishes reasonable doubt as to which of Melanie's admirers did him in. It also shoots some sizable holes in Melanie's grieving widow routine."

Charlie shot me a new look, one within an inch or two of respect. "If you're right, Jake, they're panicking. They know you still have the videotape. And that you must have gotten it from Susan." He thought about it a moment. "You might step on it a bit."

I was already doing seventy-five, but we were still half an hour from Susan's place. The rain came in gusts, sweeping out of the Glades, washing across the blacktop. Airboats were tied up in canals along Tamiami Trail, the operators sitting on the bank under thatched roofs, waiting for a break in the weather to head out for nighttime frogging. The Olds 442 roared eastward, the wet pavement hissing under its tires. I took my eyes off the road long enough to turn toward Charlie. "What's their next step? What will they try? Put the data into that computer on top your shoulders and give me a printout."

Riggs shrugged and sucked on his pipe. "I haven't the foggiest."

"Not a clue?"

"Nothing besides mere guesses. What I do is figure out things that already have happened, the hows, whos, wheres, and whens of death. Not even the whys. And you want 'What happens next.' No can do. Look at this sudden storm. Science can't even accurately predict the weather past seventy-two hours. How can we predict what men and women, perhaps psychotic men and women, will do when we have so little information compared to the data we have about pressure systems, winds, moisture, temperatures?"

I was quiet again, and Charlie blew some cherry-flavored smoke at me. "If I had to guess," he said, "it's that you're in some danger. You're the one unraveling the web they've spun. But then again, if you lose the trial, they're home free. Why should they risk it all by going after you?"

"But I know they'll try something. Melanie won't let it rest. I can predict that with virtual certainty."

"Your intuition tells you that, but your data is woefully insufficient. There is no way you can know thousands of incidents in her life that make her what she is so as to predict what she'll do."

"Whatever they are, they've made her evil."

Riggs smiled. "Correct. *Nemo repente fuit turpissimus*. No one becomes wicked suddenly. But knowing the woman is evil adds little to the equation insofar as predicting her behavior. Take my analogy to the weather. You would think that with our satellites and computers and sensitive equipment, we could gather enough data to predict the weather. Well we can't because our instruments don't collect enough information. We'll leave something out, millions of somethings out, and our predictions will be catastrophically wrong even if we leave out only a minuscule bit of data. The scientific name for that is sensitive dependence on initial conditions."

"But theoretically," I mused, "if you had enough wind gauges and satellite pictures and electronic doodads, you'd know all there is to know about the weather, and if you knew it enough times, you could see what it did the last time conditions were just the same, and you could predict weather for all eternity. So if you knew enough background about a person, you could predict his future acts."

Charlie Riggs paused to relight his pipe, an academic's trick of buying time. "For a human being, there are far too many events and no way to record them objectively. Even with the weather, Jake, you would need to know everything, the size and location of every cloud, the measurement of every bird's flight, the beat of every butterfly's wings."

"Butterflies, too?"

"The flap of a butterfly's wings in Brazil can set off a tornado in Texas."

"Metaphorically speaking," I said.

"No. Literally. It's part of the basis for the new science called chaos."

"Butterflies and chaos?" I said doubtfully. "An infinitesimal action radically affects mammoth events."

Charlie Riggs smiled, the teacher happy when a slow student catches on. "That's right. Just like the poem:

For want of a nail, the shoe was lost;
For want of a shoe, the horse was lost;
For want of a horse, the rider was lost;

And so on."

"I remember," I told him. "The battle and then the kingdom. All lost."

"Indeed."

I looked out at the rainswept street. "Then I'd better find the damn nail."

Except for the spotlights and the gentle roar of the waterfall, the Corrigan house was dark and silent on its hill. The rain had stopped just east of the Turnpike. In Gables Estates, not a drop had fallen. We jogged around the lighted path to the cabana. The screen door was unlocked, lights on inside, but no Susan. I walked into the small bedroom. Pale blue shorts and a faded Northwestern T-shirt had been flung onto an unmade bed, running shoes and socks tossed into a corner. In the galley kitchen, the oven was on four-fifty, a frozen vegetable platter was defrosting on the counter. An open can of Diet Pepsi sat on the counter. Half-empty and still cool to the touch.

We hurried onto the patio. The *Cory* was tied to the dock, lines tight, cabins dark. The pool lights were on, blue water shimmering in the night air.

The pool.

I don't know why I ran. I don't know what I felt. I don't know how I knew, but I knew.

Susan Corrigan was floating near the far end, facedown, wearing a black racing suit. I ran along the side and dived in. The taste of salt water filled my mouth. In three strokes I was beside her. With one hand, I grabbed a shoulder and turned her over. In the eerie light reflected from the water, her face was an unearthly blue, her features plastic. Her eyes were open but lifeless.

I carried her up the steps, her head slumped limply on my shoulder. A thin layer of white foam covered her lips. I gently set her down on the pool deck, Charlie helping with his hands under her back. I tore off the goggles, and my left hand lifted her neck to clear the air passage. My right hand pinched her nostrils to keep the air from escaping. Then I took a deep breath and sealed my mouth over hers. I blew hard, emptying my lungs, filling hers. Several short bursts, then one breath every five seconds. I looked for signs of life and saw none. Her breathing might have been stopped for two minutes or two hours. I couldn't tell.

Charlie knelt alongside me, letting me know with his silence that I was doing the right thing. My movements were automatic. Acting without thinking, doing what could be done. A volcanic mixture of anger and desperation fueled me. "Don't die!" I shouted at her. "Don't you die on me."

I covered her cold lips again with my mouth. I blew into her mouth again and again, trying to infuse her with oxygen, to give her some of my life. I leaned my ear to her lips.

Nothing.

I tried to find a pulse.

Nothing.

I sat on my haunches, placed one hand on her chest, just above the sternum, and pushed down hard with the other hand, trying to kick-start the heart. I kept pushing, up-down, up-down.

Nothing.

My heart was hammering. Hers was still. I paused long enough to choke back the helplessness that rose inside me. Charlie had run inside the cabana to call Fire-Rescue. I prayed for any sign of life, for a spark I could light. Still nothing. I went back to the mouth-to-mouth but it didn't work, so again I worked on the chest. I pushed harder and two ribs cracked under my hands. It didn't matter. Dead women feel no pain.

When we both knew it was over, Charlie Riggs put an arm around me and guided me to a chaise lounge. He brought two blankets from the cabana, covered Susan with one and me with the other. A numbness hit me, nailing me to the spot.

My body unable to move, the mind took over, rocketing past a hundred scenes, a thousand regrets. I had never told her what she meant to me. Why hadn't I just said that I'd never met anyone like her, a woman who was smart and sassy and strong and who thought she loved me. And died thinking I was a macho jerk. Thinking right. Dying because of me.

The numbness turned to pain.

She had been right about everything and died without knowing it. She had fretted for me, big dumb lucky stiff me who goes into the swamp and comes out wet but whole. I could have told her how much I cared, could have looked into those dark eyes and said, "Susan Corrigan, I love you and cherish you and want to be with you, now and always." But I'd held it back. And now she would never know. A step too slow, Jake Lassiter, then and now.

Charlie Riggs found a switch and turned on a set of mercury vapor lamps. The patio was doused with a ghastly green light. He called Fire-Rescue again, this time canceling the ambulance, and asking for the police. While we waited, Charlie scoured the pool deck. He found her thick-lensed glasses on a table, neatly folded, waiting for her return. Those silly glasses. I turned them over in my hands, fondled them. Charlie started to say something about fingerprints, then backed away.

"I'll look around for evidence," he said. "You stay put."

Charlie examined a pink beach towel draped over a chair. He looked in the shrubs; he crawled on hands and knees around a fifty-yard perimeter; he reached into the skimmer of the pool and came up with a handful of dead leaves; and he sniffed and tasted the water from the pool.

I watched him, letting the sorrow build inside me. When two

uniformed Coral Gables policemen arrived, Charlie Riggs gave them a step-by-step description, the time we arrived, our efforts to revive her, his inspection of the scene. I sat, still wet, still holding the glasses. Beginning to shiver.

"Is the ME sending someone?" Charlie asked.

The sergeant shook his head. "No sign of foul play. We try not to drag 'em out to the scene unless it's an apparent homicide."

"She didn't drown!" I heard myself shout across the patio. "She could swim the English Channel. I want an autopsy done, but only by Doc Riggs."

The sergeant looked at me, then asked his partner to check out the house. The younger cop shrugged and walked slowly toward the darkened fortress. No hurry, just a routine job, a drowning in a pool.

The sergeant sat down on the end of my chaise lounge. It creaked under his weight. He had a sunken chest, a beer belly, and was close to retirement. Coral Gables cops aren't the hard guys you find downtown. In the Gables, cops fish too many cats out of trees to get that cold-eyed look. Expensive cats and expensive trees.

The sergeant patted my leg through the blanket. "We take the body to the morgue. We gotta do that under section four-oh-six-point-one-one."

Charlie Riggs nodded. "Subsection one-ay-one. Then the ME determines whether to do the autopsy."

The sergeant looked back at me. "I've known Doc Riggs for twenty years, and we won't write it up, but if you want, why don't we let him have a quick look right here?"

My eyes pleaded with Charlie, and he said okay. The sergeant held a three-foot Kel-Lite and Charlie examined the body. He cupped his hands on her head, felt her skull and neck. He checked underneath her fingernails. He looked at her legs and arms.

The younger cop headed back to the patrol car to call in. The sergeant lit a cigarette and walked toward the dock to admire the *Cory,* maybe comparing it to a seventeen-foot Whaler he'd like to share with three other cops.

"Jake, I'm going to have to take off her swimsuit," Charlie Riggs said. I nodded and walked away.

After a few minutes, I heard him say, "No stab wounds, no bullet holes, no apparent loss of blood. No contusions or marks of any kind. No injection punctures. Not even an indication of a struggle."

The sergeant had come back from the dock. "A drowning, Doc. Just a drowning."

I turned around. "Charlie, please keep looking."

The other cop returned from the patrol car and told the sergeant they had to check out a ringing burglar alarm on Old Cutler Road.

"If it's the old Spanish house at seventy-three hundred, there's no hurry," the sergeant said. "Goes off every time the humidity's up, which is every week." In a few minutes, they would be roaming the suburbs, pulling over cars with missing taillights. Susan Corrigan would be just another statistic. *Accidental death by drowning.* Happens all the time.

The minutes dragged by. I watched the big house and concocted a vicious fantasy to vent my rage. Breaking down a door. Looking for them, the widow and the karate thug. Hurting them, killing them. Nice and slow.

Charlie motioned to me. "Jake, come here a second. My old eyes are failing."

The flashlight was shining on Susan's left shoulder. "Do you see any discoloration there?" he asked.

I shook my head wearily. "Maybe a faint pink. Maybe just skin color under the tan. Hard to tell."

"Hmmm," Charlie Riggs mumbled. He went into the cabana and came out with a plastic sandwich bag. Then, with a pocket knife, he cut a little square of skin from the shoulder and put it in the bag. Deep inside me, I felt every tiny slash.

"Jake, how about here on the leg?"

Same thing. A little pinkness, nothing more. I shrugged helplessly, and Charlie did some more slicing.

At the edge of the pool, the water rippled and slid under the lights. I remembered the breeze from the Gulf slapping palm fronds against

Granny's little house, the sweetness of Susan under the quilt. I wanted a second chance, to tell her what had stayed locked inside me. I stood and stared into the pool, motionless.

Charlie Riggs came over and gave me a fatherly hug. Then he looked down at the pool. "Salt water. You don't see many saltwater pools these days."

23

VOIR DIRE

"Mrs. Goldfarb, do you believe that old expression, where there's smoke, there's fire?"

Reba Goldfarb eyed me suspiciously from her perch in the front row of the jury box. She hadn't gotten settled yet, was still patting her ice-blue hair, locking it into a 1950s pompadour. She looked toward the judge for help, shrugged, and said, "Maybe there's fire, maybe just a teapot blowing its lid."

"Exactly," I said. "Things are not always as they seem. And just because Dr. Roger Salisbury is charged by the state with a crime doesn't mean he's guilty, does it?"

"Goodness no," she agreed, smiling, picking up the rhythm.

"And this indictment," I said, holding the blue-bordered document at arm's length as if it smelled of rotten eggs, "this piece of paper, this scrap, is not proof of guilt, has no more dignity than a grocery list—"

"Objection!" Abe Socolow was on his feet.

"Sustained," Judge Crane declared without emotion. "This is *voir dire,* not argument, Mr. Lassiter."

During trial I will argue over *Good morning.*

"Your Honor, I'll rephrase the question. Mrs. Goldfarb, do you recognize that Roger Salisbury, as he sits here today, is as innocent as a newborn child?"

Ignoring the concept of original sin.

She nodded.

"That he is cloaked with a presumption of innocence, that he does not have to prove anything, that the burden of proving his guilt is on the government?"

"I heard that before," she conceded, nodding again. She had seen enough television to know this stuff. My kind of juror, willing to believe that intrigue and incompetence frequently nail the wrong guy.

I liked her. Roger Salisbury liked her. She visited doctors regularly, an internist, a podiatrist, a chiropractor, and a dentist. She was Jewish, and defense lawyers from Clarence Darrow on down liked that. An old saw. Put Mediterranean types on your jury if you're defending. Jews and Italians are more sympathetic. Minorities, too. Blacks are suspicious of the police and will cut you a break in a close case. Hispanics used to fall into that group, but in these parts, they're the majority and may have lost the feel for the underdog. Keep Germans, Poles, and Swedes off the panel. Too harsh and rigid.

Anyway, that's what the book says. But nearly every defense lawyer shakes his head over a black social worker or schoolteacher who ended up leading the posse for the state. And nearly every prosecutor remembers a Teutonic male who probably once wore a Luger but carried the banner for the defense in the jury room. Go figure.

I needed Reba Goldfarb. I had lost Deborah Grossman, Dominick Russo, and Philip Freidin. All three had said that they wouldn't vote for the death penalty under any circumstances. Socolow challenged them for cause, saving his precious peremptory challenges while I spent seven of mine getting rid of guys who had blood in their eyes.

It isn't fair. Talking about the penalty phase of the case before the trial begins. Mocking the presumption of innocence. But it's legal.

"Are you in favor of capital punishment?" Abe Socolow now asked Earl Pottenger, an airline mechanic.

"Yes sir!"

Hoo boy. This guy's ready to pull the switch. Ayatollah Pottenger. Socolow smiled and moved on to a heavyset black woman.

"Mrs. Dickson, if you find the defendant guilty of murder in the first degree, and if the state convinces you that the crime is sufficiently heinous, could you recommend to Judge Crane that he impose the death penalty?"

"Ah don't rightly know," Clara Dickson said, squinting up at him.

"Do you have moral or religious objections to the death penalty?"

"It's against the preachin' ah believe in."

"Challenge for cause," Socolow said.

"Granted," Judge Crane ruled.

I stood. "Objection, Your Honor. Dr. Salisbury is being deprived of a jury of his peers. We won't have a cross section of the populace if the state systematically excludes those with moral or religious objections to the death penalty."

"Denied. The Supreme Court ruled on this in the Witt case. The state is entitled to a death-qualified jury."

I shot back. "What's Roger Salisbury entitled to, just death?"

Oh, that was dumb. Judge Crane's long, sad face sharpened and he motioned me to the bench with a tiny wave of his gavel. Socolow slid silently behind me, his invisible smile a knife in my back.

"Mr. Lassiter, I don't make the rules, I just apply them," the judge said. "Now, one more remark like that in the jury's presence and I'll hold you in contempt. *Verste?*"

"Understood, Your Honor."

We would have a bloodthirsty, gung-ho, hang-em-high jury because the law allowed it. But I wasn't doing Roger Salisbury any good whining about it. I would just try to keep some people on the panel who neither belonged to the National Rifle Association nor folded their bodies into tight balls when I asked my questions.

So here I was, bobbing and weaving, trying to seat twelve honest men and women without itchy trigger fingers. Not that I wanted to be picking a jury. I didn't want to be doing anything except feeling sorry for myself. The three weeks since her death had been a blur. Preparing for trial, arguing with Socolow, waiting for some word about Susan from Charlie Riggs. At night, when sleep came, it was filled with dreams. An expanse of water, iridescent blue, a calm seductive lagoon. But when I dived in, the water thickened into a gelatinous muck and I sank to the bottom, gasping for air. Anonymous hands rescued me and dragged me to the beach where a laughing Roger Salisbury bent over me, giant syringe in hand.

Waking at dawn, I drifted uneasily toward consciousness, vaguely aware of an undefined pain. As my eyes focused on the light, the pain took shape, a vision of Susan Corrigan. Pretty and smart and tough. And dead.

Charlie Riggs had pulled some strings, and the ME's office performed an autopsy. Salt water in the lungs. A pinkish foam in the airway. Absolute proof, Charlie said, that Susan was alive when she stepped into the pool. If she'd been killed and dumped there, the lungs wouldn't produce the foam. Death by drowning on the certificate. Nothing to dispute it.

It was murder, I told Abe Socolow. He didn't buy it, asked for proof. I told him about the cabana break-in, the theft of the drug, the widow clamoring for the videotape. Proof, he reminded me, consisted of witnesses and physical evidence. Then I told him of my run-in with Sergio and his pal with the baseball bat.

He laughed. "Ambush at Shark Valley. Sell it to Hollywood."

"Your star witness set me up."

"Not the way I heard it," Socolow said, poking a finger at me. "She says you tried to extort her. If she testifies, you play the tape. She doesn't testify, you give her the tape. Gonna get your balls whacked, Jake, you don't watch out. Could bust you for obstruction right now."

But he wouldn't. Because I was his buddy, he said. He wanted a copy of the tape. Fine with me, I told him, because it's defense exhibit number one.

He laughed again. "What's its relevance, that Melanie Corrigan is a sword swallower?"

"Pure impeachment. Lying under oath. On deposition, she denied the affair with Roger."

He wasn't impressed. "Nice try. She denied banging the doc *after* her marriage to Corrigan. The videotape was premarriage, so no lie on deposition, no impeachment. I'm filing a motion *in limine* to keep it out."

Judge Crane reserved ruling on the motion. Said he wanted to see the videotape. A couple of times. So did the clerk, the bailiffs, the probation officers, and everybody else within ten blocks of the Justice Building.

Without the tape, what would I have? Charlie Riggs saying that Corrigan died of an aneurysm, not succinylcholine. But no suspect to feed to the jury in place of Roger Salisbury. It would come down to a swearing match, beautiful widow versus spurned lover. Who said what to whom? Where did the drug come from? Who did what in Philip Corrigan's hospital room? Would the jurors even listen to Charlie Riggs's technical explanation of a bursting aorta? Probably not. Not with a black valise, two hypodermics, and a deadly drug staring them in the face.

* * *

Socolow had a tight little smile on his hawkish face as Judge Crane gave the newly empaneled jurors their preliminary instructions. Don't discuss the case among yourselves or with family members and friends. Don't speak to the witnesses or lawyers. Don't read the newspapers or watch television reports about the case.

Do jurors have the willpower not to follow *their* cases in the press? In a bribery trial a few years ago, a local columnist complained in print that the male jurors looked like they were headed for a ball game, all polo shirts and guayaberas. Next day, they all wore coats and ties.

My mind was wandering as the judge did his stuff. We would be back in the morning for opening statements. Tonight I would see Charlie Riggs. Beside me sat Roger Salisbury. Worried, a little grayer around the temples than at the first trial. His future a black hole.

"It is your solemn responsibility to determine if the state has proved its accusation beyond a reasonable doubt against this defendant," the judge gravely intoned. "Your verdict must be based solely on evidence, or lack of evidence, and the law."

I walked out of the courthouse into the blast furnace of a Miami afternoon. The blinding sun bounced ferociously off the marble steps. Thick fumes from the buses fought to rise through the soggy air.

There is no industrial smog in Miami. No steel mills, no oil refineries. Heavy industry is cocaine processing; high technology is money laundering. But a million cars in the shimmering heat add their own color to the horizon. Most days a fine red haze sprouts from the expressways and hovers over the city, hugging the ribbons of I-95 from downtown Miami northward to Fort Lauderdale. Not a thick smog, just enough airborne particles to add a counterfeit glitter to the sky, a reddish breast on the feathery clouds drifting over backlit beaches. One good blow, a cold front from the northwest, and the muck would be shoved out to sea.

But no more cold fronts. Not for six months. Until then, just broiling days and steaming nights. Purgatory for those who inhabit the swamp. My own fire burned deep inside. A score to settle. A woman had died. A woman I loved. I made a vow. When I knew for sure the how and the who of it, someone else would die, too.

24

VENOM

It had taken Charlie Riggs two weeks, but he had figured it out. Just as I knew he would. He kept it from me another week, not wanting to disturb me during trial preparations. But I badgered him and finally he told me to meet him at the morgue.

By the time I finished preparing my opening statement for the morning, it was nearly midnight. Charlie was waiting for me in the parking lot outside the new brick and glass building that looked less like a morgue than a modern office complex for a computer software company.

He puffed his pipe and scratched at his beard. I recognized the look. Acute discomfort. He took off his patched-up glasses, wiped them on his short-sleeve white shirt, and put them back on where they rode askew like a sailboat heeling in a strong wind.

"This won't be easy for you."

"Let's get it over with," I said.

The morgue was quiet. Two sheriff's deputies were hanging around the waiting area, drinking coffee, filling out forms after bringing in two bodies, a middle-aged man and his wife. The man had carved her up with a kitchen knife, then jammed a shotgun under his own chin and pulled the trigger with his big toe.

"Least he done the right thing," one cop said to the other.

"Yeah, saved us a lot of crap, blowing himself away."

A skinny kid with long, greasy hair in a ponytail sat at the reception desk, working the overnight shift. He leaned back in a swivel chair with his feet on a modern oak desk flipping the pages on a porno magazine and giggling. He kept sticking his hand in a huge bag of French fries, rooting around and popping them into his mouth, three at a time. He wore a green hospital smock and the shit-eating grin of the yahoo young. His nametag read *Curly.*

Charlie Riggs cleared his throat. Curly didn't look up. Making sure the county got no bargains on his minimum wage.

I rapped my knuckles on the kid's desk.

"Yeah?" A tone of mild annoyance, a face that needed a prescription for Retin-A.

I would have said, *Whatever happened to may I help you?* Charlie is more circumspect. He said, "We're here to see some tissue samples Dr. Kallan left for us."

Curly scowled. "Gotta name?"

I figured him for about twenty-one. If they're still sullen and whiny when they pass nineteen, they probably always will be. Another half century of bitching and moaning about bosses and girlfriends and how the other guys got all the luck.

"Riggs. Charlie Riggs."

Curly dropped the skin magazine and looked at a clipboard. "No stiff name of Riggs. Got a Rawlings."

Charlie smiled. "No, I'm Riggs. Dr. Charles W. Riggs."

The name meant nothing to him. Probably never read a newspaper, didn't know the building had a plaque honoring his nighttime guest. The kid likely was one of the astounding number of young people who can't name the century in which the Civil War was fought, much less the battlefields. On geography tests, they list Montana as an island in the Pacific.

"The deceased is Susan Corrigan," Charlie Riggs said, far more politely than the kid deserved. "Dr. Kallan was kind enough to make some slides of skin tissue."

Curly looked back at the clipboard. The month's guest list.

"Corrigan," he said. "Sure, Number eight-nine-dash-two-fourteen. Third cooler, first row."

His vacant eyes brightened. "Hey. Black-haired bitch. Love a dark bush, myself. Best looking piece of meat we've had . . ."

Charlie had a lot of quick left in him. Stepped wordlessly between us. I brushed him aside with a gentle forearm. Then my left hand found its way to the kid's neck, covered his Adam's apple, and squeezed, lifting him out of the chair. I didn't tell the hand what to do. It just squeezed and lifted. At the same time, the right hand balled itself into a good-sized fist and started coming over the top toward his pointy chin. From a deep tunnel, I heard the faraway voice of Charlie Riggs, "No, Jake!"

The right fist stopped short, uncoiled itself and slapped the kid hard. Once, twice, three times, red splotches shooting across his face. Eyes wide and white now, a scared rabbit. His feet were six inches off the floor when the left hand let him go. His knees buckled, and he crumpled to the desk, clipboard clattering at my feet. Charlie helped him up, mumbling apologies.

I walked away, head down.

Big hero.

Big tough guy.

Slapping around a pimply punk with a noodle neck and a garbage mouth. Wrapped a little too tight, are we now?

The two cops had watched it all without moving. Where they come from, an assault doesn't mean much unless automatic weapons are involved. I paced in the reception area, trying to close the spigot on the adrenaline flow. One cop looked at me and shrugged. Midnight in Miami, the crazies out. Anyway, what harm could a guy do in the morgue? Wake the dead?

The cops resumed talking, bellyaching about arresting hookers with AIDS.

"Ain't gonna wear gloves," one said. "Don't help, they bite you in the ankle."

"I hear you can't get it from somebody giving you a blowjob."

The first cop laughed. "What cocksucker told you that?"

The kid hadn't moved, but his eyes followed me across the reception area. Charlie finished apologizing and led me through the doors into a huge, brightly lit, cool room with a faintly antiseptic smell. The walls were covered with blue tile. Steel dissecting tables on wheels were rolled up to sinks. Hoses were coiled at regular intervals along the walls, and the tile floor was marked with drains.

Charlie was poking around in a refrigerator loaded with body parts and various tissues and liquids. Along one wall were five huge coolers loaded with corpses.

"What now?" I asked.

"I saw something on the skin sample I made at the scene. But my microscope isn't powerful enough, so I couldn't be sure. Dr. Kallan was my assistant for fifteen years. He took some other samples from the shoulder area, and . . . here they are."

He pulled out half a dozen slides and walked me through the procedure. If he could make a positive ID through the scope, we wouldn't have to enter Cooler Three, Row One. If he couldn't find whatever it was, we'd have to bring Susan's body out and make new dissections. My mind conjured up her body, already butchered in the autopsy, the parts tucked back inside. I told myself it wasn't Susan in the cooler, just the package that had held her spirit.

Charlie led me to an adjoining lab, where he climbed on a high laboratory stool, took off his cockeyed glasses, and peered through the lens of a high-powered microscope. Seconds later, he shook his head. He tried another slide. Nothing.

"What did you see in the samples you made?" I asked.

"I don't know, Jake. Something microscopic that disintegrated in the heat on my slide. It could be something that proves it was just a drowning. I just hope I'm not creating something from nothing—*ex nihilo nihil fit*—maybe trying too hard to prove it was an accident, to give you some peace."

He loaded another slide, took a long look, then exhaled a deep breath until it was nearly a sigh. "I thought so. Take a look, Jake."

I did. But I didn't see much, a tiny hair particle or nearly invisible twig magnified thousands of times.

"So?" I asked.

"It killed Susan," he said softly.

I looked again. "The hell is it?"

"*Physalia physalis,* one of your coelenterates, or all that's left of the one that killed Susan."

"I still don't get it."

"What you're looking at is a nematocyst, a tiny dart. Plus the remains of the sac that held the toxin. Each dart is invisible to the naked eye. She would have been stung by thousands of them, hundreds of thousands, really. The toxin is similar to cobra venom. Just about as powerful. A bad enough sting, the person goes into shock and drowns. Lots of drownings off the coast are the result of these stings. If you look at the body, nothing. No marks. So it's listed as accidental drowning. Which it is, of course. But the cause is the venom of the *Physalia physalis*."

I looked back through the barrel of the microscope. A tiny speck, that's all. But if Charlie Riggs says it's an animal's deadly dart, it is. All these years in Florida, snorkeling, scuba diving, windsurfing, and I'd never heard of a *filsailya* . . .

Charlie was still lecturing. "I don't think anybody ever got stung in a swimming pool before. Best I can figure, the Corrigans keep the water circulating from the bay. We can check it, but I'll bet there's no screen on the intake pipe. The pipe sucked water in, brought a couple of these creatures along. Susan goes for a nighttime swim. Can't see worth a darn without her glasses and swims right into one. Happens in the ocean all the time. Why not a saltwater pool? Pool bottom is painted blue. Wouldn't see the *Physalia*'s big blue sac."

Something was scratching around in the back of my mind. "What blue sac?"

"The floating sac. It stays above water. The tentacles trail underneath. They contain the darts, and when they uncoil, they shoot the toxin into the victim. The pain is intense. Horrible, really. Paralyzing. It can cripple the respiratory system and throw the victim into shock."

"A blue sac. Charlie, that sounds like a Portuguese man-of-war."

"Same thing. Forgive me for using the Latin, but it's such a beautiful language. To my ear, *Physalia physalis* sounds so much better than man-of-war or blue bottle, as we sometimes call them. Close relative of the hydroids, jellyfish, stinging corals, sea anemones."

"Man-of-war," I repeated, digging up a memory.

Charlie patted my arm and said, "I hope it's better, knowing it wasn't a murder. As Virgil wrote, *felix qui potuit rerum cognoscere causas*. Happy is he who learns the causes of things. Even if it can't bring you happiness, Jake, maybe peace."

Charlie Riggs was right. And wrong.

The man-of-war may have killed her. But it was murder just the same. Now I knew the how and the who.

Charlie was still prattling on. I interrupted him. "Melanie and Sergio killed Susan," I said, evenly and calmly. Keeping the burning rock inside.

Charlie looked puzzled. "Jake, I just said a *Physalia*—"

"I know, I know. Listen. After the malpractice trial, the two of them took a Whaler into the bay. Susan and I followed. I got as close as I could on a sailboard. It looked like they were fishing. At least they had fishing rods and Sergio was bringing something aboard with a net. But I remember this. It was one of those days the bay was covered with men-of-war. We could look up the date, I'll bet the county closed the beaches. Melanie and Sergio must have brought back some of them, kept them alive, probably in a tank on the *Cory,* then when Susan went for a swim, they dumped two or three in the pool. At night without her glasses on, goggles steamed up, she never would have seen them. Even if she managed to get to the side of the pool, Sergio could have pushed her back into the water. Before we got there, he netted the damn things and tossed them into the bay."

Still sitting on the high laboratory stool, Charlie was silent a long moment. Sifting through it. Finally he said, "It's possible. No reason it couldn't have happened. But you can never prove it. Not beyond a reasonable doubt."

"I wasn't thinking of legal niceties."

Charlie stiffened. His glasses were still on the counter next to the microscope, and he looked up at me through tired eyes. "Don't do anything foolish, Jake."

Why not? I thought. I've done lots of foolish things. Just never one that leaves you face-to-face with a death-qualified jury.

25

THE ROAD MAP

Three A.M. and wide awake. Mind buzzing, a dozen different departments tying up the lines, busy signals all round. Up front some brain cells readying for trial, still rehearsing, doing what ought to be done. Some neurons in the back running through it all, the experiences of a lifetime, roads not taken, and for now and forever, mourning the loss of Susan. Shrouding it all, a poisonous gray mist choking me with rage. Hot to inflict pain. The pain of a thousand sea creatures a thousandfold.

It was stifling in my little coral rock house in Coconut Grove. The ceiling fans were on but I was soaked. Sitting in the living room on an old sofa of Haitian cotton, more brown than its original off-white, watching rivulets of sweat track down my chest and into the top of my Jockeys. Three Grolschs didn't cool me off.

I pushed the videotape into the VCR. Same interior shots of the *Cory.* Same striptease by Melanie Corrigan, same ass-rolling act in Roger Salisbury's face. A cut, then Roger playing doctor, listening to Melanie's lungs. When she turns over, he slowly taps her ass with his thumb. Laughter all around. Then Sergio joins the party, and finally, the trick shot with Philip Corrigan shooting the scene in the overhead mirror.

Nothing there I hadn't seen before. If there was something Melanie didn't want me to see, she had little to worry about. I'd seen it all and couldn't put a handle on it. I watched it again. Nothing changed. I put my feet up on the sofa and slept for an hour. Maybe two. Then I showered, and headed to the Justice Building. Putting everything else aside, concentrating on the mission, saving a man from the electric chair.

"What I say this morning is not evidence," Abe Socolow was saying as if it were indeed evidence of momentous weight. "It is a road map, a guide as to where the evidence will go."

He was wearing a black suit. All black. No chalk stripes, no patterns. You don't see many black suits these days. Or all black ties. A white shirt. And of course, shiny black shoes. With his beakish look and sunken cheeks, Abe Socolow could have been a small-town undertaker. Or an executioner.

I wore light brown. I almost never wear it, kind of blends me into the woodwork, sandy hair and sandy suit against oak paneling. Trial lawyers always used to wear dark blues and grays, power colors. Afraid brown made them look like salesmen. Then psychologists told us we were salesmen, and brown is friendly. Ronald Reagan wore it when greeting heads of state—big cordial brown plaid or checks. For this trial, friendly brown it would be. Jake Lassiter, the jurors' pal.

Hangman or not, Abe Socolow began his opening statement in restrained and understated tones, slowly building the tempo. First he matter-of-factly described the testimony to come. He turned it up a notch when he talked about the relationship between Melanie and Roger. With motive crucial to his case, he needed the jury to believe that Roger was obsessed with Melanie and would do anything to have her.

"You will hear Mrs. Corrigan describe her long-ago relationship with the defendant," Abe Socolow said. "Yes, they had a physical relationship when she was barely out of her teens, and he already a practicing physician." Socolow shook his head knowingly. How loathsome this defendant must be. Cradle robber.

Several jurors leaned forward. Eating it up. Socolow continued, "The affair ended, and as frequently happens, their paths crossed again. The defendant tried to talk Mrs. Corrigan into leaving her husband, tried to rekindle the flame that still burned within him, but not her. She would have none of it. But his obsession, his lust, his depravity, overcame his reason . . ."

Judge Crane looked toward me expectantly. I could object here but I didn't. Socolow was arguing his case, not presenting a sterile preview of the expected evidence. The judge shrugged. If I wanted to behave like a potted plant, no problem for the court. But I had a reason. If the judge let me get the tape into evidence, Socolow had just dug himself into a hole.

She would have none of it?

Depravity?

It takes two. Or three in Melanie Corrigan's case. I would use Socolow's own words against him in closing argument.

"First, he worked his way into Mrs. Corrigan's confidence," Socolow continued. "As occurs in marriages, the Corrigans had problems. We all do. Mr. Corrigan was often away on business. She was lonely. She confided in the defendant, sought his guidance as a professional and a friend, not knowing the evil within him."

A bit melodramatic for my tastes. But no one was dozing. I could hear the gentle whir of the television camera placed at an angle behind the bar. The still camera from the newspaper clicked incessantly, despite the muffler designed to quiet it. The newsboys were scratching their notepads, soaking up the sexy stuff.

"And what did the defendant do? Suggest to Philip Corrigan that he spend more time with his wife? No! Recommend counseling? No! This defendant, who pretended to be a family friend, who pretended to mend and to cure, this Great Pretender, whispered to Melanie Corrigan time and again that she should kill her husband. *Murder* him!"

He let it hang there, knowing the silence burned his words into them. No one even coughed. It was as if jurors, spectators, and clerks all held their breaths, afraid to exhale.

"Murder him," Socolow repeated, softer this time. Juror number three, a middle-aged secretary, gasped. If Socolow had paused two more beats, she might have suffocated.

"He showed her how to do it. With a dangerous drug. An anesthetic that paralyzes the muscles and leads to a horrible, painful death as the lungs stop working. Naturally, she was shocked. So shocked that she couldn't believe he was serious. When he finally dropped the subject, she thought it was just a sick joke, a game. But then her husband died after routine surgery performed by this defendant."

For the first time, Socolow acknowledged Roger Salisbury's presence, pointing at him. The jurors' eyes followed Socolow's bony finger.

"Died after routine back surgery," Socolow said again, drawing the jurors into a cadence of repeated phrases. "Mrs. Corrigan was grief stricken. And suspicious. She sued the defendant for malpractice. The civil jury did not have the facts you will have, and he was exonerated. Still, she persisted. The defendant made advances toward her. She pretended to be interested, went to his home, and discovered the drug and the implements, the hypodermics, which you will see in evidence. You will hear testimony that a puncture on Mr. Corrigan's buttocks matches perfectly the twenty-gauge hypodermic found in the defendant's possession. You will hear evidence that this defendant surreptitiously entered Philip Corrigan's hospital room barely an hour before he died. You will hear from expert witnesses that tissue samples from Mr. Corrigan's brain and liver contain concentrations of the drug's components . . ."

It was a fine performance. Except for reading the indictment, Abe Socolow never mentioned Roger Salisbury by name, never called him *doctor*. The state's trick is to dehumanize. My job is to breathe life into the *man* who sits next to me, an innocent caught in a web of incompetence and deceit.

When Abe sat down, I walked to a comfortable spot six feet in front of the jury box. I put on a friendly smile and told them about the state's burden of proof, the burden to demonstrate *beyond a reasonable doubt* that Dr. Roger Salisbury intentionally killed Philip Corrigan. I mentioned Charles W. Riggs, M.D., and two jurors nodded, recognizing the name. How he would testify that Philip Corrigan died of natural causes. And I characterized the entire state's case as *circumstantial evidence*, spitting out the words as if describing a particularly odious disease.

I talked about Roger Salisbury, the doctor, the man. I talked about the long years of education and training, of good service to the community. Told them they'd hear character witnesses say they could believe Roger Salisbury under oath. Other doctors, community leaders. I promised they'd hear from Dr. Salisbury himself.

"You will hear a different story than Mr. Socolow tells," I said. "Not of a man spurned by a beautiful young woman. But of an ambitious, restless woman bored with her husband, a woman seeking excitement elsewhere. A woman who stood to inherit a fortune if her husband died, but would receive nothing if they divorced. You will see Mr. Corrigan's will and his antenuptial contract with this woman."

The reporters kept scribbling; the jurors kept listening. But that was about as far as I could go to toss another suspect at them. Until the judge ruled on the videotape, I was hamstrung. Still, I could put Melanie Corrigan's integrity at issue.

"You heard Mr. Socolow describe his case. He spent most of his time talking about the testimony of Melanie Corrigan. Why? She *is* the state's case. It is your job to evaluate the credibility of the state's witnesses. If you don't believe Melanie Corrigan, the state's case crumbles."

"Objection! Argumentative." Socolow stood and leaned forward toward the bench, his lean frame a javelin stuck in the ground.

Judge Crane paused and tapped a pencil against his forehead. In heavily publicized trials, he relied on signals from the press gallery to determine objections. Helen Buchman, a veteran *Herald* reporter, was the dean of the courthouse crew. But she kept a poker face this time, and the judge fended for himself. "You had considerable latitude in your opening, Mr. Socolow. Denied."

Socolow pouted and sat down. Emboldened by the ruling, I decided to finish with a flourish. "Yes, Mr. Socolow told you all about Melanie Corrigan and what she will *say*. But what evidence doesn't he have. Eyewitnesses to this alleged crime? None. Fingerprints? None. Confession? None. Just one woman's story and a prosecutor's case built on supposition, conjecture, fantasy, and whim . . ."

"Your Honor!" Socolow was halfway across the courtroom.

"Is that an objection?" Judge Crane asked.

"Yes. Improper opening."

"Granted. The jury will disregard the last statement of the defense. Mr. Lassiter, you are familiar, are you not, with the bounds of opening—"

A shout from the gallery interrupted the judge. Then a banging door. Then a woman's voice, loud: "Your grimy hands off me! I ain't walking through no gamma rays. You wanna strip-search me, fuzz-nuts, see if you're man enough. I'm with Jacob Lassiter."

Judge Crane banged his gavel and said, "Mr. Lassiter, is that lady associated with your office?"

The bailiff had her by the arm. I approached the bench. "That's no lady," I whispered to the judge. "That's my granny."

The judge looked skeptical. "Madam, are you related to Mr. Lassiter?"

"Is a frog's ass waterproof?" Granny replied, loud enough to call the hogs home.

The judge called a five-minute recess. They always last twenty. Granny Lassiter shook loose from the bailiff and smoothed her ruffled feathers. She wore a yellow print sundress, deck shoes, and a heavy Navy peacoat, a gift from a grateful sailor who once tended Harry Truman's place in Key West.

"I brought you a thermos of hot conch chowder," she told me. "Know how damned cold they keep these government buildings and don't want you getting the grippe. Hope I didn't interrupt anything important."

"Your timing was impeccable," I said. "The judge was chastising me. Why the big fuss?"

Granny balled a fist at the bailiff. "They wanted me to walk through some damn machine, see if I was carrying hand grenades. Told 'em to shove off. Might affect my unborn children, deplete the ozone layer, and curdle your chowder. You still like a dash of sherry in it?"

I allowed as how I did.

She pulled out a flask and shook in three drops that wouldn't wet the whistle of a priest receiving communion. Then she tipped the flask to her lips, drained it, glared at Roger Salisbury, and asked, "You kill that rich son-of-a-bitch who built condos in estuaries?"

"No, ma'am," Roger Salisbury said.

"Why not?" she demanded. "No balls?"

26

THE TEST

The state called its first witness, and Abe Socolow stayed in his chair. Jennifer Logan, pale and frail, stood to ask Deputy Sheriff Jack Roundtree what he found in the home of Roger Salisbury. Clever strategy. Letting the young assistant handle the preliminary witnesses. Keep Socolow from exhausting the jury with his hundred-kilowatt intensity.

The courtroom was packed. Granny Lassiter sat in the front row, doing her best not to hiss Socolow and cheer me when we emerged from the judge's chambers. I could use the moral support. Judge Crane had granted Socolow's motion *in limine:* the videotape would not be admitted into evidence. In his usual laconic fashion, the judge had merely said, "Mrs. Corrigan is not on trial here. Her escapades are not relevant to the issue of the defendant's guilt."

I had paced in his small chambers, musty with stacks of casebooks. I tossed my arms, argued, and made my objections for the record. The judge was unmoved. Socolow's face flickered with a vulture's smile.

Now Jennifer Logan peered at Deputy Roundtree from behind horn-rimmed glasses and asked about the black valise, the two hypodermics, and the vial of clear liquid. All were found in Roger Salisbury's study. In a desk drawer just where the affidavit of Melanie Corrigan said they would be.

My cross-examination was short.

"Deputy Roundtree, did Dr. Salisbury offer any resistance to your serving the warrant?"

"No."

"Was he polite?"

"Yes."

"When you pulled the valise from the drawer, what did he say?"

"Something like, 'What the hell?' "

"Anything else?"

"Best I remember, 'I can't believe she'd do this.' Something like that."

"Did he say who the *she* was?"

"Not that I recall."

Jennifer Logan called the lab technician who had tested the liquid in the vial. She asked for his findings.

"Sucks," he said.

She reddened. "Beg your pardon?"

"Sucks. Succinylcholine, a muscle relaxant used in surgery. Sodium pentothal puts the patient to sleep, succinylcholine relaxes the muscles and helps the anesthesiologist intubate the patient, get the tube down the trachea. The lungs stop working, the patient breathes on a respirator."

"And if there's no respirator?"

"The patient dies."

"A strong drug?"

"Very strong. Sort of synthetic curare. You know, the poison the Indians in South America make from plants. They dip their arrows in it. Ugly way to die."

"Your witness," Jennifer Logan said.

"No questions," I said, visions of poison-tipped arrows sailing across my mind.

"The state calls Dr. Hilton MacKenzie," Abe Socolow announced. The jurors straightened, Abe's appearance signifying an important witness.

Dr. MacKenzie was tall and ramrod straight with fine features and a forelock of straight black hair that fell into his eyes. He was not yet forty and gave the impression that he grew up with all the advantages of money, family, and education. He had a habit of jutting his fine patrician chin toward the heavens, looking down over his reading glasses, and speaking in a tone most of us reserve for pets not yet housebroken. He lacked nothing except humility.

Socolow ran through his credentials. Penn undergraduate, Harvard Medical School, internship at New York Hospital, residency at Mass General, fellowships in pathology, the whole bit. Into public service as an assistant ME in Miami, then chief canoemaker. My terminology, not his. I would ask him on cross who trained him. Charles W. Riggs, of course. Let their witness polish my witness's silverware.

"Dr. MacKenzie," Abe Socolow said, his voice heavy with respect, "let me show you what has been marked Plaintiff's Exhibit C for identification and ask you to identify it."

MacKenzie removed his reading glasses from a breast pocket, ceremoniously put them on, and studied the document. "It's our toxicology report on certain brain and liver samples from Philip Corrigan's body."

"Objection," I said, popping up, reminding the jury of my presence. "Improper predicate. No showing of chain of custody of the alleged samples."

Socolow looked perplexed. He asked if we could approach the bench. Judge Crane leaned to one side, away from the jury, and we huddled there, exchanging whispers.

"Judge," Socolow said, "I'd assumed Jake would stipulate to chain of custody to save one of his witnesses some embarrassment. These samples were in the possession of Dr. Charles Riggs, and my sense of propriety does not allow me to say on the record where he got them."

Judge Crane looked my way. I looked back. "This is a capital case, Judge, and I'm not going to stipulate to the kind of sandwiches you serve the jury. Doc Riggs will understand."

The judge shrugged. "Abe, you gotta call Riggs. I'll let you get this in now, subject to tying it up with Riggs's testimony."

That was okay with me. I wanted Charlie on the stand as much as possible. Make him their witness for purpose of chain of custody. Let the state vouch for his credibility before I call him.

Socolow went through it with MacKenzie, the finding of succinic acid and choline—two of the components of succinylcholine—in Corrigan's liver and brain. The buttock dissection showed a needle track. His expert opinion on cause of death, cardiac arrest following the injection of succinylcholine. The aneurysm? In the throes of death, quite possibly the stress on the system caused the aorta to rupture. But the instigating cause, succinylcholine, no doubt about it. The whole dance took ten minutes. Socolow moved to admit the toxicological report into evidence, and the judge accepted it, subject to Charlie Riggs tying up chain of custody. Then it was my turn.

I grabbed the report and pretended to read it, furrowing my brow.

"Now, Dr. Blumberg—"

"Dr. MacKenzie," he corrected me.

"Oh," I said, feigning surprise, "there must be some mistake. A Dr. Blumberg signed this report."

Hilton MacKenzie smeared me with his exasperated look. "Milton Blumberg is the toxicologist who analyzed the tissue samples."

"Oh," I said again, looking around the courtroom for the toxicologist.

"Blumberg works under my supervision and I am responsible for his actions," MacKenzie piped up, getting the drift.

I turned toward the judge. "Your Honor, I move to strike all of Dr. MacKenzie's direct testimony as hearsay. Further, he's not capable of responding to my cross-examination of the report, so it too must be stricken."

Before Socolow could rise and offer me Blumberg, a guy I didn't want, MacKenzie chimed in, "Your Honor, I am intimately familiar with toxicology methods and the preparation of this report based on the chromatography tests."

Ah, vanity.

"Very well," I said, "as long as we have the expert here, objection withdrawn."

He settled back into his chair. Before he could get too comfortable, I asked, "How much succinic acid was found in the brain?"

"How much?" he repeated.

"Yes, your report—Milton Blumberg's report—says there was succinic acid in the brain. How much?"

He seemed startled. "I don't know," he said.

"In the liver?"

"I don't know. It doesn't matter—"

"And how much choline?"

"Objection!" Socolow stomped toward the bench. "Judge, he's not letting the witness finish his answer."

The judge looked toward the press gallery. Helen Buchman from the *Herald* was nodding. Or maybe just chewing her gum. No matter. "Sustained. Doctor, you were saying . . ."

MacKenzie was silent. Gathering his thoughts. He shook his head, confused. "We didn't measure the amount."

My face registered shock. I spun on my heel in front of the jury box and waved the toxicology report at the witness, a toreador taunting the bull. "So it could have been ten milligrams, twenty milligrams, a quart, a gallon?"

"You don't understand," Dr. MacKenzie said, scowling. Exasperated.

"I'm sure I don't. That's why I ask questions. Now, how much choline was found in the brain tissue?"

"I don't know. Again, we didn't test for amount, only presence. It was a qualitative test, not a quantitative one."

Fancy doctor words.

"Then how did you differentiate the substances you allegedly found from the choline and succinic acid already there?"

The doctor stared at me.

I moved closer to the witness stand. "Those two substances are normally present in the body, correct?"

"Yes, of course."

"So your test may have picked up the succinic acid and choline normally found in the body, correct?"

He was silent a moment. He looked toward Socolow for help. None came. He stole a sideways glance at the jury, brushed the forelock of hair out of his eyes and said, somewhat testily, "There is insufficient choline and succinic acid normally in the body to show up in these tests."

"How much is there, normally?"

"A trace. Nothing more."

"And it doesn't show up on your tests?"

"No sir."

"Then how do you know it's there?"

"Because I know! That's all."

"Now, in your training as a chemist—"

"I never said I was a chemist," he whined. Defensive now, hunching his long, well-bred body into a corner of the witness stand.

"But you know how to do the gas chromatograph tests?"

"No." Then he added quickly, "I supervise."

"Ah," I said. I liked that. Jurors know all about supervisors, leaning against the side of the truck, drinking coffee while other guys dig the ditches.

"And of course you found succinic acid and choline near the needle track in the buttock?"

"No, I never said that. You know we didn't."

"What do you make of that?"

"I would have expected to find it, if that's what you mean."

I nodded with approval and paused to emphasize the point. "You expected to find succinic acid and choline near the needle track because the concentration of the drug should be greatest near the injection, correct?"

Again he looked toward Socolow. "Ordinarily."

"Then how do you explain the lack of the two substances near the track where the drug was supposedly injected?"

He paused. One beat, another beat. Then, very softly, a murmur barely above the whir of the air-conditioning, "Sometimes, in science, we don't have an explanation for everything."

"Quite so," I said, and sat down.

Abe Socolow had been around long enough to know how to rehabilitate a witness.

"Just a few questions on redirect," he said with perfect calm. Never let the jury sense your fear. "Now, Dr. MacKenzie. Besides looking for the presence of succinic acid and choline, what else did your tests do, and I direct your attention to page seven of the report."

MacKenzie warmed to the friendly face and followed the coaching. He flipped through Blumberg's report, got to page seven, and smiled. "We scanned for other toxins. Those tests were negative. The tests were positive only for the components of succinylcholine."

Socolow nodded. "To exclude the remote possibility of picking up traces of succinic acid and choline occurring naturally in the body, what did you do?"

Dr. MacKenzie read some more, his eyes brightening. "We tested three other bodies that recently arrived in the morgue. We performed the same chromatographic tests on brain and liver samples. None showed any evidence of succinic acid or choline."

Abe Socolow smiled too. His jury smile. To carry the message, no harm done, just clearing the confusion caused by that wily defense lawyer.

"No further questions," Socolow said, easing himself into his chair.

The judge was ready to bang his gavel and call it a day. But I had one or two more questions. Recross.

"Dr. MacKenzie, these three other bodies you tested. How many had died during or just after surgery?"

He didn't know where I was heading. But Abe Socolow did. He stood up. Tried to think of an objection but couldn't. The question was relevant and within the scope of his redirect.

"None," the doctor said, looking at the report. "Two were gunshot victims, one died in an auto accident. All DOA."

"So none had received succinylcholine within the last twelve hours before death?"

There was an inaudible mumble from the witness stand. He shook his head from side to side. Now he knew.

"You must speak up for the court reporter," I advised him.

"No, none received succinylcholine."

"You're familiar with the records of Philip Corrigan's back surgery on the day of his death?"

A quiet "Yes."

"And the anesthetics included, did they not, succinylcholine?"

"Fifty milligrams, IV drip," he said, softer than the rumble of voices from the gallery.

27

IKKEN
HISSATSU

I told Roger not to start celebrating but he was slapping me on the back. Brilliant again.

"You destroyed MacKenzie." He was jubilant.

"Maybe," I told him. "But they still have time to test someone who dies during surgery and Charlie Riggs doesn't know what it'll show. Nobody seems to know."

"Still," Roger insisted, "we won the day."

"Sure," I said, "but tomorrow is Melanie Corrigan. And the jury will convict if they believe her, acquit if they don't. Expert witnesses are just icing on the cake."

That was hard for his scientific mind to accept. "Then the trial is just showmanship," he complained, "if whoever has the best looking, most likable witness wins."

"It sometimes works like that," I said. "My job is to get the jury to dislike her or Sergio or both."

"How do you do that?"

I winked at him. Like it was a great secret. Which it was. Especially from me.

I slept well. I had prepared. I lowered my pace a bit. Tried to forget just who she was and what she had done to Susan. My first responsibility was to Roger Salisbury. Time for the rest later.

She still turned heads walking into a courtroom. Unlike the civil trial, she could not sit at counsel table. The witness rule was in effect. No witnesses present except when testifying. So the jurors hadn't seen Melanie Corrigan yet. It made her appearance more dramatic. She didn't let them down. Poised, confident, a beautiful walk to the witness stand.

Still in his black suit, the Grim Reaper asked when she first met Roger Salisbury.

She was well prepared. "I was just a kid, really. I looked up to him. He was a doctor, and I was training to be a professional dancer. We became involved. He pursued me. He was, in a way, obsessed with me. He wanted to possess me, and I gave in to him."

Then she blushed. Really blushed. It came out well, set off nicely by a navy blue, dress-for-success skirt-suit. She had the whole shtick, white silk blouse and frilly bow, hair tied back in a pony tail. Little Bo-peep. Where was the slinky temptress of the videotape? I shouldn't have been surprised. Usually, it's the defendants who do the change-overs. Street hoods shave their beards, shower, and cover their tattoos with discount store suits. A crack dealer shows up for trial looking like an investment banker. And here was Melanie Corrigan, ex-stripper, semi-pro hooker, up from the streets, blushing on cue, Abe Socolow leading off Day Two with his strength.

He took her through it all, just as he had promised in opening statement. Roger Salisbury chased her long after the relationship was over, showed her the drug, wanted her to kill her husband. She thought he was joking or half crazy, would never do it. Then Philip died, darling Philip. The beginning of a tear, tastefully done. No gushers that would interrupt the timing of the questions. After the malpractice trial, Roger asked her over, and she found the drug and the black valise in his house.

It took less time than I had anticipated. Socolow got her up there, fulfilled his prophecy, then sat down. I stood up. And the worst thing that could happen to my cross-examination happened.

Nothing.

It was uneventful.

Flat, dull.

I had worked so hard to stay in control, to bury the hatred inside of me that I buried everything else. No spark, no inspiration, no edge. Flabby questions, brief denials, no follow-up.

"Were you intimate with Roger Salisbury after your marriage?"

"No, of course not."

I had no way of disproving it. The tape was shot before the marriage, and Judge Crane wouldn't let it into evidence anyway. Roger would contradict her statement, of course, but there is something unchivalrous about that. The jury will not like him.

"Were you intimate with your employee, a Mr. Sergio Machado-Alvarez?"

"Objection," Socolow yelled out. "Irrelevant."

The judge's eyes darted across the gallery. Helen Buchman had gone to the restroom. He took a stab at it. "Granted. Same ruling as on Mr. Socolow's motion *in limine*. Mr. Lassiter, I remind you that Mrs. Corrigan is not on trial."

"Thank you, Your Honor," I said, to confuse the jury. "Mrs.

Corrigan, the black valise you testified about, was it ever in your possession?"

"No."

Again, nothing to disprove her. If Susan were alive, she could ID the valise in Melanie's underwear drawer. Destroy her testimony. I needed Susan for this and a thousand other reasons. I blinked and saw her face, nuzzling me on the way to Granny's house. I blinked again, and she was facedown in the pool. I was reeling, losing control.

"What do you know about the break-in at Susan Corrigan's cabana?"

An inane question. A preordained answer. Floundering.

"Nothing. Poor thing, to die so young."

I choked on my own incompetence, unable to muster anger or rage. I caught sight of Roger at the defense table. Catatonic. He knew I was blowing it. I improvised.

"You thought Dr. Salisbury cold-bloodedly murdered your husband and yet you went to his house after the civil trial?"

"Yes."

"You weren't afraid of him?"

"No, but . . . maybe I should have been."

I am not a mind reader. I have trouble enough understanding what people mean when they *speak* their thoughts. If I had known where she was going, I would have shut up. Instead I chomped at the bait.

"And why should you have been?"

An open-ended *why* on cross, invitation to disaster.

"He attacked me earlier at my home. He struck me right here because I would not . . . I refused to make love with him."

She was pointing to a spot below her left eye. Two female jurors looked upset. The cad. Killing a guy may be okay. But hitting a woman?

I was quiet so she kept going. "I'm sure you remember, Mr. Lassiter. You were kind enough to come over when I called you. After Philip's death, I had no one to turn to. I thanked you then, and I thank you now."

Ouch. So gracious. So ladylike. Socolow beamed. Palpable pleasure. Roger moaned. It was true, of course. Like so many big lies, this one was constructed of little truths. Roger *had* hit her. I *had* come over to keep him out of trouble. She *had* thanked me with a slippery tongue and a promise of more. Now she was making fun of me. Humbling men was sport to her. I decided to shut up before the quicksand rose above my neck. She glided out of the courtroom, elegant in her grief.

There was no time to regroup.

"The state calls Dr. Charles W. Riggs," Abe Socolow proclaimed.

The bailiff opened the door to the corridor, and Charlie bounded into the courtroom with rapid, short steps. His beard was still bushy, and his glasses still askew on his tiny nose. The bowl of a pipe jutted from the pocket of the old gray suitcoat he still kept for court appearances. He didn't need to be shown the way to the witness stand. He raised his right hand and promised to tell the truth even before the clerk asked him. He smiled at the jury and waited.

I figured Charlie wouldn't give Socolow any problems. All the state needed was chain of custody, a formality having nothing to do with Roger's guilt or innocence. Abe Socolow approached the witness stand warily. He was politic enough to skip the night in the cemetery. Just asked if Charlie had made dissections of Philip Corrigan's liver, brain, and buttock material and passed them on to the Medical Examiner's Office.

Charlie gave him the right answers and was ready to step down. Something passed behind Socolow's dark eyes. I saw the shadow of his thought. When the defense stepped to the plate, Socolow knew, Charlie would testify that Corrigan died of natural causes. Socolow wanted an extra turn at bat.

"Dr. Riggs, not to steal your thunder, but you're prepared to testify for the defense that Philip Corrigan died of a spontaneous aortic aneurysm, isn't that right?"

"Correct."

Socolow had Riggs tell the jury what that meant and Charlie took him through it, an encore of his testimony in the malpractice trial. Great. I didn't know where Socolow was headed, but if he wanted to hear my best testimony twice, fine. "Lots of things can cause an aneurysm, correct?"

"Sure. Hypertension, arteriosclerosis, syphilis, trauma."

"Trauma. How about a huge injection of succinylcholine, not the steady drip of an IV tube as in surgery. Wouldn't that cause trauma to the heart, the kind of trauma that could cause an aneurysm?"

So that's where he was going. Worried about my cross of Mac-Kenzie, trying to tie the injection to the aneurysm. Give the guy a boost of the drug, it blows out an artery. A long shot.

"You'd have to ask a cardiologist," Riggs said. "But I had a different kind of trauma in mind." He smiled at Socolow, a witness at ease with himself and his surroundings. He had testified for the state hundreds of times. If Socolow wanted to debate medicine, Charlie Riggs was happy to oblige.

"Right. You previously testified that a driver can suffer an aortic aneurysm if he hits the steering wheel following a crash, isn't that right?"

Abe had done his homework, had read the transcript of the malpractice trial.

"Yes. I've seen several of those."

"In such an accident, there's quite a shock to the system, isn't there?"

"Surely," Charlie Riggs agreed.

"And can you say conclusively that the aneurysm is caused by the impact of the steering wheel or could it be the shock to the system, to the heart?"

He was winging it now, trying to find a parallel between an injection of succinylcholine and an auto accident. It wasn't going anywhere. Not helping or hurting his case. Just one of those tangents lawyers sometimes take.

Charlie Riggs wouldn't bite. He shook his head, and several jurors did likewise. "My impression has been that it's the trauma, the impact that causes the blowout of the aorta. It takes a serious blow, but a steering wheel, or a very well-thrown punch by a trained boxer could do it."

"Even a punch," Socolow repeated, apparently happy that so many things could cause an aneurysm.

"A punch, a kick, even a karate chop."

Socolow went on, detailing every cause of aneurysm known to man, monkeys, and little white rats. But my mind stayed right there.

A punch, a kick, even a karate chop.

I hadn't thought of it before. But I did now. Nurse Rebecca Ingram said Roger left the room at ten o'clock. Sometime between ten-thirty and eleven, Melanie Corrigan waltzed in with the little hunk of martial arts skills.

A karate chop.

I didn't know whether to risk it now or wait until I had Charlie on my part of the case.

Your witness, Abe Socolow said.

I plunged ahead. "Dr. Riggs, are you telling the jury that one karate punch to the abdomen could puncture the aorta?"

Charlie Riggs looked toward the jury and stroked his beard. Say *yes,* I prayed. Say *yes,* you hairy wizard.

"Yes. The concept is *ikken hissatsu,* to kill with one blow. Some of it is exaggerated to the point of myth, but it does happen. Martial arts assassins are quite capable of it. The essence of karate is *kime,* an explosive attack using maximum power over a short distance. Of course, it would be difficult to rupture the aorta of a well-trained athlete with strong abdominal muscles, particularly if he expected the blow."

I let out a breath, awed at the range of Charlie's knowledge. Time to set the scene. "After a laminectomy, how would a patient be lying in bed?"

"After back surgery, you put a patient on his back. The pressure helps prevent further bleeding."

"With stomach exposed?"

"Yes."

"Muscles relaxed."

"Quite. The patient would be sedated."

"And, assuming a man in his fifties not in the best of physical condition was lying on his back, sedated, stomach muscles slack, could a karate expert rupture his aorta with one blow?"

Socolow leapt up. "Objection! Assumes facts not in evidence, irrelevant, beyond scope of direct, beyond witness's expertise."

"Anything else?" the judge asked.

Socolow shook his head. Already he had protested too much.

"Denied," the judge said.

"Yes. A well-placed blow, a *shuto uchi,* the sword handstrike, could burst the pipe, the aorta, that is. Perhaps even the *stoshi hiji-ate,* the downward elbow strike."

Charlie demonstrated the movement of each blow, smiling shyly toward the jury box. "I learned a little of this on Okinawa after the war," he added.

Oh bless you, Charlie Riggs, master of a thousand subjects, encyclopedia of the esoteric, bestower of life on the condemned.

"Nothing further," I said, easing into my heavy wooden chair as if it were a throne.

28

THE KARATE KING

The five of us sat on my tiny back porch swatting mosquitoes, drinking Granny Lassiter's home brew, and arguing how to use the gift imparted by Abe Socolow.

"Show a video of Sergio winning the Karate King title," said Cindy. Ever efficient, she already had fished around town and found the tape.

"Let him split your head open with a shoe-toe oochi-koochi," Granny said. "Show his mean streak."

"Drop it now while we're ahead on the point," Roger Salisbury argued. His face was drawn, and he looked like he hadn't been getting much sleep. Being a defendant in a first-degree murder trial can do that. "Socolow will be ready for anything more about the karate."

Charlie Riggs drained the dark, headless beer from a mug that was once a peanut butter jar. "Not a bad idea. That was all off the cuff today. No matter what, we can't prove Sergio struck the decedent."

I shook my head, both at Charlie and at Granny, who was offering me a refill. Too heavy with hops, like an English bitter. "You're forgetting something, Charlie. We don't have to prove anything. All we need is to create a reasonable doubt that Roger aced him."

Charlie nodded and helped Granny into the hammock where she had decided to spend the night. I didn't think there was room for two.

"But it must be a reasonable doubt," Charlie Riggs declared. "Not a possible doubt, a speculative, imaginary, or forced doubt."

I laughed. "Whoa, Charlie, when did you start memorizing jury instructions?"

"I been in trials before you got out of knickers."

"Used to wet his knickers till he was four," Granny called out from the hammock.

Roger Salisbury leapt to his feet from an aging lawn chair. "I didn't kill Philip Corrigan!" Silently, three heads turned toward him. His normally placid face was twisted with pain. "When you talk about strategy, you seem to be trying to hide something, to get off a guilty man. You all forget I didn't kill Philip! He's the one person I could never kill. He was my friend."

Salisbury sagged back into the chair and turned toward the sprawling hibiscus that threatened to overrun the porch. Everyone quieted down for a while. I thought about Roger's little speech. Something vague and fuzzy bothered me, but I let it go. We weren't getting anywhere except mosquito-bitten and drunk.

I was nearly dozing when the phone hollered. Everybody I wanted to talk to was within spitting distance. By the sixth ring, I stirred just to stifle the noise. Usually at this time of night, it's a boiler room call, somebody selling frozen beef from Colorado or solar water heaters made in Taiwan. Usually it's not Abe Socolow.

Breakfast before court? Sure. Bay Club? Sure.

"What does he want?" Roger asked, a tremble in his voice.

"Don't know. Maybe just wants to do a Power Breakfast."

Granny Lassiter snorted. "Then why call you?"

The Bay Club sits on the thirty-fifth floor of a new office building overlooking Biscayne Bay and the Atlantic Ocean. The dining room is chrome and glass, white tile, and a blinding brightness. All the charm of an astronaut's space capsule. The club was designed by a young architect adept at stealing ideas about modern design and making them worse.

Socolow was late. I looked around. There was Fat Benny Richards, all three hundred pounds of him, wolfing French toast with county commissioner Bradley Shriver. Fat Benny wore a six-hundred-dollar silk suit but looked like a ton of shit in a gunny sack. His clients called Fat Benny a lobbyist, which was a more polite term than bagman. Politicians courted him because he collected campaign contributions the way a sewage plant draws flies.

Fat Benny had the beady red eyes of an overfed rat, and his eyes were his best feature. His breath could kill a manatee and his toupee threatened to slide into his Bloody Mary. I picked up pieces of the conversation between the commissioner and the fat man. Arguing for a builder client, Benny wanted a variance from the ordinance requiring a parking space for every four hundred square feet of office space. A customary request by rapacious builders since parking garages cost a bundle and the cash return is diddly-squat compared to office space.

Fewer parking spaces, larger buildings, less green space, billboards the size of cruise ships—zoning was a scandal. But why not? In a town where William Jennings Bryan once hawked vacant lots from a floating barge, the hustle was still king.

Abe Socolow slid silently into his chair, folding his body like a scythe. He looked haggard. Black circles under his eyes, sunken cheeks, skin the color of a newspaper left in the sun. A waiter in a white vest and gloves took our order. Gloves at seven-thirty in the morning.

"Just coffee," Socolow said. "Black."

Naturally.

I ordered a large orange juice, a basket of sweet rolls, and shredded wheat with whatever fruit didn't come in a can. Let Abe suffer, I was hungry.

"That was some happy horseshit yesterday about a karate chop busting the aorta," he began irritably.

"Glad you liked it."

"Liked the bit about MacKenzie not testing stiffs who died after surgery, too."

"You ask me to breakfast to compliment my trial skills. How kind."

"Whadaya doing, Jake, just throwing shit on the barn door, seeing what'll stick?"

"Your breakfast conversation is most appetizing."

I didn't know where he was heading. He drained the coffee, and the waiter materialized silently with more from a silver pot. At the next table Fat Benny was offering the commissioner preferred stock in a cable television franchise.

"Just thought you should know," Socolow said, "I been at the morgue all night with MacKenzie . . ."

"The way you look, you're lucky they let you out."

He ignored me. "We got two stiffs out of surgery yesterday. Both had succinylcholine IVs as part of the anesthesia, and guess what?"

I didn't have to guess. No traces of succinic acid or choline. I figured Socolow would bust his balls to recoup after MacKenzie's debacle. Just didn't think he could do it so fast. Now I pictured him dashing from hospital to hospital, praying for patients to die in the OR, maybe pulling the plug in the ICU.

"As a personal favor, in a spirit of fairness," he went on, "I'll tell you about my rebuttal witness, an internal medicine guy. Feingold, head of the department at Jackson. He says a karate chop can't bust the aorta. No way. Too much padding in the abdomen, what with the fat and the stomach and all those organs."

"Kind of you to share your strategy with me, Abe. But we both know you can get Irv Feingold to say anything. I been around the rosy with him in two malpractice cases. Now, you didn't bring me here to talk about how strong your case is. What's up?"

He squinted at me through tired eyes. I smeared a large glob of butter on a heated cinnamon roll. Nearby, Fat Benny was extolling the virtues of a garbage compacting plant located upstream of a drinking well field.

"Jake, you know I'm fair. Tough, sure. But fair."

"Uh-huh," I mumbled. No use insulting him. If he had an offer, I would listen. Then I could insult him.

"We may have overcharged Salisbury," he said softly.

"Go on," I said.

"You know how juries are. Anything can happen. Hell, they can come back with Murder One and recommend death. Puts Crane in a tough spot."

"To say nothing of my client."

"Or they could compromise and recommend life."

"Yeah, and they could come back with a big fat NG."

He shook his head. "I'm not going to argue with you, Jake. Here it is. He pleads now to Murder Two, we agree to ten years. He'll be out in thirty-nine months."

It didn't take long to think about it. "No deal. A felony conviction, he loses his ticket to practice. Besides, he's not guilty. I won't plead him to jaywalking."

Socolow's jaw muscles tightened. "Jake, you're between the dog and the fire hydrant. If it's Murder One, even if no-go on death, it's twenty-five years minimum mandatory, you know that."

I knew that. And I knew that Abe Socolow was right about juries. You can never tell. I would tell Roger about the plea offer and let him decide. But I knew his answer. *I didn't kill Philip Corrigan!* It was still ringing in my ears.

"Sorry, Abe. Just dismiss the case and go away. If not, we'll take a verdict from the jury box."

"I'll see you in court," he hissed.

"In about thirty minutes," I said.

"The state calls Mr. Sergio Machado-Alvarez."

Now there was a surprise, Socolow trying to catch me off guard. Bringing the Karate King in now, figuring we hadn't had much time to work on the karate chop angle. Figuring right.

Socolow's direct examination was brief, first describing Sergio's job as the family's driver and boat captain. Brought Mrs. Corrigan to the hospital the night of October 14 to check on her husband. Clever. Blunt the jury's surprise when I show he was there shortly before the fatal aneurysm.

Sergio went through it matter-of-factly. Mr. Corrigan was fine when they saw him, sleeping peacefully. No, he never saw the doctor in the room, must have come by later. Such a shame, *qué lástima*, the boss dead, a good man. Then he corroborated Melanie's testimony about being attacked by Roger after the malpractice trial. Pulling up on his chopper in front of the Corrigan home, he saw the defendant, tires screaming, tearing out of Gables Estates. The *senora* showed him the beginning of a bruise under the eye. She was wailing that the doc struck her.

"Objection, hearsay," I sang out. "Move to strike."

"Denied," the judge declared firmly, pleased he could handle that one solo. "Excited utterance exception to the hearsay rule."

Socolow went on. "Did you ever speak to the defendant about this assault?"

"*Nunca*. I wouldn't say nothing to him. I told the *senora*, I mess him up she want. She says, no. She too kind."

"Did the defendant ever say anything to you about Mr. Corrigan when he was still alive?"

"*Sí*. He tell me Mr. Corrigan not pay enough attention to his wife, he lose her, one way or another."

"Your witness," Abe Socolow said.

I stood up and moved close to the witness stand. I kept my back to the jury and gave Sergio my best mean-and-nasty look. If we were playing poker, he saw my mean-and-nasty and raised it to cruel-and-vicious. Good. Let the jury see a hard guy up close. Too bad he was wearing a suit, covering up those slabs of muscle and malice. His shirt collar was buttoned too tight, and he kept craning his neck toward the ceiling and pulling at the collar as if to let out the steam.

"Mr. Machado, have you ever been convicted of a crime?"

He shrugged his rhinoceros torso. "No big deal."

"May we assume that's a yes?"

"*Sí,* sure. A crime, if you want to call it that."

"What do you call possession of illegal drugs?"

He snorted a little laugh. "Steroids, man. *Solamente* steroids. Possession without a prescription. Everybody I know does steroids."

"I'm sure they do. But you were convicted, were you not?"

"Yeah, sure. But I got no joo-dification."

"How's that?"

"My first offense. They didn't joo-dify me."

"The court withheld adjudication?"

"*Sí,* what I say, I got probation. I got the half-a-david with me."

He had lost me. He drew a crumpled legal-size paper from his back pocket, and sure enough, there was an affidavit from the clerk of the criminal court attesting that one Sergio Machado-Alvarez had been placed on probation, adjudication withheld.

Socolow was reading it over my shoulder. "Objection! This is not proper impeachment. That's not a conviction under Section ninety point six-ten. Move to strike."

The son-of-a-gun knew his statute numbers. And he was right. You can attack the credibility of a witness by showing a prior criminal conviction, but without an adjudication of guilt, it doesn't count.

I treaded water. "Your Honor, this is not, strictly speaking, impeachment of credibility. Mr. Machado's familiarity with the implements of steroid abuse has a direct bearing on the guilt or innocence of Dr. Salisbury."

"Tie it up quickly, Mr. Lassiter," Judge Crane ordered, turning his profile to the television camera.

I moved even closer to the witness stand. "You freely acknowledge being a user of anabolic steroids, do you not?"

"Sure, makes me big."

"And smart, too," I cracked, trying to rile him.

Abe Socolow was having none of it. "Your Honor, please admonish Mr. Lassiter not to be argumentative."

"All right, both of you. Let's get on with it."

I walked to the rear of the jury box. Let them focus on Sergio, forget about me. "How long have you used steroids?"

"*No sé.* Five, six years."

"So, at the time Mr. Corrigan died, you were a regular user."

"Sure, I guess."

"You're familiar with the studies linking aggressive, irrational behavior with steroid abuse?"

"Says who?"

"An expert witness, but we'll save that for another day. Mr. Machado-Alvarez, how do you administer the steroids?"

"Huh?"

He didn't know where I was going. Abe Socolow would have prepared him for cross-examination about his karate skills. That would come. But first . . .

"How do you take the steroids? Pills, liquids? Do they come in little doggy biscuits?"

"You inject them, man."

He took his right hand and made a little plunging motion with his thumb. He did it twice, and somewhere deep inside me, a man was hitting a gong with a sledgehammer, trying to force some rundown brain cells to match distant thoughts with nearby ones. It would have to wait.

"So you use a hypodermic needle?"

"Sure."

I walked to the clerk's table and picked up State's Exhibit Six.

"Like this one?" I asked, holding that little devil three feet in front of the jury box.

He didn't answer. He was slow but not that slow.

"Like this one?" I repeated.

"I didn't kill no old man," he said. "He's the one did that. He's the needle man." Pointing now toward Roger Salisbury. But the jury was looking at Sergio Machado-Alvarez.

Good.

Very good.

So good I was ready to stop for a while. So was the judge. He knew the evening paper had an eleven-thirty A.M. deadline. *Gentlemen, this may be a propitious time to recess for lunch.* Fine with me. Let the jurors chew over Sergio Machado-Alvarez with their roast beef sandwiches.

I returned to court early. Lugging a trial bag filled with ceramic tiles. A clerk from the law firm pushed a dolly loaded with concrete blocks. I built four stacks of blocks, leaving them far enough apart to place twenty tiles on top, the edge of each block holding a corner of the bottom tile. The top of the pile was about waist high.

Abe Socolow walked in, took one look, and began barking orders that stampeded a herd of law clerks toward the library. Socolow raced for Judge Crane's chambers, a vein throbbing in his neck. I moseyed along behind him.

It was either indigestion or our presence, but the judge looked pained. In a corner of the room, by the bookcases, Jennifer Logan scratched through the cases searching for precedent on in-court demonstrations. Meanwhile Judge Crane belched and listened to Socolow's bleating.

"Show biz," Socolow said. "Histrionics for TV. Irrelevant blather designed to distract from the issues of the guilt of the accused."

"We've laid the predicate," I told the judge. "Dr. Riggs testified that a karate blow could have caused death. This witness is a karate expert. He was in the victim's hospital room shortly before the aneurysm. Let's see how hard the Karate King can hit."

"If the witness refuses to hit these things, I can't make him," the judge said wearily. "Even if he's willing to do it, I'm inclined to keep it out. Ruling deferred for now. Let's see where the testimony goes, but Mr. Lassiter, I admonish you, no circus tricks."

Abe Socolow huddled in the corridor with his witness, instructing him, no doubt, to downplay his karate skills and to stay away from the stack of tiles. Jennifer Logan neatly refiled her research in color-coded folders. The bailiff brought the jury in, and I started earning my retainer.

I asked Sergio about his training and his trophies, his black belt and his favorite *dojang*.

"First place in Florida sports karate, we don't hurt nobody," he said, obviously adhering to Socolow's advice. "Second in Atlanta, regional competition. Training for fifteen years."

I had him tell the jury about his weightlifting, Chinese boxing, judo, and aikido.

"You're a pretty physical guy?" I asked.

"I'm okay."

Ever so humble.

"Pretty good at karate?"

"If you say so."

Evasive.

"See this stack of tiles, think you can break them all with one blow?"

"Who knows?"

"Well, on this videotape from the Florida championships, you break a stack of boards like they were toothpicks, should we take a look?"

Socolow leapt up, objecting again.

Judge Crane, more dolorous than usual, peered down at us, unhappy we needed his intervention. He looked toward the press gallery, but no one told him how to rule, so he took a stab at it himself. "Mr. Socolow, this is a capital case, and I will not unduly limit the defense. But Mr. Lassiter, get to the point. Objection overruled."

I raised my voice. "The fact is, you're not good enough to break twenty tiles with one blow, are you?"

"Huh?" Sergio looked puzzled. It did not seem to be an expression entirely foreign to him.

"Maybe Shigeru Funakoshi could do it," I suggested. "Didn't he beat you in Atlanta?"

"Home cooking. Two Japs and a Korean for judges."

"But you really couldn't break all twenty of these, could you?"

"You kidding? With my hand, my foot, or my head. Kid's stuff."

Adieu, humility. Socolow was grimacing, sitting on the edge of his chair, itching to pop up.

I said, "Let's see you do it. Mess them up. Isn't that what you said you could do to Dr. Salisbury, mess him up?"

Socolow was up again. "Your Honor. He's badgering the witness. As Your Honor said, an unwilling witness cannot be forced to take part in a demonstration. Miss Logan has handed me several cases on courtroom demonstrations that I wish to present on this issue. If the court please, in *Mills v. State* . . ."

Socolow approached the bench but I stayed close to the witness stand. The judge was going to set me down. I took a risk. It might get me another broken nose, maybe straighten out the one I had. It might get me some harsh words from the judge, nothing novel there. Or it might get me an acquittal.

I leaned over and murmured in Sergio's ear, "Stick around, Shorty. I'm gonna play a videotape of you and your friends. No wonder that bitch needs three guys. You not only have the brains of a flea, you've got the *pinga* of one, too."

Socolow was still at it, quoting the Florida Supreme Court. He couldn't hear the guttural growl that stirred in Sergio's throat. The Karate King rocked in the chair, his hands gripping the rail, his knuckles bleaching out. But he didn't get up. I leaned even closer, my mouth inches from his ear. Improvisation.

"Big pecs," I whispered, *"pero pinga chiquita, no pinga grande."*

It's important to be bilingual in Miami.

Sergio's cruel little eyes opened as wide as his brain would let them.

Incredulous that I would mock him, enraged that I could do it from a vantage point half a foot higher than he'd be in elevator heels. But I needed more, something that would cut deep into the tender meat of his machismo, something to inflame a guy who spends hours posing his bicep curls in front of a gym mirror.

"What surprises me," I breathed into his ear, "is that you're a switch hitter. A fruit. Roger tells me he could never bend over with you behind him."

He erupted. A primeval roar. Socolow turned, eyes wide, frozen. Sergio stood in the box and tore off his coat, throwing it to the floor. Short sleeves underneath, arms exploding against the fabric. He bounded out of the box toward me. I backpedaled like a cornerback on third and long. I wanted the stack of tiles between the two of us.

He looked at me. He looked at the tiles. He would have it all.

"*Shuto!*" He brought the sword handstrike down on the tiles. A thunderbolt, a thousand broken pieces, dust rising from the floor, an echo bouncing off the walls. A six on the Richter scale.

He barely paused. Two more steps and we were face-to-face. Blood streamed from his right hand, impaled by a ceramic sliver. I backed up until I was at the bar. He kept coming. Too fast. If he was ever to get good at hand-to-hand combat, he'd have to learn to control his emotions.

It would be better for Roger Salisbury if I let Sergio hit me. Just as Granny had said, let him show his mean streak. And I will do a lot for a client. I will stay up three nights in a row preparing witnesses or writing a brief. I will cajole and flatter judges with two-digit IQs. I will even cry in closing argument to win sympathy from the jury. But I will not let my head be split like a cantaloupe by a tattooed, muscle-bound, hopped-up steroid freak.

He telegraphed a roundhouse kick, and as I ducked to the right, a whirling foot breezed by my ear, a rush of air like a train through the station. He tried hitting me in the chest with a flurry of fast punches with the left fist. Later, Charlie Riggs would tell me this was the *Dan-zuki*. I deflected some of them but caught a good one in the ribs. I would feel it for a week. He liked going for the body and used a lunge punch to get one into my gut. I felt it and dropped my guard. Somebody in the gallery screamed.

He tried to come high with a looping roundhouse right. *Mawashizuki,* Charlie would explain. He had plenty of hip behind it, but I had figured he'd go for the head. I leaned to my right and the punch glanced off my ear, burning it, but not connecting.

Then I ducked inside and brought my forearm up under his chin, hard. There was a lot of shoulder in it and a good explosion from the legs. The forearm caught some neck and some jaw and lifted him off the floor. It would have been good for fifteen yards, unnecessary roughness, clotheslining a guy. The shot straightened Sergio up, made him gasp for breath that wouldn't come. Then I brought the left hook around, aiming for the chin. It took a while to get there, my timing was rusty, but that was okay. He wasn't going anywhere. The punch landed and tossed him backward onto the clerk's table, which crumbled into splinters, trial exhibits flying. State-issued furniture.

The judge was banging his gavel. I hadn't heard it during the ruckus. But there he was, banging away. And in his other hand was the .357 Magnum from under the bench. Then dead quiet. The judge looked at the gavel and then at the gun. Sheepishly. Then his eyes darted from Channel 10's video camera to the *Herald*'s still camera, whirring and clicking away. Preserving the sight for eternity, or at least until the next election.

Straining to appear judicial, he turned toward the jury box. "The jurors shall disregard the last . . . uh . . . colloquy between the witness and defense counsel."

Might as well ask the residents of Pompeii to ignore the volcano.

Then, eyeballing me, Judge Randolph Crane did a slow burn. "The Court, *sua sponte,* grants a mistrial. The jury is excused. Mr. Socolow, I assume the state wishes to retry this defendant. If so, a new trial date will be set upon subsequent motion and notice of hearing. Mr. Lassiter . . ."

He paused. He thought. His perpetual glumness was replaced with anger. It seemed real, not just a pose for the editorial boards.

"Mr. Lassiter, I have never seen such a display in a courtroom. I don't know what you did to provoke that witness, but I do know you committed battery upon his person."

Again he paused, and the courtroom waited. He was running out of steam. He shot a surreptitious glance at the press. No help. He banged his gavel three times. When no one moved, he banged it again, then looked at me sternly and in his deepest tones announced, "You have fomented anarchy in a court of law." A good quote, and from the front row, Helen Buchman nodded approvingly, her gray bouffant bobbing. Encouraged, the judge worked some righteous indignation into his voice. "In sum, Mr. Lassiter, you have flaunted . . . that is flouted . . . and in other words, you have affronted and offended the authority of this court. You are hereby ordered and adjudged in contempt of court. Report tomorrow morning at nine for sentencing. I suggest you bring counsel. And your toothbrush."

The judge bolted through the rear door into his chambers and away from the madness. A corrections officer helped Sergio to his feet. Reporters swarmed over me. From the corridor, the cameramen and grips stormed in, knocking spectators aside. A mini-cam examined my right ear. A microphone poked at my eye. I'd be the lead story at six o'clock. Good story, too. Defendant goes free, at least for a while; his lawyer heads for the stockade.

My ribs ached and my left hand was beginning to swell. Roger Salisbury hadn't moved. He sat at the defense table, probably trying to figure out if I was a great lawyer or just a guy with an adequate left hook.

Abe Socolow looked at me and said, "You went too far this time, Jake, old buddy."

"In a pig's ass!" Granny Lassiter had hurdled the bar separating the lions from the Christians, exposing gray wool socks beneath her sundress. She hugged me and narrowed her eyes at Abe Socolow. "My Jacob can whup any man in the house, and a couple weeks of county victuals never did no harm."

29

TWO OUT OF THREE

I was playing a wicked first base, stretching this way and that, digging low throws out of the dirt, trying to avoid pulling a hamstring. The shortstop was a check bouncer with a weak wing. The third baseman was a bunco artist who threw hard but wild. The second baseman was a veteran, three falls for DUI, but I didn't know much about his arm. Every grounder trickled through his legs and into right field.

Seven days in the Dade County Stockade. Like a vacation. No phones, no partners' meetings, no hearings with cantankerous judges and disagreeable clients. Almost as good as a week-long cruise to St. Thomas, although chipped beef on toast is seldom served on the *S. S. Norway*. The stockade is different from the county jail, that dungeon attached to the Justice Building. The jail is for your hard guys— robbers, killers, rapists, and multikilo dopers. Here, just a bunch of misdemeanants, including my own contemptuous self.

I had just done my best imitation of a Nureyev split, scooping up a shin buster in time to nab a three-hundred-pound grocer doing ninety days for selling pork loins as kosher lamb chops. The applause from my teammates did not break my eardrums. "Good grab, shyster," the second baseman declared for the group.

Then, a familiar voice behind me: "Did I hear something crack or you just fart?"

I turned around. Now coaching first base for the Stockade Short Timers, Abraham Socolow.

"Hey, Abe. What'd they get you for? Purloining state-owned paper clips?"

He didn't laugh. "Looks like you been working on your tan."

"Yeah, lifting, too," I said. "Gonna get strong again. Maybe even take up karate like your favorite witness."

"Funny you mention him," he said, as if it weren't funny at all. "Machado-Alvarez is in Mount Sinai, got some weird sickness."

"I'll send flowers."

"You'll do better than that. You'll go there with me while I take a statement."

"You deputizing me?" I asked, keeping an eye on the runner at second, a shoplifter who would steal anything, including third base, if given the chance.

"He was busting up some boards at a karate exhibition over at Convention Hall, suddenly gets a fever, the shits, then he's paralyzed. One of the Beach cops working security ID'ed Salisbury hanging around the stage just before macho man did his stuff. I'll need to talk to Salisbury. Thought you'd want to be present. As usual, old buddy, I'm going out of my way to do you a favor."

Next time he does me a favor, I'll probably do a month in solitary. The pitcher, a pickpocket, called a conference on the mound. He slipped the ball to the shortstop, a pickpocket, who hid it in his glove then tagged the runner leading off second. Time was called, the runner whimpered, and there ensued some plea bargaining with the umpire, a trusty.

"I can't leave," I told Socolow. "Got another three days to satisfy the judge."

"Let's go. I sprung you."

I put on my best Edward G. Robinson. "You sprung me? You dirty screw. I was going over the wall tonight with the boys. What'll they think?"

He didn't smile; he didn't scowl, just the same straight-faced look. Ten years and he has yet to laugh at one of my jokes.

With Socolow running interference, we sailed through the paperwork for my return to society. We headed east in his government Chrysler—four doors, blackwalls—toward Miami Beach. Abe wore a dark three-piece suit with his Phi Beta Kappa pin slung from a vest pocket. I wore a blue chambray shirt with a nine-digit number. If we went to a Coconut Grove club, I'd be considered highly trendy and he'd be stashed next to the kitchen with a busload of retirees from Century Village. We took the Julia Tuttle Causeway, which connects the mainland with Arthur Godfrey Road on Miami Beach. It's a great drive, high above Biscayne Bay, sailboats swooping beneath the pillars of the bridge, a fine view of the white and pink buildings of Miami Beach. From the top of the causeway you appreciate the fragility of that long, skinny sandbar with the bay on one side, the vast ocean on the other.

On the way Socolow told me he'd asked Charlie Riggs to meet us there. I thought that over a second. "Why not the ME? He's the guy on your side."

Socolow was silent. Like a good soldier, he wouldn't squawk about intramural warfare. Then he surprised me. "Maybe too much on my side."

I let it go. But he didn't. "MacKenzie's a turd," he said stiffly.

I had noticed a certain scatological bent to Abe's patter lately, but this was not the time to question whether he had been toilet trained at the appropriate age.

"A turd?" I delicately inquired.

"I can't prove it, but I think he cooked those chromatographic tests that night in the morgue, the guys who died in surgery. He wouldn't let me near Blumberg all night."

Why was he telling me this?

"You're probably surprised I'm telling you this," he said.

Mind reader.

"There won't be a new trial," Socolow continued. "The widow refuses to testify."

"You could lean on her," I suggested, hoping he'd already tried and failed. "You've done it before with reluctant witnesses."

"Not in a case like this," he said. "What's it mean, Jake, if a woman won't testify against a man she swore killed her husband?"

I thought about it. "Different possibilities. That she knows the defendant didn't do it. Or the defendant did it and she helped him. Or she knows who did it and she's afraid a trial would bring that out."

Abe Socolow didn't say a word, just nodded to himself, watched the causeway straight ahead, and kept both hands on the wheel, at ten o'clock and two o'clock, just the way they teach you. Some guys play it strictly by the book.

Charlie Riggs was standing inside the double doors of the ICU talking to a young doctor in a white lab coat. The doctor was short and pale with a bushy, unkempt beard. Charlie stroked his own beard; the young doctor stroked his. Charlie barely noticed our arrival. No introductions, we just picked up listening.

"He went fast," the doctor said with a shrug. "Ambulance brought him in, eyes bulging, stomach pain, vomiting, diarrhea, stiff joints, then paralysis. We tried to stabilize him. Barely got the IV in. Bang! Liver and kidneys fail, goes into respiratory arrest."

"Classic indicia of food poisoning," Charlie said dispassionately.

"We used to see two or three deaths a year, green beans at church picnics. Botulism."

The two doctors kept talking, ignoring us. There wasn't much two lawyers could add anyway.

"That's what we thought," the doctor said. "But we checked it out. Last two meals were banquet style for the karate convention. Three hundred people, no one else even burped."

Charlie scratched his beard. The young doctor did the same. I didn't have a beard, so I ran a hand through my shaggy hair. Socolow didn't have much hair, so he lit a cigarette, then ground it into the tile after a nurse wagged a finger at him.

"Have you checked the body for punctures, fresh injections?" Charlie asked.

"Sure did, after Mr. Socolow told us his suspicions. Nothing."

Charlie Riggs turned to Abe Socolow. They had worked together in the past, shared a mutual respect, even if Charlie thought Abe was a little sharp around the edges. "What was he doing just before he was stricken?"

"Best we can figure," Socolow said, "he just finished chopping up a stack of boards with his bare hands." Socolow looked at me. "Except nobody slugged him afterwards."

"I see," Charlie said. He was the only one who did. "I think I'll take a drive to Convention Hall."

I was sleeping in my own bed with two pillows for company when four headlights glared malevolently through my front windows, and two horns blared. I rolled over and looked at the clock. The green digital numbers flashed from 2:57 to 2:58 as my feet hit the floor. Downstairs, a flashing of high beams. Maybe the cops picking me up. Maybe I really did go over the wall.

I wrapped a towel around my waist and opened the front door. Granny Lassiter and Charlie Riggs.

"Sorry to disturb you, Jake," Charlie said, sounding not a bit sorry.

"Let me guess," I said groggily, "you want my permission to marry this woman. Forget it. Elope if you like."

"I'm game," Granny said. "Only fellow my age I know still got lead in his pencil."

"C'mon Jake," Charlie commanded, his face serious, no twinkle in his eye. "Let's take a ride and talk."

If Charlie wanted to talk, I wanted to listen. I slipped on an old pair of gym shorts, running shoes, and a gray T-shirt, stepped into the humid night, and slid into the front passenger seat of Granny's mammoth 1969 Cadillac. Over the bay, lightning flashed and distant thunder followed, a thunderstorm brewing in the southeast, headed our way. Granny had the engine running and Charlie was already in the back. Before I had dented the velour upholstery, the smell rolled over me.

"Granny, you leave a mess of last week's grouper under the seat?"

She didn't even look at me, just jerked a thumb toward the backseat and flicked on the overhead light. My gaze followed the thumb and left me staring into the waxy, dissolving face of the late Sylvia Corrigan.

"What the hell!"

"Relax, Jake," Charlie said. "Jane did us a great favor by bringing the body here tonight."

Everybody was doing me favors today. As for "Jane," the name still struck me funny, like calling Charlemagne, "Chuck."

"Weren't nothing," Granny said. "That old gal been taking up room in my cooler anyhow."

"What's going on?" I demanded.

"I found the boards Sergio had broken at Convention Hall," Charlie explained. "Easy enough. He did the noon demonstration. Slabs of pine were in the trash, stacked in nearly the same order that he broke them. I thought it quite natural to assume that the one with the cleanest break would have been the top board."

"Quite natural," I agreed.

Granny pulled onto Douglas Road, then turned right at Dixie Highway heading downtown. You expect traffic to be light after three

A.M., but it never is. You wonder who these people are, looking for a party or heading for their night shifts.

"On close inspection I could see the top board had been coated with something. I took it to Dr. Kallan at the lab, and he confirmed my suspicions. *Clostridium botulinum,* and quite a liberal dose of it."

"The stuff that causes food poisoning," I said.

"The very stuff," Charlie said.

"What'd Sergio do, eat the boards for breakfast?"

"No, he just hit one with a hand that he had cut on the tile in the courtroom. Even without the cut, the abrasion from the board probably would be sufficient to allow the toxin to enter the blood. With the wound still healing and Sergio not wanting to show weakness by wearing a bandage—I asked around—it was an open invitation to the toxin."

"And you think Roger Salisbury cooked this up?" I asked.

"Chemical companies sell the toxin to universities and laboratories for research. A doctor would have no trouble ordering some."

I shook my head. "I don't know, Charlie, a little smear on a board killing a guy."

"It's perhaps the most toxic substance we know. A thousand molecules of botulinum toxin can kill an ox. Do you know how small a molecule is?"

About the size of all the gray matter in my brain, I thought. I'm the guy who trusted Roger Salisbury. But I wasn't ready to throw him over, not yet.

"Maybe Roger's got an explanation," I suggested, sounding hollow even to myself.

"That's what we'll find out," Charlie said.

We were at the intersection of Dixie and Miami Avenue. Granny swung the aircraft carrier across three westbound lanes of Dixie and we headed north on Miami, passing under the overpass to Key Biscayne. Roger lived halfway up a long block on the right, his house surrounded by finely aged royal poinciana trees.

"What's your friend in back have to do with it?"

Charlie sighed. "If I showed you her right buttock, upper quadrant, you'd know."

"An injection?"

"Twenty-gauge needle, I'd say."

"Wait a second, Charlie. Slow down. She died in the hospital. That could have been a routine sedative, a painkiller, anything."

"Could have been. We don't have the records."

"And you've done no test for succinylcholine or any other drugs?"

"Correct."

"So you have no proof?"

"Correct again, Counselor. Your cross-examination was always your strong point."

"With no evidence, where do you get off accusing Roger of killing Sylvia Corrigan?"

"Calm down, Jake. I'm not ready to accuse. But I've been at this a long time. I have a hunch, that's all."

"A hunch! Charlie. You're a scientist. I'm a lawyer. You deal with medical probabilities, I deal with evidence. And you have us hauling a corpse around on a hunch. I don't believe it."

When I don't get my prescribed six hours of shut-eye, I can be ornery, even to friends.

"What we believe and what is true," Charlie said, "are often quite different. *Deceptio visus*. It's probably healthy up to a point, to believe in your client's cause. Beyond that point, it will blind you."

I turned around to face him, and Sylvia Corrigan toppled forward, brushing my arm with a forehead the consistency of sponge cake left in the rain. The rotten fish smell washed over me. "What do you expect me to do?" I demanded. "Even if he confessed to me, I couldn't go to Socolow. The attorney–client privilege prevents that."

"It prevents your telling the authorities about past crimes, sure. But if you had probable cause to believe he's about to kill again, there is a different obligation."

"Who's left to kill?"

"The person who first made him a killer, of course."

A flash of lightning lit the sky and a thunderclap followed almost instantly, the storm closing in. I laughed but there was no pleasure behind it. "You think Roger will kill Melanie Corrigan. If you're right, why should I lift a finger to stop him? Maybe I'll help him."

"No, you won't. I know you, Jake. I know your code. It isn't written anywhere except all over your face. You're one of the last decent men. You're a guy who looks for broken wings to mend."

"Yeah, I'm an overgrown Boy Scout."

"You won't admit it. You've created this image of the indifferent, detached loner, but I know you better than you do."

I forced the same hollow laugh. "You're a great canoemaker, Charlie, but a lousy judge of character."

"All right. We're not here to protect Melanie Corrigan or anybody else, just to learn the truth. Will you help?"

Fat raindrops splattered the windshield, prelude to a downpour. Granny slowed, then hit the brakes hard, and the old Cadillac's bald tires slid to a stop in front of Roger's house. "Tell me what to do," I said with resignation.

"Be tough with him," Charlie ordered. "He's cracking. The murder of Sergio was an irrational, bizarre act. He's crying out, perhaps over guilt, shame, who knows? He wants to be caught. But his first reaction will be denial. He trusts and respects you. You're the one who has to do it."

The house was one of those modern jobs, six concrete cubes at odd angles, a wall of glass bricks shielding an interior courtyard and a roof full of skylights. I rang the doorbell and waited. Three-thirty A.M. In Miami an unexpected visitor late at night is an excuse to set loose the guard dogs or open up with automatic weapons.

It took a while, then the intercom crackled with a sleepy, cranky, "Yeah?"

"Roger, it's Jake. Sorry to wake you. But there's news. Socolow won't refile. It's over."

Silence. Then, "Great. Call me in the morning."

"Can't. There's more. Got to see you."

"Minute," he said.

It was more like five. A hot, dank night. In the yard a row of crimson tobacco jasmine flooded us with a steamy perfume, even as the rain splashed under the portico.

Finally Roger eyeballed me through the peephole. I ducked to one side. I didn't have to move fast. By the time he turned the locks, slid the bolts, unhooked the chains, and punched the code into the digital alarm, I could have been appointed to the bench. Roger Salisbury opened the heavy beamed door to find a visitor sitting in a wicker chair on his front stoop, her head slumped to a shoulder, eyeless face melting under the ghoulish glow of the yellow bug light. Overhead, lightning crackled.

I heard Roger gag, a choking sound. I watched him slump to the Mexican tile floor of his foyer. My own stomach tossed as he clutched his throat, gagged again, and vomited. He stayed there awhile, emptying himself while the three of us stepped around him and into the house. Sylvia Corrigan stayed put.

"Why do this to me, Jake?" he whimpered, getting to his feet. Charlie steered him to a rust-colored leather sofa. Granny found a kitchen towel and helped clean his face. He sat there in a black silk bathrobe, bare feet on the floor, looking at me with vacant eyes. That bland, handsome face was gray now. "Jake, you're my lawyer and my friend. Why?"

"I'm resigning from both positions."

"Jake . . ."

"Why did you kill Sylvia Corrigan?"

His head shrunk back into his shoulders. "Why would I kill her?"

"Easy. Because Melanie asked you to. She very nearly told me you did it. When I asked her why anyone would steal Sylvia Corrigan's body, she said to ask you. It didn't make sense then, but it does now."

He cackled. Half a laugh, half a cry, a barely human sound. "I'm not a killer. You said so yourself in the malpractice trial. God you were good. I'm a healer. I took an oath. To give no deadly drug, to do no harm."

"You violated the oath, Roger. You gave it up. For flesh. You killed Sylvia and Philip and Sergio."

"I didn't kill Philip," he said softly.

Where I come from, that's an admission. Two out of three. I remembered what he said the other night on my porch. *I didn't kill Philip. He's the one person I could never kill.*

He started rocking back and forth, his head between his knees, his forearms resting on his knees. When he looked up, his eyes darted back and forth and his mouth hung slack. He cocked his head to one side and looked at me or through me, his mind somewhere on the far side of Betelgeuse. The look chilled the room. It could have frightened Sylvia Corrigan.

Then his eyes cleared. A calm voice, the old Roger Salisbury, "Jake, you remember what you said to me that first day in your office?"

I remembered fine but I didn't feel like reminiscing. "Probably that I was a lousy linebacker."

"No, that you kept looking for the good guys and couldn't find them. I admired you, wanted you to like me, to be my friend. I wanted to be one of the good guys."

He said it with sadness, finality. Knowing it was over.

"I didn't kill Philip," he repeated. "You can't believe that pig Sergio." Then he slipped into his best Cuban handyman accent: *"E's the needle man."* And he pushed his thumb against an imaginary plunger of an imaginary hypodermic just as Sergio had done on the witness stand, and there it was, the missing piece. Where it had been all along, on the videotape. That puncture in Sylvia Corrigan's backside could have been a routine injection in the hospital just before she died, but it wasn't.

Oh Susan Corrigan, you were right the first time. I am dumber than I look.

I put my hands on my knees and leaned over, my face close to Roger's. Our own little huddle. I wanted to look him in the eye. The sour smell of sweat mixed with vomit clung to him.

"Roger, I know it all now. You lied to me about when you met Philip Corrigan. You said it was after his wife had died. You were blocking it out, her death, staying a mile away from any talk about her. But you told me the truth about the succinylcholine. You did have it for two years before Philip died. And you did put an old dog to sleep with it. Plus an old lady you forgot to mention. You killed Sylvia Corrigan, and before the flowers wilted, the four of you were living it up on the *Cory*. You, Philip, Melanie, and the karate kid. A celebration cruise. Philip played cameraman. You played doctor with Melanie. After the examination, you gave her a little pat on the ass. That's what it looked like on the tape because you weren't holding anything. But what you were doing was giving her a pretend injection in the ass. She thought it was hysterical. Philip Corrigan laughed so hard he almost dropped the camera. You were showing off, letting them know how you killed her."

He stared off into space, his face devoid of emotion, without joy or pain. Charlie nodded, a signal I was playing the cards right. Granny had discovered a crystal decanter of port and a huge goblet. She drowned a look of sorrow with a healthy chug.

"One thing I can't figure," I continued, "is whether you and Melanie had it all planned. Kill Sylvia, Melanie marries Philip. After a decent interval, you snuff him, too."

"I would never kill Philip," he whispered. "Philip was my friend. I never had many friends. Philip taught me to share Melanie, something I never thought I could do. But she wanted him . . ."

"Dead," I helped out, as he drifted away again. "She wanted Philip dead. You were torn. The woman you never refused, the friend you longed for. She told you to kill him. You said you would. Just like before. But you didn't want to do it."

"I couldn't do it," he muttered, his voice thick, as if his tongue had swollen from thirst. "Philip shared his most prized possession with me. I watched him lying there in the hospital, my friend, knowing what that woman wanted me to do, but I couldn't . . ."

He floated off again, riding some inner current. I filled in the gaps. "So you duck out of the room carrying the valise. Nurse Ingram sees you. You run down the stairs to the lobby. Your pals Sergio and Melanie are waiting for the good news. But you don't have any. Melanie is furious. Sergio probably calls you a chicken-shit *cobarde*. He loves it—you're in pain—he can be the hero. You hand him the valise, and he tucks it into his bush jacket. Melanie goes with him, gives him a cover story for being there if he's seen. But he's nervous. This isn't like injecting himself with steroids. This is murder and there's a nurse right down the hall. So he hurries and doesn't get the hypodermic filled. Or he fills it and squirts it everywhere but inside Philip Corrigan. He makes a puncture, but it's a dry hole. Lucky for him and unlucky for Philip Corrigan, there's more than one way to kill a guy flat on his back. *Ikken hissatsu*. He kills him with one punch, probably the sword handstrike. Melanie keeps the valise with the drug and the hypodermics. You don't want to see it again, and you don't until she plants it in your house."

He was silent. What is it Charlie would say? *Cum tacent clamant*. Silence is an admission of guilt. Not in a courtroom, of course, but in human experience. A tremor went through Roger's body, and he wrapped his arms around himself and hugged as if to keep from splitting in two. His eyes kept clouding over, then clearing, slipping in and out of a haze like a foggy shoreline viewed from the sea.

"You knew Sergio did it," I said. "Why didn't you tell me?"

His lips moved but nothing came out. He tried again. "Because they threatened to tell Socolow about Sylvia. After the mistrial, they thought I must have told you about the karate punch. How else could you have figured it out?"

Charlie smiled, but only a little.

"Why did you kill Sergio?" I asked.

"He kept threatening me. I'll tell the cops this, I'll tell them that, I'll bust your head."

He was sing-songing it, sounding like a child. Coming and going, different people now.

I grabbed him by both shoulders. "Who killed Susan?"

"Sergio. With a poison fish or something. Melanie had him do it. She told me, laughed about it."

He said it so matter-of-factly, one woman dead, another woman laughing. Watching Roger self-destruct, I had buried it, the burning rage. The how and the who. My vow to Susan. Sergio was already dead. Only Melanie's laugh to stifle now. Melanie Corrigan, the source of the evil. Three murders, two by Sergio with Melanie's encouragement. One by Roger, same provocateur.

I let Roger go and talked to Charlie. He would take Granny back to my place. I'd babysit, spend the night on Roger's sofa.

Roger turned to me, his eyes bottomless holes. "Will you help me, Jake? Like you did before. I'm always being falsely accused, you know."

I didn't know what to say. Charlie did. "We can get you help," he said. "A very good doctor I know. In the morning, I'll make the call."

Charlie and Granny left, hoisted Sylvia Corrigan into the trunk of the Cadillac, and drove off.

Roger looked at me. Barely comprehending. I told him I would put him to bed. He didn't agree or disagree, just stood when I helped him up and moved where I guided him. He looked shrunken. So feeble and spent. His bare feet shuffled across the tile. I sat in a chair at the foot of his bed and watched him until he fell asleep. I figured the poison was drained from him now. Just the shell of a man, without the will or the weapons. Able to do no harm.

30

GREAT HANDS

I awoke at five forty-five, same as always. Tired but alert. Aware of the strangeness of the room. There is a sixth sense that tells us something has changed. Someone has passed through our space, coming or going. Our sensors—keen as orbiting satellites—track the unseen movement.

I unfolded myself from the sofa and checked the master bedroom.

No Roger.

The sheets still warm. The rest of the house, empty. I checked the garage. No Porsche.

I called my house, woke Charlie, who must have been sharing the cubbyhole bedroom with Granny. Calmly, he said, "I'll drive to the Corrigan house. You stay put in case he comes back."

I didn't think he'd be coming back. Didn't picture him running to the 7-Eleven to buy juice and eggs. Charlie called in twenty minutes from a pay phone. Nobody at the Corrigan house.

I called a cab. In Miami that's like playing the lottery. Cab drivers hail from various Caribbean islands with one coast road and one mountain road. They can never find residential addresses. I called Roger's office and got the answering service. I didn't expect to hear back, and I was right. No cab, no phone call. After twenty-five minutes, I took off.

Jogging down Miami Avenue toward the causeway to Key Biscayne, then a right turn to pick up Coral Way, the pavement still slick from last night's rain. Roger's office was on Giralda in the Gables. Five miles tops. I needed the exercise but didn't know if I had the time.

I looked for friendly drivers. Most swerved to avoid me, one or two to hit me. No takers for a big lug with a grim look and a sweaty gray T-shirt. I should have slowed that last two hundred yards, but I tried to pick it up. Sprinting. Not much left in the legs, heart going wild. Too old to run gassers, coach's delight.

Roger's black Porsche Turbo gleamed in his reserved spot in back, Melanie Corrigan's green Jaguar in the next space. Good. Melanie must have come voluntarily, Roger calling her from the house. Running here, the mind pounding with each footfall, I had pictured her in the trunk of his car. But maybe Charlie Riggs was wrong. Maybe Roger had no intention of killing Melanie, maybe he just wanted to play some more doctor games. Except Charlie had been right about everything else.

I put my hands on my hips and bent over, sucking for oxygen. It was like breathing through a wet beach towel. One of those soggy Miami mornings without air, no wind from the ocean until the sun heats up the land.

The office was a tiny one-story stucco house with an orange, barrel-tile roof. From the thirties. A lot of doctors and lawyers have gone that route, getting out of the skyscrapers downtown, building equity and taking depreciation. No other cars in the eight-space lot. And there wouldn't be, no office hours Saturday.

The back door was locked. Front door, too. On the side of the house, a brown air conditioner poked out of a blackened window. House too old for central air. I tried yanking it through the window. No go. I gave it a shoulder, braced with legs made of spaghetti, and pushed it inside where it landed on a work table with a thud. I waited a moment. No other sounds. I crawled through. The X-ray room. Dark.

I opened the interior door into a corridor that led to the examination rooms. Then I padded around to the other side of the building past Roger's office, a file room, the bookkeeper's cubicle, and finally, the casting room, where a light shone under the door. I moved close, listening to my own breathing, still heavy. An air conditioner whirred from inside, muffling voices. A man and a woman. Normal tones, no screams, no threats.

I silently let myself in. Roger wore a green gown that was splattered white. His arms were bare and splotched with plaster. He kept dipping a roll of gauze into a bowl of water. Immediately the gauze became gooey, the water mixing with the impregnated plaster. Carefully he wrapped the soggy gauze around the cotton cast padding that circled Melanie Corrigan's left arm. He smoothed out the gauze with those strong, steady hands, tucking it into place, erasing any folds or creases. Then he dipped another piece of gauze into the water and kept building.

She lay spread-eagle on an examining table, both legs already casted from ankle to hip, the right arm a heavy circle of plaster from wrist to shoulder. She was naked except for a tiny white bikini bottom. Her breasts rose and fell with each breath.

"Hello Jake," Roger said, barely looking up. "I didn't want to wake you. Melanie looks lovely in white, don't you think?"

She smiled at me luridly. Her russet hair was loose and fell over the front of one shoulder. The hair hadn't been brushed, Roger probably waking her for the early morning visit. Tiny freckles dotted her chest. She wore no makeup and looked, I imagined, much as she did a decade earlier when Roger first met her in the jerk-off joint.

"Wanna party?" Melanie said. She ran her tongue over her upper lip. "I love a sweaty man."

"Isn't she something?" Roger asked, a tone of pride. "I used to be jealous, you know. But Philip changed that. He taught me. What she gives to someone else doesn't take away from me. That's what he said. He was a great man."

Melanie Corrigan laughed, her chest rising from the table but her arms and legs staying put, weighted down by the casts. "Rog is the sentimental type," she said, derisively.

Roger kept scooping and dipping and molding the plaster. Patting it dry.

"Look at these casts," he instructed. "Smooth, eh?"

"Good workmanship," I agreed.

"Great hands," Melanie said. "He wants you to say, 'Great hands.'"

"You have great hands, Roger," I said.

"Thank you, Jake. You always had confidence in me. You knew I didn't let the rongeur slip. Not in a million years."

He leaned over a work table and picked up a small tool, stainless steel gleaming. The rongeur. He twirled it around in one hand, tossed it to the other, back and forth without looking. Great hands.

He replaced the rongeur in a tray with half a dozen others, all different sizes, from the tiny pituitary model to the bone rongeur that looked like a pair of household pliers. He patted the last of the plaster into place, pausing to wipe his hands.

"Hurry up," Melanie ordered. "Colder than a witch's tit here. Hey Lassiter, wanna go first?"

Roger dried his hands and said, "You can if you want, Jake." His eyes were focused on Mars.

"Rog, I swear I'm going to pee all over your table, you don't hurry up," Melanie said. "Are you hard or you need me to talk dirty? Bring that worm over here."

Roger untied her bikini bottom and folded it over a chair.

"That's better," she laughed. "Hurry the fuck up before my tits freeze solid. Hey Lassiter, that's a joke isn't it? Hurry the fuck up . . ."

Roger looked at me. "Jake, you're my friend, just like Philip. You can have her if you want."

"Maybe another time, Roger."

"There won't be another time," he said flatly.

A chill went through me. Maybe it was the blast of the air conditioner on my overheated body. But maybe it was because I knew. My face must have shown it. Melanie smiled seductively. "Don't worry, Lassiter. He always talks like that. We haven't fucked once the last two years, he doesn't threaten to off me."

"Only this time, it's real," Roger said.

She laughed. I didn't.

Melanie leered at me. "What's the matter, Lassiter? You afraid he'll kill me? He only kills little old ladies."

"Who do you kill?" I asked her.

"No one, smart guy. I got men friends always wanting to please me, do me favors."

"You're wrong about Roger," I told her. She looked puzzled. He hadn't told her. No wonder she was so calm. Thinking he was the same old Roger, her favorite lapdog. "Roger kills more than old ladies, and he's pretty good at dreaming up ways to do it. Painful ways."

She still didn't get it.

"Where's your pal, Sergio?" I asked, wanting her to know, wanting her to taste fear.

"Miami Beach, busting up some boards," she said, doubt creeping into her voice.

"Wrong. Dead wrong. The morgue's on this side of the bay."

Her eyes darted to Roger, who worked silently with the plaster. She looked back at me, seeking help. I hadn't moved. I could stop him any time. I was bigger and stronger than Roger, and his mind was diced into an asteroid belt of colliding rocks. He turned his back to me, oblivious. One shot to the kidneys and it would be over.

I could, but why should I? You are wrong about me, dear old Charlie Riggs. I want her dead. Stop Roger?

Why should I?

Roger stood there studying her, ignoring me, that glazed look fading in and out. He unrolled another length of gauze, dipped it into the water bowl, then slapped it into Melanie Corrigan's crotch.

"Hey, I don't need a chastity belt," she said, the voice a notch higher.

He slowly stretched out more gauze, soaked it, lifted her a few inches and wrapped it around the top of the left hip and through the crotch. He caressed it into place.

"She looks just like a little doll, doesn't she, Jake?" Another strip and then another and the two leg casts were joined. Melanie tried moving but could not, the weight was too much.

Then he pulled a white Dacron stocking out of a metal drawer, walked to the head of the table, brushed her hair back, and slipped the stocking over her head.

"Makes the plaster set more smoothly," he explained.

"Stop fuckin' around, Rog," she cried, each breath sucking the stocking into her mouth. "This ain't funny." Her voice rising, the beginning of fear.

He placed some padding over her mouth, but she shook her head and it dropped to the floor. He didn't seem to notice. He dipped another length of gauze into the water, waited a moment, and then began wrapping it around her mouth. Even through the stocking, her eyes reflected it.

The realization. The fear.

I studied that look, snapped it into place. I wanted to remember it. Susan was dead because of her, and now here she was, knowing what was about to happen, the horror of knowing probably worse than the pain itself.

She spit and coughed. The sticky mess stayed put, covering half her mouth. She breathed greedily through her nose and yelled something, muffled through the gauze. "Laschta, hughme." *Lassiter, help me.*

This time, Roger fashioned a longer piece and swaddled it twice around her head, covering both mouth and nose. She bucked up and down, involuntary thrusts from the diaphragm lifting her, the lungs searching for air. In another minute she would lose consciousness. Three minutes after that, irreversible brain damage. Then . . .

She looked toward me, eyes pleading, mouth working, the words unintelligible, her fear filling the room.

Why should I?

I didn't know. I just reacted the way I do to most things. Moved without thinking it through, doing what seems right at the time, listening to some voice inside, a smarter guy than me, someone who didn't want me to scream myself awake, seeing Melanie Corrigan turn blue under all that white.

I came up behind Roger, grabbed him by the left arm, and spun him around. From the way his right shoulder pivoted, I saw the punch coming but not the rongeur, the large one, in his right hand. His arm came hard and fast. I was going to take his punch and give back one that would sit him down. What I took was a fistful of stainless steel. It caught me on the left temple. Solid.

In the movies, guys get hit on the head all the time. Usually with a gun. Their knees buckle, they say *oooh,* and they gently fall and go to sleep. It doesn't work that way. There's a thunderclap, a blaze of lights behind the eyes, and a shooting pain, a loss of equilibrium. Then a gray fog settling.

I didn't fall down. I stumbled across the room on shaky pins, a wounded buffalo, bouncing off cabinets. Roger was standing to my left, my right, and straight in front. I took a drunk's swing at the guy in front but it wasn't him. He pushed me to the floor. I hooked an arm behind his knee and brought him down on top of me. On a good day, I could bench press him twenty times, then throw him from short to first. This wasn't a good day. He was back up and I was on one knee like a fighter trying to make the ten-count.

Then I felt the jab in my upper arm. *Déjà vu,* his thumb pushing the plunger on a hypodermic. I swatted at it and missed. He emptied it into me and I tore away from him, the needle still stuck in me, the world's largest voodoo doll.

I came at him again and took a swing in slow motion, my arms bulky girders. I didn't hit him and he didn't hit me. I just sat down at the end of the punch, then rolled onto my side, my face resting on the cool, clean tile. Then, just like in the movies, I said, *oooh,* and went to sleep.

My mouth was dry and my head was filled with barking dogs. I was cold. My face was still on the tile. It could have been hours or days. It must have been hours. Roger was sitting in a swivel chair next to me, splotches of plaster in his hair, on his face, on his gown. From the floor, I could see only the bottoms of Melanie Corrigan's bare feet sticking out of the casts. Nice feet, finely arched, clean dainty lady feet.

The feet weren't moving. I didn't need to see the rest.

"I'll help you up," Roger said hoarsely. "Don't worry about the Pentothal. You'll just be groggy for a while."

I tried to stand but he had to boost me. If he wanted to, he could finish me right there. I finally looked toward the table. The face gone, wrapped from forehead to chin, a mummy. Only the ends of her hair stuck out from beneath the plaster.

I sagged against a metal cabinet. Roger said, "You didn't mean it last night, did you, Jake?"

"Mean what?" My voice was thick; my head weighed a ton.

"That you're no longer my lawyer or my friend."

"What difference does it make?"

He swiveled in the chair to face me, his eyes dancing to a silent tune.

"Because I need you, Jake."

"Now? You need me now. What for?"

"To prove it, Jake. That I'm one of the good guys."

PAUL LEVINE is a Miami trial attorney, as well as a widely known authority on the First Amendment who has represented cases for the *Miami Herald* and Knight-Ridder Newspapers, and *Diario Las Americas*, among others. He has taught communications law at the University of Miami and authored both a syndicated television show, "You Be the Judge," and a nationally syndicated newspaper column, "What's Your Verdict?" *To Speak for the Dead* is his first novel. He is currently at work on his second Jake Lasiter novel, *Slashback*.